Queen of the World

Ben Hennessy

Inspired Quill Publishing

Published by Inspired Quill: June 2012

First Edition

Queen of the World © 2011 by Ben Hennessy

Contact the author through their website: **www.hennessywrites.com**

or through twitter: **@HennessyWrites**

Chief Editor: Sara-Jayne Slack

Typeset in MinionPro by ReallyLoveYourBook, Bridgend, South Wales

Paperback ISBN: 978-1-908600-10-3

eBook ISBN: 978-1-908600-11-0

Printed in the United Kingdom

1 2 3 4 5 6 7 8 9 10

Inspired Quill Publishing, UK

Business Reg. No. 7592847

http://www.inspired-quill.com

Dedication

This book is dedicated to the memory of my father,
Terry; the man who introduced me to stories where honour,
courage and strength of will were just as important as any
weapon. I like to think he'd have enjoyed this one.

Acknowledgements

My family and friends, for always sticking by me despite several questionable life choices.

Sara and everyone at Inspired Quill for having the guts to go with a new author peddling his first manuscript.

My initial test readers: Felicity M, John P, Carol O, Nick H and Walter W.

Amy B for the freakish character idea.

And to Illy, whose constant support and unwavering belief helped this little story idea become a written novel. For that, I will be eternally grateful.

Queen of the World

Most people say that magic doesn't exist. To some extent, they're correct. Magic is a product of human imagination. People would like the ability to fly, or conjure fire from their fingertips. Those early days of childhood, where anything seems possible, stay with us. They help form our future and linger long after we have matured. A boy may stop pretending to be a famous hero, but the dream of fame never fades completely. Neither does the ambition of being the greatest swordsman or the finest archer in all the land. The world admires those skilled in the martial arts; the ones who are able to protect the common man and keep their loved ones safe.

The world wants heroes.

Nonetheless, the reality of life dictates that admiration is earned in other, more conventional ways. A man who provides for his family is respected. A loving parent is, in turn, loved by her children. The king of a nation who rules with a fair and steady hand is given the loyalty of his subjects. These roles, among many others, are prominent within lands which have enjoyed centuries of harmony. For most, life is peaceful.

It was not always so.

The world was once savage and cruel. Respect and obedience were demanded by the strongest and the most barbaric. Loyalty was given to those who were most feared. Nations were forged by warlords, chieftains, and tyrants who ruled through brute strength and merciless punishment. Such leaders governed with iron fists and held little regard for the common wants and needs of their people, making vicious examples of all who stood against them. Those who would not fight worked the fields and were regularly mistreated by the very soldiers who claimed to protect them. War was common as opposing factions fought for territory, resources and power. Lives were short and brutal.

Then came the Four.

None could say where they came from or why. The Four walked separate from one another, each journeying to a different corner of the land. As the years rolled by, they came to each warlord and chieftain in turn. Some looked upon them with suspicion, others with intrigue. Most cast glares of derision and scorn. The Four would ask for an audience. Sometimes their polite request was granted, but often it was denied.

The Four could be persuasive.

It is said that they could do anything. Anything. *The legends tell of mountains cracked apart by the wave of a hand. Whole cities brought tumbling down with a casual glance. Rivers made to boil and the sky turned to flame at a thought. Men were shaped to appear as beasts and women as birds upon a whim.*

The warlords and chieftains listened.

The Four came with a simple message. Those in power would use their position to help their people. They would make peace with one another and focus on advancing culture, education, and science. They would protect those who lived under their rule and no longer terrorise them. They would ease the burden of taxes and let the people support themselves as well as each other. They would promote trade. They would provide sanitation and medicines.

They would do all this, or they would be removed from their rule forcibly.

One should not argue with a God.

Some did, of course. Some tried to silence these arrogant men who made demands of them. They did not live long to regret their choice. The more intelligent of the warlords, the smartest of the chieftains, were the ones who survived. They did as they were asked, and they pledged to lead their people into a new age of prosperity and peace.

The Four, once satisfied, left. They did so with a warning.

If ever your people fall back into darkness, then we shall return.

Since that time, over five hundred years previous, no nation has dared to test this promise.

Chapter One

*T*he thump against her bed brought Sarene hurtling back to reality, her dream forgotten in moments.

"Come on, girl. Those eggs won't wander in by themselves."

Wincing against the sunshine as the curtains beside her bed were drawn open, Sarene brought her arm up to shield her eyes. She shook her head, rolling over to pull the blanket around her thin shoulders.

The thump came again, rocking the frame of her bed.

"Not today. We've a lot on, so the sooner we finish breakfast the better."

Sighing, she peeked out through her dark hair. Her father was standing over her, clearly amused. He offered a hand but she waved it away.

A few minutes later, Sarene was rummaging through the small chicken coop beside their homestead. Twelve eggs. Enough for the morning but it wouldn't leave much for supper. The thought of porridge for the umpteenth day in a row made her grimace. She foraged amongst the nesting for a few more moments before rising to her feet. Brushing dirt from her knees, she looked across the valley fields, behind which their house stood at the crest of a gentle slope. Already the farmers were working through the wheat, toiling against the hard earth. It had been a few weeks since the last rains, and she could see a vague overlay of dust rise and drift in the breeze as the soil was turned. The sky above bore a single cloud, but it threatened no rain.

As she walked in the front door of her home, a small figure burst from the entrance, almost knocking her over. She stepped back, keeping a tight grasp on the basket of eggs. One of her younger brothers tore off towards the village's main street.

"Sorry!"

Sarene shook her head with a frown, turning back to the door.

"Sarene? Come on, the water's ready."

She stepped inside, moving to the kitchen area where her mother sat over a pan of simmering water. A dozen thick slices of dark bread lay spread on a platter beside her. She placed the basket next to the pan and received a warm smile in return.

"Thanks, love. Would you mind checking the pantry for some butter? I think we might have a little bit left over. Remember to wash your hands, too."

Sarene did as she was asked, placing a small clay pot beside the bread. The eggs were already in the pan, cheerfully rolling around in the bubbling water. She knelt down beside her mother, who was sewing the heel of a sock. The fabric already showed several battle scars from previous repairs.

"I sometimes wonder if Aiden has hooves for feet," said her mother after a few moments. "I've never known a boy go through so many."

Sarene yawned, rubbing at her eye with the base of her palm. Her mother gave a disapproving glance, tugging at the needle.

"Tired again?"

The girl nodded.

"I'm starting to worry, you know. It's not right for a girl your age, always waking up yawning."

Sarene shrugged in response, letting her hand drop back to her lap. She looked over at the bread, before tapping her finger against the clay pot.

"Oh, yes, if you would dear. The eggs won't be long now."

She shuffled across the floor to the platter and picked up the long knife lying alongside it. As she started scraping around the inside of the pot she heard movement behind her. A glance over her shoulder revealed her sister Taylei framed in the doorway, arms wrapped around a dripping basket.

"Have I got time to hang these before food, Mam?"

"Had better do. Your father wants all the chores done as quick as can be, so you can get over to town."

"Okay. Don't let them boys eat all the eggs before I'm back."

Sarene returned to the bread, buttering away with what little remained. Her mother bit the last of the thread from the sock before placing it beside her, tucking the needle into her apron. When both were finished they looked at each other. Sarene drew her legs up to her chest, placing her chin on her knees. She sighed softly.

"You should start getting to bed earlier. A good night's rest would do you well. You might even enjoy the mornings a little more." Her mother reached over to ruffle Sarene's hair. The girl pulled back a little in response, wrinkling her face in displeasure. Chuckling, the woman turned her gaze back to the boiling pan, absently toying with the speckled, tawny Jaithran feather hanging from a small braid behind her left ear.

"Is breakfast ready yet, Mam?" cried a voice from the doorway as two young boys scurried in. Both immediately charged for Sarene. She saw them coming a moment too late and tried to lean out of the way before they inevitably fell over her, three bodies crumpling to a heap on the floor.

"Mind out for the pans, yer fools!"

"Sorry Mam," one of the boys apologised, giggling. "Was jus' wondering cos we're both hu-ow!"

Sarene thumped him on the arm before turning to exact the same revenge on another of the writhing tangle of limbs still crawling all over her. A second yelp of alarm resounded through the cottage.

"Aiden, Astl, get off of her. Sarene, stop hitting your brothers." Their mother's voice was stern. All three obeyed, though Sarene did so grudgingly. She'd been ambushed, after all.

"Now set the plates, the pair of you. Try not to break anything as you do."

The boys did as they were told. Soon afterwards Aaron, the third brother, entered with their sister Taylei. As the food was being plated up their father Sameran also returned, his kind features marred with stress. He offered a thin smile as he took a plate.

"Problem, dear?" said his wife, Aislyn.

"Sodding wagon hasn't arrived."

Aiden put a hand to his chewing mouth, expressing shock at his father's language which elicited a giggle from the other two boys. Sameran frowned at them. They stopped.

"You won't be laughing when it turns up, lads. You'll be breaking your backs with the rest of us. The later it is the harder you'll be pushin'."

Sarene watched them return to their food without further comment.

"What do you want us to do, father?" Taylei asked as she broke a slice of bread.

"You and your sister will be making sure the men have enough water and towels. Weather like this, it'll be sorely needed."

The two girls exchanged glances, Sarene offering her first smile of the morning. She nodded her understanding, tucking a strand of hair behind her ear before continuing with her food.

"And make sure you don't pay too much attention to that Kellan lad, Tay. I don't like the way he looks at you." Sameran dragged the last of his bread around his plate, mopping up pools of escaped yolk.

"Now Sam, I don't think that's really necessary," said Aislyn.

"You haven't seen how the boys in town are acting, stripped to the waist and flexing their birdcages. Anyone would think they'd been asked to give a horse and pony show instead of hard graft."

Taylei blushed, but said nothing in reply. Sarene grinned at her.

"Would that mean pretending to be a horse, Pa?" Astl asked. His father ignored the comment.

"Come on, finish up. We should be in town before the mortar arrives."

The sun was beating down by the time they arrived alongside the mill's work site. Most of the village men who were not working in the fields were already here, along with a few of the younger women. Sameran moved towards a group of men standing around a table which had been brought out onto the grass. She recognised the town elder, Leryn, poring over a large parchment spread upon it. The three brothers ran across the street to meet the other village children. Sarene watched the youngsters as she walked beside Taylei towards the nearby well. Aiden was already the centre of attention, his animated movements accompanying a story of some sort. Those around him were giggling. Sarene smiled, wondering once again how triplets could be so different. Her trio of sibling boys were something of celebrities in the village, with Aiden most definitely the ringleader.

"Here, girls. Take one of these each, and fill them with water."

Sarene turned to see Neive, the baker's wife, holding out two battered canteens. The woman was visibly sweating; her large bulk not doing well in the early morning heat. The girls did as she asked, each taking a canteen along with a wrapped linen towel which they draped over their shoulders.

"Make sure the boys don't run dry during the day. We all know how much they can complain when they aren't being looked after." Neive winked, drawing laughter from the two girls, before moving on.

"She's always cheerful, she is. I guess being surrounded

by cakes all day would be a good thing," said Taylei as they walked.

Sarene nodded, before puffing out her cheeks with her eyes wide.

"Sarene!" Taylei made a poor job of hiding her amusement. "That isn't very nice."

The elder of the two winked, smiling. She bowed her head in a gesture of acceptance at the rebuke.

They filled the canteens, taking a moment to drink deeply from the cool, fresh water left in the pulley bucket. It tasted sweet on Sarene's tongue, as though someone had poured honey into the well.

The wagon didn't arrive for another hour, by which time the enthusiasm for the task in hand was beginning to wane. With the exception of the men around Leryn's table, who were still talking in gruff tones of discontent, the majority of those gathered were now sitting in groups on the ground, basking in the sun. The sisters made their first rounds with the other girls, handing out the canteens and offering towels to mop at sweat-beaded foreheads. Sarene could see the boy their father had warned about, Kellan, though he didn't appear to be paying her sister much attention. Taylei, on the other hand, was quite obviously keeping out of his way, being sure to move along the other groups. Sarene wondered if anyone else saw this as plainly as she did, or if Taylei would be making the effort if their father hadn't said anything.

When the delivery of mortar finally arrived, a muted cheer went up from those gathered. Sarene caught the sandy smell coming from the back of the large wagon. She moved towards it as several of the men moved to the rear with sacks ready, Leryn amongst them. His target, however, seemed to be the wagon driver. They spoke quietly, but Sarene saw from his expression that he was not impressed. Sarene turned her attention to one of the lead horses; four had been used to pull the wagon, but this stallion was the best of them in her opinion. She ran a hand over its chestnut hair, stroking at its sleek neck. The horse snorted, dipping its head to nudge at her chest. Sarene smiled.

"Watch, it, watch it!" came a cry from the rear of the wagon, before a chunk of mortar plopped to the floor with a loose thud. "Ah, by the Four..."

"It's not going to run away, Keith."

"Guess you won't need to chase it, then. Get it in the sack."

"You're meant to get it in the bleedin' sack. I'm shovelling."

"You're throwing it all over the ground, more like. Get here, we'll swap."

Sarene shrugged, patting the stallion once more before moving back towards the well to refill her canteen. By now most people were back on their feet, moving towards the work site. The first of the rocks to be used for the foundation, large slabs of granite which had been shipped to them three days previously, were carried towards the centre, where a group of the younger men were directing operations.

The morning's work was hard, but few complained. They had time to spare before the mill was required to be operational, but Leryn felt it was important to be ahead of schedule for the harvest. Sarene knew little about the mechanics involved, but she understood the importance of making sure that everything was working beforehand. The harvest wasn't looking to be a good one, judging from the lack of rains this year, but her father had explained that with the mill they could sell flour directly to Kashan, the largest city in the southern region. Cutting out the necessity for another village's assistance meant greater profits. The details were of little interest, though. All Sarene knew was that everyone had their part to play in its construction. Her part involved carrying water and handing out towels. She doubted she'd be given an honour for this task.

As the call for lunch came, Sarene glanced across the crest towards the valley a few miles distant, where the road out of the village led towards Tamiran, the capital. The hills rose sharply either side of the trail, which disappeared out of view, bending to the left. She often imagined herself walking along that path, never to return. Her imagination was vast, and she would conjure up lifelike scenarios heavy in details whenever she let her mind wander. She often considered the adventures she would experience if she ever made the journey along that trail leading to the Highway. Sarene enjoyed her life in the village, but the restrictive boundaries were a little too high. Like other girls her age, she was expected to marry off and produce children while the men worked towards the yearly harvest. In between were the occasional town dances, birthday celebrations for the elders past their sixtieth summer - which was rare, but traditionally a very special age - and the annual Shalith festival. Sarene enjoyed Shalith. It had long lost its meaning, but the stories of the Four always held her captivated no matter how many times she heard them. She didn't believe the Four had ever existed, of course. Few did these days, at least in the villages and towns out here in the country. But the stories themselves, of men with extraordinary power, were too good to ignore. She often wondered what she would do with such power, when she lay in her bunk trying to sleep. There was little else she *could* do at that time.

Sleep was becoming a problem.

It wasn't so much that she had bad dreams; if she did she never remembered them. And she certainly felt tired. But during these last few months she had found it increasingly troublesome to drift off. She felt as though her mind had to climb a mountain to reach the sanctuary offered in slumber. There was an intangible obstacle between her waking mind and her subconscious, and she couldn't figure out what it was.

"Sar?" A hand touched her shoulder. "I was calling you. Daydreaming again?"

Sarene turned to her sister, nodding with a wry smile. She lifted her hand to her mouth, mimicking a yawn, before a genuine yawn passed her soft features.

"You're just lazy." Taylei winked. "Come on, we've got bread and jam to hand out. It's that apple stuff Pledaran's aunt makes." Sarene's eyes lit up at the mention, which made Taylei chuckle. "Yeah. Try not to go silly with it this time."

After the girls had finished moving from group to group, passing out the pre-spread food, they sat apart from the rest to enjoy their own share. Sarene's dollop of the glistening yellowish compote was larger than Taylei's by a fair way, but she made no protest. They ate in silence. Around them the workers shared amiable chatter, the air occasionally punctuated with laughter. After the meal was finished the two girls removed their slippers and sat leaning back, faces turned up to the sky to allow the sunshine to radiate down on them. They sat in an almost identical pose, right ankle crossed over the left, hands spread on the ground behind them, and Taylei's long tawny hair tucked behind the right ear in the same manner as Sarene's own dark strands. Shortly before they were due to return to their tasks, a group of shadows fell over them. Sarene opened her eyes to see Kellan standing over them with three of his friends. All four of them were shirtless. If Sarene were to make a wager, she would say at least two of them were trying to tense their arms in a manner which was she presumed was meant to be casual.

"Afternoon, ladies." Kellan bowed his head, flashing a handsome grin. Sarene tilted her head to the side, appraising him for a moment. One of the larger boys behind him nudged another, a skinny lad with reddish hair and an abundance of freckles brought out by the sun.

"We'd been wondering if we'd done anything to upset either of you. We noticed that you'd kept your distance all morning."

Sarene closed one eye against the sun, pursing her lips. She looked over to Taylei, who shook her head. "My father asked me to stay clear today, is all."

"From me?" Kellan seemed impressed.

"Aye."

"What for?"

"You're a rascal."

Kellan laughed, his friends joining him with noises and claps. Sarene rolled her eyes.

"I guess I should be flattered. I think. Do you agree with him, Tay?"

Taylei turned her head to look across to the worksite. Sarene could tell she was trying to stop another of her common scarlet flushes from touching her cheeks. "I haven't worked that out yet."

"I can give you a hint, if you like." Kellan grinned, his face becoming impish.

Sarene snapped her fingers, catching his attention. She shook her head pointedly.

"Sorry, Sar. I already told you, not until you give me a song."

Sitting forward and brushing her hands, Sarene started to whistle a light melody, pulling a syrupy sweet expression; before anyone could comment she stuck her tongue out at the group and blew a raspberry. Kellan laughed.

"Very pretty, but I'd best not allow *both* of you to become enchanted with me. Your father would have my arse in a sling."

"Who said I was enchanted!?" Taylei said in a pitch which rose with each word.

"Did I say enchanted? Sorry, my mouth sometimes acts before my brain does."

"That suggests you have a brain. Don't get ahead of yourself."

Sarene grinned at the retort, as did Kellan's friends. Kellan himself simply nodded his head, spreading his hands before him. "A rascal needs to think on his feet."

Taylei opened her mouth to respond when a horn blew from the work site. The other groups started to get to their feet. Sarene reached over to her slippers and pulled them on before rising with her plate in hand. She tapped it as she looked to her sister.

"That's right. Hand over your plates." Taylei held out her hands. "I think you've got more stones to throw around."

The ginger boy at the back pointed to the lopsided stack of plates behind them. "Down there. Fetch 'em up, eh?"

"I'll fetch you a slap, firebrand. Get away." Taylei shooed

them off, sneaking a glance at Kellan as they turned. He caught it and winked in return. The blush she'd been fighting off now flourished across her cheeks. Sarene sniffed, shaking her head, as the two of them began collecting plates which had been left discarded on the grass.

"What?" Taylei snapped, embarrassed. Sarene shrugged vaguely. She had nothing against Kellan, but their father was right. He had the makings of a true heartbreaker. Taylei would do well to watch herself.

The creature giggled to itself, hidden away from the crowds passing by its hiding spot.

This was a good hiding spot. It was completely invisible to the outside world. It wondered idly if it could stay there forever, just watching. It decided that would make life fairly unadventurous, though, so such an existence wasn't really an option. Still, for now, it could enjoy the hiding spot. Hidden, watching, and giggling.

The crowds moving past were oblivious to the creature. They moved this way and that, talking in the street and waving at each other. They laughed and pointed and pardoned. They shook hands and bowed heads. They shoved and glared and swore. They bought and they sold, and all the while were blissfully unaware of the creature and its hiding spot.

The creature was hungry, and it was waiting to see what it could steal. It had no money; money was a very odd concept. It felt things would make more sense if people just took what they needed. If there wasn't enough to go around, then the strong would thrive while the weak would not. However, it was beginning to understand that the weak were often the most intelligent. The weak created ways to emerge victorious over the strong.

The creature noticed that, from time to time, an obviously wealthy little man would be followed by an obviously less wealthy large man. In a sensible world, the large man would take the little man's things for himself. Everything except the clothes, because they wouldn't fit and that would just be mean. Funny, but mean.

But instead the large man followed the little man around. The little man who had somehow convinced him to do so. He had successfully made the strong serve the weak.

The creature wouldn't ever serve the weak. It would serve only itself.

It giggled again in its hiding spot. It would do what had to be done.

And it would find the girl.

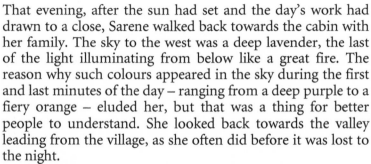

That evening, after the sun had set and the day's work had drawn to a close, Sarene walked back towards the cabin with her family. The sky to the west was a deep lavender, the last of the light illuminating from below like a great fire. The reason why such colours appeared in the sky during the first and last minutes of the day – ranging from a deep purple to a fiery orange – eluded her, but that was a thing for better people to understand. She looked back towards the valley leading from the village, as she often did before it was lost to the night.

"Shouldn't be more than a few weeks before it's up and running," her father was saying at the head of the group, his hairy arm wrapped around her mother's slim shoulders. She smiled at the sight. "The foundations were practically finished today. The walls only take time because of the trouble carrying stone upwards, but the lads did well. So did you all."

"I'm..." started Aiden, but he was cut off by a yawn. He shook his head, being nudged by Aaron. "Sleepy." He shoved his brother back.

"I think you'll sleep well tonight, lad." Sameran looked over his shoulder. "Maybe even you will, Sar."

"She prefers daydreaming to actual dreaming," Taylei said. She was using a small twig to clean under her fingernails as they walked. "I kept catching her staring off into space today."

Sarene wrinkled her nose at her sister.

"Even so, you'd all better get some rest," said Sameran. "It'll be the same again tomorrow."

As they reached their home, a figure was waiting at the gate to the chicken coop. He leaned against the wooden frame, arms folded over his chest. Sarene's eyes lit up as they drew closer, before she burst into a run. She reached the man, whose arms had opened to pull her into a tight hug, laughing as he did.

"Easy there, Sar! You'll have us both over the fence!" He ruffled Sarene's hair, looking up to the rest of the family. "Been busy?"

"Aye, but it's good to see you, son." Sameran stepped past Sarene as she drew back, reaching over to clasp the man's shoulder. "You should have sent word you were coming back. We could have prepared one of the chickens for dinner."

"Already have one over the fire inside. Thought you might appreciate it after the work in town. I did consider coming to help, but..." He winked.

"Ah, nevermind that, Jared. You must have had quite a ride."

Jared continued along the row, passing out hugs and pats to the rest of his siblings, before embracing Aislyn. "You're looking well, Ma. I didn't realise we were supposed to look younger with each passing season."

"Oh, pssh," Aislyn said, chuckling. "No need to flatter, unless that's part of your training these days?"

"There's not really much call for flattery in the Kalethi. We're supposed to stay out of sight, after all. I guess it might work if I ever got caught."

Sarene tugged at Jared's shirt sleeve, shaking her head.

"Nope, I doubt I will be either. Never lost a game of hide and seek in my life. You should know, the hours you spent wandering around looking for me."

Sarene grinned, giving him a playful jab to the arm.

"Come on. Let's get inside before the chicken burns. It

won't turn itself, as much as your fancy pose was a sight to behold." Aislyn began to usher the triplets inside.

"Will be right behind you. I need a moment with Sarene first."

Sarene peered at her brother, curious. Sameran nodded and moved in after his wife, Taylei holding his arm. Jared watched them leave before turning.

"It's good to see you again, brighteyes. Sorry I didn't write back, but you know how it is."

Sarene nodded, the corner of her mouth pulled up into a smile.

"Yeah, I'm lazy as well. Anyway, I got you something." He reached behind him, pulling a paper-wrapped object from his belt. The wrapping crackled a little under his touch. "Thought you might like to be able to sing once in a while."

Sarene snatched the object from her brother, tearing at the paper. Jared laughed at her enthusiasm as she did. As the wrapping fell to the ground, Sarene discovered a set of pan pipes. She bounced on her toes, a beaming grin on her face. A moment later she was wrapped around Jared again, giving a hug so fierce it forced a cough from her brother.

"Sar, I'm glad you like it but it's becoming a little tricky to breathe...!" He spread his arms to loosen her grip, which she did after a few more seconds. Stepping back she lifted the pipes up high, admiring them in the dim light.

"You always said you wanted a set, but that little flute you got for your birthday always sounded a bit off to me. You'll have better luck with these – I had them made especially by a crafter in Tamiran."

Sarene nodded eagerly, clutching the pipes to her chest. He was right – while she loved her flute, the instrument hadn't been of the highest quality, and it had taken so much work to sound clean she'd lost interest in playing.

"How have you been, anyway? Keeping out of trouble, I hope."

Rolling her eyes, Sarene offered another nod, this one dismissive. Her smile became amused.

Jared shrugged. "I have to ask, y'know. With the boys no

doubt causing havoc, you should be helping Ma keep an eye on them."

Sarene looked down to the pipes. Bringing them to her lips, she mimicked playing a tune on them, dancing on the spot for a few steps whilst waving an arm behind her as if leading a crowd. Jared laughed. "Aye, you could guide them around like a troupe. That would be a sight. You would strike fear into the hearts of any honest man."

Sarene gave a silent giggle, the one gesture she knew her brother enjoyed most. Holding out his hand, Jared inclined his head towards their home. "Come on. That chicken won't take much longer, providing I didn't burn it already."

Sarene took the hand in a tight grip as they walked together back into the house.

That night Sarene lay in her bunk, staring up at the ceiling. She was tired, but once again sleep would not claim her. Not yet.

Jared's visit had been a welcome surprise. She loved him fiercely. As the two oldest siblings, they had shared a special bond growing up, always exploring the village and its surrounding lands together. 'Thick as thieves,' their father would often say after yet again catching the pair doing something they weren't supposed to. Like the time they had decided how wonderful it would be to live the life of a pig, lazing in the sun all day whilst being brought meals by the owner. The pig farmer, Uronei, had found them rolling around in the mud of the sty, covered in filth. They'd noticed how the pigs liked to do so and presumed it was the common thing for a pig to do. Uronei had dragged the pair back to their shocked mother, their huge grins a statement of how they saw most things in life. Jared had explained that they weren't doing any harm, but that hadn't stopped them receiving a hiding and a good hour in the bath together, scrubbed from head to toe with a coarse hair brush.

Jared's patience with her had also been something Sarene

was eternally grateful for. With hindsight she understood how difficult it must have been for him to communicate with her, when all she could do was point and wave and cry when she wanted to tell him what she wanted to do or convey how she felt. She couldn't remember him ever taunting her, or laughing at her spitefully. He had always taken the time to work out what she wanted to say, his young features screwed up in thought.

When he had left to join the army two years previous she had cried for days. All of her family were dear to her, of course, but Jared's departure had somehow signified that their childhood was over, that the special bond they had shared was loosening with every passing season. She had begged to join him, but of course that was impossible – the Kalethi, Tamir's scouting regiment, did not take on females due to the dangers inherent in the job. Sarene had resented that, feeling she was being punished for not being a boy.

However long Jared was here for this time, Sarene was going to make sure they spent as much of it in each other's company as they could; mill or no mill.

She sighed, the breath turning into a long yawn. Right now, the most important thing was sleep.

She finally achieved it three hours later, less than four before sunrise.

The work on the mill continued for the rest of the week, Sarene's days quickly becoming tedious. She passed out water and held out towels, nodding and smiling and waiting with impatience for the horn at the end of the day. To her sister's credit, Taylei bore her absent mindedness with no complaint. Sarene was aware Taylei always felt a little pushed aside whenever Jared was around, but it was never mentioned. She had always appreciated the bond her two elder siblings had, and never tried to seek the attention of Jared over her sister.

Sarene was quick to pack up her canteen and baskets and

head on to wherever Jared was when the day was over, which was usually the tavern. He'd developed something of a reputation in the village. As the only man there who had joined the Kalethi, he was often sought out for tales of life on the frontier. Tamir hadn't endured military action for over a hundred years, but the army still commanded a respect from the general populace for its professionalism and dedication to the defence of the borders. Jared was usually sitting at the bar, talking to the patrons like an orator. He had a presence about him, his easy-going nature making people warm to him quickly.

On this day, though, as Sarene pulled open the door to the tavern, her brother was nowhere to be seen. The place was empty except for two of the elder females eating supper and Raleth, the tavern keeper, running a cloth around a clay mug. The place smelt of onions and stale beer, a combination Sarene had always found distasteful.

Raleth looked up at her, shaking his head. "He's not here, girl," he said at a volume which wasn't necessary to reach her. "Haven't seen him all day."

Sarene nodded, taking a quick look around anyway. She stepped back outside, the door to the tavern creaking at the hinges, where the first of the workers were returning to the high street. She moved back past them, weaving between the groups in search of her brother. Nothing.

After a half-hour, Sarene walked back towards her home. She held her hands together, fiddling with her fingers as she looked across the fields. It was possible Jared had simply returned home early, but he *had* left that morning with the rest of the family to head into town. She found Aaron cleaning out the chicken coop as she returned. He waved at her, and she waved back. Pointing to her eyes she held her hand above her head, as if measuring a height.

"Jared? Nope. We thought he was with you?"

Sarene shook her head.

"Oh. Don't know then." Aaron went back to placing fresh nesting inside the coop, chickens clucking around him as they waited to return to their sleep.

Stepping inside her home, Sarene saw her family sitting around the table. Her father was talking about the mill, and how much longer it would take before they could expect to have shipments of flour ready to transport out to the surrounding county. Sarene moved past them with a wave, giving a broad smile to hide her sense of disappointment. She was hesitant to let them know that she had returned for the one member who wasn't here. Moving to the kitchen area, she found two slices of bread left over, beside a couple of tomatoes and a sliver of ham remaining from the previous day. She took them to the table and started to eat.

"Where's your brother?" asked Aislyn. Sarene shrugged, looking up at her mother as she chewed. Aislyn frowned, glancing to Sameran.

"Strange. I suppose he's telling wild tales again."

Sarene shook her head. She mimicked taking a large drink, then crossed her eyes and staggered her shoulders. She then spread her hands.

"Not at the tavern? Hmph. Must be visiting friends then."

Sarene nodded. Jared had always been popular, and it would make sense there would be people from their past who would want to catch up with him. Maybe Quarin or Thastlen, two other boys who had often been caught up in their escapades together.

Sameran grunted. "I still think he would have been useful on the mill site."

"Now, dear," Aislyn replied with a fond smile. She reached over to touch his hand. "We've discussed this."

"Aye, I know," he said, placing his hand over hers. "Even so, would be good to have him there, even if only to see him a bit more often. Between Sar dragging him away and his nights in the tavern, we've hardly spoken two words to him."

Sarene winked, chewing.

"Not to say you're being greedy, girl." Her father smiled. "We know what you two are like."

"Say, now you're back, think you could help me lay the sheets on the beds?" said Taylei, peering at her sister. Sarene clapped her hands in mock excitement, before slumping her shoulders and pointing at her food, her expression pleading.

"After you've eaten, silly. Don't rush yourself. Those old beds are quite patient, y'know."

Sarene rolled her eyes, not for the first time that day.

Chapter Two

*T*he rabbit felt something hit it in the chest and it fell to the side. It flinched as it died; kicking its back legs in a useless effort to escape whatever misfortune had befallen it. As it stared, its last moments were not of a past life, or of dreams had. It simply wondered what had happened, then slept for the final time.

Kanderil, the Hunter, lifted the corpse to his belt a few moments later and tied it in place with slow precision. The leather thongs were tricky in his thick fingers, but he made no mistake before his supper was secure. Rising to his feet, he looked across the glade. No more rabbits just yet, but they would return as they always did.

Retrieving the arrow, which had passed clear through his mark, he returned to his spot behind a thick cluster of foliage. This would be a good place to set up camp for the night: Little wind, and barely fifty yards from a stream. He could hear the flowing water, mixed with occasional bird song from overhead. There was a faint scent of lavender, also. The ground was dry and the sky was clear. Yes, this would do fine.

Barely ten minutes had passed before another rabbit

hopped into view. It was sniffing the air, its eyes wild as it scented the blood of the previous kill. It didn't matter to Kanderil, who had positioned himself downwind of the glade. The fright merely made for an easier target. In one smooth motion he lifted the arrow to the string, aimed the bow, and fired. The rabbit started as soon as it heard the sound of the release, but by then it was too late. The arrow lodged in its hips, pinning it to the ground. It scrabbled frantically for a short while as its assailant moved towards it, then fell still.

Kanderil knelt, lifting his catch and pushing the arrow through it. The rabbit twitched one last time as he did. Kanderil began to tie the corpse beside the first when he heard a snap behind him. Something was moving through the trees, and it wasn't being very careful.

He remained kneeling on the floor. The arrow, sticky against his fingers, was brought to the bow lying on the ground beside him. He waited.

A few moments later, three men appeared. They walked into the clearing, fanning out to keep a clear distance between them. *Not complete amateurs then*, Kanderil thought as he looked over his shoulder.

All three had swords drawn.

"Afternoon!" called the man in the centre. His voice was cheerful, matching the bright weather. He wore leather gear in black and browns, the jerkin over his chest covering a loose fitting white shirt which billowed around his arms.

"You wear good clothes for a cutthroat," Kanderil replied. His voice was deep and rich, matching instead the trees around them.

The man laughed. "Now, why would you say that?"

"Because they are well made. Also, you advance on a man alone in the woods in greater numbers and with your weapons in hand. I doubt you have come to help me catch rabbits."

The cut throat bowed to him. "We are in the presence of a tactical genius, it seems," he said.

"Hardly. A young girl could spot you were not here to

make friends. In future I would recommend a little less haste to arm yourselves if you want the element of surprise."

"Duly noted. Still, it makes the job easier. Hand over your purse and tell us where your horse is tied, and we can all be on our way."

"I have no purse, and I have no horse."

"Odd. I suppose you walked this far out of town."

"Aye, I did. While I was, I saw you three coming. When you gallop across open terrain, it draws attention."

"Maybe he thinks he can pay us off in advice," said the man to the right, whose mouth was pulled up in a permanent sneer by a dreadful scar climbing up his cheek.

The main speaker nodded. "Either way, the advice isn't bad. We'll take it under consideration... Along with your money." He eyed Kanderil, a little of the humour dropping from his features.

Kanderil stood with his bow ready. Two of the three men took a step back.

"You're... a large one," said the man on the left. "Can't say I ever saw a man your size, not even in the ring."

Ignoring the comment Kanderil fixed his gaze on the centre man. "What is your name, lad."

"Not the kind of information I share with my customers."

"Then give me something to call you for now."

"Hawk." The name didn't fit him, but Kanderil nodded his acceptance.

"Then, Hawk. Here is one more tip. Walk away. Find someone else. I do not care who, but do so if you want to live this day."

"You think you can best three armed men with one arrow?" Hawk's smile returned for a moment as he flexed his fingers around the hilt of his sword.

"I do not need to. However it turns out between me and your two friends, you will not share the spoils." He nodded down to the bow in his hands, giving a gentle tug on the notched arrow.

The three men exchanged glances. Hawk dipped his head

for a moment, before looking to the sky. His grin was broad, lighting up his handsome features well. "Ah, but it is a good day for it!"

"Is it good enough?"

Hawk sighed. "That's a tough question, but neither can I risk losing face in front of these two bastards. I'd never hear the end of it."

Kanderil contemplated this for a moment. "Here, then." He unfastened the buckle of his poacher's belt and drew it clear from his waist. Then he tossed the belt across the clearing, the rabbits flailing behind like windsocks. They landed within three feet of the man on the left, who took another step back.

"Rabbits?" Hawk asked, his voice bemused.

"You can keep the belt."

"You pay for your life with *this*?"

"No, lad. I pay for yours."

Hawk met Kanderil's eyes, but not for long. He nodded to his companion on his right, who picked up the belt with a mutter under his breath. They looked to each other one final time before departing without another word.

Kanderil waited for another half-hour before turning his attention back to his hunt.

They did not return.

Whoever opened the door tried to do so with care, but it was a bad effort. The latch caught and the hinge creaked. Sarene lifted her head, rising to lie back on her elbows. The figure moved inside slowly, turning to close the door with the same misguided delicacy. They paused for a moment, resting one hand against the door frame, then turned to move towards a roll of bedding in the far corner of the home.

Sarene frowned. Jared was moving like he was drunk. The aroma which accompanied him supported the notion.

Her brother knelt to pull out the bedding roll. He wobbled a little, requiring a hand to steady himself against the floor. Jared took a few moments to gather himself before grasping the bedding in both hands. Flicking it out with one rough motion, the bedding offered muffled applause as it flared open.

The other end of the roll ricocheted against a mug sitting atop the dining table, which dropped from the table and clattered against the floor.

"Sorry, sorry," Jared whispered. Sarene could see him holding out his hands in a gesture of apology to the rest of his family, more than one of which were now stirring in their beds. She would have laughed had she not found the display so... Well, so...

Disappointing.

A few minutes later Jared was snoring on his bedding, not having bothered to find a blanket. Sarene went back to staring at the ceiling, something which she was becoming rather good at.

———————◄○►———————

Later that morning, Sarene was sitting on an overturned bucket watching Taylei pin up sheets to dry. Taylei was often the one doing laundry, but she seemed to enjoy it. Sarene remembered her once mentioning that she found the hanging and gathering of the house linen to be 'relaxing'. She personally couldn't see the connection.

"He's been drunk almost every night he's been here," Taylei was saying around the clothes peg held between her teeth. "He usually makes it back before the rest of us get to bed, but even then I can tell."

Sarene nodded, turning her head towards the path leading up to their house. The day was slightly overcast for the first time in almost three weeks, but there once again seemed to be little chance of rain.

Someone was walking up the path towards them. At this distance, Sarene couldn't work out who it was, but they were definitely female.

"I mean, maybe they don't let him drink in the army.

Maybe he just wants to have fun, y'know?" Taylei took the peg in her hand, clipping it into place over a bundle of blanket. "Wish he'd tell us, though. It's odd how he just disappears. He never used to."

Sarene scratched at her forearm, taking pause to inspect a frayed thread on her undershirt. She picked at it idly, still half-watching the approaching stranger.

"I hope he stays home tonight. He looked like a scarecrow at breakfast this morning." She looked over her shoulder at her elder sister, arms holding a blanket in place over the washing line. "What time did you say he got back?"

Sarene shrugged, holding up three fingers. Taylei made to respond before noting Sarene's stare. She turned to watch the woman walking towards them.

As the stranger reached the gate Sarene recognised her as one of the farmer's daughters. Claire or Clarissa or something. The light breeze was bullying the thin, reddish blonde curls which framed her pale features. Sarene noticed she was not wearing any shoes. She looked to the two sisters nervously, offering a wave.

"Hey there, girls. Is Jared home?"

Sarene looked up at Taylei, who met her eyes before responding. "Yeah. He's not feeling well though."

The farmer's daughter nodded, smiling. "He was fairly steamin' last night, yep. Can you fetch him for me?"

Sarene stood, pointing to the door and tilting her head. She raised an eyebrow, adding accentuation to the gesture.

"Oh, aye. Sorry. I'll knock if you're busy." Their visitor stepped through the gate and headed towards their home. Before she arrived at the door, though, it swung open. Jared stepped through wearing an open gown over cotton pants, and a close-fitting fur cap. On his feet was a pair of Aislyn's sandals. His sisters laughed while the visitor stared, blinking.

"Hey Carrie," he said. "Something I can help you with?"

Carrie cackled, placing a hand to her mouth. "Dress sense, maybe. Mine appears to be lacking."

Jared looked down at himself, chewing the comment over. "I do appear to have dressed in a unique manner today.

Ah well, as long as I don't report to duty, eh?"

With a gentle incline of her head, Carrie agreed. "Speaking of which, did you want to come into town for some breakfast? You look like the back end of a bear."

"Involves walking," Jared replied. He looked to Sarene, offering a wink which made her grin. "Besides, I think I'll be spending the morning at home. It's the only day these guys get away from the mill this week."

"Later, then."

"Maybe. I doubt it, though."

"C'mon," Carrie said. "We've got unfinished business, after the..." She left it hanging, raising a hand to catch a lock of her long hair, twirling it around her finger. Sarene frowned a little, trying to pick one of the many implications her words had opened.

Jared sighed. He didn't seem alarmed by their visitor's vague comment. "I'll come by if I do, but right now sitting on my arse all day seems a very welcoming prospect."

"Would be a shame, hon," Carrie said with a frown. "If you're leaving tomorrow, may as well say g'bye to us all."

Sarene's large eyes grew wide, before hardening into a glare directed at her brother. Jared caught this and looked to the ground, running a hand over his rough chin. "Thanks, Car..." he muttered under his breath. "Get out of here, carrot top. I'll catch you before I leave."

Carrie looked to the two sisters, then back to Jared. She seemed to wince. "Err, right. Make sure you do, yeah?" The girl turned and hurried towards the gate.

"Sar, that wasn't meant to be a surprise. I was going to tell you a little later." He spoke immediately, not giving her the chance to dwell over the news, but Sarene was already forming ways to berate him. She strode to where her brother stood. Jared took a step back in anticipation, steadying himself against the incoming shove which still managed to throw him off balance. Taylei walked past them, her footsteps careful but quick, and sneaked back into the house. Sarene began, presenting her sharp movements and sour expressions.

When she got going, she could be quite inventive in revealing her thoughts.

Shortly afterwards, Sarene stomped back into the homestead with Jared red-faced behind her. Aislyn looked up from her pad, a well worn collection of paper currently being used to doodle what appeared to be an oak tree.

"So you'll be off tomorrow then, love?"

Jared exhaled, his shoulders slumped as he caught Taylei's eye. "Aye, I will be. I have to be back by the end of the week."

"Where this time?"

"Can't share that, Ma. You know how it is."

Their mother nodded once, looking at her pad. She picked at the corner of the page with her thumb. "That's a shame. It's been lovely having you around, Jared."

Jared smiled. "It's been great being back and seeing you guys, too." He looked to where Sarene sat at the table, her chin resting on her folded arms. She was glaring at him from between dark flicks of hair. "I wasn't planning on sneaking off. I just didn't fancy a big goodbye."

Sarene snorted, turning her head the other way. Aislyn shook her head. "This time of year we'd have little to see you off with, save perhaps another chicken." She looked over to her eldest girl. "I think you're being a little unfair though, Sar. Your brother can't stay here forever."

Sarene made no response. Of *course* she was being unfair. She was dreading watching Jared leave them yet again; to see him walk through the valley towards the crested exit out into the larger world, to turn that winding corner. Out of sight until he next returned to the village with the hot sunshine and dusty farms and a half-finished wind mill.

She lifted her hand from the table, bending her elbow to hang her fingers in front of her head, and began to play with her tresses.

"Maybe you could go find the boys?" Aislyn placed her

pad on the floor beside her, before rising to her feet. "I'm sure they'd like to know so they can spend some time with you today."

Jared nodded, running a hand through his thick mass of untamed hair. "Aye... I'll put some clothes on. Not sure I should be wandering around town in your gown, Ma."

Taylei giggled. "Why are you wearing that thing, anyway?"

"*Thing...?*" Aislyn raised a brow. She was filling a cup with water.

Jared smirked. "I could hardly go and greet Carrie in just my briefs, girl. A gentleman has a certain reputation to consider."

"Oh, yeah." Taylei winked at her brother with amusement. "Wearing a women's gown will have all the girls talking." She rocked on her seat as if encouraging the joke to grow.

Jared shook his head, pulling the gown off and making to toss it aside. He caught his mother's stern look, however, and decided to hang the item from the back of a nearby chair.

"I'll stick to a shirt and pants. Regular uniform, like."

"Good boy," Aislyn said as she moved beside Sarene, placing the cup next to her. Sarene felt her mother's hand on her shoulder, offering a gentle squeeze.

Sarene buried her face in the crook of her elbow.

Sitting on the fence of the chicken coop, Sarene tossed pebbles in the late afternoon sunlight. She was aiming at a larger stone embedded in the ground, hitting her target maybe every half dozen attempts.

Having had some time to consider her outburst that morning, she had come to realise that it wasn't so much the news of Jared's leaving which had hurt her. She had sense enough to realise his visit would be fleeting, and they had spent plenty of time together this past week. Neither was it the way in which she had learnt of his impending departure.

She didn't know Carrie well, and it wasn't her fault that the information had slipped. The girl's reaction had suggested she clearly didn't know that she wasn't supposed to mention it.

Jared would be leaving them the same way as before, just as Sarene had imagined earlier. But she realised now that her frustration was with a different issue, one she was having great difficulty accepting.

Sarene would never get the same opportunity to leave this place for another.

They wouldn't let her. Not by herself, and certainly not in a position of responsibility. Her family, the elders, they would steer Sarene away from the notion. Her father, especially, always seemed to require assistance with some task or another when any of her friends had the option to travel out of the valley. Not even Jared, who knew her better than anyone else, would toy with the idea seriously - though he often joked about it to her, saying how she should hide in his blankets or, better yet, pretend to be a pack mule following along behind.

As much as she was accepted in every other aspect within the village, she was still too different to be trusted as an adult. At least, a *young* adult.

A young adult *female*.

She threw another stone. Missed. She ground her teeth for a moment, wrinkling her nose, before rubbing the back of her hand across her face.

"Hey, Sar."

Sarene looked over her shoulder to see Jared walking from the homestead. He deviated from the path to get to where she was sitting. He offered her a smile. She did not return it, but she did offer him one of her pebbles. He took it as she pointed towards her target. Carefully he measured the distance with a theatrical movement, sticking out his tongue and closing one eye. Sarene tried to suppress a grin. The eventual shot missed by inches. Jared snapped his fingers.

"Close! Bet if I had another ten goes, I'd hit it."

She shrugged, revealing only one more pebble in her

palm. Jared inclined his head. "Wouldn't want to waste it, eh." She nodded her agreement, her features solemn. Her brother smiled again, this one lacking in humour.

"Are you still mad with me, brighteyes?"

Sarene considered this, before shaking her head. She grinned up at him, reaching out to pat him on the head. Jared chuckled.

"Good. Listen, I was invited out tonight to say goodbye to some of the guys in town, and I was wondering if you'd like to come along? You're not a kid anymore, y'know."

She leaned back on the fence, her features lighting up at the idea. She hitched a thumb over her shoulder towards the homestead.

"They won't mind. I'll take the blame if they do. Besides, when did you start to worry about a scolding?"

Sarene giggled.

——————◄O►——————

The creature moved.

It moved with a swiftness only two people would see.

One, a merchant arriving late into town, came to a halt. His mind had told him somebody had passed him in the street, but he didn't really believe it. He presumed he had imagined it; it had been a long day's travel, and he was hungry and tired. Besides, there was nothing there now, and nothing further along the road, though he did stop to check both ways. His horse reared its head, but made no noise. The merchant shrugged his shoulders, continuing on his way. A good night's sleep would do him well.

The second, a young boy, did believe what he saw, because what he saw winked at him. The face was nefarious, impish, with a broad row of pointed teeth which reminded him of the snapper fish he saw at the market. The eyes were gleaming, and he didn't like what he saw in them. The face was gone in the same heartbeat, and the boy was left staring at nothing. He wrung the sheet he was supposed to be cleaning, his grip tight enough to hurt his fingers, before dropping the sheet and running inside his home. Like the merchant, his mother didn't believe what she was told, and the boy was sharply punished for his lies.

The creature, however, was real, and it did move. It moved fast. It continued to move west, where it knew the girl to be.

It had plenty of time, but its excitement was growing.

————◄○►————

Jared stepped from the tavern, his arm draped over Sarene's shoulders. He was singing. The song was about the famous champion of Tamir, Aldion, who had led their forces to victory against the Soraliath raiders over a century ago. The words were slurred and Sarene looked up at her brother, amused. She nudged him in the ribs, which prompted a key change which did his singing voice no favours.

"You gonna be alright with him, girl?" Carrie swung from the doorframe, swooping into view. Two men were with her, cheering at Jared with their beer mugs raised. Jared cheered back, laughing. Sarene looked over her shoulder, nodding several times. Carrie returned the gesture, her long red hair illuminated by the light from the tavern beyond, giving her a warm orange aura.

"Shame. Remember to tell him he's got to visit again soon, aye?"

"I can still hear you, woman!" Jared yelled, his voice loud out in the street.

"Then do as you're told, boy. Get back to us next chance you have." She winked up at him in a manner which prompted Jared to try and walk back towards her. Sarene tightened her grip, shepherding her brother back onto the path homewards. The two men laughed.

"Good on you! Get him back to bed before he makes a fool of himself. The amount he's had he couldn't light a candle, let alone this flamehair's heart!" They both laughed, jeering at Jared who waved them away in good humour. Carrie jabbed an elbow hard into the arm of the man nearest to her, her mild annoyance at the comment making them cackle harder.

Sarene giggled, waving at the three, before taking a hold of Jared's hand to keep him firmly in place. He leaned on her and it took a few steps to become accustomed to the extra weight. Jared began to sing a few more lines of Aldion's song, looking across the edge of the town to the valley.

"Ah, but it'll be a shame to leave!" he said finally. "I've had a wonderful time. Did you have a wonderful time tonight, dear sister?"

Sarene nodded, patting his back.

"Good, good... I knew you would. I think my friends like you. So stay away from them." He considered this advice briefly, his face frozen in thought. "No, don't stay away from them. Just stay *away* from them. You know?"

Sarene nodded again.

"Good. Good!" He grew silent for a short time. The pair of them staggered along the road leading up to the homestead. Sarene had drunk heated water flavoured with honey for the night and was glad she hadn't tried the ale. From the smell and the state it had left those around her in she was starting to think she'd never bother getting drunk. It looked like fun, but the related hassle didn't make it seem worthwhile.

"I wish you could come with me," said Jared. He stumbled a little, but Sarene kept him upright. "By the Four, the journey back to camp tomorrow is going to hurt..." He paused for a moment, then:"But yes, I wish you could come along. You'd be a great Kalethi. Quick, sneaky, silent... I mean, silent when you move." Sarene rolled her eyes, wrinkling her nose. "They're a bit old fashioned about it. Maybe in the future though. I mean, Tamir has female councillors, right? So, that means that in the future, maybe women will be all kinds of things. Like... Wrestlers."

Jared seemed to dwell on that particular thought, his footsteps growing shorter. Sarene patiently nudged him along, her features adopting a mild frown.

"Anyway, my point is, that don't let them keep you here. You..." –He waved an arm for effect – "...You just remember that you can do anything you want, yeah? *Be* anything you want. Except a gladiator. That would be quite hard, I think." He mumbled something under his breath, which reeked of ale. Sarene turned her head to avoid the brunt of it.

"I think I'd like to sleep now," he said. Then belched.

Sarene pointed towards their homestead, which stood silhouetted against the starred sky from where they stood.

Jared cheered when he saw it.

The following morning's farewells were brief but heartfelt. Jared hugged each of his siblings in turn, then his parents. There were no tears, but that was to be expected after so long. The acceptance of Jared's extended leave from home had long sunk in, for all except one family member.

Sarene held her pipes as she received her embrace, her fingers interwoven around the instrument. She smiled up at her brother, who ruffled her hair fondly. She shook her head to return the forelocks back to where they should be.

"I promise I'll write this time."

She clicked her tongue, smirking. Taylei giggled.

"Alright, well at least I'll make a better effort of it." Jared's mouth crooked into a lop-sided grin. "It's been fun, folks. Stay out of trouble."

"I'll try, son," Sameran replied, his features deadpan. This produced a chuckle from all except the triplets, who simply looked at each other as if to try and work out, between them, where the joke was.

Jared began his march back to town where his horse was stabled. They watched him, and he turned to wave once. Then, as he became smaller and smaller in their view, one by one they moved back inside the homestead.

Sarene was the last to go. She looked down at her pipes, contemplating for a moment how thoughtful it had been for her brother to have them made for her. Carefully she lifted them to her lips. She had not yet attempted to play; she wanted to be reasonably useful with them before performing for Jared. Alone now, she gave an experimental toot. The note, while off key, was wonderfully clean. Sarene repositioned her fingers, using her experience with the flute to try a few simple notes. A tune followed, one which sounded heavenly to her ears. Grinning, she pulled them close to her heart again, looking up to the sky and mouthing a thank you.

She looked back to where Jared was headed, to see that he was now lost from view.

Hawk rode with his companions along the trail leading between Tamiran and Ghellei, one of the smaller cities on the Highway. The rabbits bounced along with him, tied by the poacher's belt to his saddle.

He was not in a pleasant mood.

Hawk had garnered something of a reputation amongst others of his kind. Thieves, rogues, bullies and cut-throats. Word of mouth spread in these lands amongst a well secluded network of back-alley operatives. The Tamir national guard were by no means incompetent. On the contrary, they were known to be diligent in their investigations and took harsh penalties against anyone found taking part in criminal acts. Nothing as savage as the faraway lands, such as Katenara, where those who stole lost hands and those who spoke against their Gods lost tongues... or so it was said. But still, a set of broken fingers for a pick pocket was nothing to be taken lightly.

His own crimes were simple and straightforward, and invited simple consequences if caught: Banishment from Tamir. Banishment with blinding if he ever raped, and banishment from the living world if he murdered.

Of course, Hawk never did. He never had to. His reputation lay in the fact that, in his rather colourful career as a bandit, never had he needed to use his weapon to get what he wanted. His greatest asset was not his sword arm but his words.

Convince the victim they have already lost, and you will reap the rewards. Rare was it that it failed, and the few times that it did... well, a few missing teeth and some bruised ribs, courtesy of his two friends, never really hurt for that long.

Until recently, at least. A few days ago he held the stare of a man, a *giant* of a man, and lost. The poacher had called his bluff, and Hawk found himself having nothing to offer. No quick witted response or feigned threat. Their intended victim had simply accepted that he was outnumbered, and promised one certainly.

Hawk would have died.

This irked him. Hawk was not one used to the feeling of fear. Amongst the kind of folk he associated with, one learned to grow confident in ones skills quickly. The people Hawk worked and drank with were quick to step on those who showed weakness. But as that man in the woods had aimed his bow, and the arrowhead had gleamed in the clearing, Hawk had felt a jolt of panic which had dried his mouth and frozen his mind.

He had sneaked glances at his two companions during the journey home. Neither man seemed to hold any contempt for him, which was good. Perhaps they had not relished the prospect of charging an opponent so huge, so monumentally powerful, regardless of having the advantage of numbers and weapons.

The ride back had so far been silent.

Hawk used the rest of it to form a plan on how to redeem himself in their eyes.

He had a reputation to uphold, after all.

Sarene stared up at the ceiling.

She had played her panpipe for an hour before bed, until Aiden had yelled out the window that she was keeping them awake.

She had gazed across the valley towards the road leading out of their village, and had found it hard to drag herself away.

Now, she stared, and waited for sleep which would not claim her for some hours yet. Her eyes ached and her muscles were sore. Her shoulders felt cramped. Despite this she would not enjoy the comfort of her dreams, dreams she never remembered but always *felt* the morning afterwards.

She glanced over to where Jared had slept the night before. The bedroll and blanket had been put away that evening. Sighing, she rolled over onto her side, resting her head on her folded arm.

For a few minutes more her eyes stared at nothing, before realising there was a point of light beneath the grill of the fireplace. It hadn't been there the previous night. Sarene watched the light, unblinking, trying to work out what it was. She came up blank.

Sarene presumed it was a reflection. Her window was open, and the moon blazed pale in the cloudless sky. Maybe a pin or a button. No... Too bright for a button.

Pausing to gauge the breathing around her, certain her family was asleep, she slid out of bed and padded with soft footfalls to the fireplace. She crouched with care, and reached for where the light had been before she had stepped into the moon's silver beam.

She produced a badge. Turning to the window she held it closer to her face. It turned out to be an insignia of the Kalethi.

Jared's insignia.

Sarene turned it over in her hand. The owl's head emblem was surely made of silver, its smooth surface pleasant to the touch. It must be important for the Kalethi to craft them out of such a precious metal. The pin on the back was sturdy and sharp. Sarene winced as she tested the point a little too far, pricking the end of her finger. She lifted her hand to her mouth, sucking at the tiny wound as she considered her find.

Jared's insignia.

Sarene rose, with the same care, and returned to her bed. She lay back down, holding the badge in her palm. Her thumb stroked idle circles along the cold engraving.

She was wide awake, and her mind was full of ideas.

Aiden rubbed his eyes as he awoke, his mouth gaping as he gave a great yawn. He smacked his lips a couple of times, pulling back the sheet. Sniffing, he wiped his nose with the back of a hand and climbed out of bed.

The boy wandered to the jug of water placed out on the table and poured himself some. He made a loud gulping sound as he drank, his eyes peeping over the top of the cup.

Something was missing.

Not in the kitchen; everything was where it should be. He'd be collecting the eggs shortly, and the basket was waiting for him. The pots and pans and plates were all there. The cups and cutlery and cast iron skillet.

Placing the cup back beside to the jug, Aiden looked at his sleeping family.

His mother and his father and his brothers and his sister were all still asleep.

Sister. Shouldn't there be two?

Aiden walked to the door, pulling it open with a better attempt to stay quiet than he'd made while drinking. Outside the sun had already lit the sky, but not yet appeared over the eastern mountains. There was a dim mist across the valley below, the air damp with the morning dew. He rubbed his left eye again, shrugging his shoulders. Sarene must have started early into town.

He turned, moving back to his bed after latching the door shut again. Aiden took one last look at Sarene's empty bed, the blanket thrown across the thin mattress, before sleep returned to claim him.

Chapter Three

*I*t was only later that day, when work began on the mill, that Sameran and his wife started to worry. It wasn't unheard of for Sarene to go for walks alone from time to time, but it *was* strange for her to skip her chores. Her mauve, hooded cloak was missing as well. As she started to prepare breakfast that morning, Aislyn had discovered that one of the old satchels used for carrying chicken feed had also been taken from its hook. There were several rational explanations for where she could be - Taylei had offered that she could have gone to pick mushrooms or herbs from the nearby forests - but now to miss the mill work...

Sameran rubbed his hands together, overseeing the work of one of the groups of young men tasked with raising the granite slabs into place with a pulley system. It was slow work, made more so by the care enforced by the fact it was their sole pulley system. He'd be calling them to lunch soon, when the girls would hand out food. The girls who would number one less than they should.

"No sign of her then?" said Kalid the baker, moving up beside him. He was wiping mortar dust from his hand with a dirty cloth, his shirt sleeves rolled up to expose hairy forearms.

"Still, no." Sameran shook his head. "She'd better have a damned good reason for disappearing, worrying her mother like this."

"The girl likes to wander, just like her brother. Just like her mother used to." Kalid grinned. "Maybe a poorly timed wander, aye, but she'll be back."

Sameran gave a shallow smile. "Of course she will. Sometimes I wonder what goes through that head of hers."

"Sam, I had four elder sisters. I can tell you exactly what goes through a girl's head at your Sarene's age."

"Oh?" Sameran turn to face the stocky baker. "What's that?"

" Pimples." Kalid laughed, tucking his cloth into his belt. "S'all they ever did. Hide them, complain about them, point out each other's... Pimples. Could never work it out myself."

"Thanks. That really helps."

"Don't mention it." Kalid slapped the taller man on the shoulder, moving past him. "She'll be back by nightfall, I bet you."

Sameran ran a hand through his dark hair. He waved to the young boy sitting by the wagon, who lifted a horn to his lips as a result. A long note signalled lunch. The women started to move out towards the workers as they settled to the ground in groups.

By nightfall, Sarene hadn't returned.

Kanderil paused a few feet from the sheer drop, looking down across the valley below. He had deviated from the thin deer's trail he had been following in order to come to this outcrop of rock. The view was one of his favourites. A small village nested among the hills below, with houses and farms dotted around land which inclined slightly up to the northwest. The main centre of the village ran nearly a quarter-mile along a single street, at one end of which a construction was underway. Either a mill or a granary,

Kanderil supposed. Certainly the village was too small and too far within the borders of Tamir to warrant a watchtower or any other military outposts.

Rolling his left shoulder, rotating the joint with a certain delicacy, Kanderil looked skyward. He lifted a hand to shade his eyes. The sun indicated that the light would begin to fail around two hours from now. No hurry.

He sat down, careful to remain a few yards away from the cliff's edge. *Still acting on instinct,* he thought to himself as he pulled a battered hipflask from his belt. Unscrewing the cap, he took a small sip, closing his eyes to brace himself. The liquid burned his throat as he swallowed and he felt his cheeks flush. After a few seconds his senses returned, and he exhaled. A mild grin appeared, framed by his thick beard. Phedish Rage, the small merchant had called it. Kanderil could drink, given his constitution and extraordinary size, but this stuff still kicked him in the gut in a very pleasing way. He replaced the cap and returned the flask to its place.

A breeze kicked up, causing the canopy over the forest not far behind to breathe in response. To Kanderil it sounded like water lapping at the shoreline. He glanced over his shoulder, not expecting to see anyone. Just more of the same instinct.

It had been three years since he'd left his post with the Tamir army and he still wasn't able to simply enjoy nature as he once could. The three would-be assailants from the previous day had bothered him, also. They had picked the wrong target, certainly. Next time they would be luckier, and another victim would be claimed within the forest. Kanderil could have dealt with them, perhaps should have, making the land that little bit safer.

Not your place anymore, he thought to himself. *Not your fight.*

He sat for a while longer, enjoying the peace around him and the sight afforded to him from this vantage point. A small insect crawled over one of his wrists before either falling off or flying away. Overhead he witnessed a bird of prey, moving in large circles along the edge of the forests on both sides of the valley. He watched the construction work in the village - at least, what he could make out from this distance - and the people gathered around the work site. Aside from those labouring in the fields, it appeared that the majority of the townsfolk were gathered there.

Kanderil left an hour later, in a better mood than when he had arrived.

————◄○►————

The creature arrived.

This was the land where the girl would be. These borders and these cities and these people housed her.

It moved through the back yard of a farmhouse. Sheep bleated nervously at its approach but it ignored them. Pigs squealed as it laid one hand along the wooden pen keeping them in place, squealed at the noise that accompanied its touch, but the creature ignored these also.

At the side of the house a dog appeared. It stood proudly, with its legs straight and its ears pricked. An old wolfhound, the kind rarely seen as purebreds nowadays. It was a hundred and forty pounds, maybe. It scented the creature, same as the creature scented it.

The wolfhound growled as it took one step towards the pens. Something was worrying the animals. It had to scare the predator away. They were its responsibility.

The creature grinned at it, a terrible grin, and stepped into the dog's path.

The wolfhound died without a sound.

The creature stood over the dog's corpse for a long time. Nobody came out of the house to disturb it. The creature studied the body before looking towards where the path led deeper into Tamir. The scent of fear and blood filled the air, but the creature wasn't hungry.

Not yet.

It had a girl to find.

————◄○►————

Hawk stepped out of the Lamb and Daggers, moving towards the nearby outhouse. He spat to the side as he did, wiping his mouth. His strides were even, his movements giving no sign of the four ales he'd sunk along with his stew. The meal had been surprisingly good – the usual cook had apparently been given the night off, so for once he'd enjoyed his food instead of enduring it. He was pulling the strap of his belt loose as he reached the pisser, allowing nature to take its course as soon as he arrived.

He heard the door of the tavern swing open, the noise from within becoming louder, clearer. Moments later, it was shut. Hawk glanced over his shoulder. Seeing nobody walk by, his mild interest was gone. He returned to the task in hand.

Turning once he was done, he made his way back towards the tavern. The door swung open again as he drew close and a man stepped outside. Hawk paid him no attention until the man held his hand out, palm forward, in Hawk's path.

"He's a large man, isn't he?"

Hawk paused. "Excuse me?"

"The chap in the forest. The poacher, hunter, whatever he calls himself... Huge."

Narrowing his eyes, Hawk folded his arms across his chest. The man was old, maybe thirty summers older than he was. Closely cropped white beard, thinning hair to match. His clothes were simple but clean, while his teeth were straight and even.

"I presume you know him, then?"

"Oh, certainly do. When you meet a man like that, a man to move mountains, you should always take the opportunity to introduce yourself."

"I see." Hawk nodded his head, turning his gaze away from the stranger. Across the street, windows lit by hearth fires illuminated the few people walking through this part of the city. The hour was late, and with it came all kinds of associated troubles. "I can't say the same myself. We talked, but it wasn't what one would call friendly."

"I'm not sure, my boy. You seemed fairly civil. Just all that nasty business of weapons being involved, I suppose."

"I'm curious to know, old man. Were you watching us?" Hawk looked back to the stranger.

"I may have been passing by, yes."

"You made good time coming back to town for someone your age."

The old man rubbed his hands. "Someone my age knows a few tricks someone your age may not."

"Maybe you can fly, then."

Laughter. Then, "Not quite. Now, if we can skip the pleasantries I do have a reason for stopping you here in the street."

The tavern door opened, and a figure came out with an arm draped across the shoulders of an exceptionally unattractive woman. Hawk raised a brow. "Petar?"

"See ya in the mornin', mate!" His companion gave a wave before continuing off down the street.

Another chuckle from the old man. Irritation touched Hawk and he took a moment to suppress it.

"Good company you keep, my boy."

"Why did you stop me?"

"I have a job for you."

"Not interested, my friend." Hawk offered his own smile.

"Do you often refuse gainful employment without hearing the terms?"

"Do you often hire people you met in the street?"

"Your reputation precedes you." The stranger shrugged. "That is, I believe you're the one for me. It's a simple task, and it involves taking something with a minimal amount of violence. Your skill to adapt is just what I'm looking for."

"You followed me into the forest to watch me work?"

"It was interesting to see how you handled the giant."

Hawk paused. He stared at the stranger, lifting a hand to stroke at his chin before scratching his temple. "If you were there, you saw how that turned out. The man had strong discipline and great confidence. He bested me."

"Oh, you were trying to *mug* him." The old man waved a hand to dismiss the issue. "I need you to be a little more subtle, and he will not be your direct target. A girl, sixteen summers old, is what I need you to bring to me."

"What for?"

"Let's just say she is in the possession of something that is very dear to me."

"The poacher will be with her?"

"He should be. Soon."

"*Should* be?"

"The details are unimportant. This is your chance to redeem yourself against him."

Hawk chuckled. "The man had an arrow pointed at my heart and I withdrew. I'm not sure that counts as a life-changing experience, my aged friend."

"Do you not wish to find out if you could have had his purse, under different circumstances?" The stranger clenched a fist in front of him, taking a step forwards. "To prove you could humble the man?"

Shrugging, Hawk started back towards the tavern entrance. "If we meet again, then we'll find out. I'll not be stealing his daughter or niece for such a petty revenge." He patted the older man on the shoulder as he stepped past. "I'll be sure to ask around for you, though."

Reaching out to push the door, Hawk froze. He tried to move his hand forward but it wouldn't obey.

Behind him, the old man turned. He took a step forward, clasping his hand over Hawk's shoulder. Leaning close to whisper in his ear, the man's face was creased with dark humour. Hawk felt cool breath against his flushing cheeks.

"I believe that the giant made a mockery of you. I believe you need this opportunity to show the world that you are the better man."

Hawk felt himself becoming angry, the sensation overriding the fear which had settled upon him in his paralysed state. He tried to turn his head, but again could not.

"I believe you will prove to me that you could take

whatever you wanted from him."

He felt a desperate need building within him, and at once he had to escape. The anger was becoming stronger, and he clenched his teeth against the grip holding him in place.

"I believe you were humiliated. I believe you were made to look a fool."

Shame filled his heart and touched his soul. The emotions pouring into him were plucking at his nerves and making his head spin.

"I believe you can do this."

Tears blurred Hawk's vision, and he blinked them away.

"Show me. Show yourself. Fetch me the girl."

An image formed in his head. Shoulder length dark hair. Wide, pale brown eyes. Slim with youth, pretty without maturity.

"Bring her to me, and I will reward you in ways you could not imagine."

A scream built in his throat but he couldn't release it.

"Bring her to me, and reward yourself with revenge."

Hawk fell to his knees, the hold over him released. The rage and disgrace, the hatred and need dispersed like smoke from a quenched flame. His mind calmed within seconds. He ran a palm over his mouth, wiping away perspiration from his upper lip.

"I'll have her to you within the month," he said. His voice came out hoarse and he coughed, clearing his throat. "I'll bring her here and await your arrival."

"What of the giant?" the old man asked. The question seemed idle, off-handed, but Hawk clenched his fists at the mention of his enemy.

The poacher. The one who ruined him. The man who stole his dignity and self respect.

"The giant will pay."

Hawk stood. He moved for the tavern door, with the old man looking on, and this time pushed it open with a shaking hand.

————◄O►————

Sarene walked along the road towards Tamiran feeling quite concerned. She'd been heading along the Highway for almost two days now, on and off. At last free of the valley, she repeatedly became distracted by things along the way, her attention caught by the sheer majesty of these new surroundings. She had no idea that the trees and fields and animals she'd lived amongst all her life could be so different. The knowledge that everything around her was within touching distance for the first time was intoxicating, and she found herself brushing her fingers along bark and stroking her feet across stones simply to point out that she had done so. The sky overhead seemed somehow brighter, richer in colour. Around her she scented flowers in bloom, the smell pleasant and fresh. The few travellers who'd passed by this way had offered a wave and a greeting. At first Sarene had waved back cautiously, but as she grew more confident she'd returned these welcomes with a strong enthusiasm.

Now, however, self doubt had started to creep in. Jared had a horse and a full day's head start, while Sarene was on foot. It was becoming apparent that, in actual fact, she had *no* idea where he was headed. She'd presumed it was the barracks in Tamiran; her brother had mentioned that the army command centre was based in the capital. It would have made sense for him to go there after his break for fresh orders, but then what? She didn't believe she could stroll up to the front gates and show Jared's insignia in exchange for his whereabouts. Kalethi didn't work like that...

She guessed.

Still, the insignia could be handed in for when he returned to Tamiran. No doubt he'd be pleased. Sarene liked to think that Jared would also be proud she'd undertaken such a journey herself, even though he would have to pretend otherwise in front of the family. Her father would be fairly angry, she felt. Mother too.

But then she'd had a scalding for many a previous misdeed, and she'd only *really* be gone a week or so, providing she didn't get lost.

Sarene stepped into the forest to relieve herself. As she moved back towards the road she heard the sound of galloping hooves. Cautious, she waited behind a tree and peered along the Highway. A small cloud of dust was being kicked up behind the distant horse. No... More than one. At least three. All tearing down the road towards her.

Leaning back out of sight, Sarene wrung her hands. She'd never seen a group of riders move at such speed. Within her village, people rarely - if ever - needed to move with such haste. It seemed somehow wasteful. There were stories of course, of wars and races and messengers and the like, where great distances were covered in short periods of time. She lifted a hand to her shoulder, rubbing her neck.

She didn't like this. Risking a second look, Sarene watched as they approached. All the riders wore dark clothes. After another moment's hesitation she retreated away from the road and further into the forest line. A fallen log, layered with a carpet of mould, provided a barrier facing the road. She hurried over and crouched down behind it. The hooves of the oncoming horses could be heard clearly now, pummelling the road like thunderous drums.

Sarene ducked out of sight until they passed, but couldn't resist peeking around the log as they sped away. The horses were huge, stallions bigger than any she'd ever seen. Cloaks billowed out behind, making the riders seem just as large. They all wore their hair tidy and swept back. Every one of them looked fearsome. Sarene fell back out of view in case a rider looked back and saw her. She didn't want to become involved with a group of angry men. There were tales of cruelty on the Highway and she wished to stay as clear of it as possible.

She stood, cupping her ear, and listened to the racing men fade out of earshot. From the sounds of it they never let up their speed. The sun was quite low in the sky now, and she felt it would be a good idea to find a place to camp for the night. Again she glanced at the road. With people such as *that* roaming around, it would probably be best to sleep somewhere out of sight. There was just enough time to forage for some fruits and seeds, as well. Gently she patted her rucksack, feeling the loaf of bread within. Supplies were fine for now.

That night Sarene reclined against a huge chestnut tree, wrapped up in her cloak, staring towards the sky and wondering what she would do upon arriving in Tamiran. It wasn't long before she drifted away. Since leaving her home she'd found sleep a lot easier to come by.

Kanderil stepped between the gnarled roots, picking his footfalls carefully. The roots were twisted, smooth in some places and splintered in others. It reminded him of stories of a great octopus which terrorised sailors on the eastern seas of the world. In this case, they skulked out from the earth in an attempt to ensnare passing travellers.

He was heading back towards the woodland trail which would take him west towards Tamiran. He didn't like the city much, but there was little choice – his money was running low. A merchant in the capital was holding onto his savings, and while Kanderil rarely had the need to spend hard coin it was still necessary from time to time to collect some for his journeys. One never knew what to expect out here in the wilds.

Coming to a small clearing, one hand pressed against a crooked trunk, he found himself looking upon a young girl curled against the body of a large chestnut tree, a mauve cloak drawn close around her.

The girl watched him with wide eyes that became wider still as he halted. Her mouth gaped slightly.

"It is rude to stare, lass," Kanderil said aloud. He walked on, making to move past her. He had just reached the right hand side of the chestnut before he paused again. Sighing to himself, he took one step back and looked down at the girl.

"Why are you here by yourself?"

The girl simply stared at him

Kanderil lifted a hand to his thick mass of beard, stroking

it down in a single, slow motion. He should move on, let the girl continue with whatever she was doing before he found her. Chance often made things complicated, and that's exactly what this meeting was. A chance encounter.

The kind which could result in a similar meeting between her and a man like Hawk, whispered an unbidden thought in Kanderil's head. *A man you let walk free.*

Muttering under his breath he knelt beside her, one of his joints popping like a broken wishbone. The girl shrank away from him, drawing her cloak tighter in an effort to protect herself.

"I did not catch your answer."

The girl shook her head in response. She wasn't as young as he first supposed, but still no woman. He guessed fifteen summers. Maybe sixteen at the most.

"I am afraid that is not a proper response to the question." He offered a smile, broad and as jovial as he could muster, aware that he could be intimidating her.

The smile caused her to pull the cloak up over her face. He stopped, frowning instead.

"What is your name, girl? At least give me that much."

The girl peeked out over the hem of the cloak, sliding the fabric down over her face. A butterfly fluttered by, passing between the two of them, the sunlight piercing through its gold-trimmed wings.

Again she shook her head.

Kanderil sighed and made to stand. At this the girl's hand shot out from beneath the cloak. He paused, watching her motion to her neck, drawing a finger across her windpipe. She then shook her head once more.

The Hunter nodded. "So you are a mute."

The girl frowned at the word. She returned her hand back beneath the mauve cloak. Kanderil smirked.

"My apologies." He folded his thick arms across his chest, glancing around the woods. The Highway was maybe fifty yards to the north, not far from where his woodland trail would cross south west towards a path leading into the mountains bordering southern Tamiran. "Did you get lost?"

Shaking her head, the girl shrugged. She then considered this further before giving a small, hesitant nod.

Kanderil returned the gesture. "Okay. I can send you the right way if you need. Can you show me where you came from?" He pulled open a pouch at his side, stitched into his leggings. From it he withdrew a parchment, upon which was drawn a fairly well detailed map of the centre of Tamir. He offered it to the girl. With great caution, she reached out to take it from him. He slowly moved to crouch where he could see the map with her.

She pointed to a small village down within the Hailein Valley. The village he'd watched over less than two nights previous. Kanderil nodded. "Not too far. You can follow the Highway east, and cut off south when you see the valley appearing over the woods. It should not be hard to find since you know the area."

Again, the girl shook her head.

"No?"

The girl laid a fingertip beneath the village she'd pointed out, then shook her head once more, a length of hair slipping forward from behind her ear from all the movement. She instead gestured to Tamiran. Kanderil accepted this request calmly, taking the map from the girl and sliding it back into his pouch.

"I see. Why do you want to go to Tamiran?"

The young girl tapped the side of her nose with a finger. Her initial timidity seemed to be wearing off. Kanderil suppressed the smile which threatened to appear.

"I will need more than that. Tamiran is quite a way away, and I am not sure your parents would be happy to find out you had travelled so far without them."

The girl exhaled, air hissing from between her teeth, before looking down to the small knapsack slung over her shoulder. She fumbled around inside for a few moments before producing what looked like a broach. She held it up before her, a thin stream of light breaching the overhead canopy and bouncing from the smooth surface, making the item glimmer.

Kanderil recognised it as a Kalethi insignia. Rank Three, from the colour, meaning the original owner had probably not been a member for more than a few years. He looked back to the girl who held it up before her as some kind of talisman.

"You're going to Tamiran because you found an army insignia?"

A nod.

"Here in the woods?"

A shake of the head. The girl gestured to herself, but Kanderil wasn't sure what she meant.

"Lass, the insignias are made of treated tin. That thing isn't worth a silver piece. Whoever lost it will simply be given a new one. After a short rollicking, of course."

The words were spoken plainly, but the effect was devastating. The girl seemed to crumple before him, her features locked in a stunned expression. She lay back against the trunk of the chestnut.

"Do you know the person to whom the insignia belongs?"

A nod, after a short moment's comprehension.

"Ah, I see. Well there is no need to worry. All soldiers are shouted at when they lose a piece of uniform, but it is quickly forgotten. Your friend will be fine."

The girl shook her head slowly. She looked up at him with a glum expression, her features sullen.

"Come on. Let me show you the way back to your village."

With deliberate caution the girl pushed the cloak back away from her, getting to her feet. Kanderil did likewise, and the girl snapped out of her malaise. She stared up at him, having to crane her neck back to do so.

"What did I tell you about staring?"

She sighed. With a quick movement she plucked her cloak from the floor, swinging it around her. The mauve fabric contrasted against the browns and bronze surroundings of the trees and leaves, the heat having chased away most of the greener colours. Kanderil moved towards the highway, weaving an easy path back to the edge of the woodlands. The girl followed, head down, her hair hanging to cover the majority of her face.

Kanderil kept himself focused ahead. He had never met anyone unable to speak which wasn't the result of some sort of illness or injury. Her skin was clear and her neck free of scars, which suggested a birth defect of some kind. That he should bump into her outside of a city or village struck him as strange. One of those situations where the long odds came up.

"Just across there," he said aloud as he reached the edge of the highway. The girl came to a halt beside him, her hood now pulled up despite the bright morning sunshine. "Follow the road back for maybe a day, rest for the night somewhere safe and out of view and you will be home by tomorrow noon."

The girl nodded once, looked up at him, and then began to walk in the opposite direction. Kanderil watched her go. It mattered little to him if she went to Tamiran or not, but he knew of the rogues in the area. Most travellers would be as considerate as he had been, but those rare few...

She managed a few steps before Kanderil moved up behind her. He reached out to catch her upper arm. She stiffened at the grip, peering back over her shoulder with a mixture of surprise and fear.

"Easy now. I am not going to hurt you, but I cannot let you travel to Tamiran by yourself."

The girl tilted her head to the left. She pointed at him, then at herself, before thumbing over her shoulder.

"No, I will not escort you there. But I will ensure you make it home."

She shook her head, and tried to pull her arm free of his grip. Quickly she discovered this was a futile move.

"You do not have a choice in the matter, unless you can give me some proof your family approve of your trip."

The girl stared at him again. A faint breeze tickled her hair, which hung straight around her features. Freckles touched her cheeks and nose. Kanderil stared back, his gaze steadfast.

"I certainly have better things to do than to march you back to your home, but I will. This highway is not safe for a young girl to be walking alone."

She rolled her eyes, a wry smile tugging at the corner of her lips. She gestured down the road leading back to her valley, before pointing to herself. Then she ran a finger across her throat. Kanderil muttered once more.

"You are right. Neither way is safe." He turned, facing east and back along the Highway where the village she'd indicated on the map was waiting. "Fine. But if I must come with you then we move at my pace."

The girl was almost pulled from her boots at the sudden movement. She stumbled along behind him until she was able to match his stride, which resulted in her having to scamper along. He felt a thump of protest against his arm.

"Duly noted."

Sarene stared up at her escort for long parts of the journey home. She'd been disheartened at the news that Jared's insignia was worthless, but simply returning to her village was an even greater defeat. For a short time she'd broken free, escaped out of the valley which had surrounded her childhood, and that liberty had proven enchanting. No chores, no-one to tell her what to do, no-one to look down on her or treat her like an infant. She had a destination, a plan, and something to look forward to. Now she'd be home to face stern parents and strict punishments. The rest of the summer would be spent under the watchful eye of her father, accompanying him to pointless tasks and boring talk when there was no-one else to babysit her.

The man next to her was seemingly just like any other, although his size had frightened her at first. Sarene had never seen anybody so *huge*. Gallen, a farmer in her village, was the tallest person she knew. Her father had said he was over six feet tall, but the man holding her arm must have been another foot on top. His shoulders were like the oxen that pulled the ploughs through the fields, and his arms were double the width of one of her legs. He was old, twice her age at least. A huge longbow with bronze tips was slung over his left shoulder, a broadsword strapped to his right, so the weapons crossed at his spine. Long dark hair ran down his back and over his shoulders, and his coarse beard bushed a good six inches from his face. Why he hadn't bothered to shave she couldn't guess, but she didn't really care either. All this man represented was her failure, someone to march her back to the village where she felt she would spend the rest of her days without ever having her own adventures.

Even when they had camped the previous night he hadn't taken his eyes from her. She supposed he had watched her while she slept. The thought was an oddly unpleasant one.

The man looked down at her for the first time in an hour or so.

"Something the matter?"

She frowned in response. He looked at her for a few more steps before returning his gaze to the road. His expression was reminiscent of the characters in stories her friends used to tell around campfires in an effort to scare each other. All grim and lacking in fun. Not sad, exactly, but certainly missing some life and soul. Sarene glanced downwards, watching her feet as they walked. She was getting tired, and having to walk so quickly alongside him was becoming difficult.

The man pulled at her arm, making her jump. She peered up at him in surprise.

"Come. Off the road."

She was led into the first throngs of trees. As they reached them, he let go of her and crouched beside a chestnut which had been split at some point in the past, the wood blackened and dead. Beside the trunk was a thick cluster of blackberry bushes. He knelt low to the ground, ushering her over. She followed, unsure of what was happening but judging that his motives were worthwhile. Crouching beside him, she pulled herself close behind the bushes. The scent of the fruit was faint but sweet.

She heard horses approaching. They were moving fast. She thought of the group she had avoided the previous day, and tried to remember how that had sounded. The woodsman beside her said nothing. He merely studied the road with those stern eyes. She had a partial view through the berries.

Soon the riders came into view. It was the same group as before, a group of five, all in black hoods. They sped along the road at full tilt, their mounts breathing ragged against the bits in their mouths. She ducked back as one of the riders looked towards them, but the horses did not slow. They passed the spot where Sarene and her escort hid, and within a few minutes the sounds of their gallop could no longer be heard.

The man stood, and then walked back towards the path. When Sarene made to follow he held out a hand, gesturing for her to wait. He stared in the direction the riders had been heading for a long while. Eventually he turned to her, nodding. She stepped around the blackberry bushes, pausing to quickly snatch a cluster of them, and moved beside him.

"Come on. Road's clear."

Looking up at him, she gestured after the riders.

"Nothing." He turned back south, towards her village. "Just being cautious."

Adjusting her stance, eyes gaze fixed on him, she placed her hands on her girlish hips for emphasis.

"Come on."

Sarene didn't move. She popped a blackberry into her mouth. The man halted after a few more steps, turning back to face her.

"Do I have to start dragging you again, lass?"

She clicked her tongue. Sarene puffed herself up, standing on tiptoes, and held her arms out at right angles, as though she weighed a hundred pounds more than she did. Then she marched towards him, cheeks filled with air, trying to look angry. The woodsman simply watched before walking on behind her.

"Good girl."

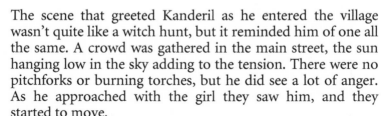

The scene that greeted Kanderil as he entered the village wasn't quite like a witch hunt, but it reminded him of one all the same. A crowd was gathered in the main street, the sun hanging low in the sky adding to the tension. There were no pitchforks or burning torches, but he did see a lot of anger. As he approached with the girl they saw him, and they started to move.

He came to a halt as the first villagers reached them. A burly man strode forward, stocky and squat. Kanderil would have guessed him to be the town blacksmith were that not a stereotypical view. Yet the Hunter towered over all them all, and he saw the initial enthusiasm of those arriving to greet him start to wane.

Not the lead man, though. "Get here, girl." He waved her over, taking point in front of the others. There were maybe twenty gathered behind him. The girl took a hesitant step forward. Kanderil nodded for her to continue, and she left him to join the group. Quickly she was steered away by some at the rear.

"Explain yourself, big man." The potential blacksmith stared at him. Kanderil found no quarter in those eyes.

"I found the girl in the woods along the road to Tamiran yesterday morning. She was alone, and I brought her back." Kanderil spoke slowly and clearly, his deep voice intended to reach all those present.

"That's a simple story, one which Sarene can't back up herself."

"I have no reason to lie, and the girl in question is in good health. She seems surprised by her welcome."

The lead man glanced over his shoulder. A woman, her broad arm draped across the shoulders of the girl they called Sarene, nodded. He turned back to Kanderil, his anger still high, as though wanting to find a reason to act upon it.

"Perhaps if you explained why you seem ready to lynch someone, I can provide more information to ease your mind." Kanderil folded his arms over his broad chest. He studied the group, taking note of those who would provide the most likely challenge should he need to defend himself. Old habits died hard.

The man considered this offer, running a hand across his jaw. Eventually he sighed, the noise regretful. "Carin, take the girl to her home."

The woman with Sarene began to walk with her, guiding her east away from the main street. The girl looked back once, her gaze meeting Kanderil's. He watched her go with no gesture, no nod of the head, waiting for the man to speak again.

Once the girl was gone, he did so. "That lass's family were attacked not three hours ago."

"By whom?"

"A group of men wearing dark clothing, on large horses. They went straight to her home, didn't pass anyone else. By the time anyone went to check, they were already riding back towards the highway."

Kanderil frowned. "Five men?"

The man opposite closed his fist, the reply perking his suspicion once more. "How did you know?"

"As I said, I found the girl near the Highway. The riders you speak of passed us by. I hid the girl out of sight."

"Scared?" A voice came up from the crowd. Male, but thin. Kanderil shook his head.

"Careful. Those riders were sent here for a reason."

Those gathered began to murmur, muttering to each other. "How could you know that?"

"Because they belong to the Gathire."

The mumbling stopped for a moment, then began again with increased volume.

The lead man spoke again, though his anger was fading fast. "Why would the Gathire come here? What business would they have with a family on the plains?"

"I cannot say. What did the girl's parents tell you?"

Kanderil nodded the way Sarene had been led.

"Little. They're with the Elders now. Tending the wounds."

"Wounds?"

"Aye." The man sighed again. "What can you do to help, exactly?"

Kanderil did not reply at first. He had no wish to be caught up in this. The Gathire were a group *any* man with sense would be reluctant to cross. This was not his problem to solve. He cursed under his breath. "I can perhaps provide some answers. I am no medic and no diplomat, but I know the Gathire."

"How?" A light ripple of accusation ran in the word, but the ire of the group before him was petering out.

"I was once with the army. I resigned."

The answer was light on detail but spoken with confidence, as if it was enough. The leader of the group hesitated before accepting the statement. "Fine. Come with me."

Chapter Four

Sarene felt Carin's hands tug on her shoulders as they arrived at her home. She turned to face the older woman. Carin was heavyset and short, with round features which seemed permanently blushed. In this dim light she seemed older than she was. Sarene looked up at her, still mystified. The gathering in the village street had been peculiar, something she'd never witnessed before. Her life was a quiet one, and she had grown and lived with peaceful people. To see them massed as they were had been strange. Disturbing, even. She'd been whisked away without so much as an explanation, and Carin had said nothing as they walked.

The woman spoke now, quietly. "Sarene, there was a..." A pause. "Some men came to your home. They did some horrible things."

Sarene stared at her. The words made sense but she didn't comprehend them. She looked towards her front door.

"You need to stay calm. Your brothers and sister are already upset. You need to stay strong. Okay?" Carin stroked a strand of hair from the girl's temple. Sarene blinked up at her again, then glanced back to the door. It seemed now more foreboding, as if a darkness lurked behind. She was reluctant to go, but at once also wanted to burst through to check on her loved ones.

Carin patted her on the shoulder before guiding her forward. Sarene moved, clasping her hands to her chest. She chewed on her lip as the door came closer, closer. The handle sat ready, waiting for her hand.

Sarene pushed the door open and stepped inside. She found her siblings sat around the table, while her father sat beside her mother's bed. Aislyn lay in it, with Sameran cupping her hand.

Her face was bandaged. The white cotton was touched with red.

Sarene took all this in as she shuffled forwards. Her brothers watched with eyes puffy from crying. Taylei's cheeks were still wet with tears. The sight of her elder sister triggered fresh ones to fall and she looked away.

Sameran stared at her with a solemn expression. He stroked Aislyn's hand once then stood from his chair. His wife's hand stayed where it was. Her mother made no visible movement at all.

As her father drew close, by the candle light Sarene could see his lip was split and swollen. She flinched at the sight. He placed a hand on her shoulder, saying nothing. Sarene found she could not bear his gaze. His disappointment was more than she could take and the scene crashed around her. She couldn't cry, not yet. Shock had misplaced every other emotion. She allowed herself to be drawn into an embrace, Sameran's arms surrounding her. She closed her eyes, pressing her face into his chest, trying to hide the sight of her mother in the bed, Aislyn's head wrapped in what could have been a death shroud.

She heard her father say "Thank you". Movement at the door as Carin left. Then he stepped back, holding Sarene at arm's length. With patience he said, "Where have you been?"

Not for the first time in her life she wished she could reply in words. She pointed north towards the road she'd taken out of the village.

"North. Why?"

It took a moment for her to remember. The insignia. Jared's. She fumbled for it, producing the tin piece after an awkward moment where she couldn't pull it free from her knapsack. Sameran took the badge from her, bringing it up to his face. He turned it over once, twice, three times. Ran his thumb across the edge. Finally he spoke, still with the insignia held up.

"Why didn't you tell us, Sarene?"

Sarene chewed her lip further. She shrugged her shoulders; what else could she do? A wave of shame and embarrassment swept over her. She shook her head and shrugged once more. Tears came in a rush, breaking free from the stunned feeling. She shook her head and spread her hands, her lower lip quivering, looking at her father whose gaze she could not hold for more than a few heartbeats at a time.

Sameran sighed, reaching out to hug his daughter again. She took it with immense gratitude, holding him with a fierce grip.

Her siblings watched them in silence.

"I'm glad you're safe. I'm glad you weren't here. They..." Sameran had to take a deep breath before finishing. "They were looking for you."

Sarene's eyes opened. She could smell sweat on his shirt, and just as clearly feel the fear in his voice. He stroked her hair, his voice low.

"They wanted to know where you were. We didn't know, but they wouldn't accept that. They hurt your mother." Those last few words came out with a tremble which Sameran fought *hard* to control.

Sarene froze, paralysed. The words were like a kick to the spine. These people who had attacked her family had come here because of *her*? What did she have to give? What possible motive could they have?

This thought gave way to something else. Something much, much worse.

Her mother was wounded, and she was responsible.

Sarene shook her head, but Sameran held it still with a firm hand. He stared at her with a raw emotion she'd never experienced from him. "Listen. Listen to me. This wasn't your fault. Whatever it was they wanted, you did nothing wrong. We'll find out in time but for now you promise me you won't blame yourself."

Animated now, she opened her mouth before shutting it again. She blinked, trying to look away, struggling to look past her father to see her mother, but Sameran's grip was too strong.

"*Promise* me, girl!"

Sarene nodded, her mind reeling. How does one react to having their life turned upside down like this? She'd never experienced anything remotely similar, nothing as devastating or visceral.

A knock at the door made her spin as the hand at her nape relented. Hathel stood there, beside the man who'd led her home. The stranger was ducking low to fit through the entrance, and when he stepped inside he seemed to fill the room. Those piercing eyes ran over the scene once only, not even lingering on the sight of her wounded mother.

"Sorry to disturb, Sam, but this here is Kanderil. He says he might be able to answer some questions about those bastards who did this."

Kanderil nodded once. Sameran did likewise.

"You picked a bad time to visit our village, Kanderil."

"So it seems."

"What is your role in all of this?"

"None, I hope." The woodsman named Kanderil held his hands before him, crossed at the wrist. "I found your girl a little over a day's walk from here. I brought her back. I felt she was somewhat young to be roaming alone."

Her father nodded. "For that, I thank you." Pausing, Sameran ran the back of his hand across his mouth. Emotion threatened to spill for just a heartbeat, but then was gone. He composed himself. "Thank you."

Kanderil took the words with no physical response. He

said, "I am sorry about your wife."

Sameran glanced over his shoulder, taking a long moment to return his attention to the newcomer. "We should step outside."

The woodsman spoke again as Sameran made to walk past him. "Perhaps Sarene should join us."

Sarene nodded at the mention of her name, mostly from instinct.

"Do you think that's for the best?" said her father.

"If this concerns her. I was led to believe so by your friend here." Kanderil gestured to Hathel, who was wringing his hands together. The balding cooper inclined his head. He seemed eager to leave.

Sameran considered this, then looked to his other children sitting around the home's sole table. "Taylei, fetch some bread and cheese for when we return." Sarene heard the chair grind against the ground a moment later.

She followed her father and the woodsman outside, closing the door behind her.

A ribbon of blue ran over the mountains to the west, framed in gold. To the east, the stars were appearing in the night sky. The moon hung thick between light and dark, maybe two days from producing a full face. The air was still warm from the day's heat, dropping only a few degrees. Kanderil enjoyed evenings such as this in most cases, content to watch the heavens turn. Not this evening.

Sameran slowed first, reaching the fencing around the chicken coop. He placed a hand upon the wood, staring out to the western range. Kanderil stopped a few feet from him, his face impassive. Sarene wandered over to her father, who reached out to draw her close to him, an arm across her shoulder. Kanderil got the impression he was making a token gesture to comfort himself as well as his daughter, an effort to protect the girl hours after the event which had befallen them.

Hathel bid them farewell. To the cooper's credit, his voice contained no pity.

Eventually, Sameran spoke. "So what can you offer, Kanderil?"

"The men who came to your home were Gathire." He paused, allowing the word to take weight in the other man's mind. Sameran reacted with a deep sigh, nodding for him to continue. "They were moving at speed along the Highway a few hours after I had found your daughter. I hid her from the road."

Sameran seemed relieved by the news, looking down to his girl. "What made you take such action?"

"Common sense, at first. Experience as a Kalethi second. Five riders moving at such pace is rare, especially in this area of the country. Your village lies between no major cities, and anyone travelling from Tamiran to Ghellei would have turned off the road your daughter and I walked miles previous."

"That was your sole reason?"

"No. I also had an encounter with some thieves several days ago who left empty handed. They also wore dark clothing, and I could not be sure they were not hunting the same route for victims." Kanderil looked at the girl, who now stared up at him. Her pale face was clear in the dying daylight.

"Dark clothing is not uncommon in Tamir."

"Neither is danger off the beaten path." Kanderil's voice was firm, speaking the truth as he saw it.

Sameran gave no immediate response. Then, "All I know of the Gathire is that they're the bodyguards of Prince Remelas."

"Not quite. The Gathire are a separate group within the military, officially under the command of the Prince. Unofficially, they are a unit of soldiers who do not answer to normal chains of command, and are essentially autonomous."

"How do you mean?"

Kanderil glanced towards the valley road. "They act

without consent. They are free to do whatever they wish to fulfil a given objective. The General of the army, currently Garonal, may assign them orders but he will have little say on how those orders are carried out."

"Lawless, then." Sameran shook his head. Understandably, he seemed tired, with dark rings around his eyes. The poor illumination only served to accentuate his haggard appearance. "What does this have to do with my family? With Sarene?"

"I do not know. I would suggest that, if she was their target, someone asked the Gathire to find her."

"The Prince?"

"Possibly. They *are* his attachment, as I said, but his command is said to be a token gesture only. Why Remelas would want your daughter, I do not know."

"Why he wouldn't just ask..." Sameran's voice was bitter.

Kanderil met the man's resentful gaze. "I presume they did ask you. I also presume they were not satisfied by your answer."

Sameran swore, tilting his head back to face the sky, before gesturing to his household. "They said they would return."

"Of that I have no doubt. The Gathire are nothing if not methodical."

"I can't risk my daughter."

"Then I suggest you leave with her."

Sameran tightened his grip on Sarene. She appeared so small and helpless against her father, much more childlike than when they'd first met.

"The nearest relative is four day's ride away. We have neither horses nor wagons, and I have little money for either."

"Your relatives will be receiving similar visits, I fear." The statement caught their attention. Kanderil shrugged. "The most logical places for a girl her age to hide would be with family. The Gathire know this."

"I thought they might... but..." Sameran fumbled for words. "Are you sure?"

"It is what I would do."

Silence fell on the three. Sameran stood there, his hands massaging the girl's shoulder. She held onto him, her arms wrapped tightly around his waist, staring at the ground. Kanderil felt a touch of compassion for them, a feeling he had not experienced for some time. He had not missed it. This was a family drawn into something they did not understand and, as far as he could tell, had no reason to endure. Their lives had been changed by a brief visit from dangerous men, and it would take a lot for things to get back to normal.

If they ever would.

"Sarene, fetch me some water." The girl blinked at her father. She looked at the woodsman, then back again. With a solemn nod she slipped free of his embrace and walked back towards the home. The two men waited until she had gone inside, the door latching shut behind her with a dull click.

Sameran ran a hand over his face. He was watching the entrance his daughter had just used. "Everything I took for granted was taken away from me today. My wife has been attacked by my own countrymen. My daughter was their target. I cannot quite work out my offence, but clearly I have wronged *someone* in a position of power."

Kanderil let him speak, feeling he was secondary to this conversation. The farmer was expressing the thoughts he could not share before his family.

"If those men had told me why they were there, what reason they had for hunting my girl, perhaps I could begin to grasp it. Perhaps I could try and make sense of this..." A pause. "All we received were questions. Then threats. Then..."

Kanderil nodded once.

"What can I do? You know how they work, how can I protect her?"

"I do not know how they work, only how they would operate as individuals."

"What does that mean, man?" Sameran snapped back.

"It means that I cannot say for sure how to keep the girl

out of their hands. The Gathire are thorough, and they will keep searching until they find her."

Sameran clenched his hands. One of the knuckles popped. The door to the home opened quietly and Sarene appeared carrying two mugs.

"By the Four... If, say, I found us a wagon and we went into hiding?"

"They would track you. I would not be surprised if they had the valley on watch soon."

"How can you be sure they haven't already?"

"I cannot. Five riders passed me – I do not know the number which originally arrived."

Sarene clicked her tongue. The two men looked at her as she hurried forward, holding out the mugs. As they were taken he held up one hand, all fingers and the thumb present and displayed.

"Yes, five."

She shook her head. Slowly she rolled her finger in a circle a few times, before pointing to the sky.

"She means earlier," said Sameran. Sarene nodded. She held up those five digits again, and waved them in one slow arc across herself. Then she pointed to her eyes, repeating the motion.

"You saw the five riders earlier in the day?"

She shook her head, bouncing her index finger twice as though a bunny hopping along.

"Two days. You saw the five riders Kanderil mentioned two days ago."

A firm nod.

"How did you avoid them?" Kanderil asked. Sarene shrugged. She tapped her temple, then gave a downward thumb. *Bad.*

"Clever."

"So they may not have put the place on watch yet?" Sameran sounded hopeful for the first time since Kanderil had met him.

"It is possible. Did you reveal how long it had been since you last saw her yourself?"

"Yes. No more than three days. We also told them the same as you; no horses, no wagon."

Kanderil sipped at his water. It had been some hours since he last took a drink, but he refrained from draining the mug. "Perhaps they felt that they would find her nearby if they believed she was on foot."

"Then we can get her out of the valley without being seen?"

"If you choose to do so, then do so quickly. I suspect they will return soon when they find themselves empty handed."

Sameran ran a palm over his face. "I could borrow a wagon, I'm sure. The Elders would approve given the situation."

"Your friend Hathel mentioned the Elders were at your home."

"They left shortly before you arrived."

Kanderil nodded. He had not seen them.

"I must be honest with you, my friend. Even with a wagon, your chances are slim."

Sameran took a long moment to answer. "Why so?"

"With seven people and possessions, you would leave a lot of tracks and make poor time. In addition, you would be easy to identify."

"Then what, damnit?" The question came out angry, but Kanderil accepted it.

"Send her alone, as she was doing anyway. Cut her hair and change her name. She can find work in one of the cities."

"Doing what? She can't speak, man."

Sarene looked to the floor, glancing away. Kanderil spread his free hand in response.

"No..." Sameran continued. "I can't send her out alone. The risks are too great."

At those words, the Hunter understood. The logical answer was obvious, but this shaken, confused man opposite was too proud to ask despite this dire situation. Their eyes met, and Kanderil felt a gnawing sense of duty clawing over his impartiality. He did not want this, but he could not accept walking away. It did not sit right with him. Not this time.

"I will take her."

The girl flinched. She shook her head, gazing up at her father. He sighed, the sound empty with loss.

"I cannot ask you to do that."

"There is little alternative. If the girl stays with you, you are all in danger. The same goes for friends and relatives. Travelling, you will surely be caught and they will take her from you. I am skilled in these lands. I can keep her out of sight."

"I could take her alone. Just us and two horses, we will make much better time."

"Then the Gathire will arrest you for trying, you will leave four children and a wife unsupported, and they will still take Sarene."

"They will have to find me first."

"They will."

Kanderil did not elaborate. This farmer, this plain man, was no match for the Gathire. He could not hope to avoid detection for more than a few weeks. In the meantime they would return to the home looking for more answers. The head of the family would be needed here... for what little good it would do. Kanderil resented that he had been placed in this position as a result of trying to do a good dead, which was in turn inspired by a moment of apathy.

Sameran ruffled his daughter's hair. She did not smile. "What of the rest of us, then?"

"In your position I would send your children to stay with other households here. Even the Gathire would not risk a national incident by attacking an entire village. You and your wife should send word to your nearest garrison asking for assistance. It may give you leverage to avoid further violence should they return."

"Why not do that anyway, and keep her with me?"

"They would still take her. The Gathire still outrank the normal military in most cases. The best they could do is object."

Sameran's mouth was drawn tight, his jaw clenched. He seemed to be taxing his mind for more options, but the most viable ones had already been discussed. When the words came they were reluctant.

"Very well. I have another son. My eldest, Jared. He is stationed in Tamiran as a member of the Kalethi. I would ask you to take my girl to him and explain the situation. He will take care of her then, and you will be free to move on. For that I would owe you a great debt, one I may not be able to repay." Sameran hesitated for a moment. "I understand you may be placing yourself in danger by doing this."

"Aye," Kanderil said. "I might."

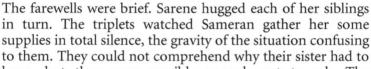

The farewells were brief. Sarene hugged each of her siblings in turn. The triplets watched Sameran gather her some supplies in total silence, the gravity of the situation confusing to them. They could not comprehend why their sister had to leave, but they were sensible enough not to ask. The atmosphere in the homestead was grave, the flickering candlelight adding to the tension. Taylei held her dearly, tears still streaming down her cheeks. Her eyes were red and shimmering, and she sniffed with every other breath. Sarene stroked her hair and kissed her cheek. She wanted to cry also, but she was holding dear to Carin's words. *Stay strong.*

Finally she moved to her mother, who still lay asleep in the bed. Her father had mentioned that she had been given a herbal remedy by the Elders, which had let her rest. Sarene held Aislyn's hand, looking down at the bandaged face. Only the nose and mouth were visible, with two larger pads beneath the bandage, each covering one cheek. Both bore two strips of blood which had seeped through the fabric diagonally from eye to jawline. Sarene could not suppress the shudder which ran through her body. Leaning forward she kissed Aislyn's brow, taking a deep breath. She didn't want to leave, and this scene made her consider refusing to go with the stranger. Sarene did not want this to be the last image she had of her mother without knowing when she would be able to return.

With great reluctance she stepped outside with her father and the woodsman. Kanderil crouched as he moved through the doorway, just as he had when he first entered.

Her father pulled her into a tight grasp, which she returned. Away from her siblings she allowed the tears to fall, making small wet dots on her father's shirt. He kissed her cheek, and as she leaned back she reached up to pat him on the top of the head, a gesture they had long associated with three words: *I love you.* Sameran returned the action.

"You be good, and you do whatever Kanderil says. He'll get you to Jared. You'll be safe there."

Sarene nodded. The thought of finding Jared after all was not the consolation it would have been three days ago. The events here at her home had not yet sunk in. It seemed unreal that at the start of the week her main worry was assisting with the mill work. Now she was being forced from her home with a man she barely knew, as a result of five others she had never met. Five strangers who had injured her mother for a reason she could not fathom.

Sameran looked to his daughter's would-be guardian. "One day I will repay you, my friend. I swear it."

Kanderil shook his head. "I do not require payment. Any man of worth would do the same."

"Then at least allow me to offer you a place to rest here, should you ever require it."

"That would be fine."

Sameran looked back at Sarene, holding her at arm's length. It took a long while to let go.

"Go on. We will see you again soon, by the Four."

Sarene stood there, unwilling to move. She clutched at the bag she held, containing the few possessions gathered for the journey. Beneath the dark fabric of the knapsack she could feel the hard pan pipes, and she closed her fingers around them as tightly as possible.

Jared would know what to do. He always did.

Chapter Five

*T*he interior of the home was like a patchwork quilt. Everything appeared warm and scattered. A broad oak table was covered in books, parchments and scrolls. A cupboard, the doors hanging open, contained an assortment of clothes in various fabrics, made double by the mirror wedged behind them. The woven rug lying on the floor was creased in the middle, the tassels along the edge tangled and knotted. A bronze-framed bed stood in one corner, covered in a thick quilt and a mountain of pillows. In the hearth, a blazing fire combined with the scores of candles dotted to throw a sepia light over everything. The place smelt of wood smoke, musk and of days gone by. The home was crafted of autumn and the colours bled into each other.

Sitting in a wicker chair was a man. The chair rocked softly beneath him as he thumbed through a book. Clean shaven and with a thick shock of silver hair, he could have passed for a man in his fifties. Wrinkles touched his brow and laughter lines ran across his cheeks, but his blue eyes were alert and clear. The man wore spectacles, the arms of which were attached to a length of chain which hung around his neck.

He was focused on the words before him. At points he would run a finger along a line, the end of his tongue poking out over a lip, and then tut or huff or murmur. At one point he shook his head and gave a contemptuous chuckle. He took a quill pen from a pot tucked into a small table beside him and jotted something in one of the margins. Once satisfied, he continued to read.

Gentle music played in the background; the sound of a harp floated through the air. The man looked up, glancing towards the window. Outside a wind was raging, and the branches of a tree rapped against the pane. It had once been suggested to him that he should remove the branch, but he enjoyed the sound of it. He enjoyed the reminder that there was life outside of his home. On clear days birds would perch there and chirp their sweet mantras. On days of harsh weather the tree would knock, seeking to come in to shelter.

There was a sound from the other side of the room's only entrance. A shuffling of feet and a small *clunk*. Then the door opened. A large man stepped inside, black skinned and bald. It was as though someone had brought to life a warrior of fable. His had a broad, flat nose and dark eyes which contrasted with the whiteness around the irises. A thick cloak of wolf's fur adorned his shoulders, and he carried a heavy staff carved with intricate detail. His torso was bare, but he wore a floor-length kilt of leather and chain. Around his neck was an amulet of gold and sapphire. He bowed his head to the man sitting in the wicker chair.

The old man closed his book and stood. He stepped forward and offered his hand. The black man watched him and made no movement to respond.

"Your home smells unpleasant," the visitor stated.

"Be thankful you only visit once every four years, then."

The warrior looked around him, gesturing with an open hand. "Could you not tidy up before our arrival?"

"What would be the point? I'd only have to mess it all up again."

The two of them locked eyes. The newcomer looked down at the hand still waiting to be taken. With a growing smile he reached out and took it, stepping forward to embrace the older man.

"It is good to see you again, my brother," he said.

"Same to you, Mubuto." The old man stepped back. "Keeping up appearances, eh?"

Mubuto looked down at himself. "There is precious little reason for me to leave my home these days. I may as well make the most of it."

Nodding, the old man stepped away, moving towards his desk. He picked up a pouch and from it withdrew a portion of tobacco, which he started to stack into a nearby pipe.

The warrior frowned. "Still smoking those weeds, I see."

Pausing, the old man looked at the pipe. "Actually, I was planning to wipe my arse with them."

Mubuto considered this. "I suppose that is one way to take in the effects."

The old man grinned. "Ever notice how you are always the first to arrive?"

"Yes."

"Do you hassle the others in their own homes as much as this?"

"Of course."

The old man brought the pipe to his mouth and bit on the clamp. "I thought as much."

For several minutes the two of them made small talk. The host puffed on his pipe, blowing thick rings of smoke towards his larger visitor, who ignored them. They spoke comfortably, both easy in the other's presence. As men they could not be more different, yet they addressed each other like family.

Eventually there was another knock on the door, which opened before either occupant could answer. A slight man of creamy pale skin, with slanted eyes and angular features, stepped across the threshold. His dark hair was cut short, his fringe just reaching his brow. He seemed much younger than the others, and wonderfully handsome with it. He wore a simple white robe free of decoration.

"Corliani," he said with a bow. "Mubuto."

"Shigasi," the old man replied. He offered the pipe in his hand. "Care for some smoke?"

"Ach, no thank you." Shigasi shook his head. "The fumes taste of burning dog hair."

"That's okay," Mubuto offered. "So does his cooking."

Corliani started to reply when a fourth figure stepped in behind Shigasi. This man was tanned, with closely cropped white hair and a tight, trimmed beard. He wore a dark robe with gold trim; intricate stitching, squares and diamonds of fabrics weaved together to form a variety of patterns. Corliani sucked at the pipe, exhaling smoke from his nostrils.

"Hello, Tyrrial."

Tyrrial bowed in response. "I see you have kept the place tidy as ever."

"Mubuto said the same thing."

"He did not listen to me either," said Mubuto as he shook Shigasi's hand. "He did not listen four years ago, or any of the years before that."

"Perhaps you could come and clean up after him, Mubuto." Shigasi turned to greet Tyrrial. "Your place is always immaculate."

"That is because there is nothing there to tidy," Tyrrial replied. "I have seen more furnishings in a tomb."

Coughing softly, Corliani smirked. "Well, well. What would the world say if they knew the legendary Four sat around discussing each other's housekeeping habits."

"To say nothing of your lacking skills as a host," Mubuto put in. "Do you not have any wine in this place?"

With a sigh, Corliani pointed towards the centre of the room. There on a small, round stand sat four pewter goblets around a silver jug. The black man nodded, moving to fetch himself a cup.

Settling themselves into various chairs after clearing away debris and stacks of study materials, the Four discussed the ongoing events in the area of the world each resided within. Shigasi revealed that the lands to the north were relatively uneventful, save for a fire in the Shu'Cha capital of Yakya.

The blaze had destroyed huge sections of the city, mostly in the poorer areas, and it had ushered in a wave of charity from the rich. The nobles had initially refused to help pay for the repairs and rebuilding, but the Emperor of the Shu'Cha had persuaded them.

Shigasi chuckled. "The ruling was that any man who owned property of worth must donate ten percent of his available wealth to the national treasury. The Emperor would then use it pay for the restoration effort. Anybody who refused would instead have all their assets removed by force and auctioned off."

"Is it working?" asked Tyrrial.

"It is now. At first the rich were simply providing a token amount and claiming it to be an accurate representation of their resources. When the Emperor received much less funds than anticipated he sent out a horde of accountants to take stock of the situation. He then declared any who cheated the ten percent figure would be fined double what they *should* have paid."

"Interesting. And the poor?"

"The majority were just thankful for help from the ruling family. A few tried to claim charity they were not entitled to, but they were simply kicked out of the city."

Tyrrial muttered. "Typical. Always a few ruining it for the rest."

Mubuto explained that far to the south an uprising in the lands of the Juu'ad had caused some unrest among their neighbours. "The Juu'ad suffered another coup. This time a man named Jubuar has taken it upon himself to murder the Chieftain and take up their Spear of Dominance. The brazen audacity of the man has many of his tribe worried."

"Should we be worried also?" Corliani asked, setting up another pipe.

"Not for now. The Juu'ad are a reckless people but they lack any real internal unity. They shake a good stick and will makes threats daily, but by the time anyone ever tries to organise an army something else happens in the capital and it all falls apart again."

"Tell that to the Maih," Tyrrial put in. "Haven't you ever considered stepping in to help them fall in line?"

Mubuto shook his head. "They are like wasps trapped in a jam jar. They will buzz and hiss but never get anywhere. Perhaps I will intervene if they ever *do* invade another nation, but for now I am inclined to let them get on with it."

Corliani shrugged when it came to news of the east. "There is really nothing to say. The lands are enduring a harsh summer, but nothing that they have not experienced in previous years. The price of wheat may rise." He thought to himself while the others stared at him. "Oh, one person invented a machine which generates its own momentum. It involves heating up water and making the steam pressure drive a piston."

"It is about time somebody thought of that." Shigasi leaned forward. "Have they developed a practical use for it?"

"Not really. It makes a lot of noise and looks awfully complicated. I wouldn't be surprised if it explodes before they make any real progress."

There was a long pause. Tyrrial scratched his jaw as the other three looked at him. His amber eyes focused on Corliani.

"Are you sure that is all?"

Corliani nodded. "All of importance."

"What about the girl?"

Mubuto chuckled, slapping his knee. Shigasi sighed. "This again?"

"The girl is still on her farm," Corliani said. "Nothing has changed."

"She came of age this summer," Tyrrial continued. His manner was calm and he leaned back in his chair, bringing a hand to his chin. "Prophets across the lands have been preaching of her existence for months now."

"Those useless mystics have been muttering nonsense for years. Nobody pays mind to them." Corliani lit his pipe again, speaking between puffs. Fumes rose up around his head. "Do you really believe anybody is going to seek her out because a paranoid fool standing on a box says she is important?"

"It is a long shot, I agree. But there is still the potential for unrest. This girl represents the reason why we must keep a tighter grip on them all." Tyrrial held up his hand as Shigasi began to protest. "Hear me out. I have always abided by our collective decisions. I have not paid a personal visit to this girl in Tamir because you asked me not to. I have refrained from getting involved in your territory, Corliani. I respect you and I trust you will handle any situation which should arise in your corner of the lands."

Corliani quirked a brow. "*Have* refrained..?"

Tyrrial gave a short laugh, glancing to his lap. "This girl is a singular risk which makes me uneasy. Should anyone take the prophets seriously and discover what she is capable of then it could develop out of control. People will start to think they can do what they like. We could be looking at a return to the old ways."

"Come now," said Shigasi. "That is a little far-fetched."

"Not at all. It is cause and effect." Tyrrial sighed. "We have discussed this many times over. You have made your arguments for letting her be, and I have made mine for removing her. Even Mubuto understands, even if he does not openly agree."

The black man smiled. "I said we should keep her under close observation, my brother. That is all."

"But you understand how she could become a threat to us?"

Sighing, Mubuto spread his hands. "If that is what you want to hear, then yes. I appreciate your argument."

"We *all* understand your concerns," Corliani pointed out. "But right now she is at home and causing no trouble. Her family is helping the village to build a windmill for the harvest. As far as I understand her father will not let her leave sight of her cottage. We have nothing to fear right now."

Tyrrial sighed. He looked towards the window as a fresh gust of wind caused the branch to tap at the glass again.

"We will have nothing to fear in the future, either."

A brief silence descended. Corliani studied his pipe

before speaking, his words measured. "You were not in Tamir. I would have noticed."

"No, I was not in Tamir. However, I decided to deal with the problem myself and suffer your disapproval."

Mubuto frowned. "What have you been up to, Tyrrial?"

"The same thing each of us has done a hundred times over. Made an independent decision for the good of the world."

"Stop being vague," snapped Corliani. "What have you done?"

Tyrrial faced him. "Do you recall the experiments I have been running these last few decades? About creating sentience?"

"You mean your necromancy," Shigasi retorted. "I thought you had given up on that?"

"I gave up on creating *life*," Tyrrial replied. "It is impossible. However, I discovered how to create a new consciousness within a host body."

The three others exchanged looks. "You mean you raised the *dead*?"

"No. I created something with self-awareness, an active thought process and its own personality. It is a little unstable, but a remarkable success."

"Using a cadaver," Mubuto said. "Necromancy."

"We can discuss this in a moment," Corliani said, leaning on his armrest. "How does this relate to the girl?"

Tyrrial tilted his head back. A light smile appeared. "I sent my creature to deal with her. She will not be a threat to us."

"Oh, for..." Shigasi covered his mouth with his hands. "You're going to murder her? But what about the studies we had planned?"

"I wanted to meet her," Mubuto said sternly. "Experience her abilities first hand."

"There are a million other subjects we can study," Tyrrial said, waving his hand. "She is too great a risk."

"You took it upon yourself to encroach on my lands," Corliani said. "And yet you talk of respect? I find this most upsetting, Tyrrial."

"I merely acted in the one instance where you could not, my brother."

Taking a deep breath Corliani put his pipe down, the embers within smoking, and placed his fingertips together beneath his chin. "Do you know if your creature has been successful?"

"I do not see why it would fail. It is the perfect assassin. You would be impressed, Corliani."

"I am sure I would be. But your actions are disturbing. Why now?" Corliani sighed. "Of all the infringements upon our rules that have occurred, why *now*? Why this girl? She is harmless."

"Harmless until someone discovered her true identity. Then she could become much more. With some utility she could lead an uprising against us. It would be a global Juu'ad."

"That I would be delighted to see," Mubuto said with a laugh, slapping his thigh. "The girl is no warrior, Tyrrial."

"In the future," Corliani announced, "I would be most pleased if you would come to us with your plans before you put them into motion. To go against the majority vote is upsetting. I am concerned by your rash decision, Tyrrial. Never before have you so openly acted against us."

"Oh, come now," said Tyrrial. "I have not gone *against* you. There was no official vote of action here."

"No, but if there had been you could have predicted the result." Corliani replied.

"I thought we were still autonomous," Tyrrial said with a sneer. "I did not realise that in times of peace we were a democracy."

"Brothers are not governments but they still respect each other," Shigasi offered, folding his hands within the sleeves of his robe. "I thought you understood that."

Tyrrial chuckled. "Very well. I apologise for my actions. But I believe I was justified. A burning building in a city of timber will not always result in a raging inferno. That does not mean one should avoid extinguishing the fire."

"I agree," said Mubuto, leaning forward with his palms on his knees. "But neither would I murder a young girl on the basis that she has the potential to injure me one day. Not without a solid reason to suspect she will."

"I feel happier debating this now the girl will be dealt with." Tyrrial shrugged. "One day you will understand that I made the right choice. My reasons were solid."

"You always have reasons, Tyrrial," said Corliani in a cool tone. "Perhaps one day you will learn trust also."

The two of them gazed at each other for a long moment. The fire crackled in the hearth, candles fluttered against their wicks and the branch knocked again on the window. The warmth of Corliani's home was lost for a moment, an icy grip descending about them until Mubuto laughed and broke the stalemate.

The rest of the meeting went along without incident. The Four talked over their recent whereabouts and the various studies they were undertaking. It was only when the three guests began to make their way back out of the door that Corliani brought up the subject again, placing a hand on Tyrrial's shoulder and speaking to him quietly.

"I will investigate this further myself," he said. "If the girl still lives, I will expect you to take no further action."

"And if she is dead?" Tyrrial asked.

"We will deal with that if we come to it. But understand this: I find your actions selfish and paranoid. Over the centuries I always felt you kept your lesser qualities under control. But in this instance you have failed us all."

Tyrrial's face darkened and he pulled his shoulder free of the other man's grip. "For a man so old you are incredibly naive. Not everyone out there *loves* us, my brother. Many are unhappy. They feel restricted by our blessed rules. Some day they will make a stand."

"When that day comes we will deal with it."

"When that day comes," Tyrrial said, "You will wish we had kept a tighter grasp on them. They have too much freedom. Crime, poverty and other atrocities are still rife out there."

"So is murder, it seems."

"Would you have stood against me? Had you known?"
Tyrrial raised a brow. "Would you have openly sought to
impede my actions?"

With a gentle smile, Corliani held the door open and
waited for his brother to leave.

Tyrrial chuckled, shaking his head as he stepped through.
"Goodbye, Corliani. See you next year."

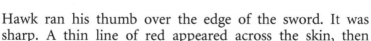

*The creature observed the two figures moving along the fields.
Soon they reached a steep incline along the edge of the valley.
They climbed. It was slow going, and the big man had to wait
for the small girl several times. He helped her with the steeper
points, all but carrying her on a few occasions. Keeping her safe.*

All the while the creature watched, grinning.

*It had seen the men who had come to the girl's home. It had
seen them leave. It had seen the villagers, petty and useless,
wandering the streets like restless lambs. It had seen the girl
arrive with her companion. It had seen everything, and it had
watched and grinned and giggled.*

Laughter like a child, high pitched and carefree.

Laughter like a killer, manic and vicious.

*It moved north, across the fields and towards the valley's
edge.*

It would be sure to keep close by.

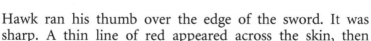

Hawk ran his thumb over the edge of the sword. It was
sharp. A thin line of red appeared across the skin, then
slowly faded.

The workmanship was immaculate. Flawless steel
shimmered in the morning light from his window. Oiled
leather had been wrapped around the hilt. Holding out an
index finger he placed the sword upon it at the very base of
the blade. It was weighted to perfection, lying horizontal

with no need for him to balance it. He gripped the hilt and swung the weapon once. It sang as it passed through air, bleeding a note around the blade. The sound was beautiful.

How it came to be in his room was a mystery, but Hawk found himself incredibly glad that it was.

He sheathed the weapon in a black scabbard similar in style to the hilt. Both were made of treated leather, with no gems or engravings except for a silver band at the tip. Placing the sword back on the table, he moved to the door and check the latch. It remained locked.

Hawk walked over to the window and looked outside. From his tavern room, he could see Ghellei's usual morning business. Markets stalls were being prepared, with merchants moving back and forth to trade and barter for that day's stock. He could smell fish and smoke from cooking fires and the filth of the people who would soon be coming to purchase what little they could afford. Sanitation was for the rich. Here in the slums, the shit mixed with the merchandise on equal terms.

The voices of those below grew quieter as he crossed the room to the small basin set against the wall. Lifting water to his face, he scrubbed hard with his palms. Droplets ran from his nose and chin as he gripped the basin. He blew air from his nose to expel the excess from his nostrils.

Hawk had not slept well.

Visions of the poacher had filled his dreams. The man seemed colossal, towering over him. Arms folded, head back, braying with a booming laugh which shook his bones and bruised his skin. Shame of such *depth* had burned like a furnace in his belly. The presence of the giant physically pained him, and he had to cower through it all despite his wounded pride.

Several times he had awoken, sweating and panting.

Several times the dream returned.

Yet that morning, after discovering the sword and placing his hand around it, he felt invigorated. The sword was his, was *him*, the part he hadn't realised he was missing. Such a weapon would grant him his revenge; would end the poacher in one blessed thrust.

Hawk was neither a vindictive man nor a coward, and yet this had to be done. Unless *he* acted the poacher would continue to walk the lands, seeking to do the same to others. To embarrass, shame and ultimately destroy them.

He looked at his hands. They trembled. A nagging thought bothered him, hanging at the back of his mind like a small raincloud threatening to burst. It felt like an itch. It was similar to waking up after an excess of alcohol, knowing you'd done something you shouldn't. Hawk tried to recall the previous evening. There was a bard singing songs. He'd had a few ales. Then he went outside for a piss and...

Nothing. He couldn't recall anything after that. Had he spoken to someone? Witnessed something?

He reached for the towel. The troubled night's rest must have affected him after all.

A knock made him turn. He reached for the sword, his fingertips just touching the hilt before a feminine voice came through the thin door.

"Good morning! I have your breakfast here."

Hawk stepped to the door, opening it. A small woman stood in the corridor, holding a wooden platter of bread and creamed cheese. A mug of juice stood beside it, its flavour unknown. She smiled up at him, revealing a large gap between her two front teeth.

"Hope you slept well, sir."

Hawk stared at her for a moment more. Then he smiled, his face brightening. "Just fine, thank you," he replied warmly. She seemed pleased by the answer. After taking the platter he rewarded the maid with a wink, then nudged the door with his foot. He caught her curtsy just as it closed.

Placing the food on the table his face soured again. Mechanically he ate, tasting little. He stared at the sword for the entire meal. The juice turned out to be watered orange, which he finished in two swallows. His eyes remained on the weapon, watching it over the edge of the cup.

Those dreams were once again whispering to him. For a moment, he believed he could still hear that laughter.

———◄○►———

The trek up the valley was slow going. Sarene was exhausted, both physically and mentally. To have marched all day towards the horror she had found within her home, only to then be made to climb up what could barely be called a path along the western side of the valley mountains, had brought her to the brink of her endurance. Her legs ached, her back roared, and her eyes burned. She stumbled along behind Kanderil, who showed no signs of slowing. If he had not been with her she would have surely fallen during the climb. Twice she lost her footing on the slim, rocky outcrops.

They hiked for another hour after breaking the top of the cliffs before Kanderil stopped. Sarene all but bumped into the back of him, her head down and shoulders slouched.

"We can camp here."

Sarene dropped to the ground, her legs curled under her. She held her head in her hands, the events of the day running at breakneck pace through her mind.

The image of her mother kept coming back to haunt her. She tried to push it away but failed. An occasional rustle of leaves around her caused her to glance up and see Kanderil collecting small branches and sticks. They were in a space of maybe four square yards between trees. The area smelt thick with nature; rich and earthy. The leaves were turning brown with the heat of the last few weeks, gold and auburn along the floor contrasting with yellows and greens peppering the branches above. Sarene brushed her hair from her face, staring at nothing.

Her mind must have shut off for a while at least, because Kanderil suddenly dumped a fair wood pile beside her, making her jump.

"Do you know how to stack this into a fire?"

She nodded. Of course she did, they had a fireplace in her home. She would help her mother prepare meals. She liked preparing the fire and bringing the flames to life. She liked helping.

"Good. Do so." Kanderil produced a small box from his pack. Holding it in one hand, he offered her his canteen with the other. She looked at it. The woodsman knelt, placing the box on the floor before unscrewing the container's cap. Crouched, he reminded her of a boulder.

Sarene took the canteen as he offered it to her again. At first she merely sipped at the water before thirst overtook her. A trickle ran down her chin as she gulped. She eventually pulled the canteen away, holding it in her lap. The liquid sloshed around inside. Kanderil reached over to take it away, replacing the cap. He placed it on the ground beside her. She heard him clear his throat, and raised her head to see him gesturing to the wood at her side.

Nodding blindly, she stared at the wood and struggled to make the connection. Tears welled, and within moments the sobs came rushing after them. Sarene buried her face in her palms and cried like she never had before, shivering and choking; the frail young girl she'd always been treated as.

She had failed to find Jared. Had run from her family and they had suffered for her. The promise made to her father to not blame herself brought no comfort.

Sarene continued to cry.

Something heavy held to her shoulder. It offered a gentle squeeze of comfort which she rejected, jarring her shoulder upwards. The weight lifted, and she was left to her misery.

She rolled over to her side, curled up in a ball, and bawled. The image of those bandages around her mother's face refused to leave her, no matter how tightly she shut her eyes.

Kanderil stared at the girl across the flames. She had cried herself to sleep roughly an hour ago. This deep into the forest, the smoke from their campfire would mostly dissipate before reaching past the canopy above, while the warm, flickering light would not be visible more than twenty yards away.

After pulling the girl's cloak around her to act as a blanket, he had watched her crying and found the accompanying sounds unsettling. No moans or wails; no words. The girl had breathed in gasps, sniffing and gulping air as if drowning. He had tried to offer some contact in an effort to console her and she had refused his hand. Deciding it was best to let her release the stress which had built up inside, he'd withdrawn.

He was disappointed to have found himself relieved to do so.

Kanderil chewed on a strip of cured bacon. The salty texture was dry now, stiff, and not as pleasant as it had been two weeks ago. In the morning he'd prepare a full meal, once the girl had slept. For now he let his belly rumble. His mind was elsewhere anyway.

He was thinking of the Gathire.

Why they would want Sarene he could not fathom. She wasn't remarkable in any way. Just a simple farmer's daughter who couldn't speak. He could detect no talents and no obvious skills. Presumably her father would have mentioned something if he had known any reason for the Gathire to seek her out. If she *did* have a great secret, would Sameran have placed her in his care? Would he endanger them both by withholding such knowledge?

Kanderil doubted it. Sarene's father seemed a good man, if completely out of his depth.

He brushed his hands together as he finished the bacon. *What, then?*

The Gathire were not sent on small errands. He had heard from his time with the Kalethi that they would openly refuse orders they considered beneath them. Something about the girl *must* be of importance. He doubted the Prince was involved. Kanderil had met Remelas once, five years ago. The Prince was still in his late teens then, but when handing out the then-Sergeant's Valour medal he had been polite and sincere with his praise. It did not fit his character to send out the Gathire to injure a young girl's family in pursuit of her.

Kanderil looked up as Sarene rolled over, pulling her

cloak higher around herself. She twitched a few times. If she dreamt then the images were not enjoyable.

What else would you expect? he asked himself.

Sarene awoke to see smoke drifting past. She smelt the remains of the campfire before she saw it, turning her head to observe a layer of white ash upon the very last of the glowing embers. The air was sombre, the first of the sun's rays hardly penetrating the thick canopy. She sat up, rubbing her temples. A fine mist had settled around them, obscuring the trees beyond. Her clothes felt damp. Sarene drew her cloak around her, shivering a little.

Kanderil was asleep, sitting cross legged on the other side of the fire. The woodsman's jaw was resting on his hand, an elbow propped against a folded knee. Sarene studied him. He looked weary now his features were relaxed. His beard was curled tightly, contrasting with the long, straight hair which reached past his chest. Even slouched, his shoulders were well over two feet across. His skin was tanned but not leathery like some in her village who toiled the fields. She wondered what he did for a living, aside from wander around in the forest.

"Are you done?"

Sarene jumped as he opened his eyes. That stare brought back the sense of hardness about his features and she struggled to meet his gaze.

"Good morning, lass." Kanderil placed his hand on the floor. With one long, fluid motion he stood. She was surprised by his grace. He wiped his hands together, gesturing to the dying fire. "Get that going again, and I will gather us some breakfast. It will not be much, sadly, but it will keep us full."

Sarene nodded, reaching for the remaining wood. Then she remembered why she was here. She froze mid-action, tears close to the surface within seconds. This time, with great effort, she managed to hold them back. Shaking hands began to lay the driest of the sticks on the remaining few embers. The girl sniffed several times as she did so, stopping once to wipe her nose on her sleeve.

The breakfast was a mixture of onions and mushrooms, with some wild garlic thrown in. Kanderil fried it in a small skillet before spreading the mixture along some of their bread. The taste was lost on Sarene; she ate instinctively, her thoughts constantly returning back to her family.

Why were they hunting her? What could these people possibly want? She had never even been outside the valley. The more she considered the question, the more answers eluded her. There wasn't a single possible reason. Not for her.

After the meal was complete, Kanderil killed the fire with his boot. He lifted his weapons from the ground and slung them in place across his back. His quiver of black-shafted arrows sat along his spine. He paused to don a headband, tying the ribbon of dark fabric across his brow to keep his hair in place. Sarene watched him while he did so, noting that at no point did he glance at her.

He turned instead to look deeper into the forest. At least, she *presumed* he did. Even with the mist around them dispersing, she was totally lost.

"We should continue on. You've slept for several hours."

Sarene took a deep breath, rising to her feet. As she shouldered her knapsack the woodsman spoke again.

"I am sorry for what happened, Sarene."

She held her thumb between the fingers of her other hand as he faced her. Her only reply was a single nod.

With that, he began to lead the way.

For two days it watched them. As they walked, as they ate, as they slept. It could smell the sweat, tasting their efforts to get away from the danger which had visited the girl's home.

The creature leapt through the treetops, watching them from above. At any moment it could have descended, but it waited. The anticipation was sweet and intoxicating. Several times it had almost given in to temptation and appeared to them early, before the perfect moment. Self-restraint was difficult and it had twitched and giggled with the effort, fighting against itself, restless like a caged animal.

Now they were tired and wary. Things would be easier this way.

It was time to meet the girl and introduce itself. Introduce her to its ways. To its claws.

It was time to make a mark on the world.

Chapter Six

*T*he travel had been difficult for the girl, but Kanderil allowed little respite. The Gathire would likely send out more than five people to search for her. There was too much open ground between Hailein Valley and the nearby main cities. If they had scouted the surrounding terrain - and Kanderil had no reason to believe they had not - they would have seen the potential routes out of the valley aside from the main road. For this reason Kanderil was leading them southwest, cutting a wide circle towards Tamiran. A direct route would increase the risk of being intercepted. The campfire on that first night was a liability, leaving behind tracks which could certainly be read, but Sarene had been exhausted from the preceding events. To deny the girl a decent rest would have made the travel torturous for her.

During the afternoon of the third day, as they walked, Kanderil carefully drew his bow. Before drawing a shaft he held up a hand, which by now Sarene understood was a sign to stop moving. She obeyed.

He knelt, eyes fixed on a point in the distance. The dense forest was silent except for a distant chirping. He waited.

A few minutes later a pheasant wandered into view. It investigated the ground with its beak before peering around. There wasn't enough time to make out the large human crouching in the distance. An arrow ended its life moments afterwards.

Kanderil walked forward to collect their lunch. He pulled the arrow free, checking it was still straight before wiping it on the feathers of the dead bird. Satisfied, he slid it back into his quiver and tied the pheasant to his bag. Sarene watched him silently, as she had done with every kill of the journey.

"Makes a change from rabbit," he said. She did not respond.

They continued to walk, stepping over dead logs and roots while ducking below branches and vines. The scent of the summer day was rich and heavy from the assorted flowers and herbs scattered amongst the grass. Kanderil turned at one point to note Sarene had paused beside a tree. She was running her hand along the rough bark, which had snarled up into a strange shape. He patiently waited until he caught her gaze. When she pointed at the tree again, he moved back to see for himself.

The bark gave the image of a grotesque face, as though melted on one side. There was a knot of wood for a mouth which split to portray a groan. One eye was detailed, a chip in the bark revealing a pupil, while the other was elongated, stretched over a few inches.

Kanderil inclined his head. "Very strange."

Sarene looked up at him in the same way she had done for almost the entire journey; lost and blank. She nodded once in return, lifting a hand to stroke her hair behind her ear. Then she walked past him, continuing the way they had been heading.

They took a break shortly after. Kanderil overturned several large stones, placing them together in the centre of a small glade. He placed kindling upon them and arranged a small fire. Looking at the girl, he pulled the pheasant free of his pack.

"You know how to prepare one of these?"

She nodded.

"Good. No need to gut it – just clear the feathers and cut some meat from the carcass." He pulled a small skinning knife from his belt and tossed it to the ground just before her. Without another word he started to gather some sticks, collecting ones which would be easy to stack. The rocks he'd laid would help to hide any evidence of them.

The girl was tired. Her eyes sunk back into her sockets, the lids rimmed with red. She rubbed at her neck often, suggesting it was tense and sore. When she *did* sleep she tossed and turned; her breathing never fully deepened. Kanderil continued to give her small tasks in an effort to keep her mind from her troubles. He doubted it would be much use, but he saw no reason to coddle her. The more he allowed her to dwell the worse the feelings would be.

This he knew from experience.

His thoughts drifted back towards his last assignment with the Kalethi. He could still smell the smoke, tainted with the salty, cloying scent of the burning dead. He saw again the image of the young girl trapped within the frame of a smouldering building, her eyes still open...

As he bent to collect the last of the wood he heard a noise behind him. The distinctive snap of a twig. He whirled around, dropping the armful of sticks and pulling free his bow. An arrow was notched in an instant. He could see Sarene, sitting by the premade fire with the pheasant in one hand and a clutch of feathers in the other. Her eyes were wide, staring into the woods opposite her. She was trembling.

Kanderil followed her gaze, taking a single sidestep.

Crouching at the base of a large oak was something that could not be human. It was pale, deathly *white*, with bright red dreadlocks of varying lengths hanging around its shoulders. Dark circles surrounded its eyes, the iris of which was a misty emerald colour. It was grinning to reveal small, pointed teeth. It wore a long, dark green coat of a similar style used by the Kalethi messengers during the storm season; the garment fanned around its small form, giving the impression of a frog sitting on a lily pad. On its feet was a pair of huge boots, the tops overturned to hang with a broad lip around his calves.

In place of fingers it had claws, three on each hand. The sunlight made them glisten.

Kanderil stepped to the side once more, then again. Its gaze flicked up to watch him approach. The broad, childish grin grew wider. It lifted one of those terrible hands and seemed to *wave* at him.

"Hi!" it said.

Kanderil stared back, pulling the string of the bow. Sarene dropped both pheasant and feathers, the latter fluttering to the ground in tiny swooping arcs.

The thing shook its head with such force that dreadlocks whipped around its face. "No need to be like that, for sod's sake. I was just sayin' hello."

"What are you?" Kanderil asked in a voice like granite.

"I'm me. I'm not you, so that's what I'm *not*." Its accent was strange, the syllables coming quick around drawled vowels.

Kanderil's eyes narrowed. "Riddles will get you killed, demon."

"Demon!" The creature managed to sound offended. "Have you ever seen a demon before? Like a really *real* demon? All fire and egg-smell and wings and stuff?"

Kanderil stayed silent except for the sound of his bowstring stretching further.

It giggled. "C'mon. You can do better than that. Demons ain't real."

"Then what are you," he replied.

"I'm your new best friend," it stated with another grin.

"No thank you."

It paused, taking a moment to pick at its teeth with the tip of a claw. It inspected its findings a moment later before wiping the back of its hand on its filthy cotton shirt.

"Oh, what? Sorry. I wasn't talking to you. I was talking to her." It pointed one of those dreadful claws towards Sarene, still rooted to the spot behind Kanderil.

The woodsman remained focused. "Why would you come for her?"

It changed expression in an instant, the humour replaced with a malicious sneer.

"I was sent here to kill her."

Kanderil released, aiming at the thing's chest.

The creature caught the arrow with one hand, the claws clicking together as it did so.

Sarene fell back, scrambling along the ground. Kanderil pulled free another shaft, drew, and released in one fluid motion. This time the creature sprung to the side, its boots kicking up dirt. The arrow *thunk*ed into the wood where it had been crouched a heartbeat before.

"Would you *stop* that?!" the creature yelled as it rolled to a halt. It was answered with a third shaft, which it deflected with the outside of its claws. Sarene turned to her front, crawling along on her hands and knees, looking for somewhere to hide.

Arms wrapped around her waist and pulled her up from the ground. Breath hissed between her teeth as she flailed her arms. She found herself tight in the arms of the creature, its stinking maw beside her cheek. Terrified, she tried to get away but the monster's grip was too firm.

"Would you bloody listen to me!" it yelled past her. Sarene looked up to see Kanderil advancing with his bow drawn. His face was grim, his eyes locked on the thing holding her. She reached out for her guardian, her legs kicking at –

At the floor. She realised the creature was barely her height.

"Look, if I was going to kill her I'd have done it by now," it said hastily. "Stop flinging those sodding arrows at me!"

"Let her go," Kanderil replied. His voice rumbled deep, the words commanding.

"If I do will you drop that bow? You're not hittin' me

anyway."

"We shall see."

"Not good enough."

Sarene kicked back, scraping her heel against its shin. It yelped, the sound oddly feminine.

"Alright, alright!" It let go and she almost fell. Catching her footing she ran towards her escort, slipping behind him to peer around his waist.

Kanderil held his arrow. "Explain yourself, devil."

"Okay, bad joke, my honest apologies." It muttered, kneeling down to rub at its shin with an open palm, the claws splayed out to avoid contact. "I just thought, y'know... you'd find it funny or something..."

"Are you saying you are *not* here to kill her?"

"Yep." It spring back up into a standing position. "I was *sent* here to kill her. But I'm not *going* to."

Sarene stared on, fascinated. Her curiosity was getting the better of her. The initial dread she had felt when she first saw the demon was fading, replaced with a strange sense of bewilderment. Bewilderment and distrust.

"Go on."

"Look, would you just point that stupid thing somewhere else? It's making me twitchy, and when I'm twitchy I do rash things. Rash things like cut people's bloody faces off." The creature actually managed to look sheepish even as its words brought images of violence.

Kanderil took a long time to respond, but he lowered the bow. He reached across to place an arm between the demon and Sarene. She patted his elbow to assure him that she was unharmed.

"Cheers, big man." It jerked its head from side to side, an audible pop accompanying both movements. A dreadlock slipped in front of its mouth and it clamped on like a fish grabbing bait, chewing thoughtfully.

In spite of herself, Sarene snickered for a moment, the noise like a hiccup. The thing noticed, spitting the lock out with an expression of bemusement. She stopped.

"Look, here's the trick. I was sent here to kill her by some guy. Tyrrial. An old fella who lives in a big tower some place over there." It waved a hand towards the east.

Sarene tensed at the name, her mouth falling open. She must have heard it wrong.

"It's taken me a while to find her, and to be honest I could use some food, so, y'know. If you'd care to continue..." It gestured towards the forgotten pheasant lying on the ground, now dirty and prickled with forest debris.

"Why have you not completed your mission?" Kanderil was insistent. Sarene flinched at the reminder.

The creature sighed in exasperation. "Listen, I'm not one of you." It clicked its tongue as Sarene blinked. "Yeah, sure, you both worked that out. Have a button. I was created by this Tyrrial guy. Made in a mad room with a bed and some rather lovely candles dotted about the place." It shrugged. "He made me as the perfect tool. I'm quicker than you, I'm more agile and I can promise you I'm a damned sight more lethal." It winked, the dark glare reappearing for a heartbeat.

Sarene shrunk back again.

"But he made a mistake, I've since worked out."

"Which was?" said Kanderil.

"He let me choose what I wanna do."

A silence fell over them. Sarene looked up at Kanderil, who exhaled slowly.

"Tyrrial. Odd for a man to be named after one of the Four."

"The old guy *is* one of the 'Four'." The creature waved its hand mockingly at the last word. Sarene gasped, bringing a closed fist to her mouth.

"Impossible," Kanderil replied. "The Four have not been seen for over five hundred years."

"Seen, no. Tyrrial rambled on a bit about how important it was to keep out of it. But yes, hark, thy masters art prosperous and liveth in thy worldetheth." It snickered at its own speech.

Kanderil shook his head. "This makes no sense. Why would Tyrrial want the girl dead?"

"Because of her..." the thing paused. It studied the pair of them, another of those bright grins crossing its impish face. "Wait, you mean you don't know? *Hah!*"

It laughed with such force that it doubled over, slapping at its knee and howling. Sarene blinked again. She exchanged a brief glance with the woodsman. His expression was unreadable.

Eventually the thing calmed, wiping away a tear with its sleeve. "Oh wow. That's magic, right there. Hehehe."

"Listen here, demon." Kanderil's voice was firm. "This girl's family was recently attacked by a group of men who were also seeking her out. Her mother was hurt, and nobody can provide her with any answers. If you truly mean her no harm then you will share this miserable joke of yours, because no one else is laughing."

Sarene's grip on Kanderil's shirt tightened as he spoke. She had forgotten about her family for the first time since the attack. The mention of it threatened to swamp her once more before the creature continued.

"Alright, thanks for the sob story. You should give pep talks more often." It muttered beneath its breath, before clearing its throat and drawing itself to its full diminutive height.

"The girl, Sarene, daughter of Sameran and Aislyn, from the village so small it doesn't have a name but is known for its wonderful position in a valley somewhere in the sticks, is the one who threatens the balance of peace within the world. The signs are correct and the prophecy shall be fulfilled."

It gave a small curtsy. Sarene stared at it in disbelief.

"What *prophecy?* She is a farmer's daughter," Kanderil snapped, suggesting he did not take the words well either.

"I don't know, I never bothered reading much," it said. "All I know is that the girl could upset the current order of things if she's left to run around causing havoc."

Sarene was at a loss. Her gaze darted from place to place, unsure of how to respond.

"How, exactly, does a young girl from a village in Tamir threaten the world?"

"I told you, I don't know." It seemed irritated by the

question. "I was meant to just come here, kill her a bit, then sod off somewhere. I never got the full briefing 'cause that wasn't really needed. The old guy did create me, after all. You tend to just do as you're told."

"Until you decide not to," Kanderil pointed out.

"Well, no, but I was there for about two days getting the who, what, where and whichever. I never got a history of the shittin' existence of things." It sniffed, its left cheek pulling up as it did.

"So why are you here now?"

"Are you kidding?" The creature sniggered, its grin wry and humoured. "If Tyrrial's as important as you people make him out to be, and he's sending things like me out to get her, can you *imagine* how many others are gonna be doing the same?"

Sarene felt fresh panic touch her chest at the words. She felt her heart rate quicken beneath the hand held over it.

"I can't think of anything else more entertaining to do than follow her around. Should be bags of fun."

Kanderil looked down to her. She bit her lip, her attention flicking back and forth between him and the thing opposite.

"No," he said.

"I'll even look out for her, like."

"No."

"Come ooo*on*. She's really gonna need some backup here..."

Kanderil clenched his jaw. "Why should either of us trust you, demon?"

"Oh, for..." It rolled its eyes, a gesture Sarene understood only too well. "Would you stop calling me that? Whatever I am, I'm not a demon, or devil, or any other silly thing you silly humans made up to scare each other. I have a name."

Kanderil raised a brow. "What would that be?"

"Spasmodic."

Silence greeted the answer.

"It's a bit odd, I know. Tyrrial told me I had a spasmodic personality, and the word made me giggle. I stuck with it.

Better than the one he was gonna give me anyway."

More silence.

"He wanted to call me 'The Deliverer'. I mean, what kind of stupid bloody name is that? Makes me sound like an evil messenger pigeon."

Nothing.

"I'd shake yer hand, but I'm not sure you'd be happy, what with these..." It wriggled claws which still shone like dark ebony. The creature seemed to blush, though it tried to hold its look of disapproval.

"My name is Kanderil," the woodsman said finally. "You already know the girl."

"Aye. I was kinda expecting more from her to be honest. At least a flaming sword or two. Maybe golden armour. That kinda thing." It frowned, before perking up again. "You're a big bastard though! Do you buggers usually grow to that size?"

Kanderil glanced at her once again. One corner of her mouth twitched a nervous smile at him, breathing a sigh. She realised she was still trembling. He knelt down to face her, matching her height, and placed a hand on her shoulder. He focused on her, which she appreciated. "Lass, I cannot begin to understand if this creature-"

"Spasmodic!" it yelled.

Kanderil paused with visible annoyance before continuing. "...If it speaks the truth, but it is here now regardless. We must press on to Tamiran to find your brother, but we should be aware of the possibility of more than just the Gathire searching for you. I hope you understand what this means."

Sarene gave a solemn nod. She understood perfectly. It meant she was in greater danger than ever. So was her family. The idea of further visits to her village conjured fresh tears. She wiped them away before they spilled.

"I will do my best to protect you. Trust in that."

"So will I," Spasmodic said in a theatrical bray, his chest puffed out as he marched over to them. Kanderil stood, turning to face the much smaller figure. Spasmodic craned his neck back to look up at him, his lower lip protruding.

"Not a chance."

The creature's firm stance wilted. "Oh, what?"

"I cannot trust you in her presence. You admitted your reason for being here."

"No, I admitted why I was *made*. I'm only *here* for the adventure!" It rubbed its hands together.

"Even so-"

"How exactly are you gonna stop me, big man?" Spasmodic sneered. "You couldn't even hit me with an arrow."

"Care to test that theory once more?"

"Pfft, no." Spasmodic waved a hand, swatting the question away. "Hardly gonna build trust if we start trying to maim each other, is it. Well, you'll try anyway. I'd do it." It gave a cheerful wink. "Give me a shot. That girl is my ride to happy times, and if she gets bumped off then where does that leave me? Stealing apples off fruit vendors. Punting a kitten around a garden. Sod *that*. So no, it's in my best interests to keep her alive and take part in all the japes and jollies she's going to find along her road."

Kanderil looked to Sarene. She shrugged. The creature seemed sincere, standing up on tiptoe like an enthusiastic minor seeking approval. She got a sense that it really *did* want nothing more than to join her for its own amusement. It made her uneasy, but she did not feel that initial terror from when it first grabbed her. Besides, why hadn't it killed her then?

Right now she felt as though she could use all the friends she could get. If she really threatened the world as this creature claimed, who else would want to walk beside her?

She nodded at the woodsman. He ground his teeth in response.

"Fine. But if I get the slightest hint that it means you harm..." The comment left hanging, he reached around his chest to sling the bow into place.

As he did he released a shaft. Sarene flinched, startled by the action.

It struck the ground no more than three inches from Spasmodic's foot. The creature jumped, its coat and locks twirling around him. It giggled with surprise.

"Alright, jeez! Full of tricks, aren't we?"

The three walked on for another two days.

Kanderil was leading them. He intended to arrive on the south eastern side of Tamiran before midnight three days hence. The dense woodland between here and there, combined with Sarene's inexperience with travelling through such terrain, made the going slower than he would have liked. The summer was in its final weeks but the heat continued unabated. Little wind breached this far into the forests and the air was cloying. She did her best, and each time a rest was called she was visibly exhausted. Her mood swayed between attentive and withdrawn. The girl's thoughts were elsewhere and understandably so. He did not press the matter or try to make her express how she felt. She would come around with time, or so the Hunter hoped.

How does one consider the fact they were potentially being hunted by one of the Four?

Kanderil had long ago believed them to be myths, no longer prevalent in a world which had long since left behind its barbaric ancestry. The Commandment of the Four, as much as it was adhered to by the religious, the political and the leaders of men, seemed to him redundant. Mankind governed itself now. They brought education and culture to the people; at least, those who could afford it. In some countries power was elected while in others it was earned. Royalty, especially, had come to understand the importance of keeping the favour of the people they ruled. He liked to believe they did so through choice and not to keep within some ancient decree which no longer applied.

To be told that not only did the Four live – at least, one of them – but also that they were actively searching for you would be unnerving to say the least. To be a sixteen-summer-old girl whose family had recently been attacked, presumably for that reason... He could not pretend to understand how she must feel. Sarene had basically been told that the Gods, as some saw them, were taking a personal interest in her.

If the creature Spasmodic was to be believed, then things were just the same. The world was still under the invisible rule of the most powerful men to ever walk the lands.

Spasmodic's mood remained, to give a conservative estimate, upbeat. Kanderil kept a close eye on it at all times. Aside from the incessant, pointless chatter it appeared to hold no threat for the moment. The initial danger it represented was fading in Kanderil's mind.

He was glad. Though Kanderil would never admit it, he was not convinced he could have stopped the demon from killing the girl if it had tried.

Now it seemed more of a nuisance than anything else. A steady stream of inane questions, terrible quips and strange observations painted a picture of a being with no real grasp of how the world worked. It didn't want to know about the Tamir people, or the history of the world, or even anything about the Four. Instead it inquired about the 'point' of snails, or why people ate rabbits but not moles, or how old people were before their hair fell out. Interrogation about Tyrrial proved useless as well – it would dismiss any questions with the explanation that he was just a 'rambling old man' who wasn't of much interest.

What he did glean from it was that it had no knowledge of the Gathire, and had not seen men of their description during its time at Tyrrial's tower. The men who had visited Sarene's home were most likely sent by another. The notion was of little comfort to him.

The sole point in its favour was its interest in keeping Sarene's spirits up. It would point out things which amused it, or make bad jokes about the surroundings. It made silly faces and sang songs, the lyrics of which were absurd. Sometimes it worked, and the girl would smile. More often she would simply nod, polite and courteous, and Spasmodic would leave her be for a short time before trying again.

Kanderil had not yet told them about his plan for delivering her to Jared. Spasmodic's appearance and revelation had changed things. For now he was content to walk and think things through, ensuring that he responded to the problem with the best possible course of action.

They camped that night in a clearing beside a small stream. The canopy above was thinner than usual, and they could see the stars of the clear night sky above. Kanderil allowed himself a few hours sleep, the first real rest he'd had in the last two days. Sarene slept fitfully, turning from side to side beneath her cloak.

The creature did not seem to sleep at all.

————◀○▶————

Spasmodic tilted its head to the side. They were moving through a thick cluster of underbrush which was proving difficult to navigate. It had been clearing the way with its claws, slashing through roots and vines and branches. The debris fell cleanly, not a leaf or twig stuck to its lethal digits.

"Hey up," it said. The giant human and the small girl stopped behind it.

"Something the matter?" Kanderil asked.

"Dunno."

They stood there for several seconds.

"Perhaps we should continue, then."

Spasmodic shook its head. "Mmm."

It turned to face them. Sarene stared at it with silent patience. Kanderil simply frowned, that stone-carved face of his stern as ever.

"Think something's coming. Not sure what though."

Kanderil listened. A bird whistled through the woods, breaking the gentle ambience of nature surrounding them.

"I cannot hear anything."

"No, not hear. I just think so."

"I see."

Sarene pursed her lips, looking around. She lifted a hand to rub at her upper arm. Taking a step backwards, she moved closer to her ward.

"Would you like me to take the lead?"

"What are you gonna do, chew through this stuff?" Spasmodic swung a hand through another collection of plants. They split, either falling to the ground or hanging from the nearest tree.

"I will keep us moving, at least," Kanderil responded.

The creature shrugged, continuing on its way. Once again, claws tore aside greens and yellows and browns. It slashed some things which wept and some things which cracked. It enjoyed the task, feeling powerful over nature. Briefly, a thought occurred to the creature that it might actually be *working* for them, a concept it found difficult to appreciate, but it put that thought aside. Work would not be fun, and it would be able to tell the difference.

Spasmodic was glad to have found the girl. She was a lot less than it had expected. The tones in which she had been described now baffled it. She was so quiet, so harmless, that it was beginning to doubt its creator's sanity. Why anyone would want her for anything it couldn't understand.

It wondered what Tyrrial would do when he realised that the girl still lived.

Tyrrial. He had been so *boring*.

No, this was much more fun. This girl was going to bring Spasmodic so much entertainment it could barely contain itself.

It halted again. Behind it, the two humans stopped.

"Another hunch?"

"You mean you don't get that?"

Kanderil stepped forward. At first there was nothing, just as before. Then the dry hiss of a branch being swept aside. Something moved through the undergrowth. A low growl, too deep for a wolf, came from only yards away. The atmosphere changed, becoming thick with menace. The woodsman pushed Sarene back, pulling free his great broadsword.

A black bear came wandering through the trees, emerging from heavy foliage. The undergrowth snapped around it. The bear paused before them, sniffing the air. Then it gave a threatening groan, saliva hanging from wicked jaws. Kanderil stepped forwards, locking his stance ready, letting his sword hang low to the ground.

Spasmodic sniggered. No way was it letting the human have all the fun.

It lunged towards the bear, landing only a few feet away. Planting its feet in the ground it *screamed*, with arms spread wide and hair whiplashing around its head, its torn coat giving a flurry of movement around its frame.

The bear reared up in response, tall and agitated, shifting from one foot to the other. Its forepaws displayed talons to equal the creature challenging it. The beast gave a roar which lacked conviction.

Taking another step forward, Spasmodic waved its arms.

"Get off w'ya! Go on, piss off! You big hairy bastard, *go!*"

The bear fell back to four paws. Awkwardly it waddled backwards, its huge head swinging back and forth. Then it turned and moved off the way it had come.

Spasmodic turned to the other two with a broad grin. It winked towards Kanderil.

"And you were gonna stab it. Where's the fun in that?"

Kanderil glared at it. "The bear was foraging. You could have just as easily been mauled."

"Yeah, but I weren't, were I? Scared it out of its stupid fur coat. Don't you ever take a gamble every now and then?"

Sarene tiptoed forward, peering out from behind the woodsman. She held her hands together at her waist.

"And you, ya chicken." It giggled as the two humans looked at each other. "Blimey. You really do need me after all. Now come on. I'm hungry. All this blinding heroism builds up an appetite." It sauntered off through the trees, shoulders rolling like a champion boxer showboating for a crowd.

In its mind it saw visions of the bear's carcass strewn across the forest floor, torn and bleeding.

Sarene gazed at the city of Tamiran, staggered by its size. From this vantage point she could see only one side – the edge of the forests at which they now stood were roughly level – but her imagination did the rest.

The walls were huge. They were a sharp grey, appearing much cleaner than the granite being used for the mill back home. Flat and smooth, the tops were covered in corrugated roofing which ran the entire length of them. The enormous southern gate was open and a guard stood sentry on either side. Dark iron framed the entrance. The red flag of Tamir, stamped with the famous golden lion, flickered overhead on a great mast. From within she could hear noises but there were so many they mingled into a faint, distant hum. It gave a general sense of *life,* life in such numbers that she could not quite visualize it.

Kanderil stepped beside her. "First time here?"

She nodded, unable to take her eyes from the scene.

"First time for me too, y'know," Spasmodic said behind them. Kanderil ignored it.

"Perhaps one day you can see how it looks from inside, as well." The woodsman shouldered his pack. "I'll meet you back here later today. If I have not returned before nightfall then move further into the woods."

Sarene peered up at him, puzzled. She tapped her chest, then gestured towards the city.

"Not this time. We cannot risk you being seen."

She stared at him pointedly.

"What's stopping me, huh?" Spasmodic angled its head so far to the side its face almost ran parallel to its shoulders. "No one's looking for me."

Kanderil adjusted the leather bracers he wore. "Aside from the claws, the red hair and the teeth, I need you to watch the girl you claim to want to help. Do this, and maybe I will trust you a little more."

"Yeah, 'cos leaving me alone to kidnap her is a *real* good move if you don't trust me," it replied.

Kanderil grunted. "Perhaps you are right."

Grinning, Spasmodic held out its hands. "If it makes you feel better you can tie me up while we wait. Not in a sexy way, though. Unless that's your thing, like. I mean, I'll be pretty useless if anyone comes along to knife her, but hey, at least I won't carry her off, will I?"

"Are you here to help her or not?"

"Listen, I never said nothing about helpin'." The creature's accent took a strange turn, becoming strained. "I just said I was following."

"Then you will have an easy job of it today. She is not going anywhere." Kanderil turned back to Sarene. She frowned at him. His tone of voice, as she had learnt over the past week, left no room for discussion and she had so far found no way to protest.

"As soon as I find out where your brother may be, I will return."

The frown lessened at the mention of Jared, but she was still annoyed. Kanderil began walking out towards the city. The length of his stride, broad and measured, meant that he rapidly covered the ground leading down from the forest.

"That bloke needs a serious slap of happy in his life," Spasmodic said as it moved next to her. She nodded absently in reply, watching him leave. A light breeze passed them, rustling the leaves clinging to the branches above and encouraging her hair to tickle her cheek. She stroked it out of the way, sighing.

"Bet he's gone to buy himself a cow. Or something to eat."

She smiled without much enthusiasm. The whole point of this journey was to find Jared. That Kanderil had denied her the chance to enter the city and look for him was irritating. She understood, of course – they would be looking for her. Whoever *they* were.

Even so.

Spasmodic plopped himself down on the floor next to her. "So, what to do?"

Sarene shrugged, watching the woodsman become smaller and smaller.

Chapter Seven

*A*s Kanderil approached the capital the noise from inside became more distinct. He could hear one voice periodically cry out from within the walls, a noise that he recognised from every city he had been to. Vendors. Market stall owners. Folk who would yell for fruit or meat, cloth or ale. They would holler in a barely intelligible language about the price, weight or quality of the goods on offer, encouraging customers to wander over in a fog. He could never understand the throngs of people who waded through the market streets day after day. As far as he was concerned a man should know what he wants, get it as quickly as possible and then move on to more important matters.

One of the guards beside the gate looked up as he approached. Kanderil noted the man's uniform – full dress and decoration. The breastplate was gleaming. The helmet plume was thick and bright, red to match the national flag. All buckles and adornments were in place, including the luscious scarlet cloak hanging from the shoulders. Kanderil smiled for the first time in three days. It struck him as amusing that, on the field of battle, the guard would be wearing maybe half of the items he'd been stuck with for the task of watching a city gate in peace time.

"Hey, friend." The guard greeted him with that look Kanderil often received; a look of wary caution. He returned the welcome with a simple nod, walking on through the gate into the city of Tamiran.

Immediately he was greeted with the scent of fish. He glanced to his left to see a stall selling goods of questionable freshness. The stall was held together with too few nails, ready to collapse at the slightest provocation. Catching his eye, the owner waved at him.

"COMEONOVERFORTHEBESTFISHINTAMIRANGE TTWOFORONEONANYFLATFISH!!"

Kanderil walked on.

As he made his way further into the city, more yells were aimed at him. Each time he ignored them. The market was heaving but Kanderil had little difficulty passing through. A man of his stature didn't need to. People tended to find space to clear a path.

He remembered a joke he had overheard during his last visit to the capital – maybe two months previous – where a drunken vagrant had said that the city needed a good war to trim the population. It was in poor taste but the sentiments were not exactly untrue. Tamiran was full. The markets he now passed were once over hundred feet within the walls, leaving a clear distance between them. People drifting in from the country, having heard of the higher standard of living, had filled the space with a vast array of goods and services. A man could have his boots cleaned, his hair trimmed, his horse tethered and his belly filled within a twenty feet stretch these days. Everyone had something to offer; everyone had something to sell.

The problem was that not everyone was buying. Goods may be plentiful but the poor had little to spend. The rich stayed away from these slum stalls, preferring to pay the extra for the higher class wares further in the eastern quarter. It resulted in thousands of people hassling hundreds more, and the city was crammed to the walls. The Council hadn't made much effort put a stop to the migration. Something had to be done, though. Such gross overpopulation was affecting the sanitary conditions for the worse, increasing the risk of disease. With people living in such close quarters the threat of plague or some other epidemic grew stronger with each season.

Kanderil reached the first of the cobbled streets, now past the worst of the crowds. He passed terraced housing and the first of the established shops. He saw the Green Tobacco sign, one of the first local points to navigate from, worn and weary as it hung from two rusted stretches of chain. The store sat at the corner of three main streets leading into the heart of Tamiran. Tobacco was still expensive and affordable by few. Green Tobacco declared its establishing year as *517* on the small glass window embedded in the front door. Twenty two years. The door itself hadn't seen a fresh coat of paint for at least five of them.

Kanderil chose the third street. He strode past the Finnegan, a tavern reputed as serving the best beef stew in town. Few would argue, but he rarely ate there. The atmosphere inside was cloying, populated with soldiers on leave and the local sloshes. He passed the sugar shop, selling candy and boiled sweets. Striped canes and squares of caramel stood in the window. Inside, a couple of children stood with their mother, pointing at the delicacies on offer with eager eyes. The young girl wore a bonnet and a spotless blue frock. The boy wore a neat white shirt over dark shorts.

A sandy haired boy sitting outside the shop, crouching beside a barrel, wore rags and a pair of shoes so thin Kanderil could see wriggling toes.

Tamiran had always retained a class divide. To see it so close together was still difficult to accept.

The boy looked at him, his face dirty. He raised a small hand and waved.

Kanderil walked on.

———————◄o►———————

He reached the Kalethi garrison forty minutes later. The building was on the outskirts of the capital's central ring, standing with bleached white walls beneath turreted roofing. As he stepped up to the entrance the man on duty looked up from his desk situated just within. The clerk wore a moustache which had clearly taken a lot of effort to grow, the results sparse and thin.

"Can I help you?" he asked in a jaded tone which irritated Kanderil. The former Sergeant leant forward, hands behind his back.

"Is there something else you would rather be doing, private? Not keeping you here against your will, are they?"

The man seemed surprised by the retort. His licked his lips, nervous.

"I'm sorry, but is there something I can help you with?"

"Where is your commanding officer?" Kanderil raised his voice, causing it to boom down the corridor leading further into the garrison.

"Err, he's not here." The clerk straightened his back in his chair and stared up, *up*. "Apologies, but if you would--"

"My name is Kanderil." *That* got the man's attention – he sat bolt upright and stared straight ahead. The name still carried weight, it seemed. "I would like to see the officer in charge here and I would like to see him now. If you can do that without keeping me waiting I may neglect to mention how lax his station duty appears to be."

The man disappeared, hurrying away. Kanderil watched him leave. He could care less about the apparent lethargy in the Kalethi non-military staff. Besides, it was reassuring to know that he was remembered. It would make his task easier.

He waited for three more minutes before the clerk returned with a large man in tow. The man wore his dress shirt and pants, but the rest of the standard Kalethi uniform was absent. His shirt was unbuttoned and the cuffs rolled back. A scar ran from his wrist upwards along the forearm, disappearing beneath the fabric curled around the elbow. Short greying hair, spiked with a glossy wax, sat over a heavy brow. His squared jaw was dark with stubble. The man did not seem to be in a good mood.

"Here he is, Mr. Kanderil."

"Sergeant Kanderil, runt." The grey haired man's voice was strong. "Gods, you're lucky he doesn't slap that terrible growth on your lip clean round your head. Locate your spine one of these days, eh?"

Kanderil allowed a small smile.

"Come on, son. Come through to my office. If this idiot had any sense of efficiency he'd have brought you himself."

Nodding, the former Sergeant accepted the invitation. The clerk made a point of ignoring him, indulging a sudden need to straighten his quill pens.

The two men walked down the corridor, their footsteps echoing with them. As ever, the pale walls lacked any signs or plaques. Kanderil understood the joke.

They passed a small garden at an intersection. The fenced area held a large tree which flourished upwards, reaching for the open skies above. A square of well-kept lawn sat around it, free from leaves or weeds. The tree had always been a focal point for new recruits; a common initiation was to climb to the top branch without being caught by the officers, who punished such trespasses with a fine of a week's wage. Kanderil himself had refused to take part as an eighteen year old trainee. None had argued against his decision.

They reached the office and stepped inside, the older man closing the door behind them. The room was bare except for a sword braced against the eastern wall and a window behind a small, plain wooden desk. Papers were strewn across the latter, atop which sat a mug and a plate from whatever must have served as lunch.

"Take a seat, my boy. It's good to see you again."

"Likewise, Rohad."

Rohad chuckled. "Makes a fine change to hear my name instead of 'Major' or 'Sir', or just plain old 'Bastard.'" He made his way around to the other side of the desk, seating himself in a rather undersized chair. Kanderil raised a brow as it creaked.

"They're working on it."

Kanderil nodded, deciding to stand.

Major Rohad was a big man in his late fifties. He carried himself well. His build was a little softer than it once was and his hair was a little thinner, but the man still held the commanding presence which had helped drill Kanderil into the Hunter he was today. Rohad took shit from nobody but gave it out in spades and carts. It took a lot to earn his respect, but once you had it, you had a friend as well as a mentor.

"So, what are you after?" the Major asked.

"I am looking for one of your men," replied Kanderil.

"Shame. I thought you were going to break out a couple of cigars and a flask of firewater."

"Sorry to disappoint, old man."

Rohad chuckled. "What's his name?"

"Jared."

"Jared? That's funny."

"How so?" Kanderil folded his arms.

"Had a Gathire fellow here not two nights past looking for him. Naughty looking bugger. Not the type you'd let your sister step out with."

"Did they say why?"

"Nope." Rohad leaned back in his chair, which creaked further. "Just asked a few questions then left."

"Did you speak to them yourself?"

"Aye, I did."

"What did you tell them?"

Rohad lifted his hands behind his head, watching Kanderil. "This is a little to the point even for you, son. Care telling me what this is all about?"

Kanderil considered refusing the request, but decided against it. "I need to find Jared as quickly as possible. His family has suffered a recent hardship, and I accepted a request to fetch him."

"Awfully kind of you, Kanderil." Rohad smirked. "Not really your style, though."

"I have my reasons."

"Of course, of course..." The Major shrugged broad shoulders. "Sorry to pry. You understand, though, that when one of my boys suddenly becomes a point of interest around here it becomes my business to ensure they haven't messed up in any way."

"No mess. Just a family emergency."

"And the man searching for him prior to you. Also dropping off bad news?"

Kanderil said nothing.

"Thought so." Rohad leaned forward, resting on his forearms. "Listen, I don't want to have to pull rank on this. Come clean, Kanderil. Why is Jared suddenly in such demand?"

The former Kalethi gave a sigh. The sound was soft, offering an odd contrast to the man making it. "I am not one for clichés, my friend. But trust me; if this was not important, I would never have come to you."

Rohad rapped his hands, interlocked at the fingers, against the desk. He glanced towards the wall adorned with the sword briefly.

"Jared was sent to the sub-border territory sixty miles due north-northwest. He should be moving between the Meadows and the village of Tilldown. Just routine patrol, nothing fancy. He seems to have a taste for ale, and there isn't a tavern within a day's ride of his markers. Should do him some good staying clean for a few weeks."

"When is he scheduled to return?"

"A month next Wednesday. He'll have a three day break, then we'll send him somewhere else."

Kanderil nodded. "Did you give this information to the other man here?"

"Had to."

"Outranked, aye?"

"Something like that." Rohad winked. They both understood. "That's all I've got."

The giant's gaze flicked to the window. "What can you tell me about him?"

"The first guy? Tall. Lean. Dark clothing like they all

wear. Had real raven black hair with eyes to match." Rohad smirked. "He didn't smile once the whole conversation. I reckon he'd have been just as happy to pull Jared's whereabouts out of me with a hook as talk to me."

"Would have been interesting for him to try." Kanderil noted.

"Aye, I would say so. Would have been more than a fine for that one, I'd think." Rohad laughed, the sound easy and rich. Kanderil found himself smiling. "These new breed are arrogant little bastards. Here in the Kalethi as much as any. Most of the new recruits reckon they were born for the saddle, or raised as a swashbuckler."

"I would expect you are having fun then."

"Oh yes," Rohad replied. The laugh railed out again. "Nothing better than giving the smug sons o' whores a decent rollicking now and then. Watching the back shoot straight and the arms flat by their sides as they try not to crap 'emselves."

Kanderil chuckled. "Always were a hard one, Rohad."

"Damn straight." The Major shook his head. "Listen, how about we go grab an ale, and I'll be happy to answer any more questions you might have."

"Not on duty?" Kanderil asked.

"Nah. Recruits have this afternoon off to study the Code, or slack as you used to put it, and I'm so tired of paperwork it would be pointless for me to stay here." He gestured to the reams of parchment cluttering his desk. Kanderil noticed one of them wore a circle from the bottom of the nearby mug.

"Come on." Rohad pushed the point. "How long has it been since you had a decent cupful?"

Kanderil muttered. It had been some time since he'd enjoyed fresh ale. Alcohol was one of the few vices he allowed himself but it was one he sorely enjoyed.

"Fine. But I need to visit the merchant holding my savings on the way." He moved for the door. "And we go somewhere quiet."

"Ashamed to be seen with me, my boy?" Rohad grinned,

rising from his seat.

"Something like that."

Petar looked into his empty canteen. He lifted the thing upwards, tilting it back towards himself. A drop of liquid fell out, landing in his eye. Then the leather strap slipped down to flap against his chin.

"Ah, yer bastard!" he cried out, lifting a palm to his face. Whiskey, evidently, stung.

"Hah!" Lug slapped him across the back. "You idiot. What did you expect to find in there, stubborn liquor?" Petar shrugged the hand away.

Hawk watched them, cross legged before the campfire, saying nothing. He was writing in his journal, scribbling down thoughts in small, quick words. Flames danced between him and his two companions, lending a flickering haze to their back and forth. A crude spit was constructed over the fire, a rabbit threaded onto it.

"Can't believe I drank it already," Petar said, his voice bitter. He tossed the canteen against the ground. It bounced once before coming to a rest. "It's not even dark yet."

"I can," Lug said. "Y'stink like a tavern pisser."

"Rich, coming from you. I've ridden horses with a sweeter scent."

"How much did they charge?"

"..What?" Petar looked perplexed. He winced as he tried to come to terms with the retort.

Lug looked over at Hawk, his face still cheered. "You get it, right?"

Hawk looked up, offering a soft smile. Lug's amusement waned, and he leaned back. He brushed his knee of dirt before exchanging glances with Petar.

"So come on. You said you'd spill the beans about that sword."

"So I did," Hawk replied, still writing.

"Well? What's it for?" Petar nodded towards the

scabbard lying within arm's reach of their unofficial leader.

"I received it as a gift this morning."

"From?"

Hawk paused to consider this momentarily. "From an old friend."

"Mighty kind of 'em," Petar said, the final word ending with a burp. He thumped himself on the chest. "Last present I got from an old mate was attempted murder. Bastard thought I owed 'im twelve gold bits from a card game last summer. Said I'd been avoiding him."

"Didn't you have his sister, though?" Lug offered, his hands fiddling with a twig he'd lifted from the ground.

"Well, yeah, but that's besides the point."

"Perhaps I simply hold better company than you." Hawk spoke softly, a wry smirk accompanying his speech.

"Pro'lly."

Hawk held his pen still and glanced down at the sword. A twinge of shame struck him, as the giant poacher's image came into his mind. His fingers tensed.

"You don't seem too happy about it," Lug said. He was using the twig as a toothpick.

"How so?"

"Dunno. You seem a bit... antsy."

Hawk looked up at him. The fire did little to warm his expression.

"How so?"

Lug met his gaze. "Like I said, I dunno. You're usually a little less... well..." He trailed off for a moment. "Less *not fun*?"

Hawk grinned. "I'm sorry that I'm not keeping you entertained, my friend. I thought that Petar here could do that by himself."

Petar sniffed, rubbing the back of his hand across his cheek, moving across the ugly scar there. He was a stocky man with long reddish curls made orange by the sunlight overhead. Hawk closed his journal.

"I am just a little tired," he explained. "A decent rest this evening will help."

Lug nodded. He was smaller, with lank dark hair always appearing in need of a wash; this he'd tucked back behind prominent ears. "Reckon so. We've been ridin' pretty hard, aye."

"That we have." Hawk smiled broadly. They had indeed made good time. At the pace they were keeping Tamiran was less than two days away, though their mounts would be exhausted. "And for good reason, my friend."

"Yeah, about that..." Petar reached for Lug's canteen. Lug tried to fend him off but was unsuccessful, instead settling for a sharp punch again the bigger man's forearm. "You never did quite tell us much about why we're heading to the capital."

"There really isn't much to say. I have a good tip about a target, one we can make plenty of money from."

"There's lots of targets we can make a lot of money from, Hawk," Petar said, before taking a swig. He swallowed, the action loud in the still night air. "But the reason we *don't*, you said, is that they're good an' protected, or at least important enough for the guard to take notice and come lookin' around."

"This one isn't, and no one else will be looking for him." Hawk shrugged. "I remember what I stated previously, but this will be worth it."

"What's the deal?"

"He's carrying something of extreme value to a friend of mine."

"Same friend who got you that sword?" Lug said, the twig sticking out from between two teeth. He chewed on it.

"Aye, the same. Call it a token of goodwill." Hawk bowed his head politely in gesture.

"Where's ours then?"

Hawk sighed, his good nature still strong. "I will handle the purse for us, lads. But believe me. You'll not be wanting for anything for a while. Good food, decent wine and women whose faces *couldn't* curdle milk, for once." He was referring to Petar, whose taste for ladies of the night was not particularly fussy. Petar acknowledged this with a broad smile. Hawk continued. "The target isn't much to be concerned about. Easy work."

"So why the sword?" Lug pressed.

"We still use swords, even if we do not *use* them."

But they would this time. The weapon he'd received would help him to expel the demons, push the shame and self loathing from his heart. A swell of excitement filled him, and his hand moved across to lift the scabbard from the ground and lay it across his lap. His two companions gave him an odd look. They seemed wary. Lug stopped picking at his teeth, and Petar screwed the cap back onto the stolen canteen.

Hawk grinned at them. In the firelight flittering back and forth in front of his face, his eyes seemed to glow red.

Sarene stared at the city, leaning against a tree. Her feet were surrounded by daisies, the stems curling around as if tugging at her ankles to gain her attention. She had tied her hair back into a high ponytail, the tip dancing just shy of her shoulders. Spasmodic had been chattering away behind her for a full hour and she'd long since lost track of what it was saying.

If her brother lay inside those walls she could be with him before sundown.

The thought of seeing Jared stride out alongside Kanderil filled her with hope, the first she'd felt since leaving her home. She had already moved forward twice as figures stepped from the city, but both times she had been mistaken. It was difficult to tell from this far away – the traffic to and from the city, while not the mad rush she had expected from the tales, was steady enough. Carts, riders and walkers arrived and departed, all while Sarene studied each as best she could.

No giant. No brother.

She scratched at her knee.

Jared *must* have all the answers. He was in the army, and

so were these other people, the Gathire. Jared would know who to ask, how to settle the matter. She wasn't naive enough to think that she would be home within the week, but perhaps whatever requirement the dark-cloaked men had of her could be resolved.

Sarene had come to believe that while the creature *was* sent to kill her, the reasons were flawed. She didn't wield any world-changing power. How could she? The idea was nonsense.

But then, was it arrogant to assume one of the Four was wrong? Was *she* misguided? The Four had changed the world. She remembered the legends describing Tyrrial as the most impatient and cruel of them. The most outspoken. That line stuck in her head, but it made no sense. If she was such a threat why would Tyrrial not come to claim her himself?

She was dimly aware that Spasmodic had stopped talking. She glanced over her shoulder. The creature was now staring at the city.

"How long d'ya think he'll be gone?" it said.

Sarene spread her hands.

"S'what I thought. How about we go take a peek?" It lifted a hand to point towards the city.

She smiled softly, shaking her head. That was a bad idea.

"Pfft." Spasmodic grinned, revealing those pointed teeth. It grinned a lot. "You wanna see what's inside as much as I do."

Shrugging, she pointed at the ground where they now stood.

"Yeah, wait here. Has he been telling you to do stuff since he showed up, or what? You take his orders pretty well."

Sarene peered at it.

"I mean, c'mon. You're the prize here. You should be in charge. I know you're only wee, like. But you should be leading him into the city, not waitin' until he decides to come back and pick you up like some kinda sick deer."

Sarene rolled her eyes, turning back towards the capital. Spasmodic was whispering beside her ear in seconds. She flinched at its sudden appearance next to her.

"You can ignore it all you like, but I think you're not thinking. I can see it in you. Smell it. You're not the type of person who *usually* just sits around waitin' for other people to fix things for ya. You're the type who asks questions later, does things first." It punched the air three times, *pow pow pow.*

Sarene deliberately mouthed the word *No.* It was trying to get her into trouble. She held its gaze, realising for the first time how its pupils shone gold when it faced the sunlight. Her eyebrow rose a half inch. *Like I need any help getting into trouble,* she thought.

Spasmodic spat to the side, muttering. "How about this, then. We wander over to the gate, look inside, then come back. No danger. Besides, what are the chances of being caught, eh? Not like these Gathire people are gonna be sitting on every street corner, are they."

Something rustled in the forests behind them. They both turned around. Nothing moved between the trees, and the only sound was of the forest itself – leaves, birdsong, crickets, wind.

"They might be behind every tree though..." Spasmodic said with a giggle. "Either that or Mr. Bear wanted a cuddle after all." Sarene shoved the creature, trying to cover her own fear.

"Right, well I'm going to take a look." The creature turned, walking towards the city. Sarene reached out grab it, missed, then hurried to snag its jacket sleeve on the second attempt.

"Oh, you're coming?"

She glared at it, trying to pull Spasmodic back towards the forest. It ignored her, and Sarene found herself being dragged along.

Dragged along, or led forward?

"I don't give two shits what you do, missy. I'm curious and I don't have any promises to keep like the big man."

She let go, standing her ground. It kept walking. Sarene wasn't sure what to do. Entering the capital wasn't an option. Kanderil would be furious if she did, and she had a feeling Jared would also be displeased. But to stay in the forest alone, if someone *did* appear...

There was another noise behind her, like a branch being swept aside. She span on her heel, staring back into the woods. Nothing stirred, nothing moved.

She shivered as the breeze picked up. Glancing back she saw Spasmodic stomping its way towards the city. It didn't look like it was going to reconsider. She couldn't imagine the kind of reaction it would get within Tamiran's walls. The creature looked... Well, it looked inhuman. *Was* inhuman.

Sarene tugged her ponytail with both hands, stamping her feet in frustration. She snatched her cloak from the ground, slung her pack over her shoulder and began running after it.

This is such a bad idea, she thought.

Behind her, from the forest, a badger wandered out from the undergrowth. Beady eyes looked skywards, unused to being out in such bright sunshine. Its ears twitched. Then it focused on the fleeing girl. It watched her catch up to the red-haired thing.

After a short time it made a noise, a hacking wheeze which could resemble a laugh. Then it turned and ambled off back into the woods, the white tip of the tail behind it twirling like water down a drain.

Kanderil sat with Rohad in the Bear's Noose tavern, nursing a mug of beer. He'd finished half the liquid in two great swallows and was now swilling the contents around. Rohad was watching him with those small, patient eyes. He'd seen the look used before on recruits who had something they should confess but were finding it hard to muster the courage. Kanderil himself was not intimidated by the look, but he understood the thinking behind it. In some ways, that made it worse.

A serving girl swished past with a tray of empty mugs.

She slid between the tables effortlessly, her elegance distracting. Her movements caught the looks of other patrons staring at her well rounded backside. One man nudged a drinking partner, nodding towards her as she left. They smirked, sharing a fairly obvious joke.

"Gonna spill, my boy?" Rohad sipped his drink.

"This place smells worse than the stables," Kanderil replied. It was true – the once fresh sawdust on the ground was simply an undercurrent to the fragrance of beer and smoke. Evidently the cook here was not of the highest quality, either. A pungent stench of burning food wafted out every time the door to the kitchen was opened. The one customer brave enough to place an order had been less than pleased with the results.

"I knew that already."

Kanderil met Rohad's stare.

"Ask the question, old man. I'm not one for guessing games."

"Nope. Never were." The Major gave a soft smile. "Alright. Tell me why you left the Kalethi."

"I grew tired of it."

"Bollocks." Rohad leaned forward onto his elbows. "You were one of the very best. Could have been an officer if you'd accepted the damned commission. No one that good at what they do grows *tired* of it. It's like a sculptor growing tired of his chisel."

"Poetic."

"Thanks. I've been reading."

Kanderil grunted. "I have my reasons."

"Oh, for..." Rohad swore, the word barked with a laugh. "You're harder to talk to than a woman with a grudge. I should know; I've been married three times. I didn't call you out for a drink so we could sit in silence."

"I came here to drink as a sign of respect. If my company irritates you, then I have other pressing matters to attend to." Kanderil took another swallow. The words were simple and honest, with no ill feeling.

"No, lad, you're missing the point." Rohad took a deep

breath. "When a man leaves my service for no good reason that I understand, I take it as a personal insult. The Kalethi are my boys, and losing one hurts whether it's to combat, illness, retirement..." Rohad waved his hands to underline the sentiment. "You just left, Kanderil. Not a word, not a thing. Badge in, payment taken, off into the forests or wherever you bloody went."

Kanderil said nothing for a long time. He listened to the quiet conversations of the few others in the tavern, hearing a word here and there but nothing to tune into. Rohad continued to stare, occasionally taking a pull from his beer.

He muttered, running a hand over his beard. "Remember Jairen Tar?"

"Strange question," Rohad replied. "Who could forget?"

"Easy to say when you just got the report. I had to walk through that burning town. I had to smell it and taste it."

"You weren't the only one. Don't tell me that's what sent you running."

Kanderil met Rohad's gaze again, but this time his expression was severe. "I did not *run*, Major."

Rohad nodded, looking to his mug briefly. "Noted, apologies for my phrase."

"Accepted."

"I just refuse to believe that a man as iron-balled as you would walk away after that. It was an atrocity in Jairen Tar, sure, and I get that. Damned raiders almost cost us another war, and we were posted along the northern border for a good quarter-year or so."

"So I heard."

"We could have used you, my friend. The team you left behind were given that dumb son-of-a-bitch Farthor. The man couldn't organise the laces on his boots. Your boys kept asking me where you'd gone and I had to make up some bullshit answer about you taking personal leave for some family emergency." Rohad finished his mug and waved to the girl leaning against the bar. "Added to that the military is recruiting like crazy. Our ranks have been increasing steadily over the last three years. All these people coming in could use a little guidance, you know?"

"Why the recruitment drive?" Kanderil asked.

"Buggered if I know. I just take the orders from those above and pass 'em on to those below."

Kanderil leaned back as a man eased past, waiting until they were alone again before speaking.

"Have you ever considered that your life would be better spent following your own wishes?"

"Deep question. No. I enjoy what I do. I thought you'd realised that by now." Rohad offered a smile which was not returned.

"I experienced something in Jairen Tar which made me reflect on my path at that time. I simply chose to walk away. I have no need for vengeance or retribution, as those raiders certainly deserved. I had been with the Kalethi for eighteen years. Half my life. Enough was enough."

"But without word?"

Kanderil lifted his drink. "It was nobody else's concern." He drained the rest of the beer. Rohad chuckled.

"My, you're an arrogant bastard, Kanderil. I forgot that about you."

Kanderil shrugged. "Kind of you to say so."

"What did you see? At least permit me that much so I don't need to keep guessing."

Kanderil rolled his empty mug between his palms, considering the question. "A young girl. Could not have been a day over ten summers old. I pulled her out of a building which had not quite caught flame, but had been ransacked. Her family were dead and she was not far behind. She had a head injury the like I have never seen without it bringing an instant end, but she was still conscious. Her eyes were open."

The maid brought over Rohad's drink, which he accepted with barely audible thanks. He took a long sip.

"She did not last long, and slipped away a few minutes after I found her. It brought things into perspective for me and I decided that was enough."

Rohad nodded. "You've seen action, and there's no

doubting your bravery. Never questioned that."

"Unnecessary words, my friend. I do not need comforting." Kanderil looked up. He had not expected the Major to try and empathise with him. It did not fit with his character.

"Perhaps." The older man gave a wan smile, reclining back in his seat. "At least I'll not wonder anymore, aye. About you, I mean. The boy Jared, though, could be another matter."

"That, unfortunately, is not up for discussion."

"I gathered. But you be careful. Those others searching for him don't play around. If they find out you're in competition they may pay you a visit."

"Let us hope they do not find out, then," Kanderil replied in a flat voice. "For their sake."

Rohad grinned as he took a drink. "This gets more interesting by the minute."

Kanderil looked to his empty mug. He took a deep breath. The conversation was beginning to annoy him. Rohad was a good man, one of the few he had time for these days, but the hints and questions were grating on his nerves. *Too much time alone,* he thought. *You've forgotten how to be social.* A laugh came up from further back in the room, and Kanderil glanced over his shoulder.

"I should be leaving," he said aloud.

"Fine." Rohad raised his mug in a toast. "I think I'll stay for a few more. Good to see you alive and well, Sergeant."

"Likewise." He reached over the table and they clasped arms, wrist to wrist. "If Jared returns, would you allow him to stay put? I will make arrangements to get word."

"Gonna be a bit suspicious to keep him here when he should be on field duty."

"I'm sure you can think of something."

With a smirk, Rohad raised a brow. "Getting me involved in your schemes without telling me about them first, aye? I have a family to think about."

"The less you know the better. Besides, when did you ever turn down a challenge?"

"Playing me to my faults, Kanderil?"

"Merely counting on someone I can trust."

Rohad shrugged modestly. "I'll do my best. No promises, though."

"None expected."

Kanderil stood, stepping back from the table. He turned sideways as the bar maid moved past to collect his abandoned mug, impressed at her efficiency.

From outside came a loud shriek, followed by some muffled cries. The entrance opened and a man wearing a filthy apron appeared with a fearful expression on his face. The man banged on the door to get the occupant's attention.

"Stop that!" the tavern keeper yelled, a short man with a bald head and a drooping moustache.

"Sorry sir, but there's a monster in the town! A real monster! He's killed a man and he's kidnapped a girl!"

Kanderil moved, his jaw tight. He shoved the messenger aside, all but knocking him to the ground, and stepped outside.

Chapter Eight

*S*arene ran alongside Spasmodic, throwing her cloak around its shoulders and forcing the hood over its head. It ducked against the action, trying to squirm free, but she held the cloak in place.

"What are you doing, you silly mare?!"

Sarene moved in front of it, place a hand on its chest. She pointed to the hood, tugged it a couple of times, then nodded.

"I'm not wearin this bloody thing. It's not my colour, doesn't match my eyes." It fluttered thin lashes in accordance with its words, before making to pull the cloak free again. Sarene thumped its chest and it snarled, making her take a step back in alarm.

"Look! I've got my own sodding hood. You put this thing on," – it hooked the flat side of its clawed knuckles against the cloth and hurled her cloak towards her –"and we won't need to worry about any of your mysterious friends spotting you on sight. We can go look-see in peace."

Sarene bit her lip. She didn't want to *go* into the city.

That wasn't entirely true. She did, of course she did, but the risks were huge and Kanderil would be angry with them.

Leaving the safety of the woods was wrong... but she felt responsible for the creature, as though any trouble it caused would be her fault. Which was ridiculous, considering it had emphasised the fact it was simply following her around, but she knew that letting it run free in the city would draw attention that they could do without.

"You're not my bloody gran, y'know," it said, reading her expression. "You don't need to come hold my hand. I'll come tell you all about it when I'm done. I might even bring you back a treat. You like fish?"

She narrowed her eyes.

"Okay. No fish."

Sarene glanced towards Tamiran. They were still quite far from the gate, but she could feel the guards watching them. Entering unnoticed seemed to be an ideal which was growing less likely by the second. She turned back towards the forests, considering heading back to the spot which Kanderil had chosen for them.

Standing where she and the creature had been waiting were three dark-clothed figures. They were all watching her. As one they began to move forwards. Her eyes widened and she started to point, back-pedalling towards the city. Spasmodic peered at her, squinting one eye.

"What?"

It looked over its shoulder. It let out a snigger at the trio heading for them.

"Heh. Ah right."

Together, Spasmodic and Sarene began to run towards the city. The three figures took up the chase. As she approached the gates one of the guards stepped to intercept them.

"Hold up there!" he called. His companion stopped slouching on his pike, taking the weapon in both hands as they drew near. "Hold, I say! What's the rush?"

Spasmodic pulled its hood up and easily moved in front of her, its speed on the run incredible.

"Coming through!"

It feigned left then dodged to the right. The man seemed

too astonished to make an effort to stop the creature. As Sarene passed he made a weak attempt to catch her with one arm. She managed to avoid him with little trouble, ducking out of the way.

"Stop those two!" she heard from behind. The voice sounded closer than she liked. Before the other guard could obey she was through the gate. Her foot slipped as she entered, causing her to stumble as the ground changed from the clean grass outside to a damp sludge. She had to swerve to avoid ploughing into a man carrying a tray of fruit on his shoulder, and then turn on her heel to slip between two men bartering in front of a stall. The sudden sights and smells distracted her and she ran aimlessly for several seconds before something snagged her cloak, tugging her towards a street leading between the markets.

"This way!" Spasmodic shrieked, its beaming face made paler in contrast to the hood now covering most of its vivid red hair. Sarene followed, sprinting as fast as she could along the unfamiliar streets. Spasmodic stayed ahead, seeming to run *backwards* most of the time, encouraging and cajoling her with great amusement.

"This place is fantastic!"

Sarene ran on. She was starting to breath heavily, her stamina failing. When Spasmodic took a sudden turn down a narrow alley she almost tripped, but managed to catch herself in time. She bolted after it, hurdling over a crate which blocked the path. Her leap took more effort than she expected and this time she *did* slip as she landed. Spasmodic stopped ahead of her, and it took Sarene a moment to realise it was actually hanging from the wall, its claws gripping onto the haphazard brickwork.

"Stop mucking around and get moving! We're nearly there!"

Sarene got to her feet and started to run again. Spasmodic dropped to the ground a short way in front of her, turning right at the end of the alley. She followed, bursting out of the lane not two seconds after.

The creature was gone. She found herself in a street

featuring rows of small terraced homes and shops. Slowing
to a halt, battering her heels against the cobblestones, she
began to panic. An anxious look back revealed nobody else
in the alley, but surely one of the dark figures would appear
soon. She spun around, catching her breath, trying to pick
the best way to go.

"Oi, girly," came a squeak. She glanced to her right to see
a wagon full of pumpkins, surrounded by filthy, moist sacks.
"C'mon, squeeze under here!" A hand appeared, gleaming
and dangerous, waving her towards the wagon. Sarene
needed no further encouragement, quickly sliding between
the wagon and the building beside. She scraped her back
against the wall, wincing at the flare of pain, but managed to
drag herself beneath the wagon, pulling some of the sacks
around her. Spasmodic was waiting, grinning at her. The
scent under the wagon was musty and unpleasant. She
couldn't tell if it was the pumpkins above or the creature
beside her.

"You're pretty quick for a human," Spasmodic said,
nudging her in the ribs. Its voice gave no indication that
their flight had tired it. Sarene did not respond. Instead she
listened; waiting for the footsteps she knew would arrive.
Her fears insisted that the hiding place was poor, the sacks
around them only offering a partial covering. She wiped her
brow with the back of her hand, blinking several times to
clear her vision. Her legs burned from the exertion of
sprinting.

Minutes passed before they were found.

The wagon above was upturned, pumpkins spilling
across the street as it *clank*ed on its side, one wheel clicking
as it span. Sarene squinted at the sudden sunlight before
becoming wide eyed with fear.

Above her stood a man wearing black clothing. Long
dark hair was tied close to the nape of his neck, drawn tight
against his head. His leather tunic was well-fitting and
seamed with white thread. At his side was a wicked hook-
shaped knife, tied to a belt with a prominent silver buckle.
The man was tanned and tall, with broad shoulders but

lacking bulk. He looked like the meanest person Sarene had ever seen, and the gleam in his eyes enforced that feeling. He seemed to relish her expression, finding joy in her terror.

"Sarene. Come with me," he said simply.

"Ah, sorry," Spasmodic said, its hands behind the small of its back and its legs waving in the air like an upturned tortoise. "I'm afraid she's a little busy right now. See, she's meant to be meeting someone."

The man looked at the hooded creature, his expression unchanging. "Unfortunate for her that she will not make that engagement."

"It's quite important," Spasmodic replied cheerfully. It sat upright, meeting the man's gaze.

The man smirked. He pulled the hook knife from his belt and knelt forward.

A second later he was dead.

Sarene blinked. The creature was giggling next to her. She was aware that blood had landed on her cheek. The man was lying sprawled amongst the pumpkins, face down. Blood was pooling around from his head, filtering between cobblestones. Spasmodic hopped up to its feet, unconcerned.

"Silly bastard. Come on, we'd better get going."

Horrified, Sarene looked up at it. It clicked its tongue, extending a hand towards her. "Come *on*! Someone might have seen that." It looked at its hand, realised what it was doing and then withdrew the offer.

"Murder!" A cry came from down the street. "Murder!"

"Oh, sod it," said the creature.

Sarene scrambled to her feet, pushing herself upright. Her mind was in a whirl, trying to process what she thought she had witnessed. The man had knelt towards them and Spasmodic had just... just *flinched*. The man had died without a sound. She stared at the corpse, a shiver beginning to grip her.

"Come *on*," Spasmodic repeated, nudging her with its shoulder.

"Murder!" the cry came again, this time louder. She heard commotion further down the street. There a man, scrawny and thin, repeated his cry. Doors were opening and others were stepping out to investigate. The scrawny man pointed towards them before cupping his mouth with his hands.

"*Murder!*"

A high shriek came from nearby as a woman cowered in her open doorway. "What *is* it!" she cried, producing an odd change of pitch on the second word.

With more physical encouragement from the creature, Sarene began to run.

———◀○▶———

Kanderil stepped outside the tavern as a mob ran past, maybe a dozen strong. Whistles were being blown; the town guard had joined the chase. Bystanders in the street gossiped about what little they knew. Kanderil muttered to himself, stepping down the road beside the tavern. He knew the mentality of mobs. They were often led by a figure that had no real sense of leadership, someone surging on adrenaline after finding themselves in charge of group of strangers. Such people often took the easiest route available, giving the false impression of purpose.

The path Kanderil followed led him adjacent to the mob. He would find the large street at the back of the tavern before they did.

Emerging at the other end of the narrow alley, the Hunter glanced around. A few of the terraced homes still had occupants in the doorways, staring along the western road. He headed that way, staying close to the edge of the street. Whistles continued to answer each other. None of them were nearby.

He followed the street for another minute, walking quickly. Reaching a crossroads, he looked left and right. Where the junction formed he saw a row of chairs displayed outside a carpentry store. One of them was overturned, two clear scratches in the wood. He moved closer. Claw marks. Kanderil followed the route on the right past the store, increasing his pace.

A child ran forward from the opposite direction. "Sir, sir!" he called. Kanderil made to move past but the child moved into his path. "Sir, you have to get her!"

Kanderil slowed, irritated. "Who?"

"The girl! She was being dragged by a blood sucker!" He pointed the way he had come.

"Blood suckers do not exist," he replied, stepping around the child and jogging forwards. He scanned the streets for any further evidence of flight. It was several minutes before one appeared – three large, pale slashes in the black-tarred doorframe. The door itself was absent. The building's poor condition suggested it was abandoned. Kanderil moved inside, studying the room within as his eyes adjusted to the gloom.

A ladder had been laid against the upper attic. Several gaps in the roof produced beams of sunlight through which dust motes were dancing. The missing door lay against the western wall. The ladder was ancient and Kanderil did not risk climbing it.

"Sarene," he said in a deep, calm voice. "If you are here, show yourself."

For a moment there was no response. Then, shuffling. The door slid across to reveal Sarene crammed within a large fireplace hidden behind it. She meekly crawled out into the open. Kanderil swore.

"You will be explaining yourself later, girl. Right now we need to leave. This will be one of the first places the guards search, if they have any sense."

"Get down before they see you!" The yell preceded Spasmodic launching itself out of the same fireplace. It tackled Sarene at the waist. She folded over its shoulder, a *whoosh* of air forced out of her lungs, and the two of them went crashing to the floor behind a broken crate. Dust flew up around the landing spot.

Kanderil waited.

"What we leaving for? The fun's just started." Spasmodic popped up back into sight. Sarene followed soon after, winded, glaring at the creature as she brushed herself down. The pair of them were filthy, covered in soot and grime. They looked like two street urchins in good need of a scrub.

The hard stare they found themselves faced with encouraged them to start moving.

Kanderil took the lead, pausing at the shack's entrance to ensure the street was clear. The guards were still blowing aimless peeps at each other as they moved around the city, searching for those responsible for the murder. The whistles were intended to coordinate a city-wide search, but they merely acted as a warning for any potential fugitive.

"What happened?" Kanderil said without looking back.

"One of those Gathire people found her," said Spasmodic.

"You sure he was Gathire?"

"Yeh, if they're the same blokes who came to her village." It pointed at Sarene. "They all dress like bloody undertakers."

Kanderil nodded. "That explains why so many of the guard are getting involved, then. You should have lost them in the forest. Less attention that way."

Silence.

"You *were* in the forest?" He looked around at the two of them. Sarene was blushing, her hands clasped together.

Spasmodic answered for her. "Some of the time, yeah."

Muttering, Kanderil moved out of the abandoned store and led them to the nearest alley. They cut between houses, pausing at each new avenue before continuing. He knew that each of the exits from the city would be on alert by now, as was the standard procedure when a public murder had been witnessed. People should be free to leave but they would be inspected first. It may be possible to get Sarene out, but the creature would be a little more difficult to conceal.

He remembered the claw marks in the doorway.

"How well can you climb?" he asked.

"Like a monkey."

"And your tracking?"

Spasmodic giggled. "I found you, didn't I?"

"Good. Find your own way out of the city then. I need to get Sarene clear."

"What, and miss all the shenanigans?"

Kanderil shook his head. "If you stay with us you increase the chance of her being detected."

"I could just kill everyone who came near her," Spasmodic replied, the statement casual.

The Hunter's response was almost a growl.

The creature muttered. "Fine. Try not to get caught, eh? She's too much fun."

"Try not to murder anyone else."

"Such a demanding fellow," it replied with a sneer. Then it was gone, slipping back the way they had come. Kanderil watched it go. Then he took a hold of the girl's hand.

"Follow my lead. Pull your hood up. And here," he said, retrieving a wad of fabric from his pack. He spat on it and handed it to her. She peered at him with a blank expression.

"Wipe the blood from your cheek."

They stepped out into one of the avenues leading to the north square. The two of them walked calmly, Kanderil adjusting his steps to match her pace. Those they passed in the street stared at him but ignored the girl. He overheard more than one conversation about the murder. The monster responsible had, along the chain of whispers, gained wings and a tail, blood red eyes and scales.

Sarene tottered along beside him, her head bowed. He glanced down at her. Whatever she'd seen had left her in a daze. To witness a death was something you never forgot. He couldn't imagine the creature had made a tidy kill, either. The blood on her cheek lent weight to that notion. Kanderil realised that he would have to talk to her as soon as they were clear. The amount of stress she had endured over the last week was astounding, and the mind could only take so much before it began to withdraw. He'd heard stories of recruits during the last conflict with Franthia; young boys drafted into service and thrown into the front lines as filler for the soldiers, making up numbers. Those who were unlucky died. Those a little more fortunate survived and learnt the necessary skills quickly.

A few went mad, unable to handle the grim reality of their situation.

The thought of consoling her was not a pleasant one. He could drill soldiers and give orders. Some on his team had come to him over the years seeking advice, and he had given it with blunt, practical words. But to offer solace to a young girl he barely knew, over matters neither of them understood, was something else entirely.

They walked on for another half-hour. Tamiran was big, and the need to remain discreet kept them to a gentle stroll. The whistles died down as the search faltered. He doubted they would capture Spasmodic. While it was likely the Gathire would be taking part in the hunt, Kanderil had no reason to believe they would be looking for *him*. A monster had killed one of their own, not a man. His meeting with Rohad should not draw suspicion either, even if the Kalethi barracks had been under surveillance. Kanderil had been one of them, and he had no ties to the girl or to Jared.

Sarene tripped. He managed to grab her arm before she fell. She caught her balance, before giving a tired smile of thanks.

Kanderil nodded as he looked across the street. It would make sense for the Gathire to be posted at the city gates. With Sarene in this condition, he doubted that they would be able to simply stroll through.

Porthouse was enjoying the day. The whistles in the city only served to cheer him further.

Whistles meant a crime and crime meant rumour. Rumour fostered conversation and conversation was enhanced by alcohol.

Alcohol was his trade.

Porthouse was a man of a shape which most people would, if asked to describe him in one word, testify as being 'round'. His body was slim of shoulder, wide of belly and thin of leg. He wore his thinning hair parted in the centre, heavy on the wax, with a curled, trimmed moustache to match. His daily uniform consisted of dark cotton trousers - tailor made, of course, to fit his peculiar measurements - a white cotton shirt and a purple waistcoat which struggled to be recognised around his flanks. A matching jacket had long since been lost in a tragic accident involving a very expensive bottle of red wine and a furious ex-wife.

He leant against his counter; arms spread, wrists forward, and watched the door. There would be no mad rush. No, that was too much to hope for. Besides, his clientele were not the rushing type. This was no stock'n'cattle tavern or beer house. Porthouse Liquor was the premier alcohol store in Tamiran for those with modest pockets and enough good sense to avoid those upper market places. The wine shops owned by the arrogant bastards serving the court attendees. Porthouse grinned at the thought of those conversations, the proprietor and the customer each at pains to try and portray a sense of wealth and sophistication to each other in the space of a five minute meeting.

I can afford your exorbitant price list, so I am clearly a person of importance.

You are indeed, but if I am providing the high quality selection, whom is relying on whom?

He could see it now. Backs straight, clothes bright, expressions reserved but cheerful. No, much better to have the ones with a bit of coin to them who didn't mind the banter, the earthy personal touch, that Porthouse provided. The stall owners, the merchants, the landlords and tavern keepers. True, he did get a few pimps and cutthroats from time to time, but even they could be charming. He didn't ask where the money came from, and he turned none away. Not even the children. They were victims, them little'uns, ragged and skinny and living on the street. It was his duty to provide them with an escape if they wanted one, and if they couldn't pay, then well... there were other arrangements.

He looked around his store. Rows of bottles on dark wooden shelves. Wine and firewater, casks of ale, spirits from across the lands. Well, the majority. Some were expensive contents from far away, covered with a label from *very* far away, but he'd yet to serve anyone who'd come back to him complaining about the difference.

Porthouse clasped a flabby hand to his massive stomach, rubbing it like a faithful pet. It gurgled at him.

"Why not," he replied aloud. He popped through the (*specially widened*) door to his back room and waddled over to the wheel of cheese sitting on its open paper wrap beside some sea crackers. Most of the wheel was gone. He cut himself a slice of the soft, crumbling cheese with the short knife lying beside the (*fake*) crystal goblet of deep Orubi wine. The slice was placed upon a cracker, and the cracker was devoured in two bites. He sipped the wine as he chewed, his face creasing up into a wobbly mound of pleasure. After swallowing, he smacked his lips together.

"Ah, that'll do. Yes, indeed."

A small bell rung as a customer entered the shop. Porthouse rubbed his hands together to remove any crumbs, carrying his great bulk back through the huge doorway.

As he saw the man standing before him, Porthouse's expression twitched, faltering. Beside the man was a young girl in a mauve hood. She seemed tiny in comparison to him.

"Kanderil, my friend!" he said in his most professional voice, the words sweet as honey. He smoothed down the front of his shirt before leaning on the counter. "It's been a long time. I heard you'd left town. *So* glad to know it isn't true."

Kanderil grunted. "Save it. I am not here for your company."

"Charming as always. May I ask after your young friend?" He gestured to the girl, his gaze running down her body. Not quite young enough for *his* tastes. Her large, dark eyes peeped out at him from beneath her hood, and she took a step closer to the Sergeant. He offered a cheery wink which she shrank away from.

"No, you may not." Kanderil nodded towards the room behind his counter. "I need to use your tunnel."

Porthouse scoffed, his laughter ringing with honest humour. "Kanderil. *Kanderil.* How many times did we go over this over the years?"

"Aye, but today is different." Kanderil stepped forward, his hand reaching for the section of the counter which lifted upwards.

"Hey!" Porthouse slammed a hand on the counter top. "This is quite out of order! I've proven to the guards time and again that there is no such tunnel leading in or out of my store, despite what... whatever *vicious* rumours may have been spread by my competitors!" Porthouse drew breath. "Now would you kindly explain to me what you think you're doing before I feel obliged to ask the authorities for assistance?"

Kanderil paused, looking at him. Porthouse wilted a little. *The man could probably fry eggs with that stare,* he thought to himself. For a moment he believed the Sergeant would respond with anger, but he knew better and allowed himself to remain indignant. Kanderil took a long, slow breath before replying.

"I am going to be clear with you, my old friend. I need the use of the tunnel which runs from your store to the imitation boulder maybe a half mile outside the walls, due north. The Kalethi," – he held up a hand to cut off Porthouse's starting protest –"... the Kalethi have known about the tunnel for around six years, as have the guards. Despite this, they have let you keep it, making the occasional visit to suggest to your competitors that they were still investigating. So please, let us not negotiate this. I am in a hurry."

Porthouse was astonished. He couldn't tell if Kanderil was certain of his words, or if he merely had a great poker face. "Look," he said. "Supposing that I *did* have some kind of passage out of the city, why would the guard not look to shut it down?"

"Because you pay off Hollandis with good bottles of wine to keep any real searches contained," Kanderil replied, smirking. "He has been sharing them from the first glass with anyone involved with your complaints. You are not the only one looking to skim a little extra out of the tax system."

His face flushing, Porthouse wrung his hands. Hot blood coursed through his veins as he felt a mixture of humiliation and rage building under his collar. "But... that's..." He shook his head. "No, that would be preposterous! Why, he would get into a lot more trouble if I were to let his sup-"

"Lad," Kanderil raised a hand. "No one would believe you. Now, my young friend here needs to use that passage."

He stared at the giant. His mouth opened to speak, closed, opened again. Realising he probably looked like a fish out of water, he shut his mouth once more and ground his teeth instead.

"Please."

The obese shopkeeper clenched his right hand, grinding it into the palm of his left. "You left them, didn't you? The Kalethi."

Kanderil nodded.

"Why?"

"That is none of your concern."

"Kanderil," Porthouse said with a clipped laugh, "if you expect me to believe your story then you've got to do better than that. I could have the Kalethi swooping in here at any moment if I gave a sign of believing your... your *lies*."

The girl, who up until this point had kept her gaze fixed on him, was now watching the Sergeant as if awaiting an answer.

"I took early retirement. I have no interest at all in your place being shut down, nothing to gain and no career to think of."

"So you're asking a favour, then."

Kanderil tightened his brow. "Excuse me?"

"You're asking a favour." Porthouse looked at his hands and held them still. "If I have nothing to lose by... by considering your *claims*, then the other alternative is that you require my assistance for yourself."

Nothing. He imagined the man's comprehension dropping into place like a rockslide.

"If I were able to get this girl out of the city by any means other than the conventional, then I would be owed something in return. It only makes sense, Kanderil."

"I could force you to tell me," Kanderil growled.

Porthouse smiled. "Ah, you could; but you wouldn't, would you?" He gave a titter of delight. "You're too much of a gentleman, my boy. One of the old school, code of iron and all that. Now, don't you worry. I'll not be asking for your first born or anything." He lifted the counter top, the hinge producing an ugly metallic squeal. "It's just a nice thing to have, isn't it? One of *your* kind on call."

Kanderil said nothing. Instead, he placed a hand at the young girl's back, encouraging her to move forward. She did so, dragging her feet.

Porthouse turned to lead the way into the back of the store. "Now," he said, halting in the centre of the room a few seconds before his flesh did. One arm came to his first chin, tapping his finger against the firmest point. "If I *were* to have a tunnel, then where would I put it..." He stood there, wincing, expecting a rough blow to the back of the head.

"Fine. A favour." The dark voice of the Sergeant was music to his ears.

"Excellent!" Porthouse scurried over to one of several stacks of crates against the far wall, straw poking through the slats of each. He lifted the top box free and placed it on the floor, four feet from the edge of the room. After appraising the box for a moment, he nudged it with his foot. Then he stacked three more boxes atop the first. Returning to the wall, he reached for one of the more prominent stones there. The work had been expensive, laying bricks and rocks in flat-packed mortar to give a very loose mosaic effect. He wriggled the stone free and dipped his fat fingers inside the newly made hole.

Something clicked.

A section of the wall swung inwards, revealing a dark tunnel. The ground had been dug out and a path lined with slate steps, beneath a ceiling propped up with wooden beams. The first twenty yards or so were visible; after that, darkness. Porthouse turned to look at his guests.

"Interesting," said Kanderil.

"Cost me a pretty penny as well, I don't mind telling you." Porthouse lifted a handkerchief from his breast pocket and dabbed at his forehead. "Unsurprising, really, that nobody has found it yet."

"It was found years ago. We just never told you."

"Never *proven*, then, if one wishes to be pedantic." His initial disappointment at the revelation was fading fast. Providing the Sergeant was telling the truth, he essentially had a free reign to transport goods through the tunnel. If the guards were aware of it and content to leave it open, then it would make sense to believe he was being given leeway to serve their own corruption. He would have to remember that when he next placed his orders. Certain commodities he had never dared to bring into Tamiran. Now...

The young girl stepped back. Kanderil knelt before her, placing a hand on her slim shoulder.

"You have to go in. I cannot bring you to the gate. I will meet you where the tunnel ends."

The girl shook her head. She seemed terrified of the passage, occasionally looking to Porthouse himself with anxious eyes. Porthouse was not displeased by the expression.

"When you reach the other side, wait. I would come with you now but I must ensure the exit is not being watched above ground. We can then get on and find him."

The girl shook her head again. Kanderil lifted his head to glance around the room. He gestured to the wall.

"Fetch that torch."

Porthouse took a moment to realise the Sergeant was referring to him. He rubbed his clammy hands together, fetching the unlit brand from its place in a riveted sconce. Kanderil took it and gave it to his young companion. The giant then produced a tinder-box from the bag slung over his shoulder. He struck the flint several times against the pitch-soaked head, the sparks eventually pulling flame. The torch erupted into life.

"Take this with you, keep walking and do not look back. I know our next destination but we have to get you out of this city first. This is the safest way."

The girl looked at him dubiously and for a moment Porthouse thought she would refuse further. Then she took a step forward, then another, moving towards the passage. She took a deep breath before crossing the threshold out of the room, entering the tunnel. True to Kanderil's request, she did not look back.

Porthouse started to return the crates he'd moved back to their original position. The door to the tunnel swung shut. Silence fell over the room. Kanderil made to leave. Porthouse cleared his throat, moving over towards the last of his cheese.

"Now then, about payment."

Kanderil stopped. "Payment?"

"How can I contact you?"

The huge man glanced over his shoulder, his face barely visible through his long hair. "Whistle."

"Hah! Oh, you're a hard man but sometimes, just *sometimes*, you show a flash of wit." Porthouse lifted a loaded cracker, the ratio a little too one-sided in favour of the cheese topping, and crammed it into his mouth. He chewed without closing his lips. "I mean," he said with a spray of crumbs, "that girl must have been reasonably important if you needed to get her out of the city without certain people knowing."

Kanderil's fingers twitched at his side.

"I do *certain people*, Kanderil. I deal with them on a weekly basis."

"You are not very good at it."

Porthouse swallowed. The comment irritated him momentarily, but he pushed the feeling aside.

"Now if you're gallivanting around Tamir after her then I can hardly call in my favour on a whim, can I? It could be years before we meet again."

"Get to your point."

"I want a share of whatever she's worth."

"She is worth nothing."

"I would disagree. Someone, somewhere, would pay for her."

Kanderil turned. He brought himself to his full height, shoulders square. Porthouse failed to contain the shudder which struck him like a lightning bolt.

"Porthouse, let me be clear. If she is followed along your tunnel then you and I shall be at odds. You do not want me for an enemy."

"Th-threats are hardly good payment for my assistance, my large friend." He padded his forehead again with the handkerchief.

Kanderil exhaled, looking away. Porthouse could tell his was wrestling with opposing thoughts. Then, at last, a nod. "Very well. Once I have delivered the girl, I shall return to you and make amends. You have a deal."

"Splendid!" Porthouse nodded several times. Morals were *such* a hindrance. "Splendid. How about we share a bottle of Orubi to celebrate this new-found partnership?" He lifted the bottle from the table and looked around for a second goblet.

Without another word Kanderil moved towards the door leading to the street outside.

Chapter Nine

Spasmodic scampered over the rooftops. Its boots, though thick of sole and heavy heeled, made little noise as it leapt from one surface to another. Anyone looking up through the gaps in the man-made canopy of guttering and overhangs would *think* they saw something, but would have difficulty comprehending what it was. Spasmodic moved with a frightening speed.

Whistles blew in the streets below. The occasional shout joined them, like a bubble rising to the surface of a stagnant pond. Humans were just stupid in swarms, blindly charging around with no real plan and no sense of cohesion. The whistles were the most ridiculous part. At least the civilians - the word *cattle* came to mind, making the creature giggle - had an excuse for their futile efforts. The guards were supposed to be trained, skilled at what they did. They were paid to keep the peace and yet they were making more noise than everyone else, adding to the panic. Spasmodic was reminded of a gull which it had attacked when it found a nest of eggs to plunder. Loud, enthusiastic, but ultimately useless in keeping its children safe.

The creature thought of animals often. It wondered if it

had some sort of weird predilection for beasts. It shook its head, snorting. Dreadlocks flew.

Spasmodic came to a halt, standing upright to gauge its position. It was maybe two miles from the edge of the sprawling capital. It could see the guard towers over the main gate to the north, flags hanging impotent against their poles in the still afternoon air.

That the humans built such a construction was astonishing. Spasmodic ran the back of its hand across its mouth before moving on, its mind wandering as it took in the architecture and design of the buildings it negotiated. It had seen villages and towns aplenty on its way to finding Sarene, of course, but nothing of this scale. It was almost impressed. Streets ran in neat spider webs, generally conforming to meet every so often at a central point. Buildings ranged from a single floor to four or five high. The majority were well maintained. It saw engraving through sheet marble, which suggested years of work, and it witnessed small gardens of incredible beauty and life appear from nowhere amidst concentrations of stone and slate. It hurdled over statues on the corners of rooftops and it sailed above the domed arch of what must have surely been a building of religious significance.

Religion was another terrible failure of the humans. Associating their lives with the will of those more powerful, despite the lack of any evidence that such entities existed.

Except for the Four.

The creature heard more whistles behind it, now much further in the distance. Spasmodic sneered. "Silly idea, letting the sheep play shepherd," it said.

Hitting one rooftop, its foot slipped slightly. It slowed again, using its other foot as a rudder to slide to a halt. Spasmodic wobbled at the waist, chuckling, waving its arms around for balance. It always surprised itself when it made a mistake. The abilities granted to it by Tyrrial were far beyond any human it had met so far. Missteps were for lesser beings.

Something cooed at it. Spasmodic looked up to see a pigeon perched atop a waist-high wall bordering the rooftop.

The bird was staring at it. To emphasise the point, the pigeon cooed again.

"You were laughin' at me?" Spasmodic asked.

The bird tilted its head to the side, peering at the creature from a ninety degree angle.

The creature chuckled in reply, noting the similarity in the gesture that it had performed itself many times.

"Lemme tell you summat. If I was a cat, I'd have eaten you by now." It extended a hand towards the bird, the sunlight gleaming from the surface of the lethal digits. The claws were smooth for the most part, blemished only by the occasional tiny hole, similar to teeth cavities. "In fact, maybe I still will. For laughing."

The bird took two steps to the left along the edge of the rooftop before cooing again.

"Pfft." Spasmodic sneered in amusement. "Cocky son of a whore, aren't ye."

A moment later the bird flapped in alarm as Spasmodic left, its shredded cavalry coat rippling like streamers as it burst into motion, leaping on to the next building. The pigeon cooed once more in annoyance at the disruption

Sarene wandered down the tunnel with her torch held out in order to ward off the evil spirits she felt sure lurked just ahead, flickering in the shadows cast by her protective flame. Twice she had tripped on uneven stones before she realised that, instead of walking, she was merely sliding her feet along the ground.

No one had bothered to ask if she was claustrophobic.

The closeness of the tunnel and the old, stale air was unsettling and strange. She was a daughter of the open sky, and she disliked the sensation of being trapped like this. The echo of the door latching shut behind her had been awful. Waiting ahead was an exit she had never seen before. What if the tunnel continued past it? She could miss her target entirely and end up lost in here for days. Would Kanderil be able to find her? Would that fat pig Porthouse come hunting for her? The thought made her shudder.

Watching the light dance back and forth across the earthen walls and beam-supported ceiling, Sarene found her mind wandering. Her endurance had reached its limit. She had been marched from her home for days and been given no real explanation why. Unable to communicate with her new companions as she had been able to with her family, Sarene was left with a sense of frustration underlining her mood. The dangers she now faced, the threats to her family and the enormity of her situation made her head hurt.

She still doubted Spasmodic to a point. How could she possibly accept the words of a creature she had issues believing existed at all? It looked like something from a nightmare, not human but similar enough to unsettle her. The way it giggled, the clawed hands, the nose which could have been a snout if one stared hard enough...

Sarene sighed. It was hard refuting the evidence. How else could such a thing be possible if *not* created by one of the Four?

Of course, that was absurd because it would suggest that one of the Four, one of the fabled mythical beings who had shaped the fate of the entire world, was searching for her. A simple farmer's daughter from the Valley with no exceptional features besides a rare vocal defect.

One thing was clear. Whoever hunted her had no good intentions. The attack on her family had proved that.

The image of her mother lying bandaged in her bed, spots of blood seeping through the fabric, made her pause. Sarene had maintained a strong effort to keep that picture from her mind but occasionally it slipped through her defences. Each instance was like a slap to the face. She bowed her head, biting her lower lip as a precaution to keep her tears from running again. The act was proving more difficult to uphold with each passing day. She felt as though all she had done for the past week was march and weep, any sleep in-between being broken and full of dreams. Dreams she did not wish to recall the morning after, with dew on the grass and sunlight breaking through the trees. Dreams best left locked away.

Sniffing, she made a concerted effort to pick up her pace, treading with increased purpose through the tunnel. The flames of the torch rippled at the sudden movement, and the darkness seemed to swirl around her as she moved. Shadows which began before her encircled the light, appearing again behind to reach with black talons towards her shoulders. Sarene ignored this as best she could, praying that the exit from the tunnel was easy to spot.

———◄○►———

Striding through the streets, Kanderil kept his shoulders broad and his head high. People avoided him that way. In addition, it was important to portray the image of a man with absolutely nothing to hide. Handily, composure was one of his strong points.

The streets of Tamiran were straight. They fell across the land contained within the huge city walls like matchsticks spilled from a box. Main streets were overlapped, dissected and framed by smaller, thinner lanes. Only the rich areas could claim to be designed and maintained with any sense of uniformity. The slums and merchant areas had simply been built upon, homes and stores opening up wherever there was room. A man with twenty yards of shop front could sell half of it to a competitor for as much as they would earn in six months of trading, such was the demand for space. Many did that, and the result was a trade district made up of small, narrow stores lined up like broken teeth. Kanderil felt more distant from society here than anywhere else. He felt a tug at his core to get back to the forests, where things made sense and nobody was looking to squeeze you for a profit or a percentage. In the woods you could eat, drink and sleep for free with a degree of luxury. Here people scraped the gutters to earn a loaf of yesterday's old bread, and Kanderil could never understand why they accepted it.

He would reach the north gate in just over an hour. The

standard procedure for a murder was to monitor the gates for a half-day, questioning everyone who tried to leave. Usually this was unnecessary, as most violent deaths came from drunken bar fights where the perpetrator was either caught at the scene or restrained by other patrons until the guard arrived.

In this case a Gathire had been killed. Kanderil could not recall a precedent, but he guessed the lockdown could be extended even further. Probably would be, in fact. The Gathire had no qualms about enforcing additional methods to look after their own. Kanderil had heard stories of the lengths taken by the faction to protect themselves or retaliate to any threat made against them. Rumours of torture, counterfeit evidence and excessive force had always lurked in the taverns and slums. Especially after a few tankards of ale. No solid proof of this had ever surfaced but, as the saying went, there was rarely smoke without fire.

Added to this was the feeling that he was being followed. Kanderil was a skilled tracker with a keen sense for these things, and he'd been unable to shake the sensation that his movements were being watched. He had decided against more than the usual precautions; he would move through narrow streets and avoid spending too long on a single path, turning corners as often as possible. Ideally he would have wanted to backtrack, lay fake trails and take other such actions to ensure he could not be shadowed, but doing so could draw additional attention.

It was another reason he disliked cities. Too many witnesses. People tended to remember a man who stood seven feet tall.

Kanderil pushed the problem from his mind as he turned another corner. He was either being followed or he wasn't. As soon as he was free of Tamiran and back into the world outside he would lose any pursuer. The city wasn't his, but the forests *were*.

The street he found himself was North Junction Road, and lead directly north for another several hundred yards or so until reaching the main gate. It passed the Courthouse of

Tamiran, its imposing front podium taking centre stage. Here, those condemned of crimes serious enough to warrant the death sentence were led to the gallows. A hanging always brought a good crowd, a fact reliable enough to attract street vendors offering food and trinkets. Human fascination with the macabre on full display, witnessed by everyone present with the sole exception of the man to be killed. He would be wearing a loose, black velvet hood. It was always *he*, as well. Females were seldom executed, and on those occasions it was done in private. The customs of the Tamir people would not allow the public death of a woman.

The next street led through to more terraced housing, each home no more than four yards in width. Kanderil ran a hand through his hair, taking a subtle look over his shoulder. Nothing in sight that alarmed him. He turned here, taking a less direct route north. Children stared at him as he passed, some with mouths wide open, whatever game being played forgotten for the moment. Adults would stare too, only they would do so less openly. Kanderil had learnt during his years working from the Kalethi base here in the capital that Tamir women were less cautious about studying him than the men.

He'd once pointed this out to an old team mate, Lotharian, who had provided an interesting explanation.

If a man offends you, then you're perfectly within your rights to break his jaw. A woman could correctly assume you wouldn't do the same to her, and therefore she's braver about the whole thing. Not that I would stare at you, personally. You're an ugly bugger.

Kanderil smiled softly at the memory. Lotharian was one of the few whose company he missed in recent years.

Eventually he reached the gate, the sun low in the sky but still a couple of hours away from hitting the horizon. Kanderil observed the security detail; five guards in uniform, and a man dressed in a long jacket which moulded around his shoulders, hanging to clear the ground by just a few inches. The high collar reached the man's chin. His clothes, boots and gloves were all black, aside from the jacket's white hems.

Gathire.

Up on the parapets of the great wall, men had been stationed every fifty yards or so. It appeared the guard had been fully mobilised against escape. The thought that they knew about Porthouse's 'secret' tunnel struck him, but it was still the safest option. Here at the gate it would have been especially difficult to smuggle Sarene through.

Moving past one unlucky citizen who had just been turned away, Kanderil appraised the Gathire Agent. The man was bald, with a straight scar running from his jawline to just above his right ear. He stood with one hand clasped loosely behind his back, the other hanging straight at his side. Kanderil noted that the guards stood in a group apart from the Agent. Even those who fought on the same side regarded them with suspicion.

One of the guards, boyish in appearance, stepped forward as Kanderil reached the gate. He held up a hand, pointing back past the Hunter.

"'Fraid you'll have to be turning around, friend. Orders of the Commander."

Kanderil nodded, making no mention of his opinion that the Commander of the Guard had nothing to do with this lockdown. "What was the crime?" he asked, keeping his voice neutral. The man before him spread his hands.

"Who cares? Whatever it was, you're still not going through this gate. Kindly step back, eh?"

Kanderil looked over at the other four. The captain was watching him with an amused smirk. He recognised the officer as Samuel, a liaison between the guard and the Kalethi over the years and a dependable man. The others with him were all young and fresh-faced; probably recruits.

The guard in front of him tapped him on the chest. "Hey, hey, don't look at them. I'm telling you to move along. Or do the rules not apply to a guy your size?"

Kanderil narrowed his eyes, clenching his jaw. He towered over the guard, who took a step back. Some of the colour drained from the boy's cheeks, the tough exterior melting away within seconds.

"I was not aware that the Tamiran guard had lost their manners recently. Do you treat all citizens with such contempt?"

The guard blinked, looking over to his companions for support. Samuel winked at him, folding his arms, while the other three stood still, uncertain of what to do. Kanderil reached inside his leather jerkin to retrieve the Sergeant pin he kept there, having relinquished the Kalethi insignia when he retired. He held it out for the guard to see. The youth reached up to scratch at the shock of blonde hair hanging from his temple, wetting his lips with his tongue.

"I believe this badge grants me immunity from the lockdown unless specific instruction is given. Did the Commander make direct mention that the Kalethi were also to be impeded?" Kanderil muttered to himself. "Perhaps you would like to explain to *my* commanding officer why I will be late arriving at my destination."

"I, uh... Sorry, sir. My mistake."

"Aye, it *was* your mistake." Kanderil put the pin away, glancing over to Samuel. "Training funds been cut or something?"

Samuel shrugged his shoulders. "This is their training. Some of them take a little longer than others to adapt, is all."

Kanderil nodded. "I hope this one gets the attention he needs." He clasped a hand on the guard's shoulder. By this point, the young man was scarlet with embarrassment. Kanderil felt him wither under his grip. "I am sure you will turn out fine, boy. Just remember you are meant to be serving the public, not your ego."

The boy's reply was hasty. "Aye, I will, sir. I didn't mean to be rude but I just saw you weren't going to turn around. I thought I should, y'know, try and stop you somehow."

"I think what he's tryin' to say is that he bit off more than he could chew, and started panicking." One of the other guards offered this, to the amusement of his colleagues. "I reckon he'd need a change of underclothes about now, eh?" The other two standing with him chuckled.

Samuel cleared his throat. "Now, lads, which one of you three there would have done any different?" The Captain ran a critical eye over them. "This man could probably pull your arm out of its socket should he so wish. At least Garlei there had the balls to step out to do his job."

The three guardsmen looked at each other, their laughter fading. Garlei smiled, some of his original cock-sureness returning to his face.

"Get on with yourself, Sergeant Kanderil." Samuel offered a polite tug of his cap. "We'll not be holdin' you up any longer."

"*Retired* 'Sergeant', isn't it?" a voice said just as Kanderil took his first step towards the gate. All six men turned to face the Gathire.

"Aye," he replied in an even tone.

"Three years now. Handed in a resignation and just... Walked away." The bald man swept a hand through the air.

A woman and her child approached the gate, the former leading a small pony. One of the guards stepped away to speak with her.

"So why, then," continued the Agent, "Should you expect immunity from the city lockdown?"

"I was given no official discharge from service, and I still retain my commission pin." Kanderil shrugged his shoulders. "If someone had wanted to cut me off completely, they could have come and found me."

"Ah, so you're simply *assuming* that you're still granted Kalethi exception. Quite an arrogant viewpoint."

Kanderil frowned. "Perhaps if we moved to the Kalethi barracks, we could speak to the officer in command there."

"The irrefutable Major Rohad, I believe." The Agent turned his head to look along the main street leading away from the gate, as if able to see the barracks from where he stood. Around the paved road before the gate a small crowd had gathered to watch the routine act of turning people away. "Your old drill instructor. Served with the Kalethi for getting on thirty... no, thirty two years now. A solid, reliable man."

Kanderil did not respond. The guards appeared uncomfortable.

The Agent turned at the waist. One arm remained behind his back while the other gestured to his left with an open palm. "May we talk in private for a moment?"

The two men walked away from the guards, along the wall east of the gate. The fortifications had been covered with mortar to remove any gap between them, providing no crack or crevice to aid in climbing. Kanderil looked up. Above them was clear blue sky, pale in colour and free of moisture.

Soon enough the Agent came to a halt. Kanderil stopped beside him. They turned to face each other. Kanderil folded his arms, a simple act he had learned long ago made most adversaries feel ill at ease. Such a posture made him seem six feet wide, with shoulders squared and his chest puffed out.

Without so much as a blink, the bald-headed man spoke. "You understand that I must ask a few questions before I even consider letting you through that gate" His voice was thin but firm, matching his hawkish features. The large, crooked nose and small eyes fit his face well. Kanderil was given the impression of a vulture that was experienced in picking the right carcass to feed on.

"Of course."

The Agent inclined his head. "My name is Chalimer. I am investigating the murder of one of my colleagues. The attack happened roughly two hours ago."

"My condolences to your faction, Justicar," Kanderil replied, keeping his voice steady. The man opposite was the highest ranking Gathire outside of the Assembly.

"Thank you," Chalimer inclined his head. "Now, we have reports of two suspects fleeing the scene of the crime. The first is a male with bright red hair, which is quite distinctive. He is described as under six feet tall, wearing a long green jacket similar to those worn by the cavalry in poor weather."

Kanderil grunted. "I have not seen him. Such a man would certainly stick in the memory."

"Yes, I believe so too." The Agent nodded. "We

understand he is the one responsible for the killing. The second suspect is either a captive or an accomplice."

"His description?"

"Her, actually." Chalimer raised his brow at the disclosure. Kanderil felt the gesture was rehearsed. "A young girl around five and a half feet in height, with dark hair to her shoulders and fair skin. The latter is a surprising trait considering the summer we have endured, no?"

"Not entirely," said Kanderil. "Street urchins will often stay out of the sunlight, finding shelter in the sewers or abandoned buildings. Pale skin is easier to colour with dirt, making them seem more sympathetic to those they beg for."

Chalimer pursed his lips. "Interesting observation. Larceny could be one motivation, though I have never heard of a Gathire being targeted for a mugging."

"Indeed. It suggests another reason. Self defence springs to mind, though revenge attacks are not unheard of against guard members. Perhaps your man acquired some enemies during his career."

"He would have been skilled to gain such a reputation so quickly. The victim had been with the Gathire for less than a year."

"Self defence seems the most likely, then. An excessive use of force when trying to escape apprehension."

"Excessive is certainly one word for it. The victim's throat was slashed through to the bone." Chalimer raised a hand to scratch at the scar on the side of his head. "I presume you have not seen the girl, either?"

Kanderil bowed his head, but kept his focus on Chalimer. "My apologies, but street urchins with dark hair are not exactly uncommon. I try not to keep a look out for young girls as I travel in case people get the wrong impression about me."

The remark elicited a thin smile from the Agent. "*This* girl was last seen heading west on Fathering Street in the company of the red haired male, around two hours ago as I said."

Kanderil spread his hands, unfolding his arms. "I cannot

help you, sorry. Two hours ago I was enjoying a tankard in the Bear's Noose."

"Alone?"

"How I spend my time has nothing to do with your investigation, unless you suspect me of something."

"Very true," Chalimer replied with another smile, this one more genuine. "It is safe to say you would have been easily identified were you involved with this crime. No, I don't think you have anything to do with this, Kanderil. It seems far withdrawn from your usual... Class."

Kanderil eyed the man. "Class?"

Clearing his throat, the Justicar of the Gathire placed both hands behind his back. As he began to speak his eyes rolled upwards, as though reciting a script from memory. "Former Sergeant Kanderil of the Kalethi. You were offered a promotion several times during an eighteen year career, all of which were turned down. You served with distinction, garnering two Lion medals for exceptional service when your scouting skills led to the removal of external threats to the Tamiran people. You also served with honour, receiving one Valour medal for bravery in the face of danger after defending four wounded team mates, single handed, following an ambush by Franthian separatists. The aggressors eventually withdrew, most likely as a result of casualties endured. You are widely regarded as one of the greatest archers in the lands, and your skill as a woodsman is highly respected by your peers. As an only child to two deceased parents, you remain unmarried and with no children. You retired three years ago, and have since spent your time in the forests and mountains of the surrounding countryside."

Kanderil unclenched his hands slowly as Chalimer focused on him again. The Agent smirked. "Was there anything I left out?"

"Only how you know so much about me."

"Of course. I am a scholar, Kanderil." Chalimer drew himself up to his full height, apparently proud of himself. "A scholar of people. I enjoy following the careers of those I admire. I actually have you to thank for that. You were given to me as a part of my initial training, as an exercise on using public records for research. Your exploits caught my imagination, and only served to fuel my interest in Tamir's historical archives."

"Interesting," Kanderil admitted. "I would have preferred not being the subject of a case study, however."

"Getting your permission first would have rendered the exercise somewhat futile, I think." With a short laugh, Chalimer reached out to slap Kanderil firmly on the arm. "Go on, be off with you. I hope you serve yourself as well as you served the Kalethi."

Kanderil nodded, turning. "I wish you luck in your investigation. Again, my condolences for your faction's loss." He made his way towards the gate, nodding to Samuel as he did. The Captain seemed relieved.

"Got your permission slip, eh?"

"Aye, you could say that." Kanderil smiled, glancing across the city one final time when something caught his attention on the other side of the road. A figure darting down an alley leading alongside a cabinet-maker's store. At the last second they looked up in his direction, and Kanderil took in two more details before the figure disappeared from view.

Greasy dark hair.

Patchy shading around his upper lip.

"You will let us know if you see the two I mentioned outside these walls..?" Chalimer's voice floated to him from behind. Kanderil replied over his shoulder.

"Of course."

Waving goodbye to Samuel he walked underneath the huge northern portcullis, keeping his long strides even, covering ground without appearing eager to get away from the city.

He would have to hurry to meet Sarene as quickly as possible, for the Gathire would be following them.

————◀○▶————

Less than two hours later Sarene and her two companions were together again. She had come scrambling out of the tunnel, her relief immense. Unsure of how to extinguish the torch with no handy supply of water, she had placed it against the large rock beside the exit from the underground passage. Kanderil had rectified this when he arrived by digging a hole in the ground with his heel and burying the flames with earth. The fire went out just as Spasmodic arrived, chewing on a carrot which was still covered in the stubborn earth it had been pulled from.

They began their journey north right away, Kanderil commenting that they should pick up their pace. Spasmodic accepted this without complaint - in truth, Sarene was starting to suspect the creature was travelling much more slowly than it usually did - but despair touched her even as she nodded in agreement. She'd been barely keeping up as it was, and was sure that another forced march would be the end of her. Over the next few hours she forced her legs to continue moving despite the cramps and exhaustion, using the terrain as a crutch wherever possible, grasping anything which came within reach. At least the forest here was not as dense as to the south of the city. There was room to move without having to crawl or hop over or under thorns, roots and vines. Shed pine needles littered the floor along with cracked moss, slivers of rock and dry, dusty earth. The browns and greens became more contrasting here, filtered amongst tones of gentle yellow and pale grey.

Kanderil said little but something appeared to be on his mind, although he was doing a good job of concealing it. If she hadn't spent the last week living in his pocket Sarene doubted she would have noticed at all. Her destiny to always listen to others had forged a skill for reading faces. Kanderil's held many questions.

Spasmodic was chattering on beside the woodsman, but by now it had learned not to expect an answer. An undeclared agreement between the two of them meant while the conversation would always flow, it would be from one direction only.

Sarene rubbed at her upper arm. Last night she had slept with her cloak pulled up only to her waist and she had been caught by the mosquitoes. Her skin itched, but she refused to allow herself to scratch. A firm rub now and then would have to suffice.

After a few miles Kanderil stopped. He turned to face Spasmodic, who paused with its mouth open mid word. It continued the vowel it was expressing.

"Ooooooooooooooooooooo--"

"If you are going to travel with us then you are not to kill anyone else," Kanderil said in such a way as to permit no further debate.

Spasmodic tried anyway. "Not gonna happen. If someone threatens me then I just react, y'know?"

"I threatened you when we first met. You did not try to kill me."

"That was different, like. I had to make friends with her." The creature pointed at Sarene, who was bent over with her hands on her knees, catching her breath. "Killing you would have made that pretty tricky."

"It suggests you have at least some control over your actions." Kanderil rolled his shoulder, lifting a hand to pinch at the thick muscle anchoring the joint to his neck.

"Listen, I'm only dicking around with you people because she's going to provide me with some adventures." Spasmodic winked at Sarene, who wasn't sure how to accept the statement. She gave a rather confused smile. It continued. "If I let some idiot take her away from me, what do I do then? No... No, better to send a message. Tell 'em they should just leave her with us for a while."

"All you have done is anger them, demon."

"Well *this* demon doesn't care. She's safe, isn't she? If it wasn't for me she'd be with that handful of bastards by now."

"The same outcome would have been achieved had you simply disabled the man, except we would not have the entire Gathire faction out for your blood with a full description of the pair of you. They are now within their rights to stick posters up in every neighbouring town, offering a reward."

Spasmodic scoffed, grimacing with delight. "Pfft. Let 'em. I ain't seen much you people can do to stop me. Sarene isn't going anywhere."

Kanderil exhaled. It was the closest she had seen to her huge guardian losing his temper. "Sarene was left in *my* care. If you insist on travelling with us then we cannot have a trail of bodies left in our wake. We will garner no sympathy for her cause that way, and we may need allies in the future. Either accept this, or travel your own way."

"Heh." Spasmodic grinned. "You think you can give out orders like that, big man? Tell me what I can an' can't do?"

"It is a request. You are under no obligation to obey. Leave if it suits you better."

"Look, the guy was tryin' to grab her! He had this evil lookin knife-hook..." – it waved its hands as it hunted its vocabulary for the right word –"...thing! He would have rammed it up me browneye and taken her to sod-knows-where!"

The creature looked at Sarene. Nodding she bit her lower lip, wanting it to agree, hating this type of conflict and the tension which went with it. Her hands came together, pleading for a positive response. The creature still had the capacity to scare her, but she was beginning to understand that it would provide her with a degree of protection she could not overlook.

Spasmodic spat noisily. "*Fine.* I'll try not to kill anyone for a while unless it's really needed."

The woodsman nodded. Sarene couldn't tell if that was the answer he was looking for, but it seemed satisfactory for now. She gave the creature a thankful smile, offering a curtsy to express her gratitude. Spasmodic sniffed, dislodging something sticky from its nasal canal. Pulling a face, she turned away. She heard it snigger.

"We will head on for another few hours before we find somewhere to camp," said Kanderil.

"We late for dinner somewhere?" Spasmodic asked. Sarene looked over to the Hunter, eager also to understand the change of pace.

"I think we can expect to be followed from the city."

With a sigh, Sarene rubbed the back of her hand across her brow, wiping away the beads of sweat which were collected there. Her hair was greasy, sticking together in dark rats tails. Snapping her fingers to get Kanderil's attention, she pointed back towards Tamiran and the way they had just come. Then she held two fingers before her eyes, before gesturing to the three of them.

"Yeah," Spasmodic agreed. "Back there she saw blind people walking in circles." Sarene frowned, clucking her tongue at it.

"I think she means we were already being watched." Kanderil looked to her for agreement, which she gave with all the mild cheer she could muster at this stage. "Aye. If the Gathire appeared from the forests behind you outside Tamiran, as you say, then it is a fair estimate that they were able to track our movements despite my best efforts. We must now assume they know our next destination, and also that they know I am travelling with you."

"What makes you say that?" asked the creature. "You weren't there when I killed that guy."

"I was questioned by the Justicar of the Gathire at the north gate. After our conversation I saw a Kalethi clerk skulking around the street opposite, making a poor job of staying hidden. I have a suspicion he followed me to the gate."

Sarene tapped her foot on the ground, thinking. She crossed her index and middle fingers over each other, before giving a *thumbs up* and *thumbs down* signal with her other hand.

"Is he... Sorry. I do not understand, lass."

Shaking her head, Sarene knelt down and started to draw in the dirt with the tip of her finger, dragging two stick figures into existence. She produced Jared's Kalethi insignia and placed it over the first figure. On the second she traced a circle around its head, followed by a triangle around its body

"Kalethi and... cloaked men? Gathire?"

Sarene stomped over to him, reaching out to grab his hand. She gave it a firm shake.

"Are they friends."

Sarene smiled, giving a triumphant nod.

Kanderil grunted. "We are supposed to be. Both factions are a part of the Tamir military and have worked together in the past. It seems odd that a Kalethi clerk would be under the hire of the Gathire, though. It would certainly be seen as espionage by the Kalethi commanders were it to come to light."

"What's up with it, then?" Spasmodic asked, disinterested. He was reclining on a partially buried rock, upon which someone had carved the initials 'M' and 'P' inside a crude heart symbol.

"I could not say at this point. As a very broad estimate, I would propose that they are aware of Sarene's relation to her brother Jared and would want to know if he returns to Tamiran."

"What about you then? You're nothing to do with her. Why follow you around?"

Kanderil replied with a voice like tearing stone. "I do not know."

Spasmodic grinned, spreading his arms wide. He gave Kanderil a cheerful wink. "Another part of the amazing journey ahead, matey."

Kanderil turned. "Come on. We should continue. I want to arrive at the Meadows before tomorrow evening."

With a deep breath, Sarene readied herself for the final part of the day's travel. She would sleep like the dead tonight. Deep enough, perhaps, to avoid the dreams.

Hawk saw the fox waiting for him in a small gap through the forest underbrush. He understood that the animal was there for him. They were five miles from the open land

surrounding Tamiran, riding along a forest trail broad enough for their horses. Having galloped down the Highway for the entire morning, men of their particular character tended to return to the less beaten path when the opportunity presented itself. Hawk reigned in his mount, which was exhausted after the past few days of tortuous pace, and called after the other two.

"I'll catch up, lads. Nature calls."

"Nature calls?" Petar called over his shoulder. "What's that, you found the silver spoon for your mouth?"

"Did I say nature? Apologies. I meant 'your mother.'"

Lug's laughter rang out like a rusty saw through oak. Petar grinned, waving.

"That's better. Tell her I hate her, silly old bag."

Turning just in time to see the creamy tip of the foxes' tail flick beneath the scrub, Hawk tied his horse to the nearest branch and followed, wading through the late summer colours which formed a dry ocean reaching to his knees. The occasional protest from the woodland tugged at his leggings and scratched at his boots.

He came to a roundish area clear of trees, with the exception of a solitary stump jutting from the ground. Upon the stump sat the old man; instantly Hawk recalled their conversation outside the tavern in Ghellei, the disquieting memory flooding back. The stranger held pieces of crushed nut in his open palm. A squirrel sat on his knee, nibbling on a portion. It froze, watching Hawk as he approached.

"Where's the fox?" Hawk asked. He ducked beneath a low lying branch which was weighed down with a full throng of leaves and buds it couldn't really support.

"Fox? Can't say I've seen one, my boy." The old man smiled at him, a natural ease to his response which suggested he was not only lying but aware that Hawk knew it. "But I'm glad I ran into you."

"Oh?"

"The girl is no longer in Tamiran. She's moved north, still in the company of two men, one of them your old friend."

The reference sparked new anger and Hawk fought to suppress it. That the mere thought of the poacher's presence could stir such overwhelming emotion in him was remarkable, even now. A slow breath preceded his reply.

"How do you know this?"

"I have my sources." The old man reached out to stroke the squirrel's smooth grey coat with the back of his fingers. The squirrel grabbed another section of acorn and continued to eat. "It's important for me to provide as much assistance as possible, considering the value of the target. Why, if it weren't for my bad back and failing eyesight I'd be right alongside you when you confronted them."

Hawk has a suspicion that the old man was perfectly capable of joining him in the search, but he chose not to voice it. "Perhaps if you shared your contacts with me I would have a better chance of approaching this girl successfully."

"Never you mind about that," the old man replied. "I'm going to be around for you. As soon as I receive further news you'll be the first to know."

"Would you at least reveal if there are others looking for her?"

The old man chuckled, as if sharing a harmless confession with a young grandchild. "I suppose I can. No, you're not alone on this, though you are the only one with a reason to confront the giant directly. His name, incidentally, is Kanderil. I intend to let you get your revenge, my boy."

"Good," said Hawk in a cold voice. "I'm looking forward to it."

"I'll bet you are. How's the sword working out for you?" The old man scratched behind his ear, closing one eye.

Hawk checked behind him to ensure that neither Lug nor Petar had come back. He felt restless. The air around him held a faint odour of cherry blossoms and lavender, of clean and crisp natural scents, but beneath that was something he couldn't quite identify. Something unpleasant.

"The sword is a fine piece of craftsmanship. The blade is perfectly balanced, the edge sharp and faultless, and the weight allows for agile movement. I've never carried a better weapon."

"Excellent," said the old man. A breeze ran through the clearing, rustling the leaves. They whispered to each other as though conspiring to commit an unknown crime. "I understand you usually avoid violence..?"

"Usually," Hawk replied. "I am a thief, not a murderer."

"Except..."

"Except when given a reason, and when absolutely necessary."

Chuckling again, the old man slapped his thigh. The loud connection between flat palm and thin muscle frightened the squirrel, which leapt away within a heartbeat. The old man leaned back, his good-humoured eyes fixed on Hawk.

"Oh, yes. You'll do just fine. Just fine indeed."

The moment hung in the air for too long, and Hawk turned back the way he came without offering a goodbye. He had taken no more than half a dozen steps when the old man called out to him.

"One last thing."

Hawk paused, facing him again with a small sigh. "Yes?"

"Well, two. Firstly, do not get short with me. I prefer a little respect from those I aid." The voice was still cheerful, still sprightly, but there was an underlying menace which Hawk understood immediately. It was more of a commandment than a threat.

Hawk nodded. He fell back on his charm, something he had done in many other precarious situations. "Of course. My sincerest apologies if I have seemed ungrateful. It was not my intention to offend a man who would provide me with such an exquisite gift." All this was said with a smile. Hawk considered offering a bow, but relented. No need to bury the retort with a pound of sugar when a sprinkling would do.

The response worked. "No offence taken, of course. Now, as I mentioned, the girl travels with two others. One you already know. The other is... not like most men. You will never meet a more dangerous hand to hand combatant, and will therefore need to make plans to deal with him."

Hawk nodded. "Identifying marks?"

"Red hair, wearing a green cavalry jacket."

"Interesting. Even with the sword, you think he's too skilled? I'm no slouch when it comes to a duel, you know."

"Hawk, I like you, but be careful not to overestimate yourself. Do not confront this man directly, for you will lose."

Hawk considered this. "I'll think on it. For now I had best catch up with my companions. That is, if you wish to remain anonymous to them."

"I don't believe that will be a problem," the old man replied. He rose to his feet, brushing crumbs and dirt from the front of his patchy green robe. "But you're right. You have a lot of ground to cover. Head north, towards the Meadows. You are looking for a Kalethi scout named Jared. Find him, find the girl. If he remains alone, then wait. Her group will turn up eventually, providing they elude their pursuers."

Nodding, Hawk started to walk away once again. "Until next time, then."

"I look forward to it."

Chapter Ten

Chalimer sat behind his hefty cherry wood desk, waiting for one of his subordinates. He reclined in his large chair, the backrest thick and straight with thin mauve padding stitched into the centre. The room was well lit by candles. Originally, paraffin lamps had stood here in brackets against the walls, but Chalimer was not fond of the scent which accompanied them.

Through the open window on the south-easterly wall, the baby blue skies were dotted with the first real clouds to form in maybe two months. They hung with patience, content to drift at an imperceptible pace, helped along by the same gentle breeze which disturbed the rows of herbs lining a small rectangular basket hanging from his windowsill.

Chalimer rested his chin on his thumbs, his two index fingers straight against the tip of his nose, his elbows propped upon the arms of the chair. He watched the door, but his mind was elsewhere. Thoughts of his assignments rolled over themselves as they often did this early in the morning.

The hunt for Sarene was progressing as quickly as it could under the circumstances. That they had not found the girl with her family during the initial search had proved disappointing, but the Gathire were receiving information at regular intervals. They knew her direction, her objective and her travelling companions.

Chalimer smiled to himself. How fate liked to throw in a twist every now and then.

The questioning of an obese, small-time crook named Porthouse - following a tip from a civilian witness seeking to claim a reward - had revealed that Kanderil had smuggled the girl out of the city. This development had been unexpected, but was one Chalimer welcomed.

He had not lied during their conversation. The huge Kalethi's military file had been introduced to him during his initial training with the Gathire, a common practice whilst learning the advantages of gathering intelligence on a target. Chalimer had continued checking up on the newly promoted Sergeant long after completing his induction. The man's skill as a scout and the respect he had earned from both his peers and superiors was rare indeed.

Kanderil's achievements, had the man wished it, would have rivalled his own.

Chalimer was the youngest Justicar in the history of the Gathire. Promoted several times within the decade, he now oversaw the day-to-day operations of the entire faction and the duties of the Agents within it. Only seven men outranked him, and they made up the Assembly. He had been invited onto the Assembly last year but had turned it down.

He could work with more autonomy outside of that collection of old hands.

Those who served him, for the most part, feared him. His appearance lent weight to that reaction. Bald soon after his teen years, Chalimer was a thin, rakish man who stood tall and straight. Never slouched, never loose. The thick, deep scar along the side of his head, a result of a lapse in concentration as a recruit when apprehending a drunken villager wielding a broken bottle, had damaged the nerves of his right eyelid. It lent him an expression of distrust, as if scrutinizing all before him. His small tawny eyes saw everything, studying his surroundings without thinking. A former lover – one he used to pay good money for once a week, beautiful and kind – had told him those eyes reminded her of a captive wolf she had seen as a child. Of course, he had disliked the use of the term 'captive', but the *honesty* in her words had struck a chord.

The reference to imprisonment had grown more accurate over time, especially during these last few years; were Chalimer made the head of the Gathire, improvements to the faction would be swift.

The Justicar made little effort to cease the rumours about him; that he killed those who disobeyed by arranging accidents or assassinations; that he had his own personal bodyguard who remained unseen at all times; that he was unsurpassed in the use of a throwing knife. Even, he had heard in recent months, that he possessed supernatural abilities and was capable of reading a man's mind.

Nonsense, for the most part. The rumours tended to fade out as a Gathire became more experienced, and those who worked with him for any extended period of time came to understand that Chalimer was no more than an intelligent, determined man who happened to be exceptional at his job. But amongst the recruits and newer members of the order, such tales lent him an air of mystery he welcomed.

A knock at the door brought him back from his reflection.

"Come."

The latch clicked. An Agent stepped inside the room, closing the door and taking two steps towards the desk before standing at attention, his head held high. The young man had a mass of blonde hair which had been tied close to the nape of his neck. The sheer *arrogance* he radiated impressed Chalimer, who delayed initiating the conversation. When he finally did, the words were casual.

"Could you please explain to me why it has taken you over a week to return from your assignment, Glaithe?"

The Agent cleared his throat. "After I had completed my original orders, I took my squad out into the surrounding areas in an attempt to locate the girl. We were successful, as evidenced by our encounter with her yesterday afternoon."

Chalimer nodded. "You had one of your squad return to inform us of your progress following your meeting with Sarene's family." He looked down to the three parchments neatly arranged upon his desk, scanning one of them. "Mm. Well, you adhered to protocol."

Glaithe said nothing, staring directly ahead. A bird chirped outside, close to the open window. Chalimer saw a shape swoop past, no doubt from the guttering above.

"Now, your report says that you made two passes through the highway between Tamiran and the girl's village, before leaving your horses at a roadside inn and heading into the forests to search for potential tracks."

A nodded response.

"Now forgive me for speculating," Chalimer said with an amiable laugh, "but it would seem that looking for the whereabouts of an inexperienced young girl travelling through dense woodland hundreds of miles square would be a little... Optimistic?"

"We had reasonable cause to expect she was travelling away from the main road, Justicar."

"Of course. You would have ridden past her," Chalimer replied. "Now, generally when tracking a subject through the woods it is a good idea to have either a suspected route in mind *or* a target's objective. Which in this case was..?"

Glaithe, his pale blue eyes still fixed on the wall opposite him, spoke in a strong, confident voice. "We believed she was heading north. Her family revealed that her eldest brother, Jared, had recently left the home to return to active duty with the Kalethi. We suspected she may have followed him."

"On what evidence?"

Glaithe look at Chalimer for the first time since entering the room. "Intuition, sir."

"I see." The young Agent's audacity to speak to him in such a tone, as if speaking to a man of limited intelligence, was surprising. Chalimer paused briefly to consider his answer. "Well, it's funny you should mention the family. As I understand it things did not go as planned...?"

"The family resisted questioning and sought to impede the investigation," Glaithe replied, his gaze returning to the wall. He had that much good sense, at least. "We took lengths to coerce their cooperation."

"According to the reports of your squad," – The Justicar reached out to trace a finger along one of the pages, reading aloud – "you 'disfigured the mother, beat the father and threatened to do the same to their children'. As in, you personally."

"We received additional information following the methods I used, sir. The other Agents gave no indication they disagreed with my approach."

Leaning forward, Chalimer folded his arms across the top of his desk.

"Glaithe, it is generally considered good policy to avoid public objection to the commanding Agent's choices. This makes me wonder why you *completely disregarded mine!*"

The Justicar slapped his hands against the desk, the chair scraping against the floor as he rose to his feet. His raised voice caught Glaithe off guard; the young man was unable to repress a twitch of shock, his left eyelid quivering. Outside, another bird took off in a flap of feathers and wings. A crow cawed in the distance.

Chalimer took a moment to compose himself before continuing.

"I asked you to search the girl's home and village and return with your findings. I did not ask you to intimidate, threaten or torture anybody at all. Thanks to you, not only is Sarene now actively seeking to avoid us, but it appears she has found the protection of an ex-Kalethi Sergeant who has the capability to make our search *much* more difficult."

Glaithe spoke quickly, his voice still firm but now laced with doubt. "We used the information gathered to approach the target in the forests surrounding Tamiran, Justicar."

"Complete luck," Chalimer retorted with a dismissive sweep of his hand. "You were minutes from simply returning empty-handed when you caught an unidentified trail which led to the girl. The resulting chase, bordering on amateur, also resulted in the death of one of your squad. Pramith. A promising young Agent who had a good future in front of him."

"He was rash to approach the subject single handed, sir. He was seeking to claim the glory of the catch himself."

"He was under your watch, Glaithe. Had you been in any way effective, you would have ensured he *made* no action."

Glaithe stood in silence, offering no more in defence. Chalimer let him stew on his thoughts for a while, taking a measured walk around his desk to stand facing the window. The walls of the room were a pale white and in need of a retouch. The window and its small herb garden were the only real reminder of the life and space outside the building.

"I do not believe I would have any objection from the Assembly were I to simply terminate your position with us. Depending on the severity of the delay to this investigation, we may also look into the possibility of incarceration for your sheer blind stupidity."

"I take full responsibility for my actions," Glaithe responded, "and I wish to be given the opportunity to redeem myself, Justicar."

"Redemption, eh?" Chalimer glanced over his shoulder. In the sunlight beaming through from outside, his scar shone crimson. "What in the name of Tamir makes you think yourself worthy of a second chance?"

"My record prior to this assignment, sir. I have always served the Gathire to the best of my abilities, and with great loyalty and dedication." This much was true, and the reason Chalimer had selected him to lead the squad sent to Sarene's home in the hopes of furthering his career. Glaithe had a growing reputation, with commendations from several officers regarding his conduct and willingness to learn. Evidently his willingness to command was even greater, and the limited power must have burst in his head like an overripe melon. Chalimer stared at the youth as he considered this. Glaithe sensibly returned his gaze to the wall, standing at complete attention.

"I expected so much better, Agent. I had high hopes for you, and this was your chance to make your mark. And, well, you certainly did that." Chalimer chuckled. "Certainly."

"Now, I cannot in good conscience send you back out on active duty. I have my own position to consider, and no Justicar in their right mind would let this transgression pass. However, you may still yet have a use for me." He returned to his desk, opening a drawer and pulling from it a sealed envelope. He raised it up for Glaithe to see. "This is your official letter of discharge from the Gathire. Inside it is also five gold pieces, minted. From me."

Glaithe clenched his jaw, swallowing.

"Now you are a civilian. Unemployed, dishonoured, and no doubt somewhat distrusted by the general populace. You know how they feel about us. However, you are also free from the laws and rules to which you were previously bound."

Looking at him, Glaithe seemed uncertain for the first time. "Sir?"

"I want you to continue looking for the girl. If you bring Sarene to me, then you will be given a full restoration of your prior status as a Gathire. Bring her to me alive and unharmed. That is my only rule. Violate this condition, and you will be hunted down and executed."

Comprehension dawned across the young man's features. "Understood, sir."

"Of course, should you be unsuccessful in locating her, then consider yourself unwelcome in Tamir."

Glaithe nodded. "One question if I may, Justicar?" Chalimer consented. "Considering the reaction to my methods, how should I conduct myself?"

"Do not make this any harder for your former colleagues, never mention our association and ensure you send word with any relative information directly to me using a five letter name of your choosing, beginning with the letter 'U'. Apart from that..." Chalimer smiled. "Well, you're no longer representing the Gathire."

"Of course, Justicar," the young man responded. He seemed comfortable with the new orders and his words came with an eager tone Chalimer could appreciate. "I understand completely."

"Good. You are dismissed." Chalimer returned to his seat, placing his elbows on the armrests once more. "Send in Jonase on your way out."

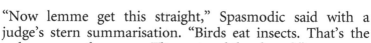

"Now lemme get this straight," Spasmodic said with a judge's stern summarisation. "Birds eat insects. That's the only purpose they serve. They eat and they breed."

The three of them were travelling alongside the forest's edge, less than twenty yards inside the tree line. The Meadows were farmlands like no other. Probably the most ideal location for agriculture in the kingdom, the fields sprawled out across miles of sloping hills and gentle inclines. The sunlight shone upon great squares of brown, gold and green, the latter colour less prominent in this late stage of the summer. Here and there, like a scattering of marbles across a garden path, buildings rose up from the ground in an assortment of small, large, old and new. The scent of vegetables, corn, roots, bulbs, *growth* permeated the air along with the musty perfume of the dry woodland they moved through. Sarene walked with her head turned to take in the stunning view as they encircled the open land by heading north-west, keeping the trees for cover.

Kanderil had made the rare mistake of offering an answer to one of Spasmodic's many, many questions. Sarene looked up as the woodsman spoke.

"Plenty of creatures exist solely to further their species. The true exception to the common rule would be those who take part in other diversions, like entertainment or art."

"But what's the point? Flying around, layin' a few eggs and then eatin' a few flies. Sounds tedious."

"I am sure it is not tedious to the birds."

"Have you asked them?" Spasmodic seemed surprised.

Kanderil sighed. Sarene was trying her best not to find amusement in his expression, but it was difficult. She went back to admiring the Meadows instead.

"Humans are more intelligent than birds, so we have the capacity to create. We have music, theatre, education, competitive games. On the base of it, however, our drives are the same. We must eat, sleep and stay warm." He gripped a young willow as he slid past it, his fingers encircling the trunk. "Our strongest instincts also involve finding a mate and producing children."

"Where's yours then?" asked Spasmodic, its words critical. It swung a hand through a nearby juniper bush. Retrieving a handful of twigs and leaves, it began picking through them for berries. A hint of bitter sap scented the air, and then was gone.

Sarene turned her head again, the question catching her interest.

"I never married."

"Why not?"

"I never met anyone I wanted to marry," Kanderil stepped over a jutting trunk, patchy with dark moss, which had been cleared for some purpose long since lost.

"C'mon," Spasmodic pushed. "You mean you've never even laid an egg?"

Kanderil stopped, the motion akin to an avalanche grinding to a halt. He turned to face the dreadlocked mutant. Sarene stumbled next to him. His response suggested he was unprepared for the question.

"Excuse me?"

"Laid an egg. You know, made a baby."

Kanderil glanced at Sarene. She shrugged, a touch of scarlet rising at her cheeks.

"Humans produce live offspring," he said carefully. "We give birth. We do not lay eggs."

"Oh, that pregnancy stuff, where the female gets fat and waddles around like a fat bitch!" The creature giggled, but the sound was cut off soon after as another question forced its way to the surface. Sarene prepared for whatever may come next, an act akin to bracing for impact.

"So... how do they get there?"

Kanderil pinched the bridge of his nose. "How do *what* get 'there'."

"The live offspring. How do they get the females fat?"

Kanderil looked skyward, his eyes wide. Sarene turned away, feeling a huge rush of blood turning her face somewhere in the region of pink.

"You... do not know where babies come from?" The sentence sounded childish, amplified by Kanderil's grave voice, and Sarene started to giggle uncontrollably.

"Nope. Never given to me. Guess Tyrrial didn't think it was important to my mission."

"Aye, that would make sense," Kanderil said, starting to move again. Sarene felt he was trying to get away from the question.

"So where do they come from then?" Spasmodic called as it followed the woodsman.

"Another time, maybe."

"Come on, I want to learn this stuff."

"Not from me."

"You do know, don't you?!"

"Yes," came the threatening reply.

"Right, well step by step then." Spasmodic clasped its palms together in a sharp *clap*. In return it was given silence, with the exception of Sarene staggering along after them, trying to see where she was going through the tears of laughter streaming down her cheeks and falling to the forest floor, joyfully providing the closest thing to rain the grass beneath her feet had received in weeks.

"Do I need any tools? How many people are involved? Do I need a permit!? Aww, c'mon mate, tell me!"

The three of them walked on until evening approached, the sunlight hanging late in the sky. Smoke from cooking fires drifted up from several of the farm cottages in view, a scene

Sarene knew well from her own village. The reminder made her feel a little homesick, and she rubbed her upper arm to comfort herself.

"There," Kanderil said. He pointed towards a farmhouse less than half a mile away. They had finally left the forest and stood in open ground for the first time since leaving Tamiran. The grass here was dry and sparse. Sarene imagined she could feel the earth waiting for a storm.

"It's a house," said Spasmodic.

"I know the family who lives there," Kanderil explained. "We will be able to take shelter for tonight."

"Great!" Spasmodic stood up from its crouched position. "Do they have food?"

"Not for you," Kanderil replied. He looked down at the smaller creature, who seemed hurt by his reply. "I will have to ask you to wait for us here."

"Because they won't have room?" it asked in a small voice, sad and sweet. Sarene hid her grin with a hand.

"Because you will frighten them. I am sorry, but until we find a way to hide your appearance you will have to keep your distance from others."

Sarene reached out to grab Spasmodic's arm, giving a reassuring squeeze. She had wondered what Kanderil would do with the creature in public, but did not expect him to be so blunt. Staring at the floor for a moment, dejected, it tucked one of its dreadlocks into its mouth and began to chew.

"Sure, I understand. No problem. I'll just, y'know..." It swung an arm in the vague direction of the forest they had just left. "Go in there and find a rock or something." Turning, it started wandering towards the tree line. Sarene wrung her hands, feeling awkward. An idea came to her. She hurried forward, reaching out to grab at Spasmodic's shoulder. The creature seemed on the verge of tears, but managed to give her a shallow smile.

Sarene reached into her pack and rummaged around for a moment. Then she produced her pipes, offering them as recompense. Spasmodic's eyes grew so round, glimmering with moisture, that it seemed ready to collapse into sobbing.

"*Ooooooohh*, for *meeeee*?" It hopped up and down on the heels of its feet. Sarene nodded, her pleasure in its reaction warming.

Spasmodic bawled out laughing, the sound shocking. Sarene jumped, taking a few steps back, clasping the pipes to her chest.

"Hahaha, sorry, I'm only shittin with ya," it cackled, wiping its face with the back of a filthy hand. "I prefer sleepin' outdoors anyway. Probably could have *worded it better though!*" The last comment was shouted past Sarene towards Kanderil, who was standing motionless with his arms folded. Only his hair, disturbed by the evening breeze, hinted that the woodsman was not a statue.

Spasmodic winked at Sarene and she got the impression of something further behind the smirk it wore. "See you on the morrow, girly." With that it skipped off into the woods, humming a tune as it did.

Kanderil watched Sarene as she returned. She placed her pipes back into her bag, deliberately taking her time to do so before she met his gaze.

"I cannot believe you fell for that," he said.

Sarene rolled her eyes, pushing past him. She heard a very brief, very low chuckle as she did.

They arrived at the cottage not long after. The outside of the building was pretty, Sarene thought. It was similar to her family home, but with some artistic touches and, though she would never admit it, a better standard of build. The outer wall were tarred, covering the gaps between the logs, giving a smooth and even finish which had then been whitewashed over with a practised hand. Each window was framed with flowers, small vines creeping around the edges. The door was large and well-maintained, no chips or markings present. A small garden, cordoned off with a low rock wall, contained a variety of flowers and herbs around a patch of turf which had received water over the dry season. Sarene was impressed with the degree of care and pride lavished upon the area.

Kanderil knocked on the door three times, each rap firm. It didn't take long for the door to open on oiled hinges. Standing before them was a man sporting a mane of blonde hair matched with a thick, straight beard. He seemed younger than her father Sameran by a fair few years, and stood short and burly, framed by the entrance to his home.

The man saw Kanderil and laughed. "Well blow me down. What the bloody hell are you doing here, Sergeant?" He reached out and shook Kanderil's hand.

"Passing through, lad. Thought I would stop by and see how you and the family were doing."

"Never had you as the type." He chortled again, releasing his surprise. "It's good to see you, though!"

Sarene glanced up at her guardian, who was smiling in a way she hadn't seen before. He seemed genuinely pleased for the first time since their journey together began.

"And who's this?" the stranger said. His gaze moved to Sarene, offering his hand once more. She took it, her grip feather light. His boldness was daunting and she fought the urge to look at the floor.

"This is Rachia, my niece." Kanderil reached over to clasp her shoulder. The contact made her flinch. She reacted by smiling up at her 'uncle', hoping she appeared sincere. "I am escorting her to her grandmothers' village in the north. Rachia, this is Fallerin, an old friend."

"A pleasure to meet you, girl," Fallerin said. "Welcome to my home. How are you feeling after a day's march with this taskmaster?"

Kanderil replied for her. "She does not speak due to an illness as a child. She is very skilled at expressing herself in other ways, however."

Sarene nodded, giving a small shrug. Fallerin, without pause, leant in towards her. "That's fine. Between you and me, I must confess my daughter talks from dawn 'til dusk and twice as much at week's end. I hope you've a good pair of ears on you, for if they aren't worn out yet they surely will be."

The comment made Sarene grin, and she produced an O with her thumb and forefinger. She was pleased that the stranger had offered such a direct response to her, something which came rarely when others learnt of her condition. The majority of the time people would offer pity or, worse, a lingering sense of unease, as though they didn't know how to treat her.

"Now, come on in," said Fallerin, stepping back into the cottage. "Erywyn's got dinner on, but I reckon we can stretch it to a couple more plates if you don't mind small portions." He looked to Kanderil again. "You look like you don't need much, anyway."

Kanderil spread his hands. "I remember Erywyn as quite the cook. Anything you could offer would be welcome."

"Well in that case she can find a couple of wheat biscuits for you," Fallerin said quickly. "Come on, let's get you settled in. I'm sure Ally will want to climb all over you both."

Ally, a shortening of Alyxendra, was Fallerin's only child; a feisty and inquisitive young girl less than ten summers of age. Kanderil caught the brunt of the child's welcome as she ran full tilt at him, attaching herself to his leg. The woodsman reached down to grasp the child beneath the arms, lifting her up into a hug. He seemed uncomfortable with the contact while she made her best attempt to squeeze the life right out of him, an effort which was like trying to crush a mountain with a folded napkin.

"You're late!" Ally said, poking him in the chest. He stared at the girl.

"Late for what?"

"My party!"

"She's talking about this year's Laysenra festival," Fallerin replied, now seated in a large cedar chair beside the room's only table. "She remembers you from when you stayed with us to build the barn."

"Quite the memory you have," Kanderil said to the child. "I am sorry that I missed your celebration. I will drop your present off when I return from my journey."

"Don't be so long this time," Ally said. "You been gone forever!"

"I will be much quicker this time."

"Promise?"

"Aye."

Ally hugged Kanderil again, more like a tackle than a show of affection, before attempting to wriggle from his grip. Kanderil placed her on the floor, where she looked up at him.

"So what did you get me?"

Sarene grinned. The girl reminded her of Taylei when she was younger, and a little of herself at that age too. Fallerin chuckled with the patient amusement adopted by doting fathers everywhere.

"Darling, don't hassle the man. He's tired. Why not play with your bracelet things, eh? I'm sure Rachia would like one."

Ally looked over at Sarene, beaming a huge smile. "I make bracelets out of things Papa finds. I have *rooocks,* and *twiiigs,* and *leeeaves,* and lots of other things too." Sarene mimed an expression of wonder, looking around the room in search of the fabled crafting materials. Ally giggled, rushing off to a drawer hidden in the far corner of the room.

"Ah-ah-ah," said her mother, Erywyn, a petite woman with kind eyes. She was approaching the table with a collection of plates and cutlery. "Not yet, dear. Food first."

"Awwwww!" Ally said with the impatience only the young could muster for such a short delay. "But--!"

"No buts," Erywyn replied. "Sit yourself down, and get some dinner in you. Then you can make all the bracelets you want before bed."

Ally sullenly made her way to the table. Sarene sat herself down next to her, pulling a silly face. It helped the young girl forget her inconvenience.

The meal was a thick, rich stew. Kanderil had been right. Fallerin's wife was indeed a good cook, the food a class above the fare Sarene had been offered the last couple of weeks. It had a strong flavour without being overbearing, the mutton pieces falling apart at her touch. Emptying her bowl quickly, she chased it down with a thick slice of bread used to mop up the gravy. Finally she leant back with a deep sigh. She hadn't been this content for what felt like an age. Erywyn smiled at her.

Talk around the table was few and far between, mostly pleasantries about the scorching weather, the roads and other such things. Sarene looked around the room as the others finished eating. The interior of the cottage was just as well kept. The furniture was good quality, polished and smooth. Every shelf was straight, sturdy-looking and adorned with mugs, pots, and utensils, all painted to match. The floor was scrubbed, the ceiling and corners free of cobwebs. A fire burned on a swept stone grill with little ash or soot visible. Even the small cross-stitch picture hanging from one wall, a scene of cottage and landscape matching the outside view, seemed right somehow.

Fallerin pushed his plate away, swallowing. "That was terrible," he said, wiping a finger around the inside of the bowl before scooping it into his mouth.

"I'll not make it again then, love." Erywyn peeked at her husband as she took a small mouthful of bread. He winked at her.

"Pay no attention to him," Kanderil said, already reclining in his chair. "It was an excellent dish." Sarene nodded her agreement. Ally had already tottered off from the table, and was gathering a handful of small bits and bobs from the drawers she had been denied before dinner.

"Kind of you to say so," Erywyn replied. She finished the last of her food before starting to gather in the plates nearest to her. Fallerin placed his hands behind his head, looking over at Kanderil.

"If ever I wonder why I married her," he said, "I just think of her skills in the kitchen, and it settles my fears immediately." He laughed as he spoke, the sound infectious. Kanderil shook his head, politely refraining from joining in.

"A shame I cannot draw the same comfort from your skills in the bedroom, dear." Erywyn bent down to kiss her husband's temple, her raven-black Jaithran feather dangling past her cheek. Kanderil laughed this time. Sarene sniggered behind one hand, the easy tone of the retort making it seem innocent. Fallerin smirked, reaching up to stroke his wife's arm as she returned to the washing pot carrying the rest of the crockery. The moment settled, and Kanderil spoke.

"How is the barn holding up?"

"Good, no thanks to you. I've made a few adjustments since you were last here," Fallerin said, amused. "Had to replace a few of the boards and one of the beams holding the roof up." He glanced at Sarene. "Your uncle is skilled at many things, lass, but carpentry is not one of them."

Sarene smiled at Kanderil, who sat with his chin against his chest. He huffed, accepting the comment. "No need for thanks," he said. "You can repay me anytime."

Fallerin's grin broadened as he scratched the back of his head. "Anyway, it's helped out a lot. With the extra storage we can hold our crop here without dragging it miles out to some other farmstead. With the wagon it used to be a good dozen trips over to Saliarn's place."

"How is the old man doing?"

"Sal? Crotchety as ever. Still brewing cider regular as clockwork, though. I have a half barrel of his stuff in the pantry, if you fancy? A bit rusty this time of year but does the job."

"Thanks, but I have to refuse," Kanderil replied, holding his hand palm-out. "We have an early start in the morning if we are to make good time."

"Shame," said Fallerin.

Erywyn, wiping plates with a cotton cloth, spoke up. "Well, maybe you can swing by on your way back. Now you've retired, I expect you have a fair bit of free time."

"Aye, what was with that?" Fallerin asked. He reached out to ruffle Ally's hair as she returned to the table. The child ignored him, dumping a varied collection of items on the tabletop along with some lengths of string. Sarene smiled when she saw tiny pebbles, flower heads, leaves and feathers. She'd made similar trinkets when she was younger. Ally offered her a piece string and she took it, along with a small round stone of grey and black.

"I felt like a change," Kanderil replied. "Eighteen years in service was enough for me, I think."

"And there was me hoping you'd found yourself a girl," said Erywyn.

"There was *me* thinking you're a cheeky bugger for retiring before you're even forty," Fallerin continued. "On the other hand I'm digging around in the farm each year and will do 'til my back is crooked and my eyesight fails, most likely."

"You are doing a sterling job providing for your family," Kanderil said. "Look at your home, man. It is bright, clean, and spacious."

"I'll give the wife credit for the 'bright and clean' part of that," Fallerin replied. "Still, I have to wonder why you're wandering around the forests like a bloody hermit."

"Who told you that?"

"Your replacement. Cocky little bugger, can't be far out of the recruits. He stopped by here last month on his way south. We ask after you, y'know. Nobody knew squat for a long while until you checked in with the Kalethi at the year's turn, apparently. Sleeping in the forests, indeed."

Sarene looked up from her bracelet. Kanderil caught her eye. "What was the man's name?"

"Your replacement? Dunno. Garey, or something." Fallerin shrugged. "Nice enough, I suppose. Just had a high opinion of himself."

"Could you describe him?"

Fallerin eyed the woodsman, a wry smile on his lips. "Is it important?"

Sarene looked back to the string she was tying.

"I might have helped train the man," explained Kanderil. "Would be nice to put a name to the arrogance."

Fallerin chuckled. "I hear you. He was about my height. Twenty-two-twenty-three summers of age, maybe. Blonde hair, blue eyes. Looks like a bit of a lady fancier."

Sarene gave no outward reaction, but she was certainly

pleased it *hadn't* been Jared. Discovering he had stopped here on the way south to visit his family wouldn't have been very helpful, and she disliked the idea of him being thought of as arrogant.

"Garat is his name." Kanderil smirked. "And you are right. Always was a little cocky."

"Aye, Garet. That's the one," Fallerin said, slapping the table. "I'm sure he'll turn out fine. I'll let him know you said hello. Anyway, my point was that I do wonder how you're able to just leave your career and walk away. I couldn't do it, and I bloody hate my work."

"Don't exaggerate," Erywyn chided. She eased herself into her chair, a clay mug in her hands.

"It's true. Up at the crack of dawn, tending to the crops, getting them watered, dragging the dirt, no days off during the harvest... It's a pain in the backside. I should move us to Tamiran and take up work as a cabinet maker."

"And leave our home behind? Not on your life," his wife said.

"You always seem to take such care in your work," offered Kanderil. "You would not have needed your barn if you were not doing a good job here."

"No need to coddle me, Kanderil," Fallerin said, folding his arms over his chest. "I'm not a boy."

"Fine. You are a lazy bastard but you do what you are told." He winked to Erywyn and, to Sarene's surprise, started to chuckle. The sound was deep; rich and loud, rumbling from his broad chest like a landslide. Fallerin and his wife laughed along while Sarene joined in silently, her shoulders quivering. Ally giggled too, even before she looked up from her bracelet. The sound of a home filled with humour was something Sarene had sorely missed. Hearing it again was a comfort she welcomed.

Welcomed to a point. Sarene sat outside the wonderful little cottage, atop the neatly stacked woodpile sheltered outside.

By goodness, *everything* here was neat! She could imagine her mother's response; impressed and full of praise for Erywyn's lovely home. Aislyn's gaze would flick aside when nobody was looking, of course, and she would seek any flaw to justify her pride for her own housekeeping. Sarene grinned at the thought, wiping a palm across her damp cheekbone. Her mother, beautiful in every way but still needing that extra tick of justification.

Her smile faltered and she fought, *clawed,* back the sobs which she felt lurking at the base of her shoulders, at the undercut of her ribs. She felt guilty at the pleasure she'd experienced at Fallerin's home, with his family, their food and warm fire. She couldn't shake the image of her mother lying in bed, bandaged up from brow to chin. Her father's puffy cheeks and swollen eye, a red tinge at the corner of his mouth where blood had been swept away. The sight of Taylei and the triplets, staring at Sarene with a mixture of emotions; she had caught gratitude, fear, shock... and blame. Taylei's look had been the worst. She could read those green eyes, and in this case they asked *What did you do? Why did you bring those men here to hurt us?*

The door opened and closed behind her with the gentle delay of someone attempting to make as little noise as possible, but the footsteps that followed made the gesture a moot point. Kanderil approached her. Who else could radiate such *presence* through the fall of their feet on the ground?

Sarene glanced up, letting her hand fall into her lap. She gazed out across the Meadows, the view shimmering like a heat wave through the tears which refused to subside. A smile touched her lips, lacking sincerity. She knew there was no chance of hiding her sadness from the woodsman, but it was worth making the effort to avoid spoiling his night as well.

Kanderil stood next to her, looking in the same direction. Sarene waited for him to speak, but he said nothing for the moment. The glow of the fireplace inside the cottage spilled from a small window just behind where Sarene sat, and in the dim light Kanderil seemed entranced by the scenery before him. With his thumbs hooked into his belt, he surveyed the land as though he owned it.

In a way, she thought, *perhaps he does.*

They remained there for a while. Not too long for Sarene to feel uncomfortable. Neither too brief for her to feel hurried.

"You should come inside soon, lass," Kanderil said finally. That voice rumbled as powerful as ever, but she was surprised by how gentle it sounded. "It is not a good idea for you to be alone like this."

Sarene nodded. She sniffed again before quickly thumbing her nose, clearing a drop of moisture from the tip. Then she pressed her sleeve to both her eyes, soaking up the remaining pools of liquid. Better for her to hide away. She agreed. Better for her to just wrap herself in bed sheets and try to forget all this. Perhaps if she was lucky she'd wake up back at home, back where things made sense and where little of importance was really her fault.

Kanderil spoke just as she placed her hands on the wood pile below her, ready to jump down.

"I once knew a girl... a little younger than you, who lived in Tamiran. Jaclyn, her name was. She was the daughter of one of my team mates. I say was... I still know her, of course. I haven't seen her since I left the Kalethi."

Sarene looked up at him. He paused, jaw twitching as he sought for the words needed to continue.

"Jaclyn was an only child. Her mother fell sick not long after she was born. Her father was at home as often as possible but he still had his duties, so the girl had grown up cared for by her other relatives, passed from home to home. When she was maybe eight or nine she started to care for her mother in turn. Her mother had never quite recovered from her sickness, you see, and she was prone to fever and other problems.

"Her father's name was Lotharian, and he doted on her. He would talk about her for hours if you let him." Kanderil smiled at the memory, looking down at his feet. Sarene smiled along with him in spite of her sadness. "She was his world, and he hers. The times Lotharian and I were assigned together, I would have the pleasure of walking back through the gates of Tamiran and seeing her run to embrace him. She would wait each day from noon until an hour past, and he would time his arrival so she could meet him. It sometimes meant spending a day camped a mile out of town, wasting time, but it was worth it. They clearly adored each other, and it was a joy to witness."

Sarene continued to smile, curious to see where this was going. She had not yet heard Kanderil speak so many words. Certainly not so candidly.

"As Jaclyn grew older her free time became limited. Her mother took on another wasting illness, and needed constant care from that point. Jaclyn was unable to play with her friends or go to school. Instead she learned how to cook, clean, administer medicine and run errands to keep the house in order. Her father took as much leave as he could, but during those years we had reports of increasing banditry on the borders to Rudacia. Lotharian was one of the more experienced Kalethi and was given his own squad, so Jaclyn was effectively left as the head of the household. She was maybe fourteen at this time.

"During a standard trek along one of the passes near the border, Lotharian was killed. His mount startled a snake lying alongside the path and it struck. The horse threw its rider and Lotharian was tossed over the edge of the pass. He landed badly and was dead before his partner could reach him. It was an accident, was all, but we all felt a sense of great loss.

"I was given the task of informing the family. I explained to them what had happened as best I could. There were tears, of course. Jaclyn's mother asked several questions, most of them trying to understand how such a tragic, meaningless death could have befallen her husband. I had no answers for her and could only offer my sympathy."

Kanderil took a deep breath. Sarene was taken aback by his words. She bit her lower lip, toying with her fingers. The

Hunter seemed uncomfortable and his voice grew quiet.

"Jaclyn had only one question for me. She said, 'Was my father a good soldier?' I said that he was respected, performed his tasks well and never let his comrades down. She nodded to me and then went to her room. I could hear her crying through the thin walls of the house. It is a sound I have not forgotten.

"Since that day I have seen her three more times. On the third occasion I ran into her at a market stall, and I asked how she was doing. Previously she had responded to the question with token replies, but this time she opened up to me. She told me that her mother had died a few months after her father. She had taken over the household and, using the pension given to her from the Kalethi, enrolled into school. In addition she working as an assistant to the book keeper at the Tamiran library, and a young man in her class was courting her. She seemed happy, healthy and lacking the sorrow of her younger years."

Kanderil paused. Sarene fidgeted in her seat.

"I, uh..." He ran a hand over his beard, tugging at the tight curls. "I suppose what I am trying to say is that I can understand how you feel, because I have seen it before. You may feel as though the bottom has fallen out of your world, or your life has swallowed you whole. Jaclyn cried with a pain I have not heard before or since, but a few years later she was full of spirit once again. They say time is a great healer, and it is true. However bad things seem now, lass, they will get better someday."

Sarene looked up at Kanderil then. The woodsman seemed smaller in the dim light, with the words hanging in the air. He was watching her, hoping for a positive response. The uncertainty in his eyes was endearing.

Smiling through her tears, she reached out to touch Kanderil's forearm. She appreciated his effort to console her, to offer some comfort during these exhausting, fearful days. The tale he'd told wasn't exactly soothing, but she understood its meaning.

Sarene was an optimist by nature, though. The story of

Jaclyn made sense to her.

The Hunter gave a smile which was barely visible through his facial hair. He half-turned towards the cottage entrance. "Come on," he said with a short sigh of relief. "There is some bedding waiting for you near the fireplace. You should have a good night's rest."

Nodding, Sarene hopped down from her seat.

Spasmodic had found a tree to sleep in. Only, sleep was the wrong word. It would be closer to the source of its condition to say it was *lucid,* or *adrift.* Any who happened to witness it in its current state would agree. The creature hung in the bough of two thick, sturdy branches growing close enough to provide a reclining seat. A leg hung over the edge of one of them, hanging limp in the air. Occasionally it twitched, the foot swinging a little. It had both arms rested over its chest, with claws interlocked in a lattice of bone. Closed eyelids quivered. Beneath, those eyes were moving and seeing and awake.

It ignored the scent of apples, for it was indeed in an apple tree. The strong, acidic thickness of overripe fruit - of which it had eaten plenty - hung around it like a cloak, shrouding the clean, fresh air of the Meadows; but it ignored this. Also it ignored the chirp of birds in a branch further overhead. It had no idea of the age, gender or species responsible for the noise which was both insistent and needy at once. This didn't matter, though, because it ignored them. It even ignored the occasional wasp which flew past, feasting on the apples. Tired and irritable at this late stage of the summer, the yellow-black things were apt to sting a stranger for no real reason, without prompting. But they left the creature alone, and in turn were ignored.

Spasmodic was lost in its thoughts. Peculiar thoughts. Something wasn't quite wired up properly inside; it knew this. Every so often it had visions. Spasmodic doubted very much they were prophesising anything, because if they *did* come true, well, that would mean the world had *much* bigger problems than a simple farmhand's daughter. Unless, of course, *she* was responsible for them. If Sarene triggered the events that ran through its head... well, that would be amazing.

Its lip twitched with excitement. Perhaps that was why it had decided to befriend the human girl instead of gutting her.

Perhaps it had always known.

Spasmodic was having a vision now, it realised. There were circles. It always saw circles. Circles of colour, of depth, of light and shadows. They twitched and glimmered and shone. Some would break into shards and then reform. They grew transparent and opaque with no real control or rhythm. The circles either radiated out or closed in, but they usually kept out of the way of the scenes behind them, through them, filtering between them. When Spasmodic was able to latch onto an image, the circles withdrew.

This time, he was watching a village. The village was not doing so well. There were corpses everywhere. Most of the homes were burning. Blood ran along the streets, in the gutters, up the walls and across flesh. Nothing moved except the flames and the smoke. Spasmodic hovered through this scene. The scent of acrid smoke touched its nose, it could *smell* its dream, and it coughed. Lingering in the centre of this dead collection of homes, it waited... The visions were never over until the circles returned.

From the smoke, from a burning home, came a familiar face. There was Spasmodic, covered in dark liquid, grinning. Terrible white teeth beamed out through a crimson mask which dripped from its chin and soaked through its hair, bright red dreadlocks darker now, dipped in sin. Its claws were a mass of torn skin, blubbery flesh, and strings of fabric. From them hung snatches of what had once made up a man, a woman or a child. Flesh and bone, clothes, blood. All the same now torn from the body. All the same now torn from the soul.

It grinned, even as it watched itself grin.

The image of itself turned, looking over its shoulder. Flames were licking at the doorway now, as the furniture and bedding and curtains and drapes and bodies began to catch fire. The vision of Spasmodic turned again and walked away. It walked out of the village, out of sight, leaving behind the flames and the death and the empty void it had created.

The circles began to rotate. Spasmodic allowed them to take over, spiralling the image out of control, the village becoming smaller and smaller until it was torn from view. The circles ran over it and with them came the sounds. It heard screaming. It heard swords clashing. It heard women sobbing and babes wailing. It heard the flames. It heard the cries of agony as wounds were inflicted. Spasmodic felt the wave of heat, the scent of sweat and bitter blood, and of horses; all musty and sloth-like in delivery, creeping up on the senses. It felt the warmth of battle upon its skin, and the scorching of the sun above, uncaring to the conflict it illuminated.

All of this swirled around, and it laughed, *roared* in triumph. Here, amongst all other places it had found, the creature felt most at home.

Most at *peace*.

Spasmodic opened its eyes.

It was sitting in an apple tree, waiting for the sunrise, to meet up with the giant human and the young girl. The Queen of the World.

The creature smiled to itself, lids drooping once more. The circles had disappeared. It took a deep breath and exhaled, shivering. This time, it did sleep.

Chapter Eleven

*E*arly the next morning Kanderil led Fallerin out to the barn they had built together four summers previous. The farmer was yawning, not bothering to raise a hand to cover his mouth. He carried a lantern with him; the first light of the coming dawn was no more than a suggestion over the far horizon.

"You still keep your wagon in here?" Kanderil asked.

"Aye, I do," Fallerin replied shortly. When the woodsman did not respond, he spoke on. "I hope you've a good reason for waking me up. I thought we established last night how much I dislike rising early."

"You are a martyr."

They reached the barn. Fallerin withdrew the bolt keeping the smaller gate-door in place.

"I expect you will need the full doorway open," said Kanderil. Fallerin gave him an odd look in the dim light cast by the lantern.

"What's this about?" he asked as he stepped inside the barn. Kanderil heard the click of a heavy latch. The two larger doors opened gradually, separating as Fallerin pushed them apart. One of the hinges gave a brief creak of protest, but they were otherwise silent. From within came the dry, musty odour of harvested crops.

"I need your wagon." Kanderil moved past his host, through the bales of hay held in storage, heading straight to the cart. "And your two horses." He ran his palm across the rim of the waist-high wheels. They were in good condition. He knelt down, looking at the axel. To his surprise there was a basic leaf-spring suspension supporting the weight of the trailer above, but the ride would still be far from smooth.

"How long for?"

"As long as I need."

Fallerin gave a chuckle of disbelief. "Well, I have to be honest. I'm not going to be able to part with them for more than a day or two. I need the wagon to transport stuff between my farm and others, and the horses are being lent to Gifford's place at the end of the week."

Kanderil stood, facing the rear of the barn where three stable areas had been installed. Only one of the chestnut mares was visible. He presumed the other was still asleep. This one was watching him.

"How much did you pay for this?" He thumped the trailer's side, turning back to Fallerin.

"I bargained it down to seven gold and four silver."

"Then I will give you twenty gold for the wagon and both horses." Kanderil reached inside his jerkin, pulling out the money pouch hanging around his neck. Fallerin raised his hands.

"Whoa, whoa, wait. What? What for?"

"I need your wagon and horses," Kanderil said slowly.

"So you're going to pay me at least five gold over the odds for them?"

"I will pay more if you think y-"

"No," Fallerin said, his voice catching a high pitch on the *n*. "No, I mean, twenty gold would be more than enough. But why? Why such importance? It wouldn't make sense to walk to the Meadows to buy a horse. You could get them cheaper in Tamiran, ones bred for travel instead of pulling ploughs."

"Rachia is not a strong rider, and I need to deliver her to her grandmother in good time."

"Your niece?"

"Aye."

"Kanderil, you don't have any siblings. You said so while we were building this bloody thing." Fallerin gestured around him.

With a sigh, Kanderil looked away. The long shadows cast by the lantern Fallerin had placed on a bundle of wheat gave the farmer an expression of accusation, with deep lines creasing his forehead.

"Rachia is not a strong rider, and I need to deliver her to her grandmother in good time. That is all you need to know."

"Is that a line I need to rehearse as well?" Fallerin asked.

"If anyone were to ask you if I had come to visit, that is what I told you."

"Who's going to ask me, Kanderil?"

"The less you know the better. My apologies for the vague answers, and if I could explain any more I would. I am very pleased to see you and the family doing so well, but now I would like to purchase the cart and horses so I can be on my way."

Fallerin chuckled, smoothing the knuckles of his right hand with the palm of his left. "This isn't some secret mission you're on, is it?" he asked with a boyish curiosity. "Does it have anything to do with all the young lads moving around?"

Kanderil quirked a brow. "Moving around where?"

"Every few months I'll see groups of lads travelling south through the Meadows on foot, with full rucksacks. Maybe a hundred or so over the course of a week. Next month a similar pattern occurs, heading north. Never seems to be the same people, either."

Muttering, Kanderil held out a large hand, fingers closed. "Fallerin, take this." The farmer reached out and received twenty round coins which shone gold by the lantern's glow. One dropped to the ground but was gathered up hurriedly.

"Take this, stop asking questions, and go back to bed."

"Fine," Fallerin said, tucking the coins into his pocket. He smiled. "But one day, when we're both old men, sitting under blankets in the sunshine and pissing ourselves, you'll explain to me what this was all about. Alright?"

"Deal. But you are supplying the cider." Kanderil was already moving towards the waiting harness hanging between the stables.

Later that morning, with the sun hanging low in the sky and the air starting to warm up around them, the three companions were following a dusty road towards the northern Meadows, staying as close to the forest line as possible. The trees stood like sentinels of nature, holding a front line against the agricultural dominance of the human farmers. Sarene lay in the trailer, her lower back propped up by a folded blanket. Spasmodic was opposite her, its hood pulled up over its head at the insistence of Kanderil, who was riding in the driver's seat. The creature had returned as soon as they were out of sight of Fallerin's home.

The two horses pulling the wagon were like the horses from her village. Both were built for pulling power, not for travel. They'd get to where they were going but the pace would be steady.

And bouncy, it seemed. The wagon rumbled with every yard, jarring her bones. Her backside had started to ache and they'd only been travelling for a couple of hours.

"So when do we get to find out your master plan, chief?" Spasmodic called to Kanderil, who responded without looking around, his voice carrying over the racket of wooden wheels grinding on compacted earth.

"The plan is simple. I expect the Gathire to reach us today. I intend to question them about the girl."

Sarene frowned at the way he spoke about her as though she were not present.

"How'd you reckon they'll do that, then?" Spasmodic

asked, looking around the wagon while it spoke. It found what it was looking for; a length of straw stuck between the planks of the trailer bed.

"I will ask them a few questions. They will answer."

"That easy, eh?" The creature held the straw between its teeth, grinning. It winked at Sarene. She smiled, tilting her head with one eye closed against the sunlight. "We might as well prepare some tea and biscuits, like. Get a little barbeque going." It jerked forward, leaning towards Kanderil's shoulder. "In fact, fu-"

"Sit down," Kanderil said bluntly. "I will explain what we are going to do."

Spasmodic complied, leaning back against the edge of the trailer. "Do I get to kick anyone in the face?"

"Remember what we agreed."

"Pfft, yes Sir!" it said with a snort. "I didn't say anything about murderin' anyone, did I?"

Sarene clicked her fingers. Spasmodic looked at her.

"Need a piss stop?"

Sarene's glare made it chuckle. Kanderil looked around for the first time that morning. Shaking her head, she held out Jared's insignia. Then she pointed to her eyes.

"Yes, we will still be looking for Jared. We need to do something about our pursuers first, however."

Sarene slapped her hand against the wagon twice, before giving a curious shrug.

"The wagon? It is part of my plan. We need to leave big enough tracks for the Gathire to find us at a certain location."

"Bit obvious, like," Spasmodic commented. "Reckon it's a bit *too* obvious. Like you *wanna* be found."

"We do want to be found," said Kanderil. "Remember, they have no reason to believe that *I* know they are on my trail. They would expect to be able to follow me without second guessing my actions."

"Why would they follow you, though? I mean, unless they're recruiting for an arm-wrestling competition." It thumbed a claw at Sarene. "They want the girl."

She reached out to nudge it with her foot. The references to her in the third person were getting irritating.

"I have to assume that they are aware I am protecting her by now." Kanderil explained. "The whelp from the Kalethi barracks would have no reason to follow me unless he overheard me asking about Sarene's brother, Jared. If that is the case I cannot be sure how much of my movements he witnessed, though I suspect he did not see me enter Porthouse's shop."

"Who's Porthouse?"

"A very unpleasant man. The tunnel out of Tamiran runs from beneath his store, and if the Gathire informant saw me enter there with Sarene and leave by myself, then the Gathire would almost certainly have followed her. Regardless, as a civilian, they should not have allowed me through the gates as easily as they did. And now, a day later, I would wager gold against copper that a witness has come forward and Porthouse has since been questioned. He has no reason to lie to them about Sarene's whereabouts."

Sarene clicked her fingers again with a crisp *snap*. Kanderil turned, and she put her hand over her eyes, shielding them from the sun. She made a slow, elaborate display of searching the horizon, like a shepherd surveying the land for lost sheep. The Meadows were still beautiful, especially in this early light, and she found it difficult to look back towards her guardian.

Kanderil smiled. "No, I cannot see them either."

"So where are they then?" Spasmodic asked through closed teeth. It was trying to hook the straw up its own nose with a ridiculous amount of concentration. Sarene creased up into laughter.

"When pursuing a target, at least as a Kalethi, it is common to give them a head start of up to a full day."

"What for?" The straw fell from the creature's mouth as it cackled. "That's a stupid idea. They'd get away."

"Letting a target think they are *not* being followed gives them a false sense of confidence. For example, if a man is smuggling banned substances or illegal weapons or other such things, you want to give them time to meet with whomever they may be dealing with, or any possible accomplices. That way you can catch a larger number of targets together."

"That's one the dumbest things I've ever heard," Spasmodic said. It waved towards Sarene. "They're chasing her, not a soddin' gang of bandits. Why let her get away?"

"I left Tamiran alone. Sarene escaped the city by other means. They never saw you leave at all. It is better to give us time to meet up again. Besides, the Gathire are skilled trackers and are said to have a strong information network. It would be very difficult to lose them."

"Pfft," Spasmodic spat, folding its arms over its chest. "So what do we do then? Wait for them to find the wagon, and then what?"

"You will see."

"Will it be fun?"

"I said there would be no killing," Kanderil looked over his shoulder again as the wagon rocked against something on the road. "I never said we would have to play nice."

Grinning, Spasmodic slid its body out until its booted feet touched the other edge of the wagon. With a long sigh, rife with contentment, the creature placed its hands behind its head, interlocking claws which *click*ed together.

"Splendid."

"This stuff stinks."

"Just dip your hand in. You do not need much."

"Ugh."

"I was not aware you were so squeamish, demon."

"Where did you get this stuff?"

"An apothecary."

"A apoffywhat? Eh, nevermind. Can't we just beat their heads in?"

"No. Now get in there, and stay still."

———◀○▶———

Kanderil, now several yards within the tree-line, stalked the trail they'd taken with the wagon.

The wagon itself sat in a stretch of clear grassland a couple of hundred yards further down the road. Picturesque and quiet, it was an ideal place to have lunch. The early afternoon sun shone brightly above. Kanderil noted that a few clouds dotted the sky. Autumn was, thankfully, only a few weeks away; it was common for rain to precede the seasonal shift, and the forests could sorely use it.

Halting behind a broad, sturdy larch, Kanderil crouched down low and retrieved the massive bow from his back. He tested the string with two fingers, before adjusting one of the bronze notches holding the string in place. Just one turn tighter. Perfect.

The bow was custom made at great expense. Sleek and smooth, it was much heavier than a standard longbow and required someone of Kanderil's prodigious strength to make full use of the near two hundred pounds of draw weight. It was able to punch through leather and hide armours with ease, and even chainmail with the right angle. He had yet to meet anyone else who could wield the weapon with any great degree of accuracy. The body of the bow had no decoration, no engraving common to personalised bows, with the sole exception of a bronze trim around the central grip. At either end of the bow, beneath matching bronze tips, an ingenious system of thread wheels on bearings kept the bowstring in place. One could adjust the tension of the string with a simple twist of the notches, or let the string slack for periods of disuse.

Though able to fire standard issue shafts, the bow came with its own set of arrows which were longer and thicker than was common. Kanderil pulled one of these now. Dark wood held both raven-feathered flights and a sharp steel point.

Kanderil listened.

For a while there was nothing. Nothing except the small

animals buzzing, flying and crawling through the woods around him. Nothing except the brush of the breeze through the leaves around him, each one caressed by a whispered kiss, rustling together in celebration. Alone for only the second time since he had found Sarene in the woods, he took a deep breath, enjoying the solitude.

If you walked away now, you could go back to your own life.

The thought came to him from nowhere. He had avoided such contemplation until now with no issues. But with a moment to reflect, he considered his situation

Kanderil had left the Kalethi for a reason. The wilds he now called his home were all he needed. Leaving behind his colleagues, his few friends, the city and the society he grew up in had been easy. He had wanted *out*, and yet here he was, most certainly back in the thick of it.

From hunting rabbits to smuggling a girl potentially hunted by the Four out from under the noses of the Gathire. All in less than two weeks. So why was he doing it? What had made him agree to this? Sympathy for a beaten man and his injured wife? A sense of duty he had regained years after gladly walking away from his commission?

Kanderil pushed the thoughts from his head. He was doing this because he had to. He had responsibilities whether he wanted them or not. While the Kalethi were certain to continue without him, the girl would surely have been found without his aid. Spasmodic may have reached her before the Gathire, but that would have been an invitation for disaster. The creature was evidently skilled as a fighter but would be a terrible guardian, likely to draw more attention than they managed to avoid.

Perhaps when they found the girl's brother. Perhaps then he could go back to his solitude.

The sound of hooves on the road drifted into range. A number of riders were coming. He estimated four or five.

Kanderil waited.

———◄○►———

The first arrow, as intended, caught the dark riders off guard. One of the five fell, the shaft jutting from his shoulder.

Another followed it less than two seconds later. The target was lucky, having slid from their saddle at the right moment. The shot missed by inches.

Kanderil notched a third arrow, cursing to himself beneath his breath as he scanned the scene along the road. He had intended for at least two of the riders to be down before they had a chance to react. The remaining four men were now using their mounts as cover, drawing weapons. None of them spoke.

This was going to be a little trickier than he anticipated.

A crossbow bolt hissed past him, *thunk*ing into a tree somewhere further into the woods. Either someone was lucky with the aim or they had him pinpointed already. Kanderil peered around the tree he crouched behind. No immediate response. That much, at least, was good. The sun was high in the air, the wind was light, and he still had the greater vantage point.

"You have attacked the Gathire, working under the orders of Prince Remelas!" called one of the riders. "Show yourself, coward, and be recognised."

Another arrow whipped over the head of one of the horses, the feathered flight stroking against the tip of one ear. The beast whinnied in fright and made to run. Its rider managed to catch the reins but was yanked along for a few yards, cursing aloud. The horse circled around as it slowed, rearing its head. Kanderil released once more. The rider gave an awkward grunt as the arrow bit into his thigh, and he quickly hopped back behind his mount.

The Hunter leaned back out of sight. His first target was now slumped motionless on the ground.

Nothing happened for the next few moments. The horses were breathing heavily, and he could hear a crossbow being reloaded. Kanderil looked at the four arrows lying in a neat row beside him, each tip covered in a greenish liquid. There were another twelve in the quiver across his back. Twelve to play with; four to make count.

"Yer only makin' this harder for yerself, whelp," yelled a different voice. This one sounded angry and rough. "When we catch ya we'll string ya'p by yer innards an' kick ya offa cliff!"

An interesting threat, but Kanderil was more intrigued by the man's accent. The Gathire were known to hire educated recruits. He was not one for stereotypes, but this yell sounded like it came from a drunkard born in the sticks, far to the south wes--

Kanderil ducked as a crossbow bolt slammed into the trunk where his head had been. He grabbed an arrow from over his shoulder and fired immediately in return, releasing blind. Snatching the four arrows from the ground, he ran along a diagonal path away from the road, keeping low. More crossbows clicked as the riders fired. One shot grazed his upper arm, carving a shallow wound.

"You two, move on!" the first voice yelled. Kanderil did not look back to identify it. He heard hooves build up speed, turning his head to catch two riders leaving the scene. Before he could look behind him another bolt from inside the forest hit the ground beside his foot, bouncing past his calf. Kanderil continued to move, sidestepping, keeping close to any cover he passed. His eyes scanned the trees but saw nothing.

He could not afford to remain caught in this crossfire for long.

Further along the road, Sarene sat on a blanket beside the wagon. The two horses had been unharnessed and were cropping at the ground with broad, flat teeth, hunting the slim pickings of grass.

She felt like a small worm on a big hook. Unable to relax, she toyed with her pipes, staring at the road.

Horses were rapidly approaching, their hooves drumming against the ground. She doubted it was Kanderil racing at such speed. There had been a few distant yells, but nothing she could make out. Trembling, Sarene forced herself to remain still. It was important, Kanderil had said, to provide both a target and a distraction. It made sense that their pursuers would be encouraged to act quickly after finding her alone in the open like this. That was exactly what he wanted.

Sarene chewed her lip, looking back towards the wagon. The trailer's cover had been pulled into place. She wanted to crawl under it and hide.

The horses were closer now. She could see them in the distance.

"Psst," said a voice. "Is it time yet?"

The question was confounding. She stared at the trailer with saucer eyes.

"Oh, wait... Heh. Nevermind."

Kanderil had found a decent cover point; the rotten trunk of a long dead tree wide enough to squat behind, covering his back from the hidden Agent while also providing a view of the road. He dropped three of the four arrows in his hand and notched one to his bowstring. A twig snapped a little over ten yards away, and he focused on the source of the sound.

Whoever approached was making too much noise to be a trained Gathire.

Kanderil saw the edge of a dark shirt and raised his bow. The rider stepped into view and he released, hitting the man deep in the shoulder. Roaring in pain and rage, he saw the Hunter and charged, wielding a short cavalry sabre. Kanderil waited until the last moment before rising, evading the oncoming blade by stepping inside the swing and slamming his forearm into the man's elbow. Before the attacker could respond Kanderil grabbed the rider by his throat and lifted him into the air, turning to throw him head-first into the dead tree. With a dull thud, the rider slumped to the floor and lay still.

Kneeling back into cover, Kanderil could see the second rider he had hit was on the ground. One arm hung from the reins of his horse like a broken puppet.

The hidden assailant would have had a clear shot if he were still in the area. Kanderil waited, counting the passing seconds. He wanted to move now, head to the wagon, but he could not risk stepping out into the open just yet.

Besides, Sarene was not defenceless.

The two Gathire Agents slid from their mounts, heading towards Sarene. They seemed nervous. Both riders were male, tall, and had their weapons drawn. One pointed the tip of his blade towards her and she flinched.

"Get up," he said in a short bark. Sarene made no movement. It was not a conscious choice to disobey. She just couldn't move.

"*Get up*, girl!" the man repeated, stepping close. "You're me ticket to a big ol' pay day." He grinned, and Sarene could see yellow, broken teeth through his tangled beard.

Spasmodic leapt from the wagon, springing towards Agent furthest away from Sarene. He barely had time to yelp before being bowled over, tumbling along the floor with the creature latched onto him. Spasmodic reached down, slid one of its claws across the man's face, and jumped up to its feet. Its victim cried out in alarm, bringing a hand to his face. The fingertips came away bloody.

"Ah, shaddap," the creature spat, measuring a solid kick at the rider's head. The connection produced a *crack* which made Sarene cringe. The man laid still, a shuddered gasp slithering from his throat.

Spasmodic looked at the remaining man, who stood nearly a full foot taller than the creature. Sarene stared with growing fascination as the man tried to hold his nerve, faltered, then stepped back.

"Wha-" he tried to say. "Wha-wh-ah-"

"Oh come on, matey," Spasmodic replied. "Don't tell me you've shit yourself already. Pretend I'm her!" It pointed. "I'm all small and innocent, like!"

"Wha..." The man paused. Sarene believed him ready to flee, but instead he gripped his sword in two hands and charged. His face contorted into an expression she could not interpret. "*What are you, demon?!*" he exclaimed in a whisper which became a roar.

Spasmodic just laughed. As the Agent closed in swinging, it ducked. The sword passed harmlessly over its head. Spasmodic lashed out, raking its claws across the man's thigh. He yelled out in pain but continued advancing. Rolling backwards to avoid the next attack, Spasmodic came up to a crouch, sneering.

"Right, you've got about a minute to catch me, beardy." As it spoke, it raised its hands. The tips of its deadly fingers were dark, as if they had been dipped in treacle.

Freezing, the Agent looked down.

"...*Poison*?" He gripped the wound on his leg as though he could halt the blood flow through sheer willpower.

"No, look, there's no need to be dramatic here," said Spasmodic, muttering. "There's no audience except the girl, and she won't tell anyone." It sniggered to itself as the man ran at it again, animated by his rage. Spasmodic sprang, actually *jumped* over his assailant's head, somersaulting clear above him and landing beside Sarene, who had managed to scramble over to the wagon. She clung to the wheel for support.

"Want a go?" it asked, prodding her with an elbow. "He's really not very good. Look. He's already knackered."

The Gathire Agent was indeed faltering. He took a faltering step towards them and stumbled, dropping to one knee. Using his blade for balance, he tried to rise.

"Just lie down," Spasmodic taunted. "Close your peepers, take a snooze. It'll be easier."

The Agent glared at him as fury turned to horror. He then crumbled to the floor.

Glaithe muttered, stepping back out of sight. He had found the girl, but that thing with her... What magic was *this*? Had she conjured a demon to protect her? The beast was lethal.

Chalimer had never mentioned that Sarene could perform supernatural acts.

Approaching her now would be suicide. The giant woodsman would not be delayed for long, and while Glaithe still had the upper hand it was not worth initiating a conflict he was not certain to win. No, better to withdraw for now. His gang had been taken down with remarkable ease. The former Kalethi had downed at least two, and this... this freak of nature with the girl had taken care of two more.

Provisions would have to be made. This changed things. Either Chalimer had withheld information about the girl, or her abilities were simply unknown. Nobody outside of the Four should be capable of summoning *monsters*...

Better to rethink his strategy.

Glaithe stepped away, leaving the others to their fate. He had an image of the girl offering their bodies to the demon for its services. With luck it would distract her long enough for the Gathire to take advantage. They could not be far behind.

"So what now?" Spasmodic asked as Kanderil approached. He had an arrow to his bowstring and was scanning the trees.

"There is another in the woods. They circled around me when the riders arrived."

"I'll go find 'em then," it said. Kanderil nodded and the creature scampered away. He approached the wagon where Sarene stood. She was nervous but appeared unharmed.

"Are you alright?"

The girl nodded, giving a weak smile. Kanderil turned without another word and moved to collect the two fallen bodies. He lifted them one at a time and placed them on the wagon, laying them side by side in the trailer. Then he gathered the two horses, harnessing them back in place at the front of the cart.

Soon all five of the riders were lined up in a row on the trailer, Kanderil having ridden the wagon back to the ambush point where he had first engaged them. He searched the travel bags of the three remaining Gathire horses - the two others had fled - and found enough rope to tie the five men around the ankles and wrists. Once finished, Kanderil sat beside Sarene on the wagon. He'd offered her a dry sweet-biscuit from his provisions and she was nibbling at it like a mouse, her gaze darting from her lap to the woods to the road in a regular circle.

Spasmodic returned soon afterwards. "Bastard," it spat, irritated. "There was someone there all right, but they left some nasty bloody smell behind. Lost the bastard's scent."

"A sulphuric capsule, most likely," Kanderil replied. "They are used to confuse guard dogs."

"Smelt like it fell out of someone's arse," it said as it hopped up into the rear of the wagon, kneeling over the restrained riders. The comment caught Sarene off guard, causing her to blush.

"So what now then? Interrogation, right?"

"No point," Kanderil turned to face the creature, throwing an arm over the back of the seat. "These men are not Gathire."

"Eh?"

"They are mercenaries." He reached down to tug at the deep, night blue shirt the nearest assailant wore. "This is not Gathire uniform. It was worn to seem so from a distance. They were combat experienced but reckless. They had me pinned down in the forests from two sides, but instead of pushing their advantage they separated to chase down Sarene, expecting her to be in the wagon they were following."

"So?" Spasmodic said with growing impatience.

"So they were going for the *money*," said Kanderil. "The

Gathire would have sought to eliminate me before heading on for the girl." He paused. "It is possible that the man you searched for in the forest was an Agent, at least. He managed to get past me without much trouble, and was smart enough to cover his retreat. Why he used sulphur I do not know. Perhaps he saw you."

"And thought I was a dog?" Spasmodic cackled, now amused.

Sarene clapped her hands. She gestured at their captives, shrugging her shoulders at Kanderil.

"I suppose we leave them here. Someone should find them eventually."

"We taking the wagon?" asked the creature.

"No," Kanderil replied. "If an Agent did get away from us, we have to assume he will gather reinforcements. Using the same plan twice would be foolish. Better to take these horses and head on towards the northern Meadows. The sooner we find Sarene's brother, the better. We can focus on discovering her importance to her pursuers afterwards."

Sarene looked at the woodsman for a long moment. The allusion to staying together after they found Jared was surprising. She couldn't tell if it was a slip of the tongue.

"I ain't ridin," said Spasmodic. "You two can get on one of those stupid things. I'm quicker meself."

"Very well. Stay close in case we need to stop for any reason." Kanderil stepped from the wagon, his foot easily reaching the ground. Sarene had to hop down from the vehicle to do likewise. She raised her head as she landed, facing the forest. Standing there, in plain sight, was a man dressed in robes of deep maroon. He seemed very old, with a thin, wispy shock of silvery grey hair. There was a long, crooked travelling staff in his hand. Sarene thumped her hand against the wagon, her eyes not leaving the stranger. Within moments, Kanderil was beside her, his bow drawn. Spasmodic placed a claw over the edge of the wagon, his wiry frame tensed and ready to spring.

"Hello there!" the stranger called, smiling. He sounded relaxed. "A pleasure to meet you!"

"State your business," Kanderil replied in a guarded voice. The words were low and threatening.

The elderly man chuckled. "Now, now, Kanderil. That's no way to greet an old friend. Come on, now, come over here."

Spasmodic peered at the woodsman with a curious eye. "You know him or summat?" Sarene snatched a glance up at her two companions.

"Come on," the stranger insisted. "I won't bite. Besides, you're in the way there."

"Excuse me?" said Kanderil. Before the stranger said anything further, the Hunter heard them. His head turned to the left. Along the road ahead more horses were approaching. They wore dark clothing with white trim and held a close V formation.

These *were* Gathire.

"Ready yourselves," Kanderil said firmly. "Sarene, get behind me." He lifted his bow, tilting his head slightly to aim along the notched shaft. Spasmodic hopped out of the cart, crouching low to the ground. It spread the claws of its right hand, leaning forward on its left, and grinned at the incoming threat.

"No, no, no." The stranger had taken a few steps towards the group and was coaxing them over towards him. "There is no need for bloodshed here. Come, join me. We have much to discuss, you and I."

"I do not know you, sir," Kanderil said through a clenched jaw, "and I would advise moving away before you are seen."

"Shit off, oldie," offered Spasmodic.

The old man merely chuckled. "Manners, boy." He shook his head. "Now look, we do not have much time to argue about this. My apologies if I startle you."

"For th-"

The sentence never really began. Kanderil had intended

to address the stranger only to find he now stood alongside him. He was still in a combat position with his bow drawn, the string taut in his grip, but now the arrow now pointed at a nearby tree.

The old man cleared his throat. "Please," he said in a gentle voice. "Follow me."

"Whoa," whispered Spasmodic.

Sarene stared at the woodsman, astounded, before it dawned that the riders were almost upon them. She broke into a run, heading for Kanderil.

The creature was torn between following the girl and engaging the enemy. It looked from one way to the other, twitching.

"Come along, boy. They wouldn't be much sport, anyway." The old man smiled.

"And whysat?" Spasmodic called. The first Agent had started to slow his horse, and was already dropping from his saddle. Spasmodic prepared to lash out at the rider, but paused. None of the Gathire had drawn their weapons.

The Agent moved past it without a second glance, moving on to the wagon. He flung open the half-folded cover sheet, then pulled the blankets crumpled in one corner of the trailer. Spasmodic remained crouched barely six feet from him.

"Nothing," he said. He gestured to the five unconscious men lying across the cart.

Spasmodic turned to look at the other four, still mounted on horses. One of them gave a grunt of annoyance. "Fan out. They can't have gotten far. I want you all back here within five minutes with your findings. I expect at least a sign of the direction they took."

Sarene sneezed.

Tensing, Kanderil brought the bow around towards the Gathire. The girl had frozen in place, fearful of being heard. Despite being less than ten yards away, not one of the riders paid her the slightest bit of notice as they rode out in different directions. None of them entered the forest.

"Now," said the stranger. "Perhaps we can get moving?"

"Ahhhhhh, shit," Spasmodic said. It hawked, then fired something from its mouth at the Agent standing beside the wagon. The man responded by putting a hand to his cheek. Confused, he looked skywards, as if trying to spot a winged culprit. Spasmodic laughed, clumping in its heavy boots towards the group.

"Is this some kinda joke? Why they ignorin' us?"

"I wanted them to," the stranger replied, walking deeper into the woods. Kanderil followed, grim faced and reluctant, placing one hand on Sarene's arm to usher her forwards. He slung his bow over his shoulder, taking one last look back towards the wagon as Spasmodic hurried past him.

He felt uneasy. This was not natural.

"So," the old man said as they came to a well nestled away from the road. The uneven structure was just a collection of large rocks stacked into place. A nearby bucket, tied with frayed rope to an iron hook embedded in one of the stones, seemed unlikely to hold much water.

The grass here was more vibrant than the dry growth by the roadside.

Sarene stared at the new arrival, unable to hide her curiosity. A stressful morning was becoming a very strange afternoon. She'd already experienced her fair share of worry, of alarm, but here was something new entirely. Kanderil had not walked away from the wagon to the old man's side, and the woodsman had looked shocked standing next to him. He now seemed uncertain in the old man's presence. If someone had pushed for her opinion, she would have guessed he was nervous.

She certainly was.

Spasmodic sat directly in front of the stranger, leaning back on its hands.

Despite the well looking as though a faint breeze might knock it over, it supported the old man's weight as he leaned against it.

"I suspect that an introduction may help us to avoid redundant questions," he said. "My name is Corliani. It is a pleasure to meet you all."

Sarene's mouth dropped open, her eyes wide.

This was Corliani of the Four.

Kanderil appeared as stunned as she did, exhaling deeply. A wry smile came to his lips. "I would guess that you are not here to claim the girl," he said.

"No," said Corliani. "Straight to the heart of the problem, eh? Bravo, young man." He chortled. "Bravo."

"She is in my care."

"Mm. Of course. Plenty of people after her, aren't there?" Corliani chuckled again, pulling his travelling staff close to his shoulder. Sarene was starting to gather a sense of deep history from the man, a depth of being she felt she was not able to comprehend.

"What happened to the Gathire?"

"I simply suggested that they could not see anyone." The old man shrugged. "It seemed easier this way."

"You turned us invisible?" Spasmodic asked. Until now it had acted indifferently to the legendary figure. "Neat."

"Not quite, my boy," Corliani replied. He reached out to pat Spasmodic's head like it were a faithful pup. Sarene blinked when it reacted in a positive manner, a contended smile emerging at the touch. He appraised the creature. "Exceptional. Tyrrial did a much better job than I realised."

"I didn't do as I was told, though," Spasmodic pointed out. The words were hesitant in coming but spoken with bravado.

"That is your choice," Corliani said with a smirk. "And that is the point, isn't it?"

The old man, this individual who had changed the world, looked directly at Sarene. He found something amusing in the way she looked back. Corliani leaned forward. Spasmodic stepped back away from him, crawling close to Kanderil as though giving them room.

"That is the point," he repeated, sounding lost in thought. Then he spoke again. "Hello, Sarene. It is an *honour* to meet you."

Swallowing, Sarene offered an awkward wave in return. *How does he know me*, she thought to herself.

Corliani studied her. She felt like a butterfly pinned to a page. "You really do not understand, do you?" he said. The comment was whimsical, as if it shouldn't have been spoken aloud. "No, of course not. Why would you?"

"If you know why she is so highly prized, then please explain," said Kanderil, some of the steel restored to his voice. "Her family has been attacked and she is being hunted. The girl has no idea what she has done, and neither do I."

Corliani looked to the woodsman. Sarene followed his gaze. Kanderil was standing at his full height, straight-backed, with his arms folded over his chest. Even in this posture he somehow seemed lesser than the old man. Corliani's presence was immense, dwarfing even the woodsman's.

"And yet you still protect her," he remarked. "You keep watch while she sleeps, you listen for danger while you travel, and you lead her without complaint." Kanderil did not respond, but Corliani bowed his head in respect. "I am impressed. You are a giant amongst men in spirit as well as stature, Windfury."

The words, coming from such an infamous name, pleased Sarene. She found herself warming to this legendary figure. It was possible he was lying about who he was, of course, but... No. Something told her he was the genuine Corliani. There was no faking *this*. At the last, Sarene raised an eyebrow. Kanderil did the same.

"Windfury," Corliani said again. "It is the name of a very old clan who used to rule this part of the land. I did not expect any of them to remain, but you..." He pointed a bony finger. "You remind me of them. You must belong to them by blood. I'll look into it for you, my lad. You may be noble yet." The old man grinned.

Kanderil nodded once in reply. "An interesting offer, sir, and without wishing to seem ungrateful I must ask again."

He gestured to Sarene. She saw again the space between them and a sense of separation prickled her skin. "What can you tell us about Sarene? Why do the Gathire hunt her?"

"More than the Gathire," Corliani replied. He stepped from the well and approached Sarene. She stood her ground, clutching her bag. "More than my brother, Tyrrial. More than the fearsome little creation who now travels with you."

"She's the Queen of the World," Spasmodic said suddenly.

Corliani gave a crooked smile. "That's one way of putting it." He reached out, the staff he'd held standing upright on its own, and placed his hands on Sarene's shoulders. She felt him give a gentle squeeze. He raised his hands to her cheeks and gently moved her head to the side, left then right. He leaned forward to look deeply into her dark eyes. His own irises were a flint grey, and as full as the sky before a thunderstorm. She believed they had seen more than she ever would, more than she could even realise.

"Bah." He reached for his staff. Sarene flinched. "Nothing. I was expecting some sign, something amazing or unique." Corliani shook his head. "You're completely normal. Now I'll need to test what they say."

Kanderil took a step towards her. "Test what who sa--" He was cut off with a raised hand.

"This won't hurt." The old man pointed a finger to Spasmodic. His lips moved. He ended the unheard sentence with a nod of the head.

Spasmodic started to rise up from the ground until it hung a good two feet in the air. It laughed, kicking its legs and waving its arms, but it was unable to drop back to the earth. Kanderil swore, bringing a hand to the back of his head.

"Well I'll be..."

"Fun, isn't it?" Corliani said, smiling. He waved his hand in dismissal and Spasmodic dropped back to its feet. The creature cackled manically, rocking on its heels.

"I gotta learn me how to do *that*!"

"No, you don't," Corliani replied. "Now, that's the

problem, you see. I've been 'doing that' for centuries. I can do anything, really. So, in theory..."

Turning to Sarene, the old man pointed again. His lips moved again, repeating those silent words. She tensed, awaiting her own journey into the air.

Nothing happened.

Corliani's eyes grew wide in revelation. He took a small step backwards as the colour drained from his face.

"Goodness..."

He laughed then. Corliani shook his hand the way one would after coming in from the cold, to relieve a numbness. He then looked down to Spasmodic and repeated the trick. Once more his lips moved. This time the creature remained where it was. Corliani gazed at his palm.

"Fascinating. I did not expect any recoil..."

The old man started to pace back and forth before the well, his sandaled feet rustling over the grass. He massaged his hand as he spoke. "Understand this. I've been manipulating things for the good of the world for a long, long time. It's been a most interesting responsibility. I've had to maintain a certain distance for extended periods, of course. I'm here to guide humanity, not lead it." The Gathire were back on the road, talking. At this distance Sarene could not make out words, but she understood the tone. They were frustrated.

Corliani waving a finger at her. "You... well, my girl, you are a whole different equation. You will change things, I think. Perhaps for only a week or so. Perhaps for decades. Perhaps forever. Who knows?" The old man shrugged. "I will, one day. I suppose. When you're all long dead. If I remain here."

Sarene glanced at Kanderil. Her guardian seemed to be growing impatient, but he kept his manners in check. Spasmodic was looking at the sole of its boot, trying to find an explanation for its brief flight.

"But of course I'm rambling still." Corliani smiled. "Sarene, the reason so many people are hunting you is because of what you represent. You have an ability no one else walking this earth does."

Sarene shook her head. The words were threatening to her despite being calmly spoken.

"What is her ability?" Kanderil asked for her.

Corliani turned to him after a moment. "Didn't you see? She's invulnerable. I couldn't lift her into the air."

Kanderil said nothing. Sarene blinked.

"Oh, for..." Corliani muttered, moving back to lean against the well again. "Sometimes I wonder, I really do. Sarene, you possess an immunity to my powers. I am certain my three brothers will also be unable to influence you in any way. It appears in addition that any attempt to use our powers on you will result in some kind of feedback." The old man shrugged. "At least temporarily. I was unsuccessful in using my power to lift Tyrrial's creation a second time."

"See--" Spasmodic said, but was cut off by Kanderil.

"Quiet. Let him speak."

"You bloody quiet," Spasmodic growled its retort. "I've met two of these Four now. Can bloody talk if I wanna."

Corliani looked from the creature to Kanderil. He inclined his head with a thoughtful, amused smirk. Sarene could read the expression well. *He has a point.*

"My apologies," Kanderil said. "Please continue."

Spasmodic sniffed, satisfied. "Thanking you, big man. I was gonna say that Tyrrial said the same thing. When he sent me out to bump her off. He said she was trouble. I never saw it before, but now I do."

Sarene and Kanderil stared at the creature.

"Well think about it," it continued. "If I woke up one day and my claws were blunt, I'd be pissed as well. What if someone stole your arrows?" It craned its neck back, peering at Kanderil.

The Hunter nodded. "She is the first. The first person the Four cannot control."

"Please do not talk about me like I'm not here," Corliani said politely. "But yes, you're right. Look, here's a better method of displaying the consequences." The old man clicked his fingers. A knife appeared in his hand. The weapon was exquisite, covered in rubies and emeralds along a golden hilt. The silver blade glimmered in the sun. It was the most beautiful weapon Sarene had ever seen. Corliani paused for a moment, smiling with relief that the conjuration had worked.

Then he threw it at her.

Sarene recoiled, bringing her hand up defensively. She raised a leg, knee bent, as she tried to twist out of the way. It was then she realised that nothing had struck her. With her heart racing she risked a look back at the old man.

"It bounced off," Spasmodic said, wonder on his pale features.

"Exactly," Corliani replied. "Allow me to elaborate. During my long life, I have produced emperors and brought down kings. I have destroyed cities, turned a clear day to a thunderstorm and raised the oceans. I have cured diseases, rendered people deaf and blind with a glance and flown through the air like an eagle. But," he said, pausing for effect, "I cannot wound Sarene from ten feet away with a knife I created by my own hand."

"So she is a threat to you," Kanderil observed.

"Not directly," Corliani replied with a shake of the head. "Look at her. She wouldn't hurt anybody. She appears to be a genuinely nice, sweet young girl. If all this soothsaying business hadn't started the whole chase I doubt she would have ever even met any of us. No, her danger is what she represents. She's a talisman to the rest of the world, and as more people discover her talent, more will come for her."

Sarene felt like she had been kicked in the stomach.

The old man spread his hands. "For centuries people have behaved, more or less, because they thought we would come back if they ruined the world we helped them create."

"There have been wars," Kanderil pointed out. "Scores of thousands have died fighting each other."

"That is the nature of mankind," Corliani responded. "You control them too much, you constrict them too tightly, and you'll have anarchy regardless of the laws. Besides, a war here and there doesn't really *change* things. No nation has ever been eradicated or destroyed since we left. Civilization marches on regardless of a few skirmishes. We monitored your progress. All these years we watched. We never found a strong enough reason to return. You have been advancing just fine within the rules we provided your ancestors."

"And now you're back for the sake of one girl."

"No, Kanderil, you're still not listening. Someone caught wind of her return. That's the problem, you see. Prophecy comes from somewhere, and even *we* cannot always control it. Someone had an idea that there was going to be a girl born when the stars aligned and the spirits sang or whatever other nonsense these witchdoctors or shaman of yours feel the need to blurt out when they actually have a vision of *some* practicality." Corliani caught his breath. "Now these people want that girl, for whatever reason, because she embodies freedom. She will come to represent a choice."

"For this entire time people have acted how we told them to act. Despite all the positives we brought to this land, some people have demanded more. Some believe Sarene will lead them to a new future, where the threat of the Four does not exist and they may act in whatever manner they wish. Some will instead try to kill her, scared of what she may bring and how she will upset the established order of things. Even Tyrrial, my hot-headed brother and blessed friend, has tried to eliminate her before she could be found."

"What do the Gathire want with her?" asked Kanderil. Corliani shrugged his scrawny shoulders.

"I do not know. I am not omnipotent, Kanderil Windfury. I know much but I do not see all. Why they seek her and under whose orders, I cannot say. But recognize that they are the first of many to come for her. Eventually there will be simply nowhere to hide."

Sarene rubbed the back of her neck. The idea was too much for her to grasp at once, and she just felt numb. Her brain was processing the information in small chunks.

Surely there had been some mistake. It sounded... well, it sounded *silly*.

"Before all that, however, I thought I should meet the

girl." Corliani sounded cheerful, as if his prior words were of no importance. "To see her in person before she becomes so famous. I believe the Gathire have left," he said, gesturing to the road unseen through the woods. "I don't think I should keep you any longer."

"Can you help her?" Kanderil asked.

"How? I can't do anything *to* her. Besides, I do not wish to upset my brothers by getting involved. Tyrrial will be fuming about his creation here joining you. I have no wish to seem similarly sympathetic to her plight." Corliani rose, leaning against his staff.

"Wait a tick," Spasmodic said. "If she's untouchable, then what's the use of sending me? If I was created to kill her, kind of thing."

"Aye," Kanderil agreed. "It is essentially a living version of the dagger you conjured just now. How could it hurt her if she is immune to Tyrrial?"

"It has sentience," Corliani offered. "I would expect that giving it the choice to harm or help Sarene must bypass whatever mystical force prevents us from affecting her."

"Oh right. Nice." Spasmodic appeared pleased by the answer. Sarene stared at the creature, aware of the conversation but unsure what to make of it. Corliani must have noticed this, for he came over to her again. He patted her arm gently.

"Have faith, Sarene. You are in good hands with a Windfury for your guide. Every story has an end. I hope yours is a pleasant one."

Nodding, Sarene offered the old man an uncertain smile. Corliani winked before turning and walking away.

"So you trotted all this way just to gawp at her?" asked Spasmodic. "What's the point of that?"

"I get lonely in my tower," Corliani called out. The three of them watched him move further into the woods. As he disappeared from sight, the well he had been leaning on began to fall apart. Soon it was just a pile of rocks.

Chapter Twelve

*G*laithe had watched his former colleagues fan out from his position atop a small crest overlooking forest. They rode north. He was chewing on a strip of cold beef, occasionally spitting out small nuggets of sinew too tough for his preference. The Gathire would not find much. Their target had gone west, into the trees.

The mercenaries had done their job. They had held the woodsman called Kanderil in place long enough for the girl to be located. If she hadn't been given the time to summon the demon they would have had her. The men must have hesitated before grabbing her, or been otherwise held off. However, it appeared Sarene had more than one trick up her sleeve. He had watched the Agents advance on her and her companions, only for them to ignore her even as she ran from the road not thirty yards from where they approached. The demon had mocked them as they stood before it.

What other sorcery did the girl possess? Why had he not been informed of these powers in advance?

Because it was preposterous, that's why. Only the Four would be able to conjure such tricks, and the Gathire were not so arrogant as to presume they could hunt down and capture one with such abilities. The people of the land did not wield magic. It was some horrific trickery, was all. It would make sense that Chalimer and the Assembly did not know what she was capable of.

Yet it would certainly explain why she was so highly prized by whoever had given the order to find her.

Taking another bite of the beef, Glaithe considered the problem. The demon would have to be dealt with. The mercenaries were clearly not up to the task; trussed up in the rear of a wagon like cattle waiting for the slaughter house. The Gathire were off in the wrong direction for now, but would prove much more useful. Useful, that is, if he had not been officially ex-communicated. He muttered to himself, rising to his feet.

There had to be another way to resolve this. He was confident he could take Kanderil given the element of surprise. The girl would be tricky, but once she was unconscious she would be a danger to nobody. He had estimated that, given her young age and rural background, she was inexperienced with the realities of combat. Neutralising her before she managed to react would be easy enough.

This left the demon as the main threat.

Glaithe stood, the sloped dirt beneath his feet crumbling. He began making his way north.

Sarene was sitting with her back against a large oak trunk. A small fire burned nearby. They would soon be out of the Meadows, Kanderil had said, and from there continue north to search the common patrol areas of the Kalethi scouts for signs of her brother. They had moved on foot, having freed the horses tied to their wagon, and she was tired. Kanderil had decided that keeping off the road was the best for now. Corliani's warning that the Gathire were the first of many had been chilling.

The sun had fallen a few hours ago and no trace of its

light was left in the sky. Instead, the stars shone far above. Her father had once told her they were spirits waving, when she'd asked why they twinkled. She had never forgotten. Sarene stared at them, her thoughts disjointed and loose but always swinging back to that one, dominating topic.

She was what, exactly? Gifted? Special? *Precious*? She couldn't *do* anything. Her hidden ability was simply a passive negation of... Well, the world-changing powers of the Four who had shaped the course of history. It was like being treasured for owning shelter against the rain. She might stay dry, but the rain would still fall.

Kanderil sat on the other side of the fire. He had said nothing, but watched her with that everlasting patience. He had spent the evening cleaning those arrows he had dipped with the sleeping draught and sharpening the iron tips with a whetstone. The gentle scraping sound was much finer than that of an axe or scythe blade on a turning stone like she'd heard in the village blacksmith's. It had a soothing effect, and she listened with her eyes closed.

It was no use. Her thoughts just wouldn't stop.

She looked to her left. Spasmodic had been asleep since they stopped for the night. It'd just dropped to the earth, laid its arm over its face and hadn't moved or spoken since. It was sprawled in a heap which looked so uncomfortable it made Sarene squirm. Regardless, neither she nor Kanderil had tried to move it into a better position. She felt they both understood that this can't have been the first time it had slept like that. It seemed disjointed in every possible place, like a living rag doll.

Eventually, after he had finished on his final arrow and slid it back into his quiver, Kanderil folded his arms over his lap and leant forward. The woodsman had tied his hair back for the first time since their journey began. She had never noticed how broad his neck was.

"Are you ready to talk?" he asked. Sarene passed on the opportunity to tease him for his choice of words. She nodded. Her lower lip quivered in a sudden flicker of frustration, but she collected herself. She hoped the fire's flicking shadows had obscured the brief lapse.

Kanderil rubbed his palms together. They sounded leathery. "I must admit I now find it hard to sympathise with your position. I cannot begin to imagine how you must be feeling about Corliani's words."

Sarene gave a thin smile. She raised her hands to either side of her head, waving them roughly a foot apart. She pulled an exaggerated, confused face. Kanderil grunted.

"Understandable... Have you decided what to do when you find your brother?"

The question made Sarene frown. She hadn't considered any changes to their plan besides having to explain to Jared this new trouble she found herself in. Now it was brought out to the open, she took a moment to reflect. Corliani had mentioned a prophecy. If the Gathire knew about it, likely others did as well. How many was anyone's guess, but it begged a question.

Would she ever find peace once word had spread?

Sarene shivered, looking at Kanderil. All she could offer was a shrug.

To his credit, Kanderil did not push the issue. "There are three main overlaps for the Kalethi along the most likely paths for travel through the country. I have a lead on where Jared may be, but if unsuccessful we can also check those. We should run into other scouts on the trail who may know which route he has taken."

Sarene nodded, then stared into the fire. The underside of the most recently placed log was glowing orange, the flames crawling over the wood. Silence reigned. Her need to discuss the issue seemed too complex, too big, and she did not know how to begin expressing herself to the woodsman. She took a deep breath, exhaling in a short, quick burst. Then she lifted her head, tapping her temple before rolling her hand at the wrist, tracing a repeating circle in the air.

"A lot on the mind, aye." Kanderil ran a hand over his leather bracer. "I would try not to think too hard about what Corliani said. Right now we have only one known direct threat. Let us focus on the Gathire, and whatever happens after that is another matter."

Laying her head back against the trunk, Sarene tugged at her sleeve. Meeting Kanderil's gaze, she ran a thumb across her throat, letting her jaw hang slack with her tongue poking out.

"No," Kanderil said after a brief pause. "I do not believe they want to kill you. If this was an assassination mission they would be a lot more discreet, I think. Only one Agent would be needed to put an arrow through your heart. I would guess they are sending squads to take you by force from the creature and me."

"I have a name," Spasmodic mumbled, face down in the dirt. Sarene grinned. It didn't move or make any other noise. Kanderil gave a quick snort.

"It makes for an interesting situation, though. Whoever is sending the Gathire out after you does not work for Tyrrial. We can presume that much."

Sarene raised a brow.

"It makes no sense. He sent the c- ...Spasmodic out to kill you. To then go to the trouble of hiring the Gathire to kidnap you contradicts his original intentions. Corliani is not responsible either. He could have taken you today. At least," he said to correct himself, thumbing at Spasmodic, "he could have removed the two of us from the equation with little trouble."

Sarene played with her hands. For a split second, she doubted there would be a problem getting away from the old man. Then modesty got the better of her. *He's one of the Four,* she realised with a smirk. *He could probably capture a girl from the countryside.*

"Something funny?"

She waved her hand in front of her, dismissing the comment.

"Do not apologise, lass. It is good that you are still smiling after all this." He spoke with a straight face, and she responded with a thumbs-up. "Anyway, I would hazard a guess that the Gathire are working for a human benefactor. Prince Remelas, maybe. Perhaps even the King. This is much better for us."

She looked at him, doubtful.

"The Four are out of my league," he said to clarify. "Men I can deal with."

"Hold on, hold on," uttered Spasmodic. It spoke first into the ground before rolling over to its side. "Ow," it said, arching its back. The action reminded Sarene of a cat.

Then it sat up, rubbing its cheek with a flat palm. "What're you gonna do, exactly? Batter your King to get some answers?"

"No," Kanderil replied. "But men have predictable ambitions and motives. They want similar rewards. They have limits."

"Y'know, you wibble on like you're not one of 'em."

"On the contrary. I have my own wants and needs, same as everyone else. But I am not tasking a division of the national military to hunt down one girl." Kanderil looked at Sarene, and must have read something in her expression. "Excuse my terms. I expect no more than a handful of Agents are involved."

She wrinkled her nose.

"How 'bout I go out there, find those Gathire chaps an' get some answers," Spasmodic said following a prolonged yawn.

"No," replied Kanderil. "The more I think of it, the less I believe those Agents even know what Sarene's capability is."

"So the previous lil' ruckus was pointless."

"At the time, no. But having spoken with Corliani of the Four adjusts our focus a little." Kanderil seemed amused by his own words. The brief lapse in his stern exterior pleased Sarene. "Let us find Sarene's brother first. Once we have them reunited, we can let them decide our next step."

Spasmodic shrugged, lying back down on the ground. Sarene folded her hands over her lap, her gaze drifting back towards the fire. The idea of receiving a hug from Jared was a comforting one, and she focused on his image up to the moment she fell asleep.

Hawk and his two companions were weary. A week without a tavern, a good meal or a few whores was wearing thin on the nerves of Lug and Petar. Hawk knew they were becoming frustrated with the lack of definite answers. So far he'd only divulged that they were going to find a young girl and bring her back to her father. He had declined to inform them of how he knew the father, or where he'd received his directions from. They were growing restless with the lack of action, as well. Twice they had come across two potential candidates for robbery, single travellers through the woodlands leading to the Meadows, and passed them both up. The three of them had not spoken more than a few words the entire morning.

Now travelling along the eastern edge of the sprawling farmland, the three of them were heading north. The sun once more dominated the heavens, with no clouds threatening to usurp its pale blue domain.

Hawk had a mental picture of the man he was to locate. Young, handsome, dark coffee hair. He had an image of a chestnut mare and a soft hide uniform of brown and green. It was as though he knew the boy, but he could not remember how. The description just emerged as soon as the old man had mentioned the name. *Jared.*

A wasp buzzed towards him, took an oddly angled turn, and hovered past his right shoulder. Hawk leant away to accommodate it.

He had not slept well the last few days. The longer he travelled and the nearer he drew to his nemesis - for that was what Kanderil represented now; a scourge, a villain, the janitor of his shame - the more agitated he became. Oh, he kept his outward facade for his partners, and remained civil in what scarce conversation there was. He continued to mention the huge rewards coming to them, the ease of the mark and the luxuries they would indulge upon their return to Ghellei. Sadly, there were only so many ways one could repeat the same promises without it becoming tiresome to hear, regardless of the gold glittering beneath the words.

Hawk ran a hand across his forehead, shaking the pointed slivers of hair bothering the upper lids of his eyes. He was hot, damp, and in need of a good bath. Had been for a few days now, in fact. Such were the hardships of an extensive ride. A man of his civility was forced to slum, smelling like a common thug.

"Hey," Petar called from behind him. Hawk turned his head to listen. "I hear the new Guide in these parts is a pretty tasty one."

"Who'd ya hear that off?" Lug replied. He sounded disinterested.

"Some old fella I lost a shitpile of gold to a few months back playin cards. Said she's a picture of good looks and bad thoughts."

"I believe the whole point of a Guide is to encourage *positive* thoughts," Hawk offered.

Petar took a moment to reply, pausing to spit to the side. He had been grinding his jaw around a huge wad of chewing tobacco since breakfast, and the sound of tarry liquid being projected to the floor was beginning to test Hawk's patience. "I think so too. Nothin like a good, hard, positive thought." He cackled to himself.

Lug joined in. "Hey, how new is new, if you found this out a few months ago."

"Who cares? Let's go pay us a visit."

"No," Hawk said casually. "We can find all the attractive ladies you need for your sordid interests once we've earned our pay."

"Why pay when we can visit for free?" Petar responded, his tone laced with steel. "I reckon this here is a democracy, and I can suggest a detour if I want it."

"He's got a point," said Lug. "We been doin' nothing but ride, eat, and shit since we started on this trip. Bit o' entertainment on the way ain't a problem."

Hawk turned on his saddle. The horse accommodated him, stepping to stand across the path.

"What are you going to do, Petar? Try and get friendly?

Steal from the Shrine? Rape her?" He shook his head.

"I can go for some spiritual guidance if I want to," Petar said, sounding petulant.

"You rob people for a living. I think your spirit's past the way of guidance."

"Hey, now. You're no better than me, despite your pretendin'."

"Yeah," Lug offered. He rode in beside Petar. "All this tellin' us what to do is getting mighty boring, Hawk."

"Reckon if you want us to come along for this bountiful reward," Petar stated, "you should be a little less of a dick."

Cursing under his breath, Hawk looked to the forest line in front of him to gather his thoughts. The trees stood without response, minute differences in shades of the bark and leaves giving an oil painting effect as their branches swayed in the faint breeze. He felt a swell of anger pass through him, like a wraith walking over his grave. It swept through his shoulders, filled his lungs, before being pressed out as Hawk exhaled.

"Fine. A quick visit. And I apologise if I have seemed demanding these last few days. I..." He gave a tired smile. "I need a break, is all. The reward we'll get will let me live well for a few months, and I suppose I'm anxious. I hope you can forgive me."

Petar shrugged. "Sure." He spat another plume of brown saliva before kicking his horse forward, riding past Hawk without another word. Lug followed, but he halted beside Hawk to clasp him on the arm.

"Never you worry, old pal. It's been a long season this year, and I reckon we could all do with a rest."

Hawk nodded in agreement, but as Lug moved past his features hardened. He reached over his shoulder, fingers brushing the hilt of the sword. It had whispered to him. He had heard the words in his mind. Words telling him to show his friends exactly how much control he really possessed; how little they could resist him should he wish to make an example.

Ignoring the sword hadn't been difficult, but that the

communication existed at all bothered him.

It took another day and morning to find any trace of Jared.

Kanderil was guiding them along one of the routes he used to patrol, skirting the borders of the Meadows. The trail overlooked Horhai Lake to the northwest, the largest body of water in Tamir. Having never seen so much water in one place Sarene was in awe of it.

Less than an hour after noon, they spotted a Kalethi scout cresting a hill less than a mile distant. Spasmodic was asked to retreat out of sight, and it complied with minimal fuss.

The scout steered his mount and trotted out to meet them as Kanderil raised a hand in greeting. Sarene noted that he appeared no more than a few summers older than she was. Bright eyed, with skin tanned from exposure to the year's hard summer, he had waved as he approached. His horse was a fine animal, but she suspected it was a tad large for its owner.

"Ho, there!" the scout called. "Lovely morning, isn't it?" Sarene nodded her agreement. A single cloud in the morning's sky ribboned across the sun. The day was still bright but it lacked the biting heat of the previous few weeks. The view from the north end of the Meadows was wonderful. She could see the silhouette of mountains in the distance, clustered on the horizon; she imagined the knuckles of a god trying to pull itself into view. The land was less flat here, and it rose and fell in deep swathes of natural countryside, sweeping from west to east like the tide of the ocean she had never seen but often heard about.

"Aye," was Kanderil's concise reply. Sarene frowned at him. "How's the patrol?"

"Easy enough. Nothing much going on out there. I've spent the last few weeks just enjoying the view, truth be told."

"Nothing wrong with that, lad. Provided you also fulfil

your duties."

The scout looked Kanderil up and down. "Do I know you?"

"I doubt it. I left the Kalethi three years ago."

"Oh right. Yeah, before I joined, then. Still, reckon you're familiar. At least, a chap your size would be difficult to forget." The youth laughed, then caught himself. "That is, no offence mean-"

"None taken," Kanderil said, raising a hand. "Now, while we have you, I was wondering if you knew another Kalethi named Jared. He is on the Meadows -to-Tilldown route."

The scout glanced at Sarene before responding, offering her a polite bow of the head. "Jared?" he chuckled. "Yeah, I know Jared. May I ask why you're after him?"

"I am his uncle. It is something of a family matter."

"Ah," said the scout with certain solemnity. Sarene had learnt over the years that 'family matters' were often respected without ever demanding much explanation. You could use it as a handy excuse to get out of boring situations if needed. Taylei did it all the time, so much so that their village tutor had once asked her mother about the 'ongoing problem' in the family. Her sister had been kindly asked to stop soon afterwards.

"Have you seen him?" asked Kanderil.

"We crossed paths maybe a week back. That route he's on covers the Shrine, though. Maybe you could ask the Guide how long it's been since he dropped by. Her Shrine isn't too far; less than ten miles or so." The scout pointed towards the east.

Kanderil nodded once. "Thank you for the tip. We will head that way and see if we can pick up his trail."

"Not a problem. If you have no luck, try the barracks. It's about a day's walk from here. Follow the road north towards Fasherai, then go west at the Swan Inn. You can't miss it. Might get lucky when he drops in to report. You remind him he owes me two silvers, aye?" The scout laughed. "Caught him red-handed with a straight flush. Should have seen his face."

"He never was much of a card player," said Kanderil, chuckling. He glanced at Sarene before speaking again. "I was not aware there was a barracks up that way?"

"No, built recently," the scout replied, scratching at his neck. "A lot of recruits up there. Military thought it would be a good place for training exercises, is all. Kalethi drop in patrol reports every so often. At least when there's something to report, like. Gets a bit quiet in this area."

"Aye, I remember."

The scout tugged on the reins of his horse, which had taken a few steps forwards. The mare reared its head. "Anything else I can do for you today?"

"No, thank you. Enjoy the rest of your day. Safe travels."

"And to you both. Take care!" The scout heeled his mount forwards, riding south west. Sarene watched him go, waving goodbye when he turned in his saddle some forty yards distant. She tugged at Kanderil's sleeve, pointing at the departing youth. She then gave a thumbs-up.

"Yes, he was," agreed the woodsman. "Even if he did break every non-disclosure protocol there is."

Spasmodic caught up with them soon afterwards, toying with a large pine cone it had found. Kanderil was leading them east. They were passing an expanse of sparse woodland, the trees tall and straight with creamy bark criss-crossed with dark indentations. To be able to walk between the trees with a straight back and direct footsteps was a relief. The ground here was level too. Sarene removed her slippers before long and grinned as she skipped barefoot over the hard earth. The earth was warm and the dry grass tickled her soles.

It was late into the afternoon before Kanderil pointed towards their destination. Sarene had heard of Shrines and their Guides; Kaltor from her village had made the pilgrimage to see one not long after his wife had died of fever. He had returned calmer and in control of his emotions, though unable to discuss much of what the Guide had said. Sarene had never worked out whether he had been asked to remain quiet about it. At a distance the Shrine looked lovely. The walls were pale stone with two front columns either side of the large brown door. A domed roof crowned the building. The windows seemed glassed, but it was difficult to tell for sure.

Before they drew too close, Spasmodic was once more asked to find somewhere to wait. "You wanna buy me a bloody collar and a lead," it said as it walked away. "What's the point of following her around if you're gonna whinge at me to shit off every time we meet someone?"

"Just until we find solution for your appearance," Kanderil had replied. Sarene had given it her most sympathetic look. It had responded with a curse, stomping through the trees.

Side by side, they soon arrived at the Shrine. Kanderil rapped his knuckles against the door. The noise was sharp but made only a faint echo inside the building. They waited for almost a full minute before hearing footsteps. The latch clicked on the other side and the door opened to reveal one of the prettiest faces Sarene had ever seen.

The woman smiled at her before looking up at Kanderil. "Welcome, both of you. Please, come in."

"No need," he replied. "We were hoping you could he-"

Sarene nudged him hard, her elbow connecting with his hip. It was like striking a wall and she forced herself not to wince. Though she smiled up at the Hunter, her eyes divulged her true thoughts.

"...Thank you." Kanderil turned his attention back to the pale haired woman, who stepped back to open the door.

"My apologies, but I have few refreshments left," the woman said as they entered the Shrine. "An earlier visit consisted of three hungry travellers, and I haven't gotten around to preparing more."

Sarene barely heard her. She was transfixed the interior of the Shrine, her hand at her throat. It was *beautiful*. Two rows of polished wooden pews, six deep, face an altar which had been covered in gold leaf. The Shrine was perhaps forty yards long; twenty wide. The decorations of precious materials along the walls and the smooth marble flooring underfoot were exquisite. She started to walk along the left-hand aisle, admiring every detail. The windows were glassed, after all – all eight of them – and had been stained with the golden lion of Tamir, each displaying a different pose.

The woman bowed her head to Kanderil. "My name is Katanchi. It is a pleasure to meet you." Her voice was clear and melodic. She wore a simple full-sleeved dress of white cotton, tied at the waist. Her eyes were slim, slanted in a way Sarene had never seen before, while her long hair was so blonde that in the sunlight it seemed as pale as the dress.

"Kanderil. That is Sarene."

"An honour," Katanchi replied. "I am the Guide here, and I would be happy to discuss anything on your mind." She glanced over at Sarene, who was investigating an oil painting hanging between two of the windows, a finger running along the frame. "Both of you."

"Our thanks, my lady. We are hoping you could provide some information for us. We are searching for a Kalethi currently patrolling your area of the north. His name is Jared."

Sarene looked over at the mention of her brother. She scurried back towards them, keen to find out if the Guide would be able to help.

"Jared..." Katanchi replied. She gave an odd smile. "Yes, I know him. He was here no more than two days past. He stopped by to introduce himself."

Sarene clapped her hands, beaming a smile. Katanchi gave her a fond look.

"I am presuming that was the right answer, dear?"

"Jared is her brother," Kanderil explained. "She has news of a family emergency and it is important we find him."

"I see. Well, he said that he would complete his circuit once a week, give or take. There is a small quarry town a few miles to the east. Maybe you could wait there for him?"

Kanderil nodded. "Thank you." He made to turn, but

Sarene tugged at his arm again. He stopped, this time with a mild frown.

"Yes?"

Sarene pointed to Katanchi, using her other hand to gesture talking, clapping her thumb and fingers together. The Guide's smile was humble.

"We do not have time," Kanderil replied. He turned his attention to the woman. "My apologies. Perhaps we will return here on our way south."

"Perhaps," Katanchi countered. "Whenever you wish to talk, someone will be here to listen. That goes for both of you." She winked at Sarene, who giggled.

"I wish you well the rest of your day," said the woodsman.

"Thank you," said the woman, bringing her hands together. "I think I will get on with my sewing, then."

Sarene shoved her guardian as they walked away from the shrine, succeeding only in pushing herself off balance. Kanderil regarded her, his features unmoved.

"We do not have time for pleasantries."

She levelled her gaze at him, shaking her head.

"You want to find your brother, yes?"

Pointing back towards the Shrine, she held up one hand with fingers and thumb spread. Kanderil ignored her. Enough time had been wasted. They had been looking for Jared for almost two weeks now. Had he been travelling alone he would have already made contact.

The girl huffed, but made no further protest. As they followed a thin line of worn grass, an unofficial road crafted by the feet of many passing pilgrims, she looked across the countryside. Above, clouds were clustering, and the first of the autumn rains threatened. The glow from the sun hanging beneath them gave each a golden belly. She seemed pleased by the sight, for it made her smile.

Soon enough, Spasmodic appeared. The creature always

approached from behind, and Kanderil heard it coming only moments before it was beside them. He was starting to understand what it had meant about not requiring a horse.

"Did ya get me anythin'?" it asked.

"We are on the right path," Kanderil replied.

"Great. I was hopin' for puppies, frankly."

They walked as they often did; he in the lead, with Spasmodic beside Sarene, chatting nonsense at her. She was in the mood for it today, laughing her silent laugh along with several of its observations. This in turn encouraged it to giggle with her. Kanderil was curious that she had warmed to the creature so quickly, considering it had been created to assassinate her. It sometimes treated her with a complete disregard, but more often it acted pleased to have her attention.

As darkness fell they withdrew a short way from the road. They camped without a fire and ate stale bread with a sprinkling of salt and pepper. In the distance, lit windows stood out from a roadside tavern. Lanterns hung from outside, illuminating the stables and front garden.

"I'll keep watch," Spasmodic said aloud after Sarene had nodded off to sleep.

"No," said Kanderil. "I shall do it."

"C'mon, big man," the creature protested. "How much sleep do you get a night?"

"Enough to see me through the day."

"Bollocks. Maybe if you got more than a couple of hours you wouldn't be such a grumpy guts."

Kanderil did not reply. It smiled.

"Alright, forgive me there. But still. If we're gonna work as bestest friends here, you're gonna have to trust me at *some* point. I piss off when you ask me to, I didn't kill any of those buggers by the wagon back there, I done everythin' you said. When do I get a chance?"

Kanderil studied it for a long moment, searching for any hint of deception. It spoke the truth; it *had* done everything asked of it since Tamiran. And he was tired. He had pulled no more than six hours sleep in the last three days since leaving Fallerin's. He considered the dangers against the benefits, and decided it was important to be clear headed for their meeting with Jared. There was a lot to discuss.

"Fine. Wake me in four hours. If anyone comes, you know what to do."

"Yeah. Wave."

Kanderil did not laugh.

"Alright, alright. I get it."

The creature waited until Kanderil had closed his eyes and started to breathe heavily. Soon his face relaxed and his eyelids flickered.

Then it moved towards the roadside tavern, no differently drawn to the lights than the moths banging themselves against its windows.

Petar was drunk. He was sitting in the tavern garden, propped on a stool. Lug had staggered to bed a half-hour previous. Hawk had not been seen since supper. The tavern was almost empty, with no more than half a dozen guests. With some difficulty he ran a hand through his ginger hair, which reflected the lantern light above him. He had given up singing and was instead concentrating on sitting without falling over.

It was an interesting feeling to be this drunk. Balancing it was a delicate process. He was only a few sips of alcohol away from slumping over and passing out. He could entertain himself by merely being awake. The act of existence was hilarious and he would find himself just smiling, smiling on the verge of laughter, as he swayed this way, that way, back and forth. He would try and find the cloudy liquid falling from his cup as it splashed on the floor, but give up soon afterwards and go back to swaying.

It took a while for Petar to notice someone was standing in front of him.

Hawk was being a right bastard, to be sure. They had

been companions for a long time. To call themselves friends was perhaps a stretch, but Hawk had always been a confident man, someone who got results. The fact he had introduced them to a manner of theft which did not involve bloodshed was a definite positive. Petar was not adverse to violence; on the contrary, he enjoyed a good, honest brawl. But robbery with murder was a hanging offence, and he didn't much fancy departing this life from the end of a rope.

Hawk's recent manner grated on his nerves. He hated the feeling of being spoke down to, the sense that he was somehow inferior to his peers, and Hawk had certainly been stoking *that* particular fire over the last few days. Ever since he'd come to them with this current job, he'd been acting weird. Gone was the witty, cultured thief. Instead was a brooding individual who seemed to be hiding something.

He looked up and saw Hawk. "Hey," he slurred, his head lolling to one side. "Hey, you starin'? Moster, mister bloody Highnmighty? Hmm?"

Hawk giggled brightly. The sound didn't match him. "Nah mate, not starin'."

Petar blinked a few times. He tried to focus by closing one eye, glaring at Hawk over his own nose. Only, it wasn't Hawk. The figure was shorter and wore a long cavalry jacket. The hood was pulled up, and in this dim light Petar could see nothing but shadow where the face should be. It held its hands behind its back. He thought he could see blood red locks hanging either side of its chest.

"So what ya want?" Petar leaned forward, propping himself up on elbows crossed over knees. "What ya want there?" He felt one of those brief waves of sobriety which he knew would fade in seconds. It was as if the brain sometimes took control, realised the state of the body, and gave it back to the booze. *Call me when you're done with it.*

"What happened to you?" the figure asked. It sounded amused.

"I'm drunk," Petar said in a way which suggested that should be obvious. "An, an' if ya had any sense, y'would be as well."

"Why?"

The response caught him off guard. He understood that he had made a questionable statement, but perseverance was the key now. Backtracking was for weaker men. Petar decided to use a tried and trusted method to gain the upper hand when given the oldest question in the book. Why indeed.

"Why not?" he chuckled. The sound was thick with phlegm. "It's me bloody right to 'ave an a- (*cough*) an ale now an' then if I so please."

"So you *made* ya'self like this?" Another giggle. "You've gone idiot on purpose?"

"Aye!" Petar stood suddenly. His body protested, and it took another few seconds to collect his balance. "Who ya callin stupid, short-arse?"

The figure shrugged. "You. Now, don't bother gettin all hot, chuck. I just come to see what this place was like. Looks a bit dingy, eh."

Petar glared at the stranger a while longer, before turning one half-step to look at the building. He studied the architecture as bets he could; a simple tavern, with mortar covering log walls. A slanted roof, broad and thatched, dominated its shape. The windows were shuttered. He caught a lungful of the nearby stables and the fragrance made him wheeze again.

"Yeh, it's shit. But it's cheap, aye, an' it serves booze. 'Sides, me foot 'urts a bloody mighty. Grown-in toenail. But s'all good!""

"Right. Say, you ain't seen any sheep or summat round here?"

"Ya lost one?"

"Nah, I don't own any. I'm just hungry."

Petar's body caught still. As soon as he spoke, he started staggering again. "Oh, I geddit. Haha. One o' those, eh? Lonely in the night an want a bit o' warmth, aye- Haha, I yeah. Yeah, no. Haven't seen any. I prefer women. Big, fat women." He grinned, showing uneven teeth, and made some lecherous gestures with his hands and groin.

"That how you eat, mate?" the figure responded in a rush

of laughter. It bent forward with its legs stock straight, peering at him like he was some kind of exhibit.

"No, I tell you what I did see tho'," Petar continued before realising he was speaking to his own hand, which was now in front of his face. His other hand crossed it at the wrist, limp. He closed his eyes, not wanting to deal with them. "I tell you what I did see. I saw a woman today who was... was well, she was f'in *lovely* she was. Had those strange eyes, she did, all narrow and big at t'same time. Blonde, like, really blonde." He spat, but the saliva landed on his sleeve. "Couldn' see her tits tho. Was a bit disappointed if I tell t'truth."

"Sorry," said the stranger abruptly, "but you're probably the greatest human I've ever met." It laughed, the sound so infectious Petar couldn't help but join in.

"Aye, same to you!" he called in response, stepping back to fall onto his stool. He cheered, looking at his mug, which had tipped over during the talk.

"Keep on now, tell me more about this lady friend of yours."

Petar nodded, mumbling something even he didn't understand. He sniffed, slapping at his cheek as something buzzed against it. There was more speech, and he dimly heard a question being asked of him. When he looked up, the figure was gone. Petar wiped a string of drool from his mouth and made for the tavern door. It was hard work.

Spasmodic returned to where Sarene and Kanderil slept. It settled in near to them, leaning its head back so the hood came down past its nose.

"Something the matter?" Kanderil asked without opening his eyes. The voice was firm as ever.

"Alcohol is underrated," it responded.

Kanderil sniffed the air, but said nothing further. Spasmodic peered at him for a moment, waiting until the deep breathing resumed. Then it shut its eyes, allowing the waiting circles to descend.

Chapter Thirteen

"*W*e need a horse."

Kanderil spoke as they ate breakfast. Sarene had pilfered the last of the oat cakes on offer at the Shrine the day before, keeping them hidden until now. She'd feared a reprimand for taking them from the Shrine, but he had accepted his share with no more than a sideways glance.

"I don't need one," replied Spasmodic. "I'd quite like a sheep, tho'."

Kanderil ignored the comment. "Jared is travelling on horseback. We need to catch up."

Shaking her head, Sarene pointed to Jared's insignia - which she had pinned to her sleeve as quick reference point for him when signing - before mimicking a rider racing a horse. She then wagged a finger.

"You mean he will not be riding hard?" As she nodded, Kanderil placed another portion of his cake into his mouth, chewing and swallowing before continuing. "You are right. However, we still need to catch up with him before the Gathire do. Also, there is little dense cover in this area of Tamir. We might as well make good time if we have to move in the open." He brushed stray crumbs from his beard.

"So where do we get one, then?" asked Spasmodic around an entire cake it'd stuffed into its maw.

"How many were there at the stables?"

The creature choked on its oats. "Bats. What?"

"Last night, when you went there. How many?"

"No idea, weren't there. Wasn't me. These cakes are shit."

"You are a terrible liar." Kanderil was staring at him. Sarene had joined in, lacking the certainty of her guardian but making up for it with enthusiasm.

"Look, I just went to peek. I saw a drunk bloke having the *best* conversation with himself. I can't have been more than fi--"

"Irrelevant at the moment. How many horses were in the stable?"

"Dunno. Four?"

Kanderil nodded. "As long as there is likely to be one we can take."

Sarene exchanged glances with the creature. Eventually Spasmodic cackled, bouncing where it sat. "Wait, you're gonna *steal* one?"

"Yes. Purchasing a mount would leave further evidence of our whereabouts. Theft is simpler."

"Bollocks. You'd moan it was 'dishonourable'," the creature said in a poor imitation of the woodsman's low, rumbling speech.

"Perhaps under normal circumstances."

Blinking, Sarene closed her bag and reached for her cloak. She focused her attention on the toggle to try and mask her surprise. *I'm turning him into a thief,* she thought.

Wiping a cloth over his mouth Hawk sighed, pushing his plate away. The tavern wasn't much, but the food was decent. Fried ham with eggs over bread certainly set the foundations for a good day. He assessed the damage caused by the previous night's drinking. Lug seemed to be dealing with his hangover, but Petar was a mess. They'd had to pound against his door to wake him. He said he couldn't remember the final number of cupfuls, or what time he had called it a night. Lug recalled that when he went to bed Petar was still going strong by himself. Petar mumbled something in response before forcing down his breakfast along with a large pitcher of water.

"Do you serve coffee?" Hawk called to the barman, who was wiping down his service area.

"I do, but it's expensive," came the reply. "Pick it up off a merchant who makes t'run down Tamiran from Helais a few times a year."

"Bring him a cup," he said, nodding to Petar, who sat with his face buried in his hands. "I think he's willing to pay the price this morning."

"Ain't paying golds for it," muttered Petar through his fingers.

Hawk chuckled. "I will pick up the tab, my friend. Soon enough, money will be plentiful."

As the barman lifted a kettle from the fire and stepped into the kitchen, Lug watched Hawk closely. He seemed to be searching his for something. "You're convinced this is going to be the king of all paydays, aren't you."

"Yes," Hawk replied.

Lug held his gaze for a while longer. "Sod it," he said finally before raising his voice. "Make that two coffees."

"Not a problem," the bartender called through the doorway.

With the decision made, Lug turned back to his two associates. "So where we headed today? We got no real destination, have we?"

"What makes you say that?" asked Hawk.

"Well, we been riding north for a while now. If we were going to a town or summat, I reckon you would have said."

"True. And honestly, I have only a general idea of where to look. But I'll be able to tell if we have taken a wrong turn."

"How?" mumbled Petar.

"I had a good informant," Hawk replied, his voice smooth.

The light perfume of boiling coffee beans began to drift around them. Lug glanced towards the kitchen, a touch of excitement in his eyes. "I've never had this stuff before," he explained. "Always fancied but never thought it worth the silver."

"Silver?" Petar blurted out in a panic.

"Ease your mind," said Hawk. "I said I will pay for it."

They waited until the tavern keeper brought over two cups of steaming hot coffee on a tray. Beside them were a pot of sugar and a tiny jug of thin milk.

"What's this?" Lug asked, pointing to the accessories.

The tavern keeper shrugged. "Summat t'fancy places in Tamiran started doing. Makes t'coffee sweeter. Don't ask me. I just do what they do, since they sell the stuff like water t'rich folk."

Lug lifted one of the cups, inhaling deeply. He closed his eyes. Hawk tried hard not to laugh.

"Good?"

"Aye, 'tis." Grinning, Lug took his first sip. That grin froze in his eyes, and he hissed as the expression slowly turned to surprise, then disgust, resting finally on horror. He swallowed.

"Wha' hell is that?" he managed to say. "It's like bitter mud. Bugger me, I burnt my lip as well. Is it meant to be that hot?"

Hawk chuckled this time. "Try it with the milk and sugar. They make it much more palatable." He turned his attention to Petar, who was simply staring at the remaining cup. "It will make you feel better," he offered.

There was a noise from outside. A horse whinnied, and Hawk heard a muffled young voice yell.

"*Stop! S'not yours! Thief!*"

The three of them looked at each other before scrambling to their feet. They ran towards the exit, Lug first, Hawk just behind. As they rushed through, a horse came bolting past them from the stables, across the garden and out towards the road.

Hawk saw two figures on his horse. The passenger, slight with a purple hood pulled up, he did not recognise.

The rider he did. Kanderil.

"Get the horses," he said as Petar joined them.

"Weren't that yo--"

"*Get the horses!*" roared Hawk, furious that the poacher was escaping him again. He pulled free his sword, as if it were possible to engage the giant in combat from where he stood.

More mockery. More shame. More *hatred.*

Lug ran for the stable.

Chapter Fourteen

Without a second glance back, Kanderil rode hard. The horse was a fine animal and it was covering ground at a considerable pace given the weight it carried. His experience with horses left him keenly aware that he must to be careful not to overwork the animal. Kanderil's bulk came with some drawbacks.

Sarene leaned forward against his back, holding on tight. He'd never asked if she had ridden before. It made sense that she would have, coming from a farming community. Handling horses was a regular part of such a lifestyle and it was rare to meet a citizen of the countryside who could not ride to some extent. The way she gripped him, however, suggested she was unfamiliar with letting the horse run.

The shouts behind them had been disappointing. He had hoped to make a clean getaway. While the theft had been necessary, such knowledge would give little comfort to the owner of the horse. Something in those cries concerned him, though. There was more than anger or frustration. More than disbelief. There was a definite *rage* there.

If they were being pursued then they would do well not to get caught.

Scanning ahead for trails or walkways as a means to get off of the main road, he urged the mare on. At this speed, turning across the grassland was dangerous. A pothole, a rabbit warren, an embedded stone could all easily injure the mount. Better to wait a short while until they could make a smooth transition away from the road.

"Hey," a voice yelled through the air whipping at them as they rode. "You're being followed."

Glancing to his left, Kanderil saw Spasmodic running beside them. Each step it took carried it several yards. Its coat rippled against its thin frame and its dreadlocks flailed around its head.

"How many?" he called back.

"Three, on two horses. Man, they're pissed. Well, one of 'em is. He keeps waving his sword around and raging about you." It looked behind him and grinned. "Oi, stop starin', miss."

Kanderil could not see Sarene, but presumed she looked just as astonished by its movements as he felt.

"I can go and deal with them if y'want," Spasmodic continued. The words came as casually as they could under the conditions.

"No," Kanderil replied. "I'm going to turn off the road soon. When I do, I need you to get rid of the tracks."

"What? How d'ya expect me to do that? They're not miles away, y'know."

Raising a brow, he indicated the thing's current speed with a small nod.

The creature giggled. "Oh, right. You people can't do this." It eased its pace, dropping out of sight.

A few minutes later a small trail cut open in the grass. Ahead was a cluster of woodland some half-mile across, encircled by dead stumps, nestled against an old logger's cabin. Kanderil steered the horse off the road and thundered across the plain, heading for the trees. The mare's hooves kicked up dust as they drummed against the dry ground. Kanderil did not risk looking behind, hoping the creature was able to do its job.

He slowed at the last second, pulling on the reins as they neared the trees. The horse snorted in irritation at the sudden command, catching its breath. Kanderil encouraged it to enter the woods as Sarene relented in her fierce grip, separating from him. As soon as they were hidden from the road, he motioned for her to slip from the saddle. The girl looked a little pale but otherwise fine.

As Kanderil led them further into the woods, Spasmodic returned.

"Done. Road looks buggered now," it said. "No hoof-shapes left, anyway."

Soon after they heard more horses on the road. Kanderil placed a hand on the hilt of his great sword, listening for any change in the sound to suggest the riders had left the road and were crossing the grass. The air around them was still; none of the leaves around them rustled, and even the crickets appeared to hush.

After what seemed like hours, the sounds of pursuit began to fade. Kanderil patted the horse's flank. "This beast deserves the credit for escaping."

"Yeah, cos the fuckin thing did good hiding its own dirty tracks," Spasmodic said with a sneer.

"You did well."

The creature eyed him momentarily, suspicious. Then a grin sneaked across its chalk white face. "Cheers."

Kanderil nodded. "They will be looking for us along the road. We will have to be careful."

"Heh. They can join the back o' the line. Though, what's the point of a horse now? We're back to where we started."

"That's where you come in." He looked down at it, folding his arms across his chest.

"See, when you do that, you generally say something bad." Spasmodic folded its own arms in imitation, pulling a rather good facial impression of the Hunter. Kanderil did not laugh.

"Ever wondered what it's like to be a scout?" he said.

"No." Spasmodic waited, but no further words came. Kanderil continued to stare. It resisted for as long as it could.

"Oh. I mean, yes. Eh, what's she got?"

Kanderil followed the creature's gaze to where Sarene stood. The flap to the travel bags tied to the horse's saddle was open. The girl was looking through a small journal, her gaze running along the pages as she flipped through them.

"I was not aware you could read," Kanderil said. Sarene merely nodded as her fingers came to a rest roughly in the centre of the book. After a few moments of silence she bit her lip, concern sweeping her adolescent features. Hurrying over to them, holding out the journal with pages displayed, she pointed insistently at the words scrawled across them. Kanderil reached over and took it from her. He started to read.

> *-ace at which my heart beats. His face haunts me and i long for the day i will end him. Kanderil laughs each time i close my eyes. He stares at me while i sleep, and he will not let me rest. I cannot bear the shame of his taunting and how he seems to know my every thought and what i intend to do to him. But i know i will be the end of Kanderil. I will place the sword deep into his gut and wrench it twist it and draw it clear with blood and fire. I will make him scream as he makes me scream. The shame will pour clean from me as his life falls free of his body. I hope you can hear me Kanderil, for i am the bringer of death. I will send your soul from this world to the next. The days of y--*

Kanderil looked up. His tried to recall a name or a face of anyone who could possibly harbour such a deep hatred of him. He came up blank. Whoever wrote this meant to kill him. That much was clear. He flicked through a few more pages. The text, spindled and blotched with ink, looked to have been scribbled at high speed, bordering on unintelligible. Words tended to repeat themselves. There were several references to the writer's guilt, his shame and embarrassment. The author focused on ways in which Kanderil would be made to suffer. His name appeared every other sentence. There was a recurring mention of revenge.

Curious, he looked back at the earlier entries in the journal. These were much calmer, written with a patient hand. They spoke of everyday thoughts, the commentary being of travel plans and recent encounters with travellers on the road. Along the border were numbers with a date. There was no mention of Kanderil at all.

He realised Sarene was watching him. Spasmodic turned its attention from her to him and back again.

"So is someone gonna tell me the joke?"

"It appears," Kanderil said, "that I have an enemy."

They left after an hour. Spasmodic took off ahead with instructions to return should it discover any sign of the men who had chased them from the tavern, the Gathire or any Kalethi scouts. Kanderil still had reservations about trusting the creature to perform the task, but he was inclined to believe it would. He was beginning to realise that Spasmodic generally *attempted* to do what was asked of it. It seemed to get distracted sometimes, was all.

Sarene sat behind him as they rode, reading the journal. To learn that she could read was a plus point. A thought occurred to him.

"Can you write?"

Sarene looked up as he turned in the saddle. She nodded, hair bouncing around her face.

"Why do you not carry a journal of your own?"

The girl shrugged, going back to the words in her hands. Kanderil turned back around. There was nothing up ahead, so he kicked the horse into a gallop. He felt Sarene grab onto his jerkin with one hand.

That anybody would wish him such harm came as something of a shock. Kanderil had no enemies he could think of. He had served in the Kalethi with honour and distinction, aware of the respect with which he was viewed. There had been no ongoing conflicts with which to become somebody's nemesis. Bandits and raiders seldom took personal offence to confrontations with the military. It was a hazard of their chosen profession. He had never courted another's wife, cheated someone out of money or possessions - *besides this horse*, he thought - or humiliated another man with his fists. Try as he might, he could not understand why someone would despise him so utterly.

Kanderil rode in a sensible manner. He would push the horse hard for short periods before dropping back to a canter. The beast had shown few signs of protest so far. Kanderil had stopped at a small cluster of buildings along the road to pull water from a well, allowing the horse to drink. The well was in the centre of a simple rest stop, the buildings providing a few basic needs such as food and blankets. No children played in the street, and the two men he saw were both well into their senior years. The place had an air of depression about it and Kanderil soon moved them on.

It wasn't until a few hours past noon that Sarene knocked on his broad back. He started to turn, but stopped just before he hit the journal with his cheek. He took the offered book, slowing the horse to a walk before reading.

Today was a poor day. We found a poacher in the woods. We had him three to one but were foolish to approach while he held a bow in his hands. The man was huge, bigger than any I have seen before. He appeared closer to some sort of ogre than a human. He spoke with a confidence I must admit to being swayed by. We asked for his money and he refused. We threatened to attack but he promised that one of us would die before we reached him. The way he held himself, such an argument was difficult to resist. Perhaps we would have left, but he proceeded to insult us by throwing his days catch to us. Offering to provide our lunch, he said. I almost attacked him then, just to prove a point, but we left. We took the rabbits. This encounter was humbling, to say the least. Hopefully our next mark will be more rewarding.

"You can understand all of these words?" said Kanderil.

There were a few that he had trouble with himself. She simply nodded, giving another of those casual thumbs-up. "Well, you are correct. This is me. I remember that encounter. It took place a few days before I met you. Though, why the man would be so furious over this..." He handed the book back. "I do not know. But this is not important. We must focus on finding your brother."

The next afternoon Spasmodic returned. He had not come back when Kanderil and Sarene had made camp for the night, or during the morning after. Kanderil had readied the horse soon after dawn and they rode much the same as they had before. The ground was not as even as it had been in the Meadows and much of the ride was along a mild slope. The road they followed would eventually lead to Fasherai, several days north. Tilldown, which was the end point of Jared's assigned route, could be reached by the late evening if they rode hard. Around them, the forests were receding away to the east, revealing a great expanse of open moorland, like a carelessly strewn quilt of jade velvet. The land appeared folded up, like some great being had gently pressed the ground from beneath.

Sarene had finished the journal, giving up halfway through the period where the writer had started raving about her guardian. The language became ugly and hateful within a single page, and was so vicious and mean that she'd closed the book and tucked it back into one of the saddlebags. They had found some provisions there the previous evening, and she'd been delighted to discover a fresh apple along with some more oatcakes, all wrapped in a handkerchief. Apparently, oatcakes were popular amongst travellers.

Kanderil reined in the horse as the creature approached. It was out of breath for the first time since they'd met; its pallid, hollow cheeks were flushed with colour.

"I think I found her brother," it said.

Sarene blinked, hesitant to believe it. Her heart raced.

"Where?" asked Kanderil.

"Up ahead. Might take you three-maybe-four hours or so to get there if you run that thing properly." It gestured to the horse, which ignored it.

"What makes you think it is him?"

"He looks like her," Spasmodic replied with a smirk. "Same hair, same stubby nose, same 'orrible smell. You have any clue how much you humans stink?"

Sarene choked back a laugh. She didn't want to accept this good fortune just yet. Didn't *dare*. Not until she had seen him for herself. She patted Kanderil's arm, encouraging him to get going.

"Get back there. Tell him we're coming to meet him."

"What about that whole 'ooh, I'm scary' thing?"

"Once he finds out what trouble his sister is in, your appearance will be the least of his worries." Kanderil dug his heels into the horse's flank and the animal kicked into a run. Spasmodic hurtled past them in a blur of motion and was soon out of sight.

Sarene clutched onto Kanderil as they rode. Her thighs were burning and her spine was aching from bouncing in the saddle for so long, but she ignored the discomfort. She thought of what she would do when she finally caught up with her brother – and then grinned. The *first* thing she wanted was her hug, and for Jared to tell her everything was going to be alright.

Excitedly, she whacked Kanderil's side with her palm. Hard.

Kanderil yelled at the horse in response and flicked the reins harder. The rate at which the road passed beneath them increased. Above, the clouds which had been building over the last day finally opened and a delicate rain started to fall on the eager plains below.

Glaithe was nothing if not observant.

He had located one of the horses which had fled during

the confrontation with the giant and the demon. Overtaking his former Gathire colleagues was imperative, so he had ridden hard to the north, out of the Meadows. He never drifted more than a few miles apart from the dark riders, keeping them in sight with his small telescope.

Once he was confident the Gathire were heading towards Fasherai, the largest city in the north of Tamir, Glaithe pushed on. He swapped out his horse at a roadside way station, paying a small amount of coin for the privilege. The replacement he took was hardly good stock but it was fresh. He forced the animal to gallop for a full afternoon until he reached the crossroads splitting the northern moorland from Horhai Lake. There he relented, his mount exhausted, and waited.

He had called in a favour from the Gathire informant working for the Kalethi before departing Tamiran. The weasel of a man knew plenty about the patrol areas in this region, and revealed that this crossroads was a common crossover point for the scouts. Glaithe had deduced from the Kalethi assignment schedule that the girl's brother, Jared, should be nearing this point of his circuit barring any reason to be delayed or hurried.

He could not work with possibilities. He preferred meticulously careful estimates.

This was one such estimate. Glaithe had a likely location, a description, a timeframe and a known route for backup if required.

So the next morning, when Jared appeared on the main road, he was already prepared to follow. He maintained a good distance, using his telescope to keep watch on the unsuspecting Kalethi. It was obvious that Sarene was still trying to contact him; why else would the young sorcerer be travelling this way? Northern Tamir offered little in the way of hiding spots. If the girl was looking to flee the country then south towards Franthia would have been the more efficient choice from Tamiran. Kanderil would know this.

Besides, her father had mentioned that Jared could be the reason for her initial disappearance. Right after Glaithe had split the man's lip open and then stared, deliberately, at his three terrified sons.

He smiled at the memory.

Glaithe had been following since the previous afternoon, watching the Kalethi trot his way along the road which snaked through the undulating terrain, the young scout devoid of urgency. Still, it made him easy to follow and it allowed the following Gathire squad to catch up.

What *hadn't* been anticipated was the red haired demon appearing first, without the girl. The monster, covering ground at a frightful pace, caught up with Jared and stopped him in his saddle. Glaithe adjusted his telescope and focused in on them.

They appeared to be having a conversation.

———◄O►———

Jared wheeled his mount around when he heard the sharp whistle. Something was approaching him at an incredible speed. He pulled free his sabre, the weapon hanging low by his side. There was a low whispering coming from the blurred object, silky and textured. The thing was almost upon him. His horse reared, and Jared raised his weapon as the drizzle turned to rain.

The blur turned into a man. Only, it wasn't a man at all. Whatever it was had vivid crimson dreadlocks and wore a deep green cavalry coat. It had claws where its fingers should be and grinning, pointed teeth. Jade green eyes fixed on him as it slid to a halt, the damp gravel beneath its booted feet crunching as it did.

"Now," it said in a curious voice, "what is it 'bout me that makes people pull out their weapon as soon as they see me."

As soon as the horse dropped back to all four hooves, Jared charged. He swung the sabre down towards the creature, his mount swerving to the left at the last moment. The creature whipped an arm up and deflected the blade with the back of its hand. The connection was like striking steel. Jared gripped with his calves, tugging on the mount's reins to keep himself facing the sinful looking creature. The gelding snorted, nostrils flaring in fear.

"You, heh," the thing said before giving a short chuckle. It tilted its head, eyes gleaming. "You really shouldn't be doin that, matey."

"Give me one reason why," Jared demanded.

"Well, apart from the fact I'd *kill* you, I'm on your side." It dropped its aggressive posture and stood up straight, offering an animated wave. "Hi! My name's Spasmodic."

Jared shook his head, tightening the grip on his sabre. "I tend not to make friends with those who rush me. Especially when they're inhuman."

"Oh, c'mon. I didn't rush you, I'm just working to a schedule here." The creature muttered to itself, seeming to forget all about him.

Jared squirmed a little in his saddle.

"I'm presuming," he said hesitantly, "that since you're introducing yourself that you're not going to attack."

"Hah, attack you? Do I give off that vibe?" The creature asked, clearly amused. Then, a quick gesture with one of those terrible hands. "Actually you kinda answered that a moment ago. Nevermind." It coughed. "No, I'm not here to hurt you. I've been lookin for you for the last couple o' weeks. Well, we have."

Jared sat back, water dripping from his chin. "Go on."

"Look, there's a whole load of shit gone on, but the basics of it is I'm with Sarene. She's in a bucket of mess and she's been looking for you. She's back down th-"

"Whoa, wait," said Jared quickly, raising a hand. "Sarene? Where is she?"

"I was about to say, she's back down the road. She's with an older guy. They're sharing a horse." Spasmodic thumbed over his shoulder.

"You're not making any sense, demon. What ab-"

"Oh, you can cut out the *demon* gubbins right away," Spasmodic barked at him. "I'm gettin a bit tired of it. Maybe you're all demons and I'm the normal one, ever think of that? Huh?"

Taking a deep breath, Jared sheathed his sword. "Please. Start again."

Spasmodic sighed. "Your little sister, Sarene – you know her, right? – Well, she's back down the road. She's in trouble, she's being chased by some right shady buggers and she needs your help. If we go back that way we can meet her and the big man who's lookin after her. Geddit?"

"Why should I trust you?"

"Because it's your *sister*, you tit. What bloody reason would I have to come and make all this stuff up? I don't even know you. Besides, aren't you meant to serve the public?" It held its arms wide, beaming, and shook its hips. "Well, I'm public, baby. Come serve it up."

Jared considered this. It was a fair point. But the thing looking at him... The way it spoke, the way it never stood still, the way it *grinned*... He fought down a sense of discomfort. He leant forward to whisper to his mount, trying to soothe it. It was scared of the creature. Jared could relate.

"If you're tricking me," Jared said, "I'll send you back to the pit you came from."

"Actually came from a table," replied Spasmodic as it turned and started jogging south along the road. "You ride, I'll match your speed," it called.

Jared complied with one hand on the hilt of his blade.

Glaithe's horse galloped across the plains, heading south. He was running over several calculations to determine the direction he should move and the instructions he would need to give to his former associates.

The fact that the demon had reached Jared first was something he should have expected. Sent out to do its master's bidding, no doubt. He was certain the dreadlocked Familiar was responsible for Pramith's murder back in Tamiran. The girl had fled with it. Everyone, including the Gathire, had assumed she'd been kidnapped.

On the contrary.

At this speed he had to rely on his natural vision rather than the telescope. It didn't matter. The estimates he'd made were correct. He saw the Gathire cantering across an area of grassland, heading toward the road. They were spread wide but drew together as Glaithe approached. He wore dark clothing but not the uniform of his old faction. It was standard protocol to meet any unknown approaching figure as a unit.

As he closed into range the central Agent held up his hand. He was a stocky man. The fact that his stirrups came only to the second notch announced that he was not very tall. Glaithe reined in his mount.

"Greetings, my friends."

"Glaithe," replied the Agent. "Fancy meeting you here. Word is you've been retired."

"Perhaps," Glaithe responded with a smirk. "I am presuming you are still open to information, Jonase."

Jonase considered this. He glanced to his right. Another of the Agents nodded. "Do you have any to give?"

"Well, I would not be this far north on my own time."

The Agent paused. "Go on."

"I believe the man wanted for Pramith's death is heading south. If you head south east from here and hold a steady line you'll intercept him."

The Gathire looked at each other.

"Why tell us?"

"I have no sword," said Glaithe, producing a sheepish smile. "I was merely tracking the man. I would hope a full squad of Agents could bring him down."

Jonase smiled. "And you would take the credit, of course. I know you too well, Glaithe."

"Come, now. Why would I seek credit as a civilian? I simply want justice for a friend."

"How noble." The words were thick with sarcasm.

"Believe what you will. Pramith died under my command. If you want to cut his killer off you'll need to leave now. Take it or leave it." Glaithe held Jonase's gaze.

Neither man backed down.

"Form up," Jonase said finally. "Let's get going. We shall see if our old comrade here is worth his word." The Agents turned their mounts, keeping in formation. The horses were well trained; only one snorted as it wheeled around. As they galloped away, Glaithe offered a wave.

As soon as they were a fair distance, he proceeded further south, also edging towards the road.

The demon had to have come from somewhere.

◀◯▶

Spasmodic ran alongside Jared. The horse's sluggish pace was irritating. It could not understand why the beast couldn't match its speed; why *nothing* could, for that matter. Was making the effort so difficult? Spasmodic sniffed, peering up at Jared, who was pointedly ignoring it. Fair enough, it thought. Maybe the boy needs some explanation from another human.

They'd been moving for well over an hour when the dark riders appeared. They were heading in from the west, seeking to intercept them on the road. Five of them in a V formation. Spasmodic whistled. When Jared looked down at him, the creature pointed.

"Hey, check it out," it yelled.

Jared did so. "Gathire," he replied over the sound of hooves beating the ground. He made to pull up.

"Yeah. They're chasing you and your sister."

"What!?"

The mount neighed but did not slow.

"Yeah. Keep it casual, like. Maybe they'll ignore us." Spasmodic lifted its hood up over its head and tugged, concealing as much of its face as possible.

"Why are they after her?"

"Look, the less I have to yap the happier I'll be. For now, just keep movin', aye?" It waved one hand as if it were a sprinting prophet, providing revelation. "Big man will explain all."

"Who's 'big man'?"

"Kanderil." Spasmodic giggled. "Oh, you'll love him."

A horn blew a single, protracted note. It ignored the sound, but Jared looked over. "They're coming to cut us off," he exclaimed anxiously.

"Helpful of ya to say so, thanks."

"Maybe I should stop and find out what they want."

Laughing brightly, it kept running through the rain. Jared matched pace with it. It could hear the Gathire fall in behind them, hooves thundering along the path. Spasmodic called up to Jared.

"You get goin'. Sarene'll be along here somewhere. Look for a huge fella riding a brown one of these things."

"What are you going to do?" asked Jared.

"Public relations." Spasmodic skidded to a halt, a shower of damp gravel erupting from its heels. Jared accelerated away from it, the horse neighing as the creature dropped from sight.

It rubbed its hands together in anticipation, turning to face the five Gathire, dropping low to a crouch. With one arm between its bent legs it leaned forwards, claws splayed out on the ground. It grinned as the Gathire approached. It giggled as they slowed to a halt.

"You there," the lead Agent called. "You're under arrest, in the name of the King and of the Assembly."

"What for?"

"Murder and kidnapping."

"Well, shit." Spasmodic chuckled. It knew only the lower half of its face was visible beneath the hood. Rain was dripping from the rim. It could smell fear on at least two of them. "Didn't know your laws applied to me. Y'know, being a *demon* an' all."

"You'll be executed publically," one of the other Agents yelled. "Burnt at the stake."

"Have to get me there first."

"Where is the girl?"

"Ate her."

Swords were unsheathed then. Spasmodic heard the

blades sing as they were pulled free. It looked up to see five gleaming points aimed at it. A shiver of excitement ran up its spine.

"Hey, you better mean it when you do things like that," it said playfully.

"Give yourself up," the lead Agent warned, his upper lip curling into a sneer.

Spasmodic stood suddenly. Its coat tails fluttered down around its calves, the thin leather rippling like a ship's sail. It held out its arms straight, wrists together.

"Come get me."

The five Gathire dismounted. They stepped around the hooded creature, maintaining at a safe distance, forming a circle around it. Their swords remained extended, the rain making the steel glisten.

"You have no idea who you're facing," said one of the dark riders.

"See, I'm sure your mate in the city thought the same thing," Spasmodic replied. "Right up until I slashed his throat."

The five men charged. Spasmodic leapt upwards towards the first of its targets. It rotated in the air, avoiding the five sword points as they came together. One taloned hand flicked out at an amazing speed. There was a solid connection as it somersaulted over the victim. A cry of agony made it grin as it landed –

Landed directly in the path of an oncoming attack. Spasmodic ducked, rotating at the hip, but it failed to avoid the Agent's strike completely. The sword cut through his jacket, leaving a shallow gash in its forearm. Blood oozed from the wound. Spasmodic cartwheeled away from another assailant, this time from its right.

The man it had clawed fell to the ground, clutching his face. His cries were becoming difficult, as though he were trying to breathe through mud.

"Pfft, that all ya got?" it spat as the four remaining Gathire fanned around him. They moved in unison, blades twirling, unfazed by the pouring rain. *These buggers are well trained,* Spasmodic thought; *must have practised for ages.*

Spasmodic surged towards the Agent to its left. It used its claws to backhand the man's attempted block, spearing him to the ground with its shoulder. As soon as they hit the floor Spasmodic mounted him, tearing open the man's throat with a flick of its wrist. Blood sprayed into the air, splashing red across the dull yellow grass. The creature just managed to see the fear in his eyes before they went vacant. It grinned, rolling off of the body just as a sword sliced the air, aimed at its neck. The blade connected with hair only.

Spasmodic came up to one knee, turning, just as two of the remaining three Gathire rushed it. It hurdled over the first blade, the lead Agent dropping to one knee to aim his swing low.

It didn't quite clear the second, as the waiting Agent had concealed his attack with an elaborate feint. The man whirled around at the last moment and, with both hands, brought his sword up in a viciously sweeping arc.

Already in flight, Spasmodic was helpless.

The blade carved into the left side of its chest. Pain exploded through its torso as several ribs separated. It saw its own deep red blood spill out of its body. In response, Spasmodic screamed.

The sound was pure, frenzied rage.

Landing in a crouch, the creature immediately sprung backwards towards the two Agents. One of them managed to block, retreating in alarm, but the other man was too late. Spasmodic was upon him, raking and clawing, the man shrieking in abject terror before collapsing to the ground with a score of appalling gashes across his upper body. Spasmodic kept moving, ducking an attack from behind only to spin on its heel, rounding a kick at the Agent's head. Its boot impacted with such force that the man's jaw shattered. He fell unconscious to the ground, dropping his weapon.

Spasmodic turned on the last Gathire standing only to find that he had drawn his crossbow. It roared in bloodlust as the man fired.

———◄○►———

The bolt hit the horse high in the neck, just behind its right ear. The mare's legs buckled. Kanderil turned in the saddle, his feet slipping out of the stirrups, and grabbed Sarene. He managed to wrap his huge arms around her just as the horse rolled. They hit the ground hard with him taking the brunt of the impact.

"Are you okay?" he asked, catching his breath. The girl nodded, dazed. He let go. "Stay here. Do not get up."

Kanderil stood to discover three men were heading towards them on foot. They were not Gathire. Beyond them was a small outcrop of rock where they must have hidden. Kanderil reached for his bow; he'd attached it to the saddle instead of wearing it across his back, to make room for Sarene sitting behind him. Before he could grasp it he heard the twang of a crossbow. He threw himself to the floor, the bolt whistling over his head.

"Kanderil!" someone yelled. The call was venomous. Kanderil pushed himself up to observe the approaching men. The lead one he recognised.

The man from the forest. The bandit. Hawk.

"*Kanderil!*" Hawk had his weapon drawn and was only yards away. Kanderil rose to meet him as he vaulted the horse. The sword came slashing down, ringing out a note in the air. Kanderil leaned out of the way, backing off. Pressing the attack, Hawk kept swinging wildly, his eyes livid. There was no coordination to the assault. Kanderil had to keep retreating, drawing his assailant with him, avoiding the singing blade. To his relief the cut-throat was ignoring Sarene, who had huddled against the still body of the horse.

The two other bandits were reloading their crossbows.

"No!" yelled Hawk as he heard the pull-string click into place. "He's mine."

Kanderil narrowed his eyes. "How hav-"

Catching his breath, Hawk stepped towards him. "You keep your mouth shut, you *bastard*!" He swung again.

Kanderil was ready this time. He dived to the side, the blade missing him by inches. Rolling to his feet, coming up with a long smear of dirt along his arm, the Hunter waited. The ground was damp and he caught the scent of the earth.

"This is your last day, poacher," snarled the cut-throat through gritted teeth. Kanderil could sense the man's hatred emanating like heat from a bed of coals. "I've been looking forward to this."

When Kanderil said nothing, Hawk came for him again, swinging low. A faint glow was visible around the sword as he hopped back away from it. Hawk rolled his wrist, ripping the blade across Kanderil's stomach. He barely managed to avoid it, the steel tip scoring a mark through his jerkin.

In his peripheral vision, Sarene jerked in fright.

"Where is your laughter now?" Hawk said. The words were like a curse, born of loathing. "Where is your grin, huh?" He swiped the blade between each question. "Why aren't you *laughing?*"

Kanderil moved a fraction too late, his upper arm caught by the edge of the blade. He heard a cracking hiss against his skin. Kanderil grunted, but kept his focus. Hawk laughed.

"Look, poacher. Look well. You'll be losing more than this."

"You talk too much."

The reply infuriated Hawk once more, who launched another frenzied assault. He lashed out again and again, as though having to fight through the rainfall to reach him. Kanderil bent at the waist, doubling over as the blade *whoosh*ed past his midriff. The flurry of attacks continued. Backing off, Kanderil led his opponent in a circle. He refused to be pushed too far from Sarene--

Sarene, who was now in the grip of Hawk's two companions. She was being held around the waist, her arms flailing against the flame haired man who restrained her. The other bandit still had his crossbow in hand.

Capitalising on the distraction, Hawk managed to score another wound, carving the muscle of the giant's thigh with another bizarre *hiss*. Kanderil was tiring against the smaller and faster cut-throat, each dodge requiring a little more effort. The longer this took, the more perilous his situation became.

Hawk knew this too. With a terrible grin he charged at Kanderil, the blade at his side. At the last moment Hawk swung the sword around high, seeking to cleave through Kanderil's neck.

Sarene looked away, shutting her eyes.

The Hunter stepped in to meet the attack. He shoved a hand out to palm the flat of the blade upwards, glancing it away. A searing heat flared at the point of contact. With all the strength he could muster, Kanderil whipped a ferocious backhand into Hawk's cheek. There was a sickening crunch as the man's head snapped to the side. The cut-throat fell to the ground, his body limp.

The other two bandits winced.

Aware of hooves on the road, Kanderil looked up. A Kalethi scout was approaching fast. Spasmodic was nowhere to be seen. Kanderil bent down to pick up the sword Hawk had dropped.

It burned his hand when he gripped the hilt. Kanderil recoiled in pain.

"Let the girl go!" the scout yelled as he drew closer, pulling free his sabre.

"No!" replied Petar, the man holding her. He drew a knife and held it against the side of Sarene's throat. "Back off!"

"He'll do it!" said Lug in support of his friend. "Get away!"

"They won't kill her," said Kanderil, limping towards the dead horse. He shook his hand a few times, trying to relieve his singed fingers. "She's worth too much money."

"I will!" Petar protested. "I'll finish her off right now!"

"Let go of her," the scout demanded. He dismounted as he reached them, running for Sarene. When Petar pressed the knife against her neck, however, he halted.

"We're gonna back off nice an' slow," said the bandit. "If you try an' follow us, she'll be bleedin' on the ground."

"I seen him do it," said Lug, nodding and shaking his head at the same time. In this rain, the bandit smelled rank as a wet mongrel. "All nasty like, I wouldn't push him!"

Kanderil reached the horse. Casually he retrieved the bow and one of the arrows from the bound quiver beside it.

"Hey, uh," said Petar with panic quickly rising in his voice.

"You will not kill her," Kanderil repeated. He notched the arrow. "We have had this discussion before; if you do, you die also. So you let her go and walk away."

The two bandits looked at each other. "No, we, uh..."

"Who hired you to find her?"

"We..." Petar looked blank.

Lug spoke up. "Hired him." He pointed to the still body of Hawk. "He was hired. We're working with him."

"So you do not even know where to take her?" asked Kanderil in a patient voice despite his heavy breathing.

The two bandits looked at each other. Neither of them spoke.

"Then it seems you are at a loss. Let her go, walk away."

"Bu-- *Ow!*"

Sarene stamped on Petar's foot. Yelping in pain, he hopped back. The knife fell harmlessly to the ground.

"S'mah bad foot!" the man cried. "You lil'-"

Kanderil pulled the bowstring. Tension produced a creak from the body of the huge weapon. "Walk away," he said in a manner which made the two bandits freeze. Petar still held his foot. Lug licked his lips. Eventually the latter pointed to Hawk's form.

"What 'bout him?"

"He comes with me."

The bandits looked at each other. Eventually Lug spat, then wiped his mouth. "Forget it. Ain't no job worth dyin' over." He grabbed Petar's shoulder, encouraging him to follow. Together they started walking back to the rocky ambush site where their horses were no doubt tethered.

Sarene ran towards the scout. She all but knocked him over with the force of her impact. The Kalethi swept her up into a deep embrace, swinging her around in a circle.

"Brighteyes," he breathed. "What are you *doing* here?"

With a smile which reached from ear to ear, Sarene lifted her arm to show him the Kalethi insignia pinned to her sleeve. He took a step back, his handsome features producing a lop-sided grin. Just as Kanderil had pointed out when first meeting the girl, he clearly understood that the item was almost worthless – and yet he reacted well, intuitively understanding *why* Sarene had ventured so far away from home, and pulled her into another tight hug. If this man wasn't her brother, he certainly had a talent for empathy.

Once Lug and Petar had ridden away, Kanderil checked the extent of his injuries. The skin of his palm was blistered slightly, so he wrapped his hand in a linen bandage recovered from one of the saddlebags. He was at a loss to explain why Hawk's blade would have scalded him. Satisfied his other wounds required no immediate attention, he leant on his bow.

"I presume you are Jared," he said in good time.

The scout nodded, one arm around Sarene's shoulders. The girl was beaming up at him with relief, clinging on as though he might otherwise disappear.

"Yeah, that's right. I was told to come here by that demon..." Jared paused, looking over his shoulder. "Oh, wait. He didn't make it?"

"What?" Kanderil replied.

"He stopped to face a squad of Gathire who tried to head us off. Told me to keep riding until I reached you. What is all this about?"

"I will explain when I get back," Kanderil said, limping towards Jared's horse. "Stay here with your sister. How far away was it?"

"Can't have been much more than three miles."

He hauled himself into the saddle, wincing. Steering the horse around, Kanderil flicked the leather reins hard, digging in his heels. The horse sped off along the road as Jared and Sarene watched, arm in arm.

Chapter Fifteen

*G*laithe approached the devil lying on the road. Scattered around it were five Gathire bodies. At least four of them were dead. They looked like they'd been mauled by a pack of bears.

He dropped to one knee next to the dreadlocked creature. Oh, but it was a *fearsome* thing! Lethal in combat, he had seen it in action and scarcely believed his eyes. The Gathire were among the best swordsmen in the land, with rigorous training exercises a part of everyday life. They learnt to fight as a unit, to cover each other's backs and join together to attack the same target from multiple sides and angles at once. If a man couldn't fight he couldn't be an Agent, regardless of his skills in other areas. It was that simple.

The demon had torn them to shreds within two minutes.

Glaithe reached out with one hand, grasping the demon's shoulder. He started to turn it onto its back, pulling his dagger from his belt inch by creeping inch. *Better to make certain*, he thought.

The creature rolled over suddenly. Glaithe jumped, sheathing his dagger again. It was the correct move, for the thing opened its eyes. They took a moment to focus before taking him in.

"Ahh... shit," it uttered. "Do I have to kill you as well?" Its voice was strained and low. The filthy shirt it wore was now a deep scarlet as blood seeped through the cotton.

"No," Glaithe replied coolly. "I saw them attack you. I'm here to help." His mind was racing as he considered the situation he found himself in.

"Well ain't you the-" it coughed. The action brought a twisted grimace of pain and it wrapped an arm around its chest. "...Shit," it said again, snarling.

So where are we going with this, he thought to himself. *Making friends with the devil?*

No. Once he had the demon's confidence it would relax. Then he would cut its throat.

"Lay still. Try not to talk." Glaithe stood. "I have a needle and thread in my packs. We should close that wound." He walked back to his horse. The air was motionless around them despite the rain. The terrain was picturesque here and the colours were full and rich, the moors glistening with precipitation, but the world felt somehow empty, like a landscape painting. He pulled a roll of bandage and a leather pouch from his saddlebag and then returned to the creature, which had closed its eyes again.

He started to stitch. The chest wound was deep. As he pulled the flesh together he felt the ribs beneath shift. When the monster growled in response, Glaithe shushed it as though it were a child.

"I need you to brace yourself. If we're to stitch you up properly I have to apply pressure. This is going to hurt."

There was no reply. Glaithe started to work. He could feel it tense under his hand, and its jaw clamped together. The wound was grave and Glaithe was surprised that it had not bled to death already. As he pushed the needle through its skin he saw it grin from time to time. One time it giggled, lips curled with dark humour. Glaithe stitched as quickly as he could. When he was finished he grasped one of its wrists, his other hand hooking under its arm.

"We need to lift you. I am going to bandage your chest tightly to help prevent those ribs from doing any more damage."

The creature, astonishingly, just sat up. It barked a curse word before slumping forwards. Glaithe removed its overcoat, slipping the sleeves over its arms, and unbuttoned its shirt.

"Do you often undress guys you find lying in the dirt?" it asked, opening its eyes. Emerald irises sparkled.

Glaithe chuckled. "Not without offering them money first."

The thing laughed, grimaced, thought better of it. Glaithe pulled its shirt free with care. The demon's body was wiry and thin, with not an ounce of fat on it. The muscles underneath its milk-white skin were like steel cord. Its spine was clearly visible, as if each vertebra was trying to burst free. He started to wrap the creature's chest with the bandage. It complained at the firm tugging without much conviction. A few spots of blood were already oozing through the white fabric as he finished, but the stitches had stemmed the majority of the bleeding.

"Do y'ave any whisky?" it asked.

"No," Glaithe replied.

"Hurr... Shame... thought it was common for--" it pulled a pained face, catching its shallow breath "- a cripple to drink whisky."

"You'll live without it," he said. The thing did not speak further, instead closing its eyes. Glaithe considered for a moment why he had not attempted to kill the devil where it lay. It had been a danger when awake, certainly, but it had allowed him to stitch and bandage it. The second or so it would have taken him to draw his dagger and plunge it into the thing's throat would have been plenty. Did he fear it could smell his intentions? That its reactions were so fast that it would retaliate before it realised it was dead?

No... It wasn't that. It was all about the estimates. The demon was foolish to accept such help from a stranger. As expected, it'd left itself open; sitting with its arms at its sides, eyes shut. Glaithe's fingers closed around the hilt of his knife.

A horse was approaching from the south, galloping at a fair clip. He let go of the dagger for a second time, presuming that the rider must be one of the creature's companions. Rising to his feet, he saw the giant he had bested in the forests. Glaithe smirked. For such a respected ex-Kalethi, the woodsman had been surprisingly easy to outmanoeuvre.

If he'd been holding his crossbow, he could have slain the woodsman and the Familiar within moments of each other.

The huge man pulled up next to them, dismounting. His strides favoured one leg, and Glaithe noted several light wounds across his person.

"Who are you?" he asked.

"My name is Glaithe. I came across your friend and tended to his wounds."

"Why?"

"Seems an obvious answer. He is injured."

Kanderil stared at him a moment longer before kneeling beside the demon. "How bad?"

The thing opened one eye, looking back with incredulity.

"Well..." it wheezed. "It's not bloody *good*, is it."

"You are not dead yet, lad. Can you ride?"

"If you steer." It held out its arms to be aided to its feet. Kanderil grabbed one arm, Glaithe the other. Between them they helped the creature, which swore mightily as they did, into the saddle; exhausted with pain, it leaned upon Kanderil, who had already mounted in front of it.

"I would accompany you," Glaithe said before they could depart.

Shaking his head, the giant looked down. "No. My thanks for your charity, but I must refuse."

"I have information of importance to you."

Kanderil's eyes narrowed. "Which is?"

"Let me come with you. I'll explain everything to you and to Sarene."

"If you are another one chasing her down..." The words

were stone cold.

Glaithe spread his hands, smiling. "On the contrary, my large friend. I am here to see her safe."

At first it appeared that Kanderil would decline, but eventually he pointed to Glaithe's horse. "Give me your weapons first. Then you may ride with us. We will need to return to hide the bodies also."

Nodding, Glaithe unclipped his dagger, passing it sheathed to the woodsman. He returned to his horse, mounted, and rode back next to Kanderil. Finally he relinquished his crossbow, which had been attached to his saddle.

"If I suspect at any point that you intend to do Sarene harm, we will have a falling out. You do not want that, so mind yourself."

Glaithe bowed his head, resisting the urge to retort in kind. Together they headed back south, to where the girl would be waiting.

His mind racing, the former Agent started making some mental calculations. There had to be a way to turn this to his advantage.

The five of them took refuge in a traveller's cabin found nestled amongst the woodlands east of the road. Heading to the nearest town was out of the question. With four Gathire bodies having been dumped in a shallow cave less than a mile away - the fifth Agent was alive, though his jaw had splintered into a dozen pieces; they'd left him beside the road, unconscious and stripped of all his official documents and identification - there was going to be a military presence in the area soon after they were found.

The cabin was empty and the previous occupant had kept it in order. It was customary within Tamir for public cabins to be treated with respect, and it was uncommon for the interior to be anything less than neat and tidy. The fireplace was prepared and the bed was made. The pine table was clean with four chairs slid into position beneath it. Only the bare shelves and an absence of personal belongings hinted that the cabin was not a permanent home.

Spasmodic had been laid out on the bed. It was still talking from time to time, but the words came weak and subdued. Having accepted the fact that it was injured, it had given up trying to act with its regular enthusiasm. Sarene fussed over it, ensuring its head was propped up and the blanket was tucked in around it. The creature teased her for the efforts but the insults lacked malice. At last she patted it on the cheek before making her way over to Jared, tucking herself under his arm.

To be in the company of her brother at last was wonderful. She stared up at him with another beaming smile, and once more he returned it. He ruffled her hair for the sixth or seventh time and she nudged him with her elbow.

The trials of the last few weeks had worn her endurance to the limit. The violence she had witnessed, the constant pursuit, the revelations from Corliani... that she'd at least achieved her original objective and found her brother was a significant personal victory. Sarene was determined to enjoy it for as long as she could.

Just how long that would *be* remained to be seen. Again she turned her attention to the dark-clothed stranger who had returned with Kanderil. He was leaning against the wall beside the entrance. The way he studied them made her uneasy; she was under the growing impression he didn't want to get caught looking at her, rarely meeting her eyes.

"You have a lot of explaining to do," said Jared. Sarene glanced up, expecting to see him addressing the stranger. Instead, he was looking down at her.

She blushed, nodding. *You have no idea.*

"What manner of creature is that?" the stranger asked, gesturing towards the bed. Sarene peered over her shoulder at Spasmodic, who seemed asleep for all of a second.

"I'm a shark," it mumbled.

Jared smirked. "Whatever it is, it has a sense of humour."

"I'm right here, y'know," it snapped, turning its head to glare at them, and then winced. It refrained from moving further.

Sarene tapped Jared's arm. She pointed at Spasmodic, then at herself. Crossing her arms at the wrists, she brought them close in front of her chest.

"It's protecting you?" Jared said to clarify. Sarene nodded. "Where did you find it!?"

"It found her," said Kanderil as he entered the room, closing the door behind him. The door had swelled due to the summer heat and squeaked against the frame. He moved to the far wall, beside the fireplace. "But before we get into that, we need to ascertain what his role is." Kanderil folded his arms, focusing on the stranger with that unforgiving stare.

The man cleared his throat. "My name is Glaithe, as I said. I am a former Gathire Agent." At the words Sarene gripped Jared's arm, stepping behind him. He looked at her, puzzled. Kanderil's expression became hard as stone.

Holding out his hands in submission, Glaithe continued. "Before you judge me, know that I was discharged for disobeying orders. You see, I was one of those deployed to Sarene's family home."

A tightness enveloped Sarene's throat. Jared opened his mouth but the words were delayed. He licked his lips. "You went to our home?"

"I objected to what happened after we discovered she wasn't there," Glaithe explained with a distinct calmness. "We were supposed to ask some questions and then leave. I tried to stop the Agent in charge from doing what he did, and was taken into custody for it. The Assembly relieved me from duty when I arrived back in Tamiran."

Jared looked from the man to Kanderil and then to Sarene. She recognised the effort he was making to keep the concern from his face as he spoke. "What happened? What happened at home?" He gently shook her shoulder. Biting her lip, she looked across at Kanderil.

"The Gathire paid your family a visit, searching for

Sarene. They attempted to extract information through violence. Your mother..." Kanderil paused, looking at Sarene. She nodded for him to continue. "Your mother was scarred across the face."

Jared took this information in silence. Sarene wrapped an arm around him but he did not reciprocate.

"I tried to prevent it from happening," repeated Glaithe. "For that I was put on report for 'hindering the investigation'. Officially I was discharged, but the truth of it is that I quit. I was disgusted that such methods were used during a simple interview."

"She returned to the family home not two hours after you left," said Kanderil. "Had your friends been patient, you would have had her."

"Another reason why violence was a foolish method," Glaithe replied, eyeing the woodsman. "And they are not my friends."

"So why are you here?"

"I came to help her. I have a way of making this better."

"Do you know why she is being hunted?"

"I do not. That information is restricted and I could discover little before I left the city. I know that it takes a lot of gold to hire the Gathire privately, however. Whoever took out the contract is wealthy."

"Doesn't take a genius to work that out," said Jared, with hostility. He was shaking softly. Sarene laid her head against his chest, trying to comfort him.

"A fair point. I should warn you, though. Once the Gathire accept a contract, regardless of the source, that contract is a bond which will never break. They will continue to hunt Sarene until they find her." Glaithe shook his head, giving a sardonic smirk. "With four dead Agents out there, you're all implicit. Me as well, if they find out I helped your strange friend over there instead of bringing it in for trial. Whoever wants the girl isn't going to let her disappear."

"There has to be somewhere we can take her. Out of the country, maybe" Jared 's grip tightened against her shoulder. She offered a weak smile in return.

"That may not be a permanent solution," Kanderil said slowly.

"Why? Their jurisdiction ends at the border. Let's get her somewhere safe until this all blows over."

"The Gathire have operatives in other countries," Glaithe explained. "They will still hunt her. Besides, there's nothing to say that the person who hired us... Sorry, I mean *them*, will not simply hire further factions to search for her abroad."

Jared swore. He turned his attention to Kanderil, rubbing the back of his neck. "I suppose you're allied with them in some way, to agree with this guy so easily?"

"No," the Hunter replied. "I was formerly a Kalethi. I have no attachments to the Gathire but I know a little of how they work."

Jared turned his attention to Sarene. She shrugged, letting her expression speak for her; *What is a girl to do?*

With a sigh, he gently stroked her hair. "Why are they hunting you, brighteyes?" he breathed. "What do they think you're worth?"

"So what is your solution to all this?" Kanderil asked.

Glaithe examined his fingernails, replying with confidence. "I can seek out the Regent, Nichai. I met him as a trainee after winning the long distance run during the Shalith Games three years ago. We have remained on good terms since. He will listen to me."

"The Regent?" said Jared. "He's just royalty by blood. He hasn't any influence over the Gathire."

"But he *does* have the ear of both his brother and the King. I believe that once they hear of this outrageous hunt and persecution of your sister, they will step in."

"I do not like it," said Kanderil after a pause. Sarene peered over at him. He seemed older than his years following the confrontation with the bandits, with deep lines running across his forehead. "We cannot rule out the possibility that the Prince ordered this search in the first place."

"True enough," Glaithe conceded. "For what it's worth, I think that is unlikely."

"Why?"

"The contract was for a paid sum of money. Prince Remelas is the acting commander of the Gathire. He wouldn't *have* to pay anything to send Agents on a mission for him."

"He could be covering his tracks," said Jared.

"From whom? The only person to outrank Remelas would be the King. On paper this is a simple search and retrieve mission. He would have no reason to question it unless he verifies everything his eldest son does, which given his increasing senility seems improbable."

Sarene snapped her fingers. They all looked at her. She pointed at Glaithe before raising a hand to grasp the back of her own collar. She yanked it as if she were child caught misbehaving, before pointing at the former Gathire a second time. Looking at Jared, she was relieved to see him nod as though he had considered this as well. "How do we know you will not just hand her in to your former colleagues?" he said. The question was loaded with accusation.

Glaithe gave a disarming smile. "You are welcome to travel with me. I cannot assure you my protection, however. As you have no doubt already realised the Gathire have an informant in the Kalethi barracks." At Jared's look of puzzlement he continued. "This is how we discovered your large friend here was travelling with Sarene."

"Aye," Kanderil agreed. "When I next see him I plan to relieve him of his position. Perhaps a few of his teeth as well."

Behind them, Spasmodic giggled.

"Anyway, this will mean you are on the Gathire's black list. If we are stopped you will be taken into custody."

"What about me, then?" said Jared. "Nobody knows I've met with you. Officially I've nothing to do with this so far save family ties." Sarene tightened her grasp on him, shaking her head. She had gone through so much to find him and the thought of losing him again so soon filled her with sudden dread.

"A much lesser risk, I agree, though you could likely be arrested and taken for questioning. But since you wouldn't know anything I cannot see much reason for an extended delay if you are brought in. If there are no objections, we could set off immediately." Glaithe leaned away from the wall, his boots loud against the wooden floorboards.

Shaking her head again, Sarene stamped her foot for emphasis. A dull thud reverberated around the room. She pointed at Kanderil while tapping against her ear, before then waving a dismissive hand towards Glaithe.

Kanderil exhaled slowly. "Glaithe, would you give us a few moments? I believe we have a few things to discuss in private."

"By all means," Glaithe replied. A pause. Then, "If this is information on why Sarene is being hunted, it could be helpful for me to hear it. Perhaps I could provide some answers."

"Trust me," Kanderil said. "This is a situation there *are* no answers to."

Sarene held up a hand. She stared at Glaithe for a long while, contemplating what more he could possibly know. Nobody spoke; the only noises were the rain pattering against the roof and the ragged, sticky breathing of Spasmodic.

"I already suspect the girl is... gifted," said Glaithe finally. Sarene's eyes widened.

Jared looked from person to person. "Would someone *please* tell me what it going on?"

"Explain," said Kanderil, ignoring Jared.

"Well, why else would she travel with a demon?"

"Get knobbed," Spasmodic exclaimed from the bed.

Jared laughed, the noise heavy with frustration. "The man has a point," he said as Sarene nudged him with her shoulder. "Well, why *is* it here? Creatures with claws and fangs don't turn up every day, Sar."

"If I inform the Regent that the Gathire are searching for a girl travelling with a demon who has slain five of my former brothers in arms, she will receive little sympathy."

"Why would you mention Spasmodic at all?" asked Kanderil with a tone of menace.

Glaithe chuckled. "I may be on your side, but I am not completely naive. I have my own curiosity to satisfy. If you know why the girl is so highly prized, then I would like to hear it."

Kanderil faced her. "It is your call," he said simply.

Sarene wrung her hands as she mulled it over. The fact Kanderil had asked for her decision was a welcome one, but she was anxious not to make the *wrong* call. Suddenly an idea came to her. Tugging Jared's sleeve to get his attention, she hooked her thumbs around each other and flapped her fingers, mimicking a bird flying away. She then scribbled an imaginary note on her hand.

Jared snapped his fingers. "Of course. The message service. We could send a note back to the Regent. That way we can witness the information this man writes firsthand."

"No," said Kanderil. "The note would pass through several hands and then the Kalethi garrison before it even reached the Regent. Each note is also marked with the point of origin. The risk of someone taking a look is too great."

"If the note is sealed with wax it is a felony to break it," Jared continued. "I have the necessary tools to send a private note."

"Even so. I dislike having vital information concerning Sarene's whereabouts tied to a pigeon," Kanderil replied, deadpan. "I will travel with Glaithe. We can make an arrangement as we travel on how to avoid detection. It shouldn't be too difficult."

"You should not underestimate the Gathire," warned Glaithe.

"They should not underestimate me."

"Duly noted," said Jared. "Satisfied, Sar?"

She gave him a firm thumbs-up.

"Good. Now maybe we can share your little secret?"

Sarene sighed heavily, tasting the musty air. Having Glaithe hear her story didn't matter too much. The way things were going, she guessed the news wouldn't remain secret for long.

The Hunter stepped from the cabin after they had finished discussing Sarene's immunity to the power of the Four. Her unique way of signing was easily read by her brother and, with Kanderil elaborating at certain points, the two of them had described her flight from home and the arrival of Spasmodic. They covered her encounter with the Gathire in Tamiran, the pursuit through the Meadows and the meeting with Corliani. Jared had asked a few questions of interest here; it was not every day that one of the Four appeared for a chat.

Glaithe had not said a word, only nodding in places with his hand covering his mouth as he considered all that was being revealed. As Kanderil left the room the man had been deep in thought. He wasn't sure what to make of the former Agent, who had so far offered them assistance and done nothing to suggest an ulterior motive besides satisfying personal curiosity. But there was certainly something a little... off. Kanderil couldn't quite put his finger on what that was.

Attached to the side of the cabin was a small open-sided shed. The rain was still spitting as he approached it. The group's two horses were tied there, beside a stack of chopped logs. It had taken several trips to hide the corpses of the Gathire and bring everyone to the cabin. The other new member of the group had yet to offer his perspective on things.

Kanderil knelt in front of Hawk, who was bound and gagged in front of him. The blonde haired bandit was still out cold. He reached over, pulling the gag free. A huge bruise was forming on the right side of Hawk's face, beneath an eye now circled with a dark blue sheen. Kanderil sometimes forgot his own strength.

"Wake up," he said, reaching out to prod the man's forehead.

Groggily, Hawk opened his eyes. As soon as he focused on Kanderil, he began to struggle against the ropes binding his arms to a thick wooden pillar holding the shed roof in place. One of the horses complained at this disturbance, stroking its hoof against the ground.

"Untie me, you bastard," Hawk hissed. "I'll kill you where you stand!"

"Hardly the best argument there," replied Kanderil, rising to his feet. Moving over to one of the horses, he pulled Hawk's sheathed sword from the saddle. He'd had to ask Jared to retrieve it from the ground. Kanderil could feel the burns on his fingertips as he held the weapon. With the scabbard on it didn't hurt, though warmth still radiated from beneath the leather cover.

"This is quite a weapon you have here," he said. "Must have cost a few gold."

Glaring at him, Hawk said nothing. Kanderil continued as he began to wander back and forth in front of his captive.

"See, this suggests that someone paid you to come for me, while your anger would make me think this was personal. Therefore, either you really do not enjoy leaving a victim with his purse – and remember, lad, *you* tried to rob *me* - or, there is something more to the story."

Hawk spat at him. Kanderil must have busted a tooth or two out of place, for the spray was not clean. He kneeled down once more. "So which is it?"

"You think this is a joke?" Hawk said with a low growl. "All you've done to me? And you ask *why*?"

"Refresh my memory."

"I wouldn't give you the satisfaction." Hawk strained against his bonds again. "Having me recount your crimes would no doubt amuse you further."

Kanderil nodded towards the saddlebags hanging from a hook embedded in the cabin wall. "In there is a journal. The young girl you were looking to kidnap found it. She showed me all the wonderful and flattering prose you wrote about me."

"Deserved words, and I would write a thousand more for

each second of your demise!"

Kanderil gave a polite smile. "Poetic. You have a bard's tongue. Now, let me repeat our previous encounter as I recall it." He shook the sword for a moment. "You came at me, armed, in a forest in southern Tamir. You and your two friends outnumbered me. You asked for my purse and I refused. I gave you my catch for that day, a-"

"*The ultimate insult!*" Hawk roared with such ferocity, his voice wavering with emotion, that Kanderil had to lean back. "You preached to us like children, tried to buy your life with a miserable offering!"

Shrugging his shoulders, Kanderil sought to make his point. "The whole meeting lasted a few minutes at most. You took my catch and left. Now, to my knowledge we have never met before or since. How did I come to be such a figure of hatred for you?"

Hawk fought against his fastenings for a while. Kanderil let him. The ropes were thick and the knots secure. Eventually the bandit's strength failed, his body sagging in defeat. Tilting his head back, catching his breath, Hawk spoke with the hushed reverence of a condemned man giving forced confession.

"The laughing. You haunt my dreams, you bastard. All I ever hear when I close my eyes is your mocking laughter. You have taunted me for damn near a month. I must destroy you to save myself." Hawk's lip started to quiver. "I just want to sleep without the *dreams*. I just..."

Kanderil thumbed his jaw. Reaching to his belt he pulled free a small sack of coin. He held it out with one arm straight before letting go. The pouch landed beside Hawk's hip with a small *chink*.

"There. You have my gold."

"This isn't *about* that anymore!" Hawk yelled, his self pity drowned in a fresh wave of anger. "It's *you* I want, Kanderil; not your money. I will cut you down and the sword will drink deep of your blood. That will end this cursed nightmare, and I can live again!"

Kanderil looked at the weapon in his hands. He

considered the matter as Hawk babbled more elaborate threats. Looking out from the makeshift stable he realised that the rain had stopped, with drops of water forming and falling at the edge of the shelter. Sunlight was beginning to break through clouds which were packed together like huge wads of fresh cotton dipped in mercury.

Slowly he stood. "Someone will be out to bring you some food soon."

"Give me back my blade," Hawk replied. Even this was threatening.

"No. I will be keeping this for now."

The air was filled with curses as Kanderil walked back towards the cabin, tapping the sword's hilt against his thigh. Each time there was contact he felt a spot of heat through his leggings.

This was a most interesting weapon.

"Ready?" Kanderil said, opening the door. The cabin interior was dark and dingy in comparison to the growing afternoon sun outside. Glaithe rose to his feet, taking one final bite of the oatcakes Sarene had produced.

"These are good," he said, pointing at the remaining cakes lying upon the table.

"She found them."

"Ah, well. Beggars can't be choosers on the road."

"Aye. Listen, we need to make a detour on the way back to Tamiran."

Jared frowned. "What for?"

"To speak to the Guide. I want her to take a look at this weapon." He lifted Hawk's sword. "I have a feeling it is enchanted somehow."

Jared shared a glance with his sister, who was picking crumbs from the table between thumb and forefinger before poking them into her mouth. "Enchanted like the fairy tales?"

"Yes. There must be reason why I cannot wield it." He

revealed his palms to display the burn marks.

"Here," said Glaithe. "Let me try."

Kanderil offered him the sword and Glaithe took it, cautious fingers closing around the hilt. "Nothing," he declared, his grip becoming firm. "I can hold it fine."

"So could Jared," Kanderil replied. "It only disagrees with me."

"Enchantment isn't *real*, though," said Jared. "Magic doesn't exist, except that done by the Four..." He trailed off. Sarene grinned at him. "Yes, I haven't forgotten," he said to her quickly.

"Exactly," said Kanderil. "It would not be a huge shock to find an enchanted weapon used in this hunt."

"Come on then," said Glaithe. "We should cover as much ground as we can before sunset. The sooner we arrive in Tamiran, the sooner we can negotiate Sarene's safety."

Kanderil nodded. "We will meet you back here in ten days. Keep her of trouble, Jared." He pointed with the scabbard towards the bunk at the back of the room. "You must move the creature somewhere safe, also, in case anyone else shows up."

"I can do that," said Jared. "All part of the training."

"Good. We shall leave your horse. I can pick one up for myself in the nearest town."

Sarene pointed to the wall adjoining the stable outside. She then held her wrists together.

"Aye, he must remain here as well. I have a feeling our merry prisoner has more answers for us." With that, he stepped aside to allow Glaithe through the doorway. The two of them left with no further word. Kanderil did not see Sarene waving him off, so she banged her fist on the table. He turned. She pointed at him first, then to the floor. She then held out all fingers and thumbs.

"Yes. Ten days."

She brought her hands together over her heart. The girl pursed her lips, clearly worried. He smiled, hoping the gesture conveyed enough sincerity to comfort her.

"Promise."

With that the woodsman stepped into the damp outside, closing the door behind him.

For Sarene, the first few days went by at an agonising pace. They'd moved Spasmodic to the back room, presumably intended for use as a pantry. The thin mattress barely fit on the floor. The creature slept the entire time, its body twitching frequently. Even in sleep it was restless. Its countenance would drift into different moods. Most of them were joyful, amused or relaxed. Sometimes, though, there was a discernible shift in tone and a profound malice would emerge from its dreams. Sarene tried not to take notice if this was the expression greeting her when she tended to it.

The injury was becoming a concern. The Gathire blade had cleaved through at least two of Spasmodic's ribs and torn the muscle over them. It was a severe wound, Jared had said, but not life threatening in itself. Infection was the main worry. The skin around the wound had scabbed and a pungent, whitish liquid was seeping out, sticking to anything which came into contact with it. Sarene washed the area four times a day, sparing the limited bandages as much as possible. Its skin felt feverish. She hoped it would wake up soon.

The man named Hawk remained in bondage, but Sarene was polite when providing him food and water. Now that Kanderil had left, the prisoner was rather sullen. He took his spoonfuls and his cups with no comment, allowing Sarene to dab at his chin whenever she spilled something. He would stare at the wall opposite for hours at a time. Whenever Jared spoke Kanderil's name, however, Hawk would scowl at them. It was the only time he seemed to take any interest in his surroundings.

Spending time with her brother was the only real positive of the situation. They conversed in their own way. Jared would talk unless Sarene began to gesture with her arms, hands and face. She was very expressive with her family, much more so than with strangers. Jared rarely had to spend more than a few moments working out what she was saying. They had spent so much time together as children that she often believed they had invented their own one-sided language; she would communicate, he would understand.

He asked her questions that Kanderil never did, and the chance to discuss how she truly felt ever since her flight from home was wonderful. She told him, over the course of an afternoon during which she both laughed until she wept and wept until she choked, why she had left home in the first place. About the horror which followed the attack on the family. Her thoughts of Spasmodic and Kanderil. Her fear of capture. How it was to witness the death of a man not two feet from where she stood.

More importantly, she tried to put into words her feelings about discovering her unique gift. Jared had offered some gentle reassurances, but on this he could provide little support. The gravity of her situation was growing with each passing day and the weight of it was not pleasant.

On the fourth afternoon, a group of men arrived at the cabin. Jared stepped out to meet them. They'd spoken for a short while as Sarene hid with Spasmodic and Hawk in the back room. It wasn't long until Jared came back to them, smiling.

"Standard military," he explained. "Someone called in the guard after finding the survivor we left beside the road. They took my word and left. It seems they think he's a civilian. Bloody lucky as well." He grinned, holding up his Kalethi insignia. "The Gathire would have searched this place all the way through."

In the evenings they amused themselves with cards. Jared carried a pack with him and practised simple tricks and sleight of hand illusions. They played simple five-match for a few hours before bed. This was the time where Sarene would feel the most nervous. It was a sensation which she imagined must be like awaiting trial. Unable to run until Kanderil returned and unable to relax in case they were discovered here. Jared talked often during the game but he did little more than distract her for short periods.

The idea of asking the Regent personally for assistance struck her as a huge gamble. Truth be told, she knew very little about the Regent at all.

"Please, come in." Katanchi the Guide stepped back from the door as Kanderil entered the Shrine, with Glaithe behind him. "I did not expect to see you again so soon."

"Aye." Walking a short way inside, Kanderil took in the splendid interior for the second time that week. While Sarene had clearly been impressed by the aesthetic value of the lavish furnishings, he enjoyed the *ambience* within the building. There was a profound sense of peace here. Travellers from all over Tamir would walk hundreds of miles for a single visit to the Guides dotted around the country. All of them sought comfort or counsel; an impartial soul willing to listen. Here, none were judged and none were turned away. That tradition of serenity must have seeped into the stone walls themselves.

With a deep breath, Kanderil addressed his host. "My apologies if I seemed rude during my last visit, my lady. I was in something of a hurry."

"I suspected as much," the woman replied with a smile. "I also suspect your travels are not quite over, Kanderil."

"You could say that." He was unsurprised that she had remembered his name. It would make sense that the Guides were trained to memorise the little details. After all, repeatedly having to ask a pilgrim's name while trying to comfort them would be rather awkward.

"How is Sarene?"

"She is well. Enjoying a deserved rest."

With a nod, Katanchi turned her attention to Glaithe; he was leaning against the backrest of a pew, arms folded. She greeted him politely and he responded in kind.

Kanderil had conversed little with him during their ride, which suited them both fine. Glaithe would have made a most compatible travelling partner had Kanderil not known his past. The fact he was a Gathire, discharged or otherwise, remained a concern. They had only the man's word that he had resigned from the faction.

When they arrived in Tamiran, the Hunter would have to remain vigilant.

"How can I help you gentlemen today?" asked Katanchi, her arms disappearing into the sleeves of her white robe. This one was embroidered along the hemlines with a vibrant blue stitching.

"I was hoping you could take a look at this sword." Kanderil walked over to a waist-high table, the legs of which had been carved to resemble doves. He grabbed one of the candlesticks there and shoved a platter of fruit aside before the Guide spoke.

"Please, not there. The table is offering appeasement to the spirits, and disturbing it will bring bad luck."

He paused, blue wax dribbling from the flame, before placing the candle back where it was. "I did not realise. Please accept my apologies."

Solemn-faced, Katanchi sighed as he turned. Then she broke into a smile, stepping towards the table. "I jest, Kanderil."

"I did not take you for a fool, my large friend," said Glaithe as he joined them, wearing a distinct smirk. Kanderil grunted.

"Who knew the Guides had a sense of humour."

"Funnily enough, you are not the first person to say that," Katanchi observed. She removed the objects from the table and placed them on the floor. Kanderil laid Hawk's sword in their place, unwrapping it from the shabby blanket it had been carried in.

The woman traced a fingertip along the smooth, featureless scabbard. "Why don't you tell me a little about the item," she said.

"It hates me," Kanderil stated. "A man seeking revenge against me carried it with him. I cannot touch the sword directly, for it burns my skin." He held up his right hand to show her the scald marks along his fingers and palm.

Before replying, the Guide sought for any sign of deception from him with a measured gaze.

"Interesting. I have never heard of such a thing existing for centuries." She reached out to gingerly touch the hilt. When it failed to harm her, she seized it and pulled the weapon free. She held the blade out before her, admiring the craftsmanship. Stepping back from the two men she gave a few swings, the sword arcing in a graceful butterfly pattern in front of her. Kanderil looked on with appreciation.

"I was not aware you could handle a weapon."

"I would not expect you to be." She held the sword up straight in front of her.

"Formal training?"

"Something along those lines. A Guide should be able to defend herself." She smirked. "Not that we ever face any trouble, of course." Katanchi brought the weapon close to her, running a thumb to test the edge. As she did her expression changed. She withdrew her hand from the pristine steel of the blade and moved back to the table, whereupon she placed the sword back in its sheath. Then she wiped her hand on her robe as if it were filthy.

"Something the matter?" asked Kanderil, exchanging looks with Glaithe, who arched a brow.

"You say a man carried it against you?"

"Yes."

"Did he wound you with it?" she inquired.

"Yes, but not seriously. Two shallow cuts."

"May I see the injuries?"

Kanderil frowned. "Something I should be concerned about?" He lifted up the short sleeve of the shirt he wore beneath his jerkin. There the wound inflicted by Hawk streaked across his upper arm. Katanchi reached out, prodding the shallow wound.

"Did you not notice this before?" she asked. "The wound is cauterised."

"I had, yes. After the hilt burned my hands, however, I thought nothing more of it."

Glaithe chuckled. "Do you often regard mysterious developments so plainly?"

"It would be a waste of time to concern myself with it," Kanderil replied with a shrug.

Katanchi moved to an oak chest in the corner of the large hall. She pulled the lid open and rummaged through the contents, stacking papers and ledgers beside her until she pulled free a leather-bound tome. The volume was worn out, the covers battered and scarred from repeated wear and tear.

"You mentioned not having heard of a weapon like this in modern times," Glaithe called after her. "Am I right in assuming weapons like this once existed?"

"Yes." She walked back towards them, passing through a beam of sunshine piercing the western window. The book's pages fluttered over each other as she searched them. "During the years immediately following the journey of the Four, magical weapons were not unheard of. It was theorised that they were given as gifts to the rulers who abided by the Four's mandate. Over the centuries almost all of them have been lost to history. Only five are known to remain, kept either by foreign kings in their personal treasury or in well guarded museums to the north of the world. Those five have simple enchantments on them. There is an amulet which grants an increased sense of hearing in Kae'cha, for example. A staff which emits its own light source in Edabouis. A sword providing greater strength in... Well, you get the idea. It is also said that after so many years the powers of each have faded significantly."

Katanchi paused with a fingertip running along fading scripture. She then flipped back a few pages, forward one more and finally settled on the contents displayed, tapping the yellowed paper.

"Here," she said, offering the book to Kanderil. Revealed was a detailed sketch of a sword which closely resembled the one he now carried. "The book describes how these blades were given to those chieftains who agreed to the Commandment of the Four but were facing subjugation from larger clans in the area."

"The Four dealt with any clans who fought against the new way of things," pointed out Glaithe.

Katanchi shook her head in response. "They punished the *leaders* of those clans, it is true. But as far as we know they couldn't simply relocate themselves at will. If a faction decided to go back on their word after, say, Shigasi had departed their lands, it would take time for him to return again and set things right. Therefore the smaller clans needed some kind of deterrent to being conquered in the meantime. Weapons such as these were one such device."

"What ability did it grant?" asked Kanderil. The scripture of the tome was spidery and difficult, and he could not understand much of it.

"In most cases they were said to produce flame around the blade. The effect was most intimidating and granted the wielder a certain presence in diplomatic relations. That would explain your wounds." She looked at Kanderil pointedly before returning to the text. "And here; occasionally, a clan's most skilled warriors would receive them due to the 'sudden bloodlust and tireless energies bestowed upon them' by the weapon. Similar to the barbarian rage-masters in the Skolpase mountains, I expect."

"Those savages?" Glaithe said, scoffing. "They're not intelligent enough to fight tactically. Blind fury is all they have."

"I would rather not face one head on, regardless," said Kanderil. He shrugged. "So the bandit found one of these blades and came for me. Implausible, but not impossible."

"But that's my point," continued the Guide. "That sword has been created *recently*. I felt it as I touched the steel. There is a..." she paused, rolling her hand as if encouraging the correct word to come. "There is a *purpose* there. Who did you take it from?"

"A cut-throat named Hawk. A man who came for revenge after I prevented him from robbing me."

"Sounds reasonable," said Glaithe.

"I thought so."

"The man didn't find it," said Katanchi. "Not like this,

and not unless he stole it from one of the Four. If I had to make a guess, I would say he was given the blade to hunt you down."

Kanderil looked at her. "Nonsense, lass. That suggests one of the Four wants me dead."

"Would they have any reason to?"

He considered the question. The others watched him in silence. The first name that came to mind was Tyrrial, who had created Spasmodic to murder Sarene. Kanderil had surely not been in the girl's company for long enough to warrant a magical weapon being forged to kill him off, though. Corliani would have simply killed him when they met. The other two legendary names, Shigasi and Mubuto, had so far been absent in the situation or at least subtle enough to avoid direct implication.

Which of them, then?

"I have no reason to believe the Four would be seeking to do me harm," Kanderil said at last, his voice firm.

"Making the mystery all the more confusing," offered Glaithe.

The woodsman ignored this. "Would the sword have any permanent effect on the man wielding it?"

Katanchi placed the book on the back of a nearby bench, the weight of the thing producing a dull *thump,* before bringing her hands together. "I cannot say for certain. I suppose it is not beyond the realms of possibility that the weapon was created to fill this bandit with the same fury that the warriors of old experienced *and* give them a specific target. Of course," she noted with a peculiar little smirk, "a weapon created by the Four could be capable of *anything.*"

With a bow of the head Kanderil laid the sword against his shoulder. "Thank you for your time, lass."

"Indeed," said Glaithe in agreement, already heading for the exit.

The Guide smiled. "You are both most welcome. Just leave a donation in the box."

Their footsteps echoing in the Shrine as they left, the two men did just that.

"Feel free to return at any time," Katanchi called after them from the doorway. "I would be most interested in learning more about the weapon."

"Should I find anything further," said Kanderil as he pulled himself into the saddle of his newly purchased mount, "I'll be sure to get in touch."

"Make sure you do. And oh, Kanderil? Tell Sarene to be careful."

Kanderil and Glaithe heeled their horses forward out of the small garden surrounding the shrine, and were soon galloping along the road at pace, onwards towards the great city of Tamiran.

Chapter Sixteen

*T*he dagger hit the tree at an angle, sliding across the bark and penetrating nothing but air. Sarene's thumb jarred against the crossguard, and she hissed at the sudden pain.

Jared smiled. "You'd certainly hurt someone like that, but only the Four knows where on their body."

They were outside the cabin, standing before one of the broader trunks encircling the area. The heat of the summer had returned, and Sarene wiped the back of her hand across her brow. Having spent the last five days cooped up indoors, it was refreshing to be outside again. It had taken almost an hour of relentless badgering before Jared had agreed, and even then it was for the purpose of learning how to handle a dagger. If she was destined to avoid people who would wish her harm, it was time she learned how to defend herself. While Kanderil was more than capable of protecting her, she was determined not to remain the vulnerable waif that she had unwillingly become.

"You're just swinging your arm," Jared said, reaching out to grabs her elbow. "There's no power in your swing, and you're not defending yourself. Stand with your left leg slightly forward, keep your left hand out in fr- No, not that far out. Yeah, that's right. Now keep your forearms facing your body. That way you're not exposing yourself to attack."

Sarene did all of this, pulling a face. When Jared had stopped tugging her hands and nudging her ankle with his foot, she poked her tongue out at him.

Chuckling, he took this with good grace. "Hey, you *asked* me to teach you."

She rolled her eyes before focusing on the tree again. Shoving the dagger forward, the point dug into the bark with more authority, metal once again scraping against her knuckle. She swallowed down her frustration, stepping back into her protective stance.

"Better," said Jared, "but you're losing your shape as soon as you step forward, and you're still extending your arm too far. Remember, you're meant to be closing the distance with your body. If you keep your arm sticking out like that someone's liable to cut it off."

Frowning, she drew her free hand across the opposite elbow, before dangling the limb as if the tendons had been severed. Jared laughed, which in turn made her grin.

"Exactly like that. Now come on. Try again. Left foot forward, hand out to protect yourself."

They went over and over the basics for more than hour. With each repetition she better understood how to keep herself protected when advancing on a target. Jared had suggested that her best chance of surviving a close encounter was to try and finish her opponent quickly, while she had the element of surprise; few would expect a young girl to know the basics of military training, he'd explained. Jared showed her two techniques to deflect an assailant's strike, allowing defence against both a direct thrust and a downwards stab.

When she was able to hold her stance consistently they practised sparring, having substituted the real weapon for a length of branch. Jared attacked while Sarene countered. As she became more comfortable with the fundamentals, she encouraged her brother to approach with less restraint.

"Don't push yourself too soon," Jared said, pinching his

shoulder and rolling his arm after having taken a fierce jab to the underarm with the menacing stick. "We can practice again tomorrow."

But Sarene shook her head. She wanted to get as much practice as possible. Jared lunged suddenly, seeking to strike her ribcage with the heel of his palm. Sarene, caught off guard, didn't quite manage to cleanly avoid the blow and it bounced against her lower rib. The stick feebly poked at his shoulder in response.

"Ah, sorry," said Jared quickly, as Sarene's face tightened at the dull throb in her side. She waved the apology away, irritated by his immediate concern. Gritting her teeth, Sarene shook her hand to relieve the ache there. The blister forming between her thumb and forefinger was evidence enough that when it came to taking care of herself, she really had no experience at all. Of course, there had never *been* any requirement before now. Back at home Sameran watched out for her, and the village as a whole protected itself. There were no raiders so far within Tamir's borders that she'd even been under threat from outsiders. Sarene had never considered herself feeble or helpless before. Yet ever since this journey began, others had fought on her behalf; Kanderil, Spasmodic, and now Jared would continue to put themselves in danger, believing her incapable.

The reality was as plain as the circular swelling between her knuckles. She poked the fluid building beneath her skin.

Now, that situation would change. No more hiding behind others. She was tired of it.

"Sarene?"

Jared's voice brought her from her thoughts. Clicking her tongue, she wiped the sole of her bare foot against the ground to dislodge a tiny pebble before taking up her stance and inviting him towards her.

"No," said her brother. "Come on. You're exhausted. Let's wrap things up for today and make some food."

Sarene scrunched up her face in disagreement, urging him to approach.

"Tomorrow. I promise we'll carry on th--"

As he spoke she sighed, then began to close the space between them with small, rapid footsteps. He grinned, preparing himself. When she was close enough Sarene brought the stick forward, and Jared reached out to grab her wrist. She used her free hand to whack her palm against his elbow, angling the stick under his grasp. The pointed end jabbed into the skin over his ribs, just below the heart.

"*Ow!*"

Grinning, still gripping his arm, Sarene stared up at him in triumph. He licked his lips as he disengaged, rubbing at his chest.

"Fine. But I'm not playing around anymore." He sounded annoyed, but that was fine. Sarene bowed her head in agreement, then prepared herself for another attack.

Porthouse was in something of a fluster.

In his line of business, certain customers became regulars. Everybody liked routine. Drunks, especially, had a way of staying loyal to a particular venue. It was how tavern keepers and publicans became minor celebrities. Serve the same drink to the same face at the same time every morning and you became a part of their life. Porthouse was no different. He served the little extra for those who enjoyed alcohol in the comfort of their own home. He, too, was well known in this district of Tamiran... and that fame brought with it a degree of expectancy.

His tunnel was becoming a source of concern.

The Gathire had paid him a visit a fortnight back. They'd inquired about a visitor he'd had. A 'man-mountain' known as Kanderil. Long hair the colour of mahogany. Thick, coarse beard. Very distinctive size, quite difficult to forget. They'd asked if he could recall such a figure. Porthouse had nodded, reaching for his handkerchief.

He remembered the visit.

The shipments of his special goods had ceased ever since. He had expected at least three deliveries by now. Nothing had turned up. He had customers of a particular reputation inquiring about his stock. When would it be arriving? What was the hold up? What were they expected to do without the supply to meet the demand Mr. Porthouse-sir-you-know-how-business-works-around-here. Questions which became more insistent as the days passed. Associates who had treated him as an equal over the years were growing impatient.

Porthouse crammed another piece of smoked sausage into his mouth. He chewed with his mouth open, adjusting his collar yet again. One of his business partners had scheduled a meeting for this afternoon. He'd promised them that a shipment would be waiting for collection. The best tax-free, black market, A-grade brandy from Cho'Nanj. The finest hand-rolled, moisture-preserved cigars from Janchar. Great wines sold free from the clutches of the state they was brewed in. Sweet liquors prepared in the basements of otherwise legitimate operators. He invested a good part of his takings into them and earned a tidy sum more by selling them on.

When there was nothing *to* sell on, those on the street got anxious. Porthouse brought in so much of the stuff that, when his supply ran dry, there was fierce competition for the goods of other smugglers in the city who could then command a much higher price. Regardless of who bought them, profits would be minimised.

The criminals of Tamiran were not the kind of people a man should disappoint.

Pacing across his shop floor, Porthouse waited for his associate to arrive. This time they would be angry for certain. The promised goods had not arrived. A spent supplier was a useless supplier. A useless supplier was a liability, a source of names and faces for the authorities.

Authorities such as the Gathire, who had paid him a visit a few weeks ago.

Silence was golden. When silence could not be bought, it would be ensured.

————◄○►————

Glaithe walked out from the damp tree line beneath an overcast sky, directly towards the two sentries stationed around the entrance to the tunnel. They were chatting to each other. One of them was resting on the artificial boulder housing the 'secret' doorway. When they saw him they straightened up, hands moving to the hilts of their swords. Glaithe held his palms facing out before him to show he carried no weapon.

"Ho there," called the older of the two. "Identify yourself."

"Glaithe. I am an Agent of the Gathire." He tugged on the faction medallion hanging over his shirt from a thin leather cord.

"Shoulda guessed from all the black he's wearin'," said the other sentry. He grinned to show yellowed teeth. "How can we help you, mister Glaithe?"

"On the contrary, I'm here to help you," Glaithe replied. "I have orders to relieve you both."

The two men looked at each other. "Excuse me?"

"We believe another wagonload of illegal goods is due later this afternoon and intend to question those bringing it in."

"Ah, right," said the guard with yellow teeth. At this distance Glaithe could smell his matching breath, which reminded him of fermenting onions. "Makes sense, n'all. Why don't you just arrest the fat bastard in the shop?"

"Porthouse?" Glaithe laughed. "Why would we do that? He's the biggest link between the smugglers and the black market. Arrest him and we'll waste months learning their new schedules."

"So why post us here then?" the other guard said. The man had the weary look common to career soldiers. "Nothing's come through here for weeks. Eventually they'll find other suppliers anyway."

"Even the most simple minded of criminals realise that all traders are checked by the local law enforcement at some stage. An operation of Porthouse's size which wasn't *ever* investigated would be more suspicious. They'll wait, and they'll keep trying." Glaithe shrugged his shoulders. "Like today, for example."

The two sentries shrugged. "Alright. Well, show us the orders and we'll get back to the barracks then."

Glaithe tensed, but kept his expression calm. "Orders?"

"Aye. Cap'n said we aren't to move from here without a written order."

"I'm here to relieve you from your post and you want a written order from my superior?"

"Standard practice. If you were with the guard, not a problem. But you're a different department." The elder soldier spread his hands in apology.

"And if I do not have these orders written down?"

"Written down and signed," said Yellow-teeth. "Just coverin' our own backs, y'know?"

"We can wait here 'til you're back."

They shuffled their feet under his withering gaze. Glaithe was taller than both men. He straightened his back, drawing up to his full height, and smiled.

"So, let me clarify this. You want to send me back to Tamiran, which is a good hour on horse through these woods. You want me to pick up a copy of my orders, which will take another hour with all the other tasks my faction is handling right now. I'll wait on an old, leather bound couch until the papers are signed and stamped. Maybe I'll flick through a book from the collection on the shelf beside our clerk's desk."

The sentries looked at each other warily.

"I'll pick up the orders and ride back here. Maybe another hour. In the meantime my fellow Gathire, set in specific places in these here trees" – he waved an arm to the woodlands around them –"will wait for my return before taking any action that may be required, because frankly the sight of two fully uniformed guards outside the entrance to this here tunnel will prove something of a deterrent should the smugglers see you."

"Bu-" one of the guards tried, ultimately in vain.

"When I arrive, you'll get your orders *if* there is still anyone here to apprehend. You can go home to your Captain, safe in the knowledge that *you* did your part to help, and Tamiran can sleep easy knowing such disciplined men are on duty. That's what you want, correct?"

Glaithe fell silent, irritated now. What he had said was nonsense, but the words were based in truth. Those who valued protocol over initiative and action were fools. It was easy to give a solid performance under the circumstances.

After all, such backwards thinking contributed to his ejection from the Gathire.

"Look," said the older guard, heavy with caution. "I don't wanna cause any fuss here, like, but if we turn up back at the barracks without orders we'll get roasted. Your superior or whoever it is should *know* all this. He's the one who'll get it in the neck."

"Oh?" Glaithe grinned like a cobra. He'd won. "My superior is to blame here?"

"Well, not in so few words, but he should have known we'd need the orders. It's standard practice," the guard repeated.

"Right. Fine. I'll just go tell Chalimer that he forgot my orders."

The guards looked at each other. Yellow-teeth shifted his weight nervously. "Chalimer?"

"Yes. He's organising this operation. Sorry, what were your names again?"

"Wait a minute here," said the elder guard with an edgy laugh. "Let's not be too hasty."

"Oh, it's not a problem," said Glaithe, rubbing his hands together. "I'm sure Chalimer will be *most* pleased to hear about formal guard procedure. He would not want to make such an oversight again, being such a thorough man." He turned to walk away.

"Err."

"Let's hope his plans aren't foiled by bureaucracy in the meantime, eh?" Glaithe ended with a laugh. "My, that would be embarrassing."

"Wait!" called Yellow-teeth. Both sentries hurried to catch up with him, their armour *chink*ing encouragement with each step. Glaithe slowed, adopting a facade of utter astonishment.

"We, uh... We wouldn't want to inconvenience mister Chalimer, now, would we? I'm sure he can do the paperwork *after* you're finished here. We'll, er..."

"We'll wait until he's ready," the elder guard finished for his partner.

Glaithe considered this for a moment. The guards fidgeted like schoolboys outside the head tutor's office. "Fine. Wait for a courier at the Salmon Run."

"The food place?"

"Yes, the food place. Someone will be there before sunset with your orders signed, stamped and sealed."

Yellow-teeth sighed. It was a mannerism best avoided, thought Glaithe, given the odious stench which accompanied it. "Couldn't we just pop to your garri--"

"Gentlemen, please. Enjoy a meal and a cup of tea. Here," he said, "I'll even pay for it." Glaithe fished a few silvers from his pocket before pressing them to the elder guard's palm. "As a reward for your cooperation here."

"Oh, right." The man smiled at last. "Well. We'll be off then, eh?"

"Have a pleasant afternoon," said Glaithe. He watched the sentries walk away, their silence speaking volumes about their lack of comprehension. A few minutes after they were out of sight Kanderil stepped from the tree line, his leather garb blending in with the natural tones around them.

"Nice work," said the giant as he approached.

"It pays to be a Gathire."

"So it seems. Did you not hand your insignia in when you were discharged?"

"I did," Glaithe lied smoothly. "This here is a fake."

"Interesting. Let us hope your ruse works at the other end."

"You think Porthouse's horrible little shack will be guarded?"

"No," said Kanderil, shoving open the heavy tunnel entrance. It fell inwards with a strained, rusty groan. "But I expect the palace will be."

Porthouse swallowed as the front door opened. Three men entered his shop. None of them were the type one would feel comfortable meeting late at night when walking the streets alone. The two at the rear of the group seemed stitched into their clothing, and Porthouse felt that everything in the world was just a little too small for them. They had jaws carved of granite and fists the size of watermelons. Both needed a shave. Both were bald. For a moment Porthouse wondered if they were related.

The lead man was smaller. It seemed inevitable, but it was true. The leaders of the underworld were often smaller, smarter and more ambitious than their peers.

In most cases, they were capable of much more cruelty as well.

"Porthouse!" he brayed. His voice was rich, like a classical actor. In fact everything about the man suggested a love for the theatrical, from the flawless goatee beard to the billowing silk shirt and tailor-made pantaloons which *flowed* from his calf-length boots. He could have been a great performer, a marvelled sculptor, or a fanciful lord. Someone whose presence lingered after he had strode past you in the street--

Porthouse forced a welcome. The man's name was Morai, and he was a man to be feared.

"So glad you're here, Morai," he replied. "Can I get you anything at all?"

"Only the goods you promised, my man." Morai smiled at him. It was a winning smile, a smile intended to make him feel more comfortable.

"Indeed, indeed." Porthouse lifted his handkerchief, dabbing at his round head. He felt saturated by his own sweat; the shirt he wore was damp against his blubbery skin.

"Now, before we get to that, I would like to discuss some of the details. Ugly business really, you know, but something we should just knuckle down to before we carry out your merchandise, hmm?"

Morai quirked a brow. He was still smiling, and his gaze was still warm. "Now, now. There's no need to be nervous." The man walked slowly forward and placed an arm over Porthouse's shoulder. "As long as you have what I want, I will be happy to talk with you about anything your greedy little heart desires. It has been a while, after all, and I would want to keep my favourite partner happy, wouldn't I?"

Porthouse laughed as Morai patted his cheek, which wobbled. The laugh was anxious and high in pitch. "Yes, yes, of *course!*"

"But, since it *has* been so long, I would most like to see what you have for me beforehand. After all, there would be no need to waste my time further if you are indeed lacking in stock once again."

His heart racing, Porthouse wrung the handkerchief in his hands so tightly that the sweat he had just mopped up dripped from the end.

"No, no, of course!" he said, the words hurried. He moved to his counter, swinging the door up and sliding his frame along the wall towards the door to his back room. "It would be most ridiculous of me to bring you here and have nothing to show you, haha, oh my that *would* be silly..."

He reached his stock room, the three men close behind. Porthouse looked around for something, anything, he could pretend was contraband. Some of his expensive whisky, perhaps, or flavoured burnwater. He whispered a quick prayer to the Four for assistance.

"Porthouse, you're sweating." Morai stepped beside him. Porthouse giggled.

"Yes, I am, aren't I? Most odd, really." He glanced over to the huge brutes standing either side of the door. One of them winked at him. "Most, uh..."

"I'm going to go out on a limb here," said Morai, stepping forward to inspect a few of the unmarked crates lined up against the wall. His voice was resonant in the enclosed space. "I would say, judging from your nerves, the absence of your usual haste to the placement of gold in your pocket *and* the considerable lack of stock you have here, that you have nothing for me. Again."

"Well," Porthouse replied, "let's not be hasty here. I have plenty of liquor for you to--"

"Liquor I can get anywhere," Morai interrupted. He turned, smiling again, but this was like the grin of a wolf before it leapt for the throat. "Porthouse, I like you. I really do. But I need goods the people *want*. Goods from across the border, goods which should cost the common man five times what they pay *me* for it. And the longer you continue to disappoint me, the longer I must disappoint my customers. Disappointed customers are *lost* customers. This is how trade works. Our trade."

He snapped his fingers.

The two men stepped to either side of Porthouse. They grabbed one arm each, their grip tight as a bear trap. He struggled out of instinct, knowing it was pointless.

Morai stood before him. "Can you provide me with my goods this day?"

Porthouse tried to grin. What appeared was a cringe. "N-no, Morai, my supplier did n-not arrive. He must have b-b-been delayed for some reason."

A nod. "So, you do in fact waste my time. And then you proceed to waste more of my time by declining to tell me as soon as I arrive. Very poor form, my fat friend." He reached into his breast pocket and produced a thin, pearl-handled tool. With a single hard flick of the wrist, a straight razor appeared. To Porthouse it looked like the sharpest blade in the world.

"Very poor form indeed. It hurts me to do so, but I have to ensure that you never disappoint me like this again."

Porthouse braced himself, wriggling against his captors. He started to plead, stammering his words. As the razor was brought up, the candlelight reflected in the blade, he turned his head and squeezed his eyes shut.

A sudden ringing made all four men turn their attention to the back wall of the stockroom. There, a small bell fixed to the ceiling was dancing in response to a string being tugged inside the hidden tunnel.

Morai chuckled, all ill feeling lost in an instant. The razor was closed. "There we go!" He laughed like the swashbuckling hero of those ghastly stories sung by bards across the lands, even going so far as to place his hands on his hips. "You tease, Porthouse! Stringing me along like that. Cutting it fairly close, if you will excuse the pun!" He slapped his knee, tossing his head as the joke spilled over.

On hollow legs, Porthouse staggered over to the wall. He shoved a stack of crates to the correct position on the floor and pressed the necessary stone to open the entrance, which swung inward. "About time you got here!" he yelled into the tunnel, a shade shy of hysterical. His voice rebounded along the tunnel, giving him a natural reverb.

From the passage came two men. One he did not recognise; a stranger sporting a thick growth of long blonde hair tied at the nape of the neck, clad in black riding gear. The other was Kanderil. The man was easily a full head taller than the two bullies accompanying Morai and broader with it. The latter pair looked at each other with grim faces.

"Were you expecting us?" the stranger replied casually.

"Of course he was," said Morai. "We all are. Do you have the stock?"

The stranger and Kanderil exchanged glances. Kanderil smiled. *Perhaps for the first time*, Porthouse thought.

"They think we are couriers," muttered the stranger. "Wonderful."

"You mean to say you aren't?" Morai's voice was low and dark. "Porthouse, what is this?"

"I, eh," Porthouse began to jabber. "I c-can assure you, that this w-was not part of the operation, and it is n-not *my* fault that the men who were s-*supposed* to bring me the goods aren't... well, that is to say that I s... oh..."

"Problem?" asked Kanderil as the words trailed off.

"Whoever you are," said Morai, "please turn around and

go back the way you came. My colleague and I have some business to conduct." He opened the pearl-handled razor again. The henchmen grabbed Porthouse by the arms once more. "I would not wish for you to get involved."

Stepping forward, Kanderil loomed over the three linked men; one fat and struggling, two solid and mean. "I am afraid we cannot do that. This man here is my cousin."

Morai stared at the Sergeant incredulously. "Your *cousin?*"

"Aye. I cannot allow you to injure him."

"Your cousin? I do not believe it for a moment."

"He was ill as a child. Most men in our family grow to be around my size. Unfortunately he did not live up to expectations due to the fever. While we grew upwards, he grew outwards." Kanderil spread his hands. "Such is life. Now please, have your men release him."

"I cannot do that," replied Morai in a cold voice.

"Then you and I are at odds, lad." Kanderil cracked his knuckles, tilting his head back.

"He failed to uphold an agreement. I have my reputation to consider." Morai seemed unafraid of the newcomer. "If I let him go unpunished more will follow his lead."

Kanderil sighed. "Porthouse, what have you gotten yourself into this time? Aunt Freida will be most upset when she hears of this."

The stranger coughed at this. Porthouse tried to crane his neck around to look past Kanderil but the thugs holding him tightened their grasp.

"I will ask you again," the woodsman continued. "Please release my cousin. He will answer to me, and I shall arrange a compensation of sorts for collection tomorrow. I have friends in high places who will aid me if needed."

Morai chuckled, admiring his razor for a moment. "High places... Kind of you, I'm sure."

"Not a problem."

The razor slashed through the air. The blade whistled. Morai took a step towards Kanderil, barking in anger. Even now it seemed his wondrous voice recited a dramatic script.

"I *am* high places, you ingrate! How dare you speak to me as if you do *me* a favour?" He span on his heel, stepping back in front of Porthouse, a deadly tension around them all. "Guran, Tarhas... Break his arms."

Porthouse started to yell, fighting against the grip. For the longest moment of his life he waited to feel his bones bend and crack.

Nothing happened.

He looked up to see two huge hands on the shoulders of the brutes restraining him. Kanderil leant forward.

"If his arms break, your necks follow."

The pair looked at each other. They released their captive. Porthouse stumbled away quickly, all but falling against the doorway. One of them - Porthouse decided it was Guran - turned on his left heel, throwing a huge right hook towards Kanderil's jaw. The punch thundered home, rocking the Sergeant. Kanderil took a step back, lifting a hand to wipe his mouth. He smirked, spitting to the side.

"Good effort."

He lunged, throwing a straight right hand in retaliation at the man who struck him. Guran's nose exploded and he staggered back in shock. Kanderil followed this up with a left uppercut which hammered into his sternum. Guran dropped to one knee, winded.

Tarhas charged then, tackling Kanderil around the waist. The impact was like a sledgehammer striking cement. The two goliaths seemed to crumble gradually downwards. As they did Kanderil grabbed Tarhas in a headlock, hooking his other arm under the thug's shoulder before planting his feet against the stone floor. The result left Tarhas with only his forehead to cushion the hard landing. There was a sickening crack as skull met brickwork.

Morai swore. He made for the exit, leaping over the prone form of Guran - then cried out, skidding to a halt. A knife was at his throat. The stranger had stepped between him and Porthouse, whose bulk still filled the exit.

"Let me guess," the man said. "You're not one for bargaining now your meatshields are down."

Morai licked his lips. "A hundred gold to let me leave."

The stranger stepped forward and swung his elbow against Morai's temple. The blow was ferocious and delivered with a spiteful look of enjoyment. Morai staggered to his side, tried to grab something to steady himself, found nothing and fell to the ground.

"Cheap bastard," the stranger sneered. He was prowling, fists clenched, like a hyena before a fresh kill.

Kanderil dusted himself off as he got to his feet, looking towards his partner. He seemed displeased with something he saw there.

"You take me to the most romantic places," said the stranger with a grin.

Kanderil ignored him. "You know the favour you wanted?" he said to Porthouse, lifting a hand to his jaw. Porthouse nodded, too shaken to respond.

"Consider it given."

As the two of them stepped through to the shop, the fat smuggler slid to the ground, his legs giving way. "W-what should I do with them?" he said to nobody in particular.

"Call the guard," called Kanderil as he opened the front door. The bell gave a cheerful ring. "Tell them you fought off a robbery."

The door closed behind them and Porthouse was left in his dusty old stockroom surrounded by three unconscious men. Men who would be *very* upset when they awoke.

Kanderil and Glaithe stepped into an alleyway two stores along from Porthouse's place. The day's trade was coming to an end, at least outside of the market, and the afternoon's hustle and bustle was dying down. The sounds and smells of Tamiran were all around them; stalls clanking as they were dismantled, people calling to each other, the dirty streets musty with the recent rains. Kanderil looked across the cobbled streets, taking a moment to adjust. It was always these initial few minutes that made him remember why he had left for the wilderness in the first place. Too much noise, too many people, too much of everything. There was no room for a sense of self amongst it all.

Glaithe nodded the way they had come. "So much for a quiet entrance."

"They were crooks," Kanderil replied. "They will not report us."

"Well, not lying face down on the floor, they won't." Glaithe grinned. "Alright, so now we need to get you to the Regent."

"How do you propose we do that?"

"Simple, really. I'll pay a visit to the palace and get myself an audience. Shouldn't take too long. I'll then accompany him out for a ride in his carriage and you can meet us at a predetermined spot."

"Not a chance."

"What?"

Kanderil shook his head. "I did not come all this way only for you to speak to the Regent in private. We meet him together."

Grinding his teeth, Glaithe reached around the back of his head to retie his hair in place. He said nothing until he finished, and when he did the words came out tetchy. "All right then, what's *your* plan?"

"How great is your friendship with the young Regent?"

Glaithe shrugged. From his breast pocket he took out a selection of three smoke-sticks tucked into a strip of matches. He placed one stick between his lips, and then struck the match. "Nichai looks up to me," he said, lighting the stick. After puffing a few mouthfuls of thick, pungent smoke, he flicked the match away. "I already told you I won the long distance run a few years back. When he presented my scroll he invited me over for afternoon tea, of all things. I may have elaborated on my successes to some extent, and since then he's been fascinated with my brief but colourful career."

"I did not know you smoked," Kanderil observed.

"I don't make a habit of it," the man responded, taking

another drag. "I carry them for when I need to think in times of stress. Before smuggling a fugitive into the royal grounds, for example." Glaithe exhaled another plume, smiling.

"So Nichai would consider you an equal, then," said Kanderil, picking up his track of thought.

"He's only a couple of summers younger than me, so yes."

Kanderil looked up, gazing down the road. Glaithe did likewise. As one they saw an approaching carriage for hire. The vehicle was large, the sides embossed with decorative adornments while the horses were snow white with feathered headpieces. The driver sat bolt upright, his spine rapier straight, with one of those terrible top hats to elongate his height. He wore an embroidered jacket of velvet blue with silver stitching.

Kanderil snatched the smoke stick and tossed it aside. "Follow me."

Glaithe watched him leave. "What are you going to do," he called in a low voice as he hurried after. "Drive through the bloody gates?"

They exited the carriage not thirty yards from the square surrounding the House of Tamir. Keeping low and out of sight, they snuck from the carriage to behind a covered handcart parked alongside one of the surrounding buildings. The rear of the palace had a wonderful garden spanning almost two hundred square yards. Kanderil had heard it described by a Kalethi team mate years previous who had returned from an assignment within the House. Perfectly kept lawns dotted with small ponds, beautiful trees of many varieties and flowers of every imaginable colour. Around this ran a wrought-iron fence twelve feet high and topped with gilded spikes. Kanderil presumed the gardens were also patrolled. It would be foolish if they were not.

At the front of the palace was a simple reception area. A paved, arcing road ran from the front gate to the main entrance. Security here was tight, with four guards at the gate and another four at the palace doors. A watchtower stood no more than twenty yards either side of the gate also; within both were two fine archers, selected for their skill and vigilance.

Getting in would not be easy.

"We are going to bring him out," Kanderil whispered aloud.

Glaithe peered past Kanderil towards the House. "How?"

"You are his friend. He would come to meet you somewhere if you requested it."

"Perhaps. Bit of a moot point if you won't let me leave your sight to fetch him."

"We can get him a message."

"If we can get him a message why didn't we send a damned messenger pigeon?" Glaithe hissed in that quiet-angry tone used when having a disagreement while trying to avoid attention.

"Do you believe the Regent would have come to meet you a five-day ride away with no given reason?"

"No," Glaithe admitted. "Our relationship is not that strong."

"Right. But he would come meet you at, say, a coffee house? We only need to get him outside those walls. There is no need to include any delicate information. Once he arrives we can get down to business."

"How, then?"

Kanderil considered this, his chin resting on his chest. "I was once told that the Regent is generally on good terms with his staff."

"He has to be," Glaithe replied with a grin. "With no official responsibilities, people of importance generally ignore him. He's basically public relations."

"So he would receive a note from one of the servants?"

"Probably. Why, have you got one in mind?"

"Not yet."

They waited, stepping away from the cart back into the nearby alleyway. Twice they were passed, once by a woman with her child, the other by a man carrying a painting under his arm. Kanderil watched the latter. The man never met his eyes and had tensed as he approached, relaxing only once he was well clear. It struck him as odd that a person could fear being mugged so close to a large number of armed guards, but that was life these days. The Four may have stamped out barbarism and war, but apparently petty crime was so common even they could not hope to put a stop to it.

"There," said Glaithe, pointing along the road. Approaching from the north eastern corner of the square was a woman dressed in a black apron over a plain brown dress. Her hair was pinned back in a bun and a black scarf covered her forehead. She was carrying a small satchel with her.

"What makes you think she is palace staff?"

"She's kitchen staff," Glaithe replied. "Every time I met with the Regent he would have some sort of refreshment delivered. Probably good manners or something. Anyway, that's the uniform of those who brought the stuff in for the butlers to carry over. I guess the drab colours help them blend in with the furniture."

Kanderil nodded. "Fine. Fetch her over here."

Glaithe stepped out from the alley as the woman neared. "*Psst.*"

She looked over just as he raised a gold piece, which glittered in the late afternoon sun. The woman scurried across the road towards them.

"What can I do for you, sir?" the woman asked politely, though her eyes remained fixed on the coin.

"Do you not earn much in there?" Kanderil inquired. The woman peered at him, her eyes at first scornful but growing wide as he rose from his crouched position.

"They pay enough to keep me and my young'uns fed," she said. "But when a man waves gold at you, you come to see what they want." The woman blushed and she bowed her head. "Providin' it's nothin' shameful, beggin' your pardon."

"We need you to get a message to the Regent," Glaithe said. "Quite simple. Tell him I want to meet him at the

Acorn coffee house as soon as he is able."

"The Regent?" She sounded wary. "If I go off disturbin' him, I'll be for a lecture off Mr. Goss. He's already got it in for me."

Kanderil and Glaithe looked at each other for a moment as the kitchen hand mumbled something in distaste.

"Would you do it?" asked the former.

"Why you want him? It ain't nothin' terrible, is it?" She paused, then gasped. "Wait, you're not gonna kidnap him or anythin', are you? Oh, I wouldn't want to be involved with anythin' like that!"

Folding his arms, Kanderil cleared his throat. "We just need to speak with him. I promise you on my honour that we do not intend him harm."

"Well, now, your honour ain't much to a woman like me," she retorted. "We only just met. You could be a right bastard."

"Madam", Glaithe said with a touch of humour, "will you help us or not? I will give you this gold piece here and now if you pass on the message for us."

"'Madam'," she said with a small giggle. The act reduced her age by a decade, dispelling the spidery wrinkles at the corners of her mouth. "Ain't you the flatterer... Okay. I'll do it for two gold."

"*Two?*" Glaithe exclaimed in muted anger. "You want to *bargain*?"

"Ain't like you're gonna keep askin' people who come by, are you? If I tell the guards someone's trying to bribe staff to see the Regent they'll be sniffin' around here quick, like."

"Alright," said Kanderil.

"Besides, I doubt you folks are spotless in reputation, otherwise you wouldn't be sneakin' around like this, would you? Could just walk right up to the gates and sa--"

"Alright," Kanderil repeated, reaching for his money pouch. His fingers grasping nothing, he looked down. He cursed.

"Hawk."

"What?"

"I left my money pouch behind." Kanderil shrugged. "I donated my last coin at the Shrine. You will have to pay her."

Glaithe scoffed in disbelief. Rigid with protest, he took his time fishing around in his pocket until he found another gold coin. The kitchen hand snatched them out of his fingers before stuffing them into her satchel.

"Alright. What was it? Coffee house when?"

"The Acorn, yes. As soon as possible" Glaithe's voice was sullen. "Tell him Glaithe will be waiting there."

"Will do. You chaps take care now." She hurried off along the road towards the front entrance, glancing this way and that as if she feared capture.

"Quite a formidable woman," Kanderil said after she left. He chuckled as Glaithe muttered something viciously offensive beneath his breath.

They arrived at the Acorn shortly after. The place was quiet. Only two other customers sat inside, reclining in wicker chairs as they nursed dark liquid in ceramic cups. The interior of the coffee house was arranged similarly to the others found in Tamiran: sparse, dark, and aromatic. The decor was deep marbled oak and walls painted in the same colour as the drink they served. Only the seating was lighter, giving a creamy contrast to the general gloom.

Kanderil inspected one of the free seats, which was designed to be low to the ground with a sloping backrest. Glaithe eased himself into the chair opposite.

"Something the matter?"

Kanderil nodded. "The furniture is too small."

"You must get that a lot. I'm not sure what to say. It is the only style they have."

"Why would anybody need a seat that low?"

"I suppose it encourages relaxation. They're quite comfy, really." Glaithe leaned back with a satisfied sigh, crossing his legs. The cushioned seating beneath him squeaked. "Could get used to this, if the drinks weren't so damned expensive."

"A true shame you are buying them, then."

The remark produced a lop-sided smirk from the former Agent. "Nice. This little trip is turning out to be a drain on my funds, Kanderil."

"I will repay you when we get back to the cabin."

"That's what they all say."

Kanderil narrowed his eyes, looking down at the man. "You doubt my word?"

Glaithe stared back for a moment before breaking out into laughter. "Easy, there. Of course I trust you. Just a figure of speech, is all." He settled himself further into the chair. "If I'm paying, you're ordering. I'll have a single."

Kanderil looked over at the service desk. A bored looking woman was leaning on her elbows, watching them. She had grey hair and a fair collection of wrinkles and creases on her face. He judged that she would have been pretty in her youth.

"I can hear you fine," she said aloud. "No need for either of us to walk."

"Two singles," Kanderil replied after a pause. The woman nodded, getting up off her stool and disappearing into the back room.

"Well that was easy," said Glaithe. "You drink here often?"

Kanderil shook his head.

"Well, there's singles and doubles, with milk or without. You can ask for it hard, also, but people tend to agree that tastes like cow dung."

"Why order it, then?"

"Because it keeps you going for hours," Glaithe revealed as if this were a secret. "Look, if you're not going to sit can you at least stand next to the wall? You're making me nervous."

They waited; the coffee came. The woman served them with respect, each cup presented with the handle facing the customer, a sugar bowl and a small jug of milk equally distanced between them. Kanderil lifted his cup between thumb and forefinger. For the cost of it, the amount of coffee received was laughable. He took a sip. The bitterness hid a rich, nutty texture beneath it. Kanderil held the hot liquid on his tongue. The taste was fine. He swallowed, nodding his head.

"Like it?" Glaithe asked, his eyes encouraging a positive answer.

"I have drunk worse."

"Good!" Glaithe lifted his own cup in a toast. "Cheers, then."

They passed the time without further conversation. While Kanderil savoured the rest of his drink, Glaithe relaxed in the chair with his eyes closed.

Kanderil was beginning to like the man, albeit reluctantly. Glaithe was well-mannered, intelligent, and witty. When speaking his words came quick and clear; otherwise, he did not say much at all. So far he had done nothing to suggest that he was planning to betray them, or give Sarene's position away to the wrong people. He seemed sincere in his dealings and was confident enough in his own abilities to speak to Kanderil as an equal, something which was rare indeed.

Most couldn't get past the woodsman's size or reserved manner. Glaithe had.

Even so, something still tugged at Kanderil's subconscious. A nagging thought which he could not quite identify. If he was a paranoid man, he would have said that the trip had been...

Easy. It has all been too *easy*.

The door opened. Two Royal Guards, resplendent in red and silver, stepped inside. Their swords were sheathed.

Sheathed until they saw Kanderil. Blades flashed into the air. Kanderil clenched his fists and turned to face them.

"Nichai!" yelled Glaithe urgently.

A third man appeared between the two guards wearing a childishly inquisitive expression. Kanderil recognised him immediately. The Regent of Tamir was a young man of around twenty summers. He was handsome aside from a large, hooked nose. His hair was oiled flat against his head and tied back. A touch of makeup accentuated his lips and eyes, and his luxurious clothes were of varying shades of blue silk which reflected the dim candlelight of the coffee house.

The Regent looked at Glaithe and Kanderil. At the latter he raised a plucked eyebrow. "My, my... Goodness!" He gave an excited giggle before turning his attention to the other customers. They were staring at the scene before them in a state of shock, their expensive drinks forgotten.

"Oh, my apologies!" said Nichai, gushing the words. "I did not mean to interrupt your evening's peace. However, if you would be so kind as to grant us some privacy, I would be *ever* so grateful. I will, of course, pay your bills."

The two other patrons nodded, exchanging looks. They got up from their low chairs and moved for the door, squeezing past the Regent who uttered fond compliments as they passed.

"Nice to see you again, my lord," said the old woman after they had gone. "Same as always?"

"Of course! That would be a wonder, my dear Garsha." The Regent bowed and the woman smiled before disappearing again. Evidently she was no stranger to this kind of ruckus when the Regent graced her establishment.

The two guards, who were still bristling with swords in hand, reminded Kanderil of attack dogs awaiting the command to leap. The Regent placed a gentle hand on a forearm of each, his voice soothing.

"Oh, come on now. There's no need for all this hostility, is there?"

"This man is a wanted fugitive," one of the guards growled. "There's a reward on his head in connection with a murder and kidnapping."

The Regent's eyes grew wide as he observed the woodsman, fascinated. "*Really?*" He took a step closer, his hand raised to his mouth. "Well, yes, I can certainly see it in him. What a brute!"

Kanderil's jaw tightened.

Glaithe stepped forward, offering his hand. "Nichai. It is good to see you again."

"Oh, Glaithe, my friend!" Nichai pumped the ex-Agent's hand with both of his own, smiling. "What on earth are you doing having coffee with a known fugitive? And why invite me?" He chuckled then, leaning in close. "Anyone would think you're getting me into trouble!"

Garsha returned with a steaming cup of coffee. The Regent took it with good grace, offering more elaborate thanks. He then asked the woman to leave them alone, which she did without looking back. One of the guards closed the door and locked it. Nichai sat in one of the chairs. Glaithe took the seat opposite, with Kanderil standing beside him.

The other guard stepped forward. "My lord, I must protest again at the presence of this criminal!"

"Nonsense," the Regent replied. "I trust you can keep me safe. Let's hear what this is all about, eh?"

The guard grit his teeth, stepping back and shooting a look of exasperation at his partner. Both of them sheathed their blades, pommels hitting home with a sharp *dink*. Kanderil could sympathise. The boy's disregard for any threat the Hunter *could* possess was naive in the extreme.

"So," said Nichai, "what *is* this all about? I was expecting something most interesting, to be summoned away from my home like that at short notice. Having one of the servant girls come to me, as well! I thought to myself, 'Nichai, why would Glaithe not simply pay you a visit?' After all, you are most welcome, my friend. As I hope you know..?"

Glaithe nodded. "Of course, your Highness."

"Oh, I told you already, none of this formal address business. It gets very tiring." Nichai paused to sample his coffee, which Kanderil noted had already been sweetened with milk. "Anyway, *I* presumed that you had a surprise of some sort for me. And, well, I suppose you did!" The Regent snorted, holding his cup steady. The liquid inside rippled perilously close to the rim.

"Indeed," replied Glaithe, placing his hands together. "Forgive me for speaking bluntly, my friend, but we are short on time. How far do you trust your men?"

"Cembri and Savarn?" The Regent leaned back in his seat. "These two men have served me since I was nine years old, Glaithe. I would trust them with my life."

"I would not," stated Kanderil. "What we need to discuss cannot leave these walls. They must leave."

The two guards took a step forward each in protest, fingers once again hovering over their hilts. The Regent shivered. "Forceful, isn't he?" he said to Glaithe. "How wonderful. What a *presence* he has!

"Now look here, my man." Nichai gazed up at Kanderil, craning his neck back further than was necessary. "If I say these men can be trusted, then you'll do well to listen. You cannot expect me to sit unguarded with a wanted man, if what they say is true. If you have business with me, then you have business with them." The Regent crossed his skinny legs, lifting his cup to his lips with both hands. "Though, bear in mind, if we are not to talk then my men shall have to arrest you." He sipped.

Kanderil glanced toward Glaithe, who shrugged. There was little else in the way of options. While he could refuse, escape and leave the city, doing so would bring Sarene no closer to safety. He should have expected that it would have been difficult to keep their secret between Glaithe, the Regent and himself for the entirety of the journey. That he had believed he could was now irritating.

"Fine."

Glaithe turned back to the Regent. "This is Kanderil. He has spent the last few weeks protecting a most special young girl. They have been chased halfway across the country by several factions, including our own Gathire."

"What for?" The Regent asked. His curiosity grew with each moment, making him look more and more juvenile. "For the murder?"

"No. I believe you mentioned her to me during our last meeting. The girl mentioned by the Seers."

Kanderil looked at Glaithe for a long moment. His companion did not return in kind.

The Regent considered this, murmuring different

subjects and names as he recalled them. The words made no sense and Kanderil chewed the inside of his lower lip to keep from voicing his irritation.

Then Nichai's eyes went wide and he took a sharp intake of breath, sitting bolt upright. "You mean *her?* The one who's going to change everything?"

"Yes."

"You *found* her? Goodness me!" The Regent laughed long and loud. "Oh, my!"

Kanderil exhaled before he spoke. "You have heard of her."

"Oh, yes, *yes,*" came the reply. "Have you never heard of the Seers?"

"I have," said Kanderil. "I never believed they held any true skill, unlike the Guides."

"Well a lot of it is nonsense. They have to have *something* to say to the crowds, after all. But from time to time a lot of Seers start saying the same things at the same time. In recent years they've been going on and *on* about a girl who is going to change the world. But," Nichai concluded with a sudden, deliberate care, as if a rational thought had just forced its way to the surface, "How can you be certain it is her?"

"I have it on fairly good authority. Trust me." Glaithe smiled. "However, with so many groups pursuing the girl, we need to get her somewhere safe. I was hoping that you would be able to help?"

"*Me?*" The Regent squealed his answer. "How on earth can I keep her safe? I do not have my own army or palace or anything."

"You have *a* palace," Glaithe observed. "The House of Tamir. We only need keep her safe until she has had some time to think and consider her future. As you can imagine, this has all come as quite a shock to her."

"Oh, of course!" The Regent waved his hands in a feminine way, his shirt cuffs flailing around his wrists. "Of course, poor thing. She must be quite worrisome. What about her family?"

"They could be summoned," Kanderil said as Glaithe

looked to him for an answer. "They have already been visited by the Gathire. The visit was not friendly and her family were beaten."

"Oh." The Regent brought a fist to his mouth. "Oh, that *is* a shame. Glaithe, that is a shame. Why would they do that?"

"I protested gravely," said Glaithe. "I was relieved of duty for doing so."

The Regent stormed to his feet. His cup fell to the ground and cracked, bleeding coffee across the slate tile floor.

"*RELIEVED OF DUTY!?*"

Kanderil winced. He was surprised the boy's yelp did not shatter all the ceramics in the shop.

Glaithe held out both hands. "Please, Nichai, that isn't the issue here. We can discuss my situation later."

"But how *dare* they remove you from your position? You being such a commendable Agent and all that. And a Games champion!" Nichai looked at Kanderil, gesticulating. "Did he tell you he was a Games champion?"

"He mentioned it."

"Oh yes, I am sure he did so in passing. Very modest. Now, we must have this sorted out as soon as possible, Glaithe. I shall speak to the Assembly at once."

"Your Highness," said Glaithe soothingly, "there is no need to fret. First we must assist Kanderil and the girl. That is why we are here. After that, perhaps we can speak with the Assembly."

The Regent stared at both of them, the compromise offered to him eliciting a war of responses across his powdered features. "Didn't I say modest?" he said, measuring his words. "Thinking of others before yourself. Yes, fits you. Fits you completely, Glaithe." He looked at the floor. "Oh, bugger. I've lost my cup."

"So will you accompany us to find her?"

Nichai grinned. "Of *course!* I would be most honoured to meet her. I have never met anyone who has been prophesised by the Seers before. Sounds wonderful." He glanced over his shoulder. "Savarn, would you leave payment on the till? Thank you."

Glaithe raised an eyebrow. "Are we done here?"

"We are going to meet the girl, I thought?"

"Well," Glaithe protested with as much civility as he could. "I thought perhaps we could have a night's rest bef--"

"Leaving now would be fine," said Kanderil. The words were stated in a way which Glaithe found hard to argue with. The man sighed instead, nodding once.

"Splendid." The Regent clapped his hands together. "We shall travel by carriage. Most comfortable. It has something called 'suspension' on it. Have you heard? The wheels bounce but the carriage does not. Remarkable!"

"Horses would be preferable," Kanderil suggested. "We would attract less attention to ourselves."

"How far is the ride?"

"Five days." He studied Nichai for a heartbeat. "Maybe six."

"Hmm." The Regent considered this. "First tell me if you murdered whomever they say you did."

"I did not," Kanderil replied.

"Did you kidnap anyone?"

"No."

"Then why would they say you did?"

"I cannot say."

"A man of few words, are you?"

"Where possible."

The answer made the Regent laugh brightly. "Oh, I think I like you. Very well, we shall ride. My retinue of guards will, of course, accompany me. Allow me an hour or so to gather my things. Where are your horses?"

"We left them outside the city," said Glaithe. "We had to enter by other means."

"Not a bother. I will bring a couple spare. Your friend Kanderil will be under my protection, so we ca--"

"No," said Kanderil.

Somewhat taken aback by the blunt rejection, Nichai eyed him up and down. "...I beg your pardon, sir?"

"No. Glaithe and I must leave the same way we came. If we are seen by any of those hunting the girl I protect, they will follow us regardless of your involvement." He straightened his back as an afterthought. "Your Highness."

"Oh." The Regent knit his brow, tapping his forefinger against the side of his vast nose. "Yes, of course. Secrecy is paramount. Well, where can we meet you?"

"Ride north from the city. We will find you along the main road soon afterwards."

"Very well." The Regent turned to his two guards, who seemed to have relaxed slightly over the course of the discussion. "Isn't this *exciting*? We get to have an adventure!"

The two guards nodded, giving strained smiles. Their reaction forced a cough from Kanderil to camouflage his amusement. The Regent left, sweeping through the door onto the street. One of the men, presumably Savarn, stepped past to leave a gold coin on the table. He avoided meeting Kanderil's eyes.

Glaithe brought his palms together, smiling once they were alone. "Well, that went well."

"The boy is an idiot."

"He's enthusiastic. Do not confuse excitement for stupidity."

"He is an idiot," Kanderil repeated.

Chuckling, Glaithe shrugged. "Regardless, he can give Sarene the help she needs. Come on. We'd better get back to the horses before he leaves. Otherwise we'll be dragging the roads for them."

Stepping from the Acorn, the two men headed back towards Porthouse's store, sticking to the alleys and side lanes as much as possible.

As it turned out, Porthouse had taken Kanderil's advice. They arrived at the store just as Morai and his two men were being led away by the Tamiran guard. Lying low until the street cleared was time they could have done without losing, but there was little choice. Roughly a quarter-hour later the last guard departed, having questioned the hefty complainant at length. Kanderil noted that the guard taking the statement scratched at his head often, glancing the way the prisoners had been taken.

Kanderil smiled.

The two of them entered Porthouse's store, ignoring the 'Closed' sign. Porthouse had forgotten to lock the door. They asked for the tunnel to be opened for them. The fat man complied with no argument.

"The authorities didn't believe me," Porthouse sulked as the door swung open.

"No shit," replied Glaithe.

"They think I have an accomplice somewhere. I've been warned that Morai will most likely walk free as well. They advised me to lay low for a while. What am I supposed to do now?" The smuggler shook his head, his jowls wobbling. He threw up his hands. "I'm done for."

"If you trade with people like that, eventually you get stung," said Kanderil. "You should know this."

"Stung? I'll b-be murdered, more like!" Porthouse snapped back.

"Go and stay with relatives," said Glaithe. "Wait until you can offer some sort of reparation. It'll blow over eventually."

"Besides, he knows who your cousin is now," offered Kanderil. "Tell him to take it up with me."

They jogged along the tunnel holding one torch each. They were back to their horses within a couple of hours of leaving the Regent, Kanderil the more out of breath. Finding the geldings still tethered in place to a low cropped branch, they mounted and headed for the road. The Regent would be arriving soon, with luck.

Chapter Seventeen

Jared pushed the door open with his foot, his arms hefting a fresh set of logs. They'd decided to use the last of the tea they had. The copper kettle was already hanging in position, its base blackened from extensive use. Placing the wood on the floor beside him, Jared started to set the fireplace.

Sarene was sitting at the table playing a game of solo with the cards. She was gnawing on her lip as she considered her next move. The deal had been unkind, giving a deeply unbalanced game. Three dark Queens looked at her from the seven rows. She turned the next three cards from the pack. As a dark ten revealed itself she snapped her fingers in frustration.

"Not going so well?" Jared called over his shoulder. Sarene peered at him, clicking her tongue when he started to laugh. "Nevermind. You can always start again." He stacked three logs, which *clunk*ed together as they were placed in position. Whistling to himself, he threaded some more kindling between them before working with his tinderbox. A few minutes later the first flames were licking around the dry wood. It hadn't rained for four days and the last of the summer heat now baked the land without respite.

Jared stood, moving to join her at the table. She leaned forward, resting her chin on her hand, and watched him. He cleared his throat and she raised her brow. That was usually a sign he was going to say something meaningful. She wasn't wrong.

"I've been thinking. You weren't running away just because of me, were you?"

She shook her head, the gesture wary.

"And you understand that if you hadn't left, you would have been found at home with Ma an' Pa."

A nod.

"So the Gathire were probably on their way before you even decided to leave. Your little wander had nothing to do with what happened. You know that, right?"

Sarene looked at her hands, tugging on her thumb. If she had been at home the Gathire might not have cut her mother. They might not have hit her father. If she'd never left, then this whole sorry mess could have been avoided. She felt that she had *something* to do with the resulting tragedy in her little valley home, but she remembered her father's words. Her promise to him.

She nodded her head again.

"Good. I wouldn't want you to blame yourself for any of this." He offered her a smile, which she returned. "The more I think of it the more I believe we'll fix everything. You'll see."

"I don't suppose for a moment you would share the secret with me as well?" said a voice from the corner of the room. They looked over at Hawk, who was still bound at the wrists and ankles but had been given a folded cloak to sit on to ease his sore bones. Jared gave a lop-sided grin.

"So you're talking to us now?"

"Call it professional interest." The words sounded as dry as the wood spitting on the fire.

"One would think you'd know, bandit. Or do you often chase down young girls for money?"

"No," Hawk replied. "Just her."

Sarene's face twisted in displeasure and she averted her eyes. Jared took a deep breath.

"You never told us who hired you," he said.

"No. I did not."

"Perhaps we can share some information."

"I'm not sure that is wise," said Hawk, reclining back against the wall.

"How so?" Jared turned his chair to face their captive. He was leaning forwards with his elbows on his knees, hands folded. "Scared of what your employer may do to you?"

"Boy," said Hawk, gazing up towards the ceiling. "I've had some time to think, sitting here on this floor. My mind is a little clearer. I've be considering the very question you now ask, and I'm inclined to believe that I am scared, yes."

He sounded tired, and Sarene found herself looking at him again.

"So you're a coward. You chase after a young girl, you try and kill an unarmed man protecting her, and you do the work of men you fear." Jared scoffed, turning to Sarene as he sat up. "If this is the sort of man hunting you, sister, you are quite safe."

The bandit cleared his throat gently. "Have you ever been at the mercy of something you cannot quite explain?"

Jared laughed in a way which she found ugly. "A most relevant question. I think I speak for both of us when I say yes."

"Speak for both of you. Good one."

"Watch your mouth, you bastard."

Sarene tapped the table with a finger to grab Jared's attention, before placing her hands against her chest and taking a slow, calm breath. He nodded in return, taking a moment to compose himself. It was difficult to believe her brother was so easy to anger. She watched him as he turned back to their prisoner.

"Anyway, you ask why I did it," continued Hawk. "I cannot say. The reward was good, yes, but that is secondary. The girl wasn't even my main priority. I only wished to see Kanderil dead." He spat the name as if it were a curse.

"Why?" asked Jared.

The question drew out an expression which Sarene found sad.

"I cannot quite explain it," said the cut-throat.

There was a noise from outside. Horses were coming to a halt, followed shortly after by the sound of several people dismounting. Stirrups jangled and feet hit the dry earth.

"My sword," Hawk murmured.

Sarene stood up, her excitement growing. It had been eleven days now. Her brother waved her back down as he stepped towards the door.

"No. Not until we're sure it's them."

Suddenly the door opened. Filling the frame was Kanderil, the sunlight fierce behind him. Sarene ran forward, beaming. Before the woodsman could stop her she had caught him in a fierce hug. He patted her on the back in reply. She glanced up and he nodded to her. She thought she could see a smile beneath that great beard.

"Good to see you again, lass." As she stepped back, grinning, Kanderil narrowed his gaze. "Where did you get that?"

She blinked, looking down. For a moment Sarene was at a loss before she realised her new dagger was still attached to her belt. She tapped it with a finger before thumbing over her shoulder towards her brother.

"Sarene asked for it," said Jared as he stood beside her. "I couldn't think of a good reason to refuse, everything considered."

"Interesting. All went well, I presume?"

"It has been quiet," Jared replied. "You?"

"Productive. The Regent has agreed to meet with Sarene and offer her protection. Her, you and your family."

Sarene bounced up and down on the balls of her feet, bringing her hands together. A break of good news at *last*. She returned to Jared's side, hugging him also. Jared threw an arm across her shoulders, laughing.

"That's a relief." He raised a hand towards the window. "So, err. Where is he then?"

"Waiting patiently behind this huge beast," said a new voice. Sarene peered at the door as Kanderil stepped inside. Revealed was a man not much taller than she, clad in a riding outfit of soft leather and a fancy white shirt a few sizes too big for him. He had a rather large nose, and Sarene had trouble keeping her attention away from it.

Jared stood to attention beside her. She regarded him like he'd done something stupid.

"Sarene, this is the Regent of Tamir," said Kanderil.

A jumble of different reactions gripped her in unison. She tried to bow, curtsy, salute and offer her hand all at the same time. The result was reminiscent of a seizure. The Regent took her confusion in good spirit, offering a high-pitched laugh. As she righted herself, her hand still flat to her forehead with her hair feathered over it, she produced a broad smile.

"What a charming young girl," he said to Kanderil, nudging him in the ribs. The Regent bowed to her, his form regal and practised, before rising and clapping his hands together. "Great! There's no need for any more of that. Between you and me, it gets *very* boring waiting for people to finish all their fancy greetings. Just call me Nichai." The Regent winked at her, and she sniggered again as he watched Jared try and relax his salute as casually as possible.

Glaithe appeared from behind them, moving to the far wall. He checked over Hawk's bindings, testing the knots. The bandit was watching the proceedings without comment. His eyes were on Kanderil and he seemed to be searching for something.

"Well then," said the Regent, gesturing towards the table. "Shall we get started?"

They seated themselves with the exception of Kanderil, who stood behind Sarene and Jared. At the doorway, one of the Regent's guards stood at attention. She had seen another half-dozen men milling around outside as Nichai had entered.

"Now," Nichai started, "I have it been told that you are the girl I've heard so much about. It is quite an honour to meet you, my dear." He smiled at Sarene, who looked first at Jared and then at Kanderil. The familiarity with which he'd addressed her was unanticipated, and she blinked.

"One moment, please." Kanderil walked away from the table without another word. Curious, she turned to watch him stop beside Hawk. He reached down to lift the brigand up by his belt and shoulder, carrying him like he was a toddler. Hawk kicked out at the indignity.

"I can stay!" he protested in anger, writhing in the Hunter's grip. "I already know enough! The Regent and the demon! There's little left to hide!"

"There is enough," Kanderil replied. He tossed the man through the open doorway. Hawk landed with an awkward thump on the hard forest floor. "Put him somewhere safe, will you?" he said to the men outside. Sarene heard the shuffling of footsteps. Hawk's voice became more indignant, but faded into silence.

Kanderil closed the door. He then returned to the table. "Continue."

"Something the matter with him?" asked the Regent.

"He tried to kill me and kidnap Sarene."

"Oh." The Regent glanced at the doorway. Then he shrugged. "Anyway, what were we saying?"

"Apparently your arrival has been prophesised, lass," Kanderil repeated, looking towards her. "Seers."

The Regent adjusted his collar, his features joyous. "I must admit, when they said someone was going to arrive who would change the world, I initially thought it would have been a man." The honesty was disarming. Sarene reached out to grab her brother's hand.

"Change the world?" Jared repeated. "How?"

"Well, I was hoping you could tell *me* that," the Regent said with a dazzling smile. "Kanderil here – lovely man, by the way, if a little gruff, has he always been like that? – kept his cards close to his chest. All he and Glaithe suggested was that she was the one the Seers have been raving about."

"Actually, Glaithe can take sole credit for that," said Kanderil. Sarene picked up on the tone of the statement. Her guardian was displeased.

The former Agent spread his hands. "I remember Nichai mentioning it, is all."

"What have the Seers said?" asked Jared.

"Oh, the usual. That this person will unite nations and bring a new prosperity to the lands. Blah-blah-blah," said Nichai, batting at an imaginary annoyance. "Now, forgive a silly young man like me, but you do not *look* like you could change the course of mankind, sweetie." The Regent's eyes grew still as he studied Sarene. Anxious under his gaze, she shifted in her seat.

"Sarene?"

She looked up at Kanderil.

"Before we go further, do you agree to his offer? Protection for you and your family for as long as is needed to sort this situation out."

Sarene pursed her lips. She began a hesitant nod, but then changed her mind and started shaking her head. Her hand came out, patting air in a request for time. Kanderil merely waited.

The Regent's face grew apprehensive. "Something the matter?"

In response she pointed towards the back room. Then she brought her wrists together, as though, splaying her hands as if in bondage.

"Ah." Kanderil motioned towards the pantry. "We have another with us, who is also wanted for the murder I am accused of."

"You said you did not commit murder, Kanderil." The Regent was looking at him in astonishment, as if he had been lied to for the first time in his life. "Did your friend?"

"Yes."

"Oh, goodness." The response was somewhere between shock and excitement. "Tricky, that one. Why does he not show himself? Is he worried we are here to arrest him?"

A noise came from the back room. There was the sound of fabric shifting position, then a heavy *thump*.

Nichai shrugged. "Apparently not. Well, I am sure

provisions can be made. I will do what I can to ensure your friend is kept away from the gallows."

Kanderil exhaled. "It was self defence. He was protecting Sarene."

"I will do what I can, sir. That is all I can promise."

Sarene considered this. She supposed that if Spasmodic was guilty of murder it would take more than just this man's word to keep him safe, even if he was royalty. Besides, she thought with a sudden grin, she could not imagine Spasmodic waiting patiently as he went through the court process her mother had told her about. Sitting in a cell, being summoned to court... The creature would just escape and leave town if it came to it.

She nodded. Kanderil cleared his throat.

"Very well." A pause, then, "Sarene cannot be affected by the Four. She is immune to their magic. In attempting to cast anything against her they are rendered powerless for a time."

The Regent stared at him. The corner of his mouth twitched. He studied Sarene again for a long moment. She rubbed her upper arm, fidgeting.

"I say. How could you possibly know that for certain?"

"Because Corliani himself paid her a visit."

The Regent started clapping his hands like an excited child. "Oh, good *form*!" Then he stopped as suddenly as he had begun, caught by his own paranoia. His face shifted from delight to suspicion. "Wait. How can I know you are telling the truth?"

Kanderil levelled his gaze at the Regent. The motion was like aiming a crossbow. "Why would we lie?"

"Well, you have admitted that you are wanted for murder. It would be a fairly good ruse to trick me into offering asylum, would it not?"

"*Sarene* is not wanted for murder, Nichai, and I do not ask for sanctuary. They think we have kidnapped her. Why would we come to you asking for her protection if she was my captive?"

"A good point. Yes, I see." Nichai tapped his considerable beak. "Glaithe, do you think this girl is what she claims?"

"She claimed nothing," said Glaithe. "Kanderil explained everything on her behalf. With respect to the girl," – he regarded Sarene as he spoke, his ghostly pale eyes fixing on her – "it would be difficult to make up a story such as this and convince a man of Kanderil's good sense to believe it, given her condition."

Sarene raised a brow at the word 'condition' but otherwise made no response to the explanation, which she felt was a good one.

"Oh, yes. The lack of a voice. Poor thing, poor thing." The Regent looked at her with the kind of pity reserved for those who were in some way crippled. She wrinkled her nose at him.

"My lord," said Jared, "Sarene most certainly *does* have a voice. She just speaks in a different way to you and me."

Sarene smiled. She pointed to herself first, then tapped her temple with one hand as she mimicked a quacking mouth with her other. The Regent laughed, slapping his thigh as he rocked in his chair.

"Oh, yes. Haha, yes, I expect you talk all the time in there!" He looked around the sparse room trying to share the joke, his mouth wide and his eyes creased. Only Glaithe gave a genuine smile. Jared grinned in confusion, and Sarene shrugged, amused.

With a cough to sever the moment, Nichai rapped his knuckles against the tabletop. "Back to business, then. Glaithe tells me that you are being hunted. I can at least understand why you would ask for my assistance in this matter. The Gathire do not readily give up, after all!"

"What exactly are your terms?" asked Jared, giving her hand a squeeze.

"I will send for your family to be brought to the House of Tamir. You shall all be placed under protection from my own retinue of guards. We can be assured they need not fear any further attacks against them." The Regent's smile was broad. Sarene couldn't help but return it.

"What will we do about the Gathire?"

"I think I can handle them. It should be simple to call off the search."

"They've hunted this girl down for almost a month," said Kanderil. "Agents have died trying to capture her."

"That is unfortunate, of course. But you forget that my brother, the Prince, is their commander."

Glaithe spoke then, cutting off Kanderil's response. "Prince Remelas is in effect a figurehead of the Gathire. We work for our own council." He ignored the stony look he received.

Sarene reached up to wind a lock of hair around her finger.

"However," the former Agent continued, "it is very rare that the Gathire decline to follow a specific order given by the Prince. All the Prince would have to do is inform the King of any refusal, since he *does* command the Gathire as he does all wings of the military. Anyone who dared to overrule the Prince would require some very persuasive arguments to keep his post."

Kanderil leaned his head to one side, scratching at the underside of his jaw. It occurred to Sarene that his mass of facial hair must get very itchy.

"How can you be sure your brother is not behind this search in the first place?"

"He would have told me," said the Regent simply.

"Is he required to?" asked Jared.

"No. But... well. I have to confess I have been interested in the Seers for some time. I generally enjoy the nonsense they spill out. It has become something of a hobby of mine, as I think I may have mentioned in Tamiran." Nichai punctuated the final word with a pointed finger. "Anyway, I have become something of an expert in picking out the occasional truths from their rather profound warbling."

Sarene stared at him like he'd just grown an extra mouth.

"Seers," Glaithe explained, "are semi-religious folk who claim to see visions of the future. Most are just mad or stupid, but a few show enough promise to be accepted by the established prophets."

"Fools guiding fools, for the most part," said Kanderil. He glanced down as the Regent peered at him, his young features hurt. "No offence, your Highness."

"Hmm. None taken." Nichai broke into another grin. "Anyway, because of this I tend to chatter about their divinations to my brother. I foster hopes that he will one day share my enthusiasm." He sighed. "More often than not he ignores me, but in a polite way, of course. You know how it is to talk at someone and know they are not listening, but they allow you to continue anyway? For your own benefit?"

Sarene nodded. *Better than anyone else here,* she thought to herself.

"Well, that's how it is with Remelas. I've been talking about these revelations of someone who would, as I say, come to change how the world worked. I have never experienced so many Seers blabber about the same visions. I kept mentioning this to my brother. I'm sure he must have heard it a score of times. If he had organised a search for this person then I'm sure he would have told me. He knows how curious I am about it."

"Besides, as we mentioned before," said Glaithe, "the Prince doesn't need to pay for a Gathire search. Whoever hired them gave gold and plenty of it."

"Something I was curious about," said Jared, interlocking his hands. He looked at Glaithe closely. "How do you know the contract was bought and not directed?"

"It was mentioned in passing when I was ordered to your home," replied Glaithe. Jared tensed, and Sarene laid a hand on his forearm.

"On the subject of Remelas, we *must* go and pay him a visit before we proceed to the palace," said Nichai with a clap of his hands

Sarene's pursed her lips to one side of her mouth. She tapped the table, giving a pointed shrug.

"Is she inquiring why?" asked Nichai, amused by Sarene's direct response. When she and Jared nodded in unison, he tittered. "How remarkable. Well, it is a little embarrassing for me to say I do not have the authority to give you official diplomatic protection. Only my father and my brother can do that."

"Are neither at the House?" asked Kanderil. He sounded unconvinced.

"No. My father is away on a state visit somewhere to the south. Can't remember where." The Regent sniffed. "My brother is at the garrison in Leithar Grove... East of here, I think."

"Aye," said Glaithe. "About two days ride."

"You should have mentioned this back in Tamiran," stated the woodsman, his jaw jutting out with irritation.

"Would it have changed anything? I had to ensure this was genuine before revealing the location of the Prince. You're a suspected murderer, Kanderil. Besides, this is a quicker journey than marching her to my father."

"We should hide her in the palace until one of them returns."

"That could be weeks, perhaps months," said Glaithe. "Besides, the palace has too many staff. Someone would talk, either about seeing her or about not seeing her at all. If the Four consider her important enough to look for, someone will eventually decide she's worth trying to snatch away from you. The Gathire would likely walk right through the front gates if she was without the Prince's formal protection. Even the House of Tamir has informants inside." He shrugged his shoulders as the Regent gasped. "Sorry, my lord, but it's true."

Nichai cleared his throat, sniffing his perfumed handkerchief. "My brother can provide us with a stamped document to say that Sarene has royal immunity. The Gathire will no longer be able to touch her, and no son of Tamir in their right *mind* would try and kidnap her from Remelas' direct protection!" Nichai laughed at the very thought, rocking back in his chair and bringing his hands together, limp at the wrists. Sarene laughed in a way which sounded like a sneeze. She covered her mouth, suddenly feeling self conscious, and looked around the room to make sure nobody was watching.

"I dislike this," the Hunter growled.

"You must trust me, Kanderil," cooed the Regent. "Besides, I insist. I am eager to see my brother and explain in person what is transpiring in our kingdom. If you allow me that concession I will do everything I can to provide Sarene and her family with a safe haven."

"Then what about Tyrrial? Dragging Sarene to Leithar Grove prolongs her exposure. He won't be swayed by some damned signature your brother provides you." Kanderil's voice was unyielding and Nichai seemed taken aback.

"You can't mean the Four are here in Tamir, hunting her *directly*?"

Another noise came from the back of the cabin. Sarene turned her head with the others around her and watched Spasmodic shuffle gingerly into the room. The creature popped its neck, tilting its head to the side. Its appearance made her think of a filthy, miniature bear emerging from hibernation. The cavalry coat it owned was draped over its shoulders like a cloak. Its upper body was bare except for the dirty bandage around its chest, patches of maroon blotted through the fabric. One spindly arm was cradling its stomach. The creature stopped, staring at them through the mass of dreadlocks hanging over its face. It gave a horrific snort, chewing on whatever it produced, before it barked at them all.

"'Ey! Whose bits do I have to tickle to get some fuckin food round 'ere?"

"Oh my!" squeaked the Regent, bringing a hand to his mouth.

"Yes," Kanderil said. "They are."

They spent one night in the cabin with the Regent and his entourage. Kanderil argued for departing that same evening but had been outvoted, the opposition led by Glaithe, who argued that he had been riding for seventeen straight days and needed a decent rest. Nichai took the bed; the rest had stretched out on the floor, while the Royal Guards slept on their blankets outside, Hawk with them.

It appeared that Spasmodic possessed some remarkable powers of recovery. Sarene watched as Kanderil checked over its wound. The ribs had knitted together and the deep gash over them, while still red and angry, had sealed itself well. The wound should have kept it bedridden for well over a month, but it was practically healed within the fortnight. When Spasmodic was unable to provide any answers, Sarene explained that the creature had slept straight through Kanderil's absence and that the wound had oozed a milky liquid. In the end, the accelerated rejuvenation had been chalked up to one of the mysteries of the creature's origins. Spasmodic found this new development most inspiring.

Glaithe and the Regent had stepped outside to talk for a while, as Sarene was growing tired and fighting to keep her yawning to a minimum. Kanderil watched them leave, his eyes fixed on the door until they returned a few minutes later. He and Glaithe exchanged a look she couldn't interpret, but nothing was said. The way they were with each other suggested to Sarene that their journey had been a positive one. They spoke to each other plainly and without tension, which was a sharp contrast to how Jared addressed the former Agent. Her brother remained suspicious, speaking to Glaithe in the fewest possible words. Sarene herself was still in two minds; despite her natural affinity for following Jared's lead, she also valued Kanderil's opinion. She therefore treated Glaithe cordially, overlooking the fact that he frequently avoided her gaze.

The Regent, on the other hand, was simply delightful. He had her laughing for the most of the night. She had never quite met anyone like Nichai. Seemingly oblivious to how others saw him, he laughed without inhibition and made wild, exuberant gestures to match his vibrant words. He talked at length without becoming boring or repetitive; no subject was tedious for him and nothing was phrased in ten words where a hundred would do. He appeared to take a delight in everything, though Sarene had eventually asked him to stop with the steady flow of compliments he threw in her direction. The Regent possessed a flattering remark for everyone and everything, even Spasmodic. Nichai had been fascinated with the creature, who took the subsequent inspections with good humour, but after numerous questions had been answered with close variants of *don't know* and *don't care*, the Regent eventually left it in peace.

The plan for the following morning had been to set out at first light. With the large number of riders – fifteen in total, with one prisoner – it was estimated that they would reach Leithar Grove around noon of the third day.

Beneath a gloriously sunny morning which scattered shadows on the ground from the sparse woodland canopy overhead, the Regent explained again to Kanderil why the trip was necessary. The woodsman remained unconvinced at the idea of heading further away from Tamiran.

"As much at the reality of the situation irritates us both," Nichai said as he watched his retinue prepare the horses for the journey, "I have no official power to stop the Gathire from arresting her, even in my own home. If you want her secure, we need my brother's seal."

After swinging himself into his saddle, Glaithe spoke up in agreement while patting his mount's broad neck. "We could wait outside the city until either the Prince or the King returned, but that just leaves Sarene in the same position as she is now, only with a much larger group to track. While we're out here we may as well take steps to ensure her safety."

"Do you two often agree so easily?" asked Jared, his gaze directed at Glaithe. Nichai laughed at the suggestion, and that was that.

Kanderil evidently found the question rather less amusing. Sarene looked to him for his reaction, which was stoic to say the least. The woodsman had taken Spasmodic aside a little earlier, speaking to it quietly. Sarene was able to lip-read a few of the words used, and she suspected the creature was being asked to travel out of sight of the group.

Her interpretation had been correct, for when the riders formed up into a column and rejoined the road, Spasmodic was nowhere in sight.

Sarene sat behind Jared for the ride. It was a tight fit on his Kalethi saddle, which was designed to keep one person secure and comfortable for long rides. She had watched the surrounding countryside as they trekked east towards Leithar Grove. Despite having seen so much of Tamir over the last month, she was satisfied to know that it retained a degree of wonder for her. The grass of the plains weaved into a carpet with the occasional flourish of dark green and lavender; the effect crisp and sweet to the eye. The trees, with blistered bark and scattered limbs, stood ancient and majestic before her, alive with possibilities of what memories resided within. Even the sky, the same sky she had lived beneath all her life, felt alien and fresh this far north, as though she rode under a different shade of blue. She watched it all pass by with a fond smile.

Later that afternoon, as they took a brief stop for food and to refresh the horses, Sarene tapped her brother on the arm. He looked around, a piece of bread stuck in his mouth.

"Hurrrgh?"

She pointed towards a thin road leading to another of the small villages they were passing, clusters of houses which looked like miniature replicas of themselves in the distance. A crude sign had been erected a hundred yards or so along the road. At the base of the signpost sat a fox, its orange fur seemingly animated in the strong sunlight. Sarene believed it was looking directly at her.

"Oh," Jared said as he removed the bread, chewing. "That's unusual, to be out in the daylight." He bit his serving of cheese.

Sarene nudged him again before shielding her eyes from the sun, making a point of looking around them. She then swept a hand towards the only visible trees, at least a mile north of where they sat, which broke over the horizon like a convoy of refugees.

Shrugging, Jared finished his mouthful and swallowed. "I don't know, Sar. I'm not an expert. Maybe it thinks we'll leave some food behind."

"What's that?" asked Glaithe. Sarene peered at him, gesturing at the signpost. He was arching his back in an effort to relieve an ache of some sort.

"A fox." Jared pointed absently, turning his attention back to his food.

Glaithe winced before looking in the direction indicated, exhaling as he relaxed. "Where?"

Sarene and Jared both returned their gaze to the signpost. The fox was no longer there.

"That's weird," said Jared. "There was a fox sitting right there not a second ago."

"Sure," said Glaithe, twisting his body to the side, rotating at the hip.

"It was there," Jared insisted. "Sar saw it as well."

"Well it isn't there now," said Glaithe, unconcerned. Jared stared at the signpost for a while longer. He took another bite of his bread.

"Weird," he repeated.

Sarene scanned the horizon for signs of the fox. She saw none at all. Before long she gave up, her curiosity still nagging at her, and broke off a piece of her lunch, her gaze wandering.

It was then she noticed Hawk.

The bandit was sitting, still bound at the wrists, holding a piece of bread halfway to his mouth. He wasn't moving a muscle. His eyes were fixed in the direction of the signpost, and his face was as pale as the flour which had made his food.

Sarene watched him, chewing, her hair rustled by the breeze.

They pulled in to rest at a guesthouse in the village of Shaiman, a location which was ugly but functional. Every building was squat and heavy, each a muddy shade of brown due to the clay used to smooth down the walls. While the horses were stabled, Nichai entered the guesthouse to pay for everyone's lodgings. Sarene followed. The interior was simple and lacking in luxury. Only an abundance of candles kept the common room from becoming depressing, the owner having been heavy handed with the wood varnish. These two elements combined to give the place an eerie atmosphere which Sarene found enchanting.

Two of the Regent's retinue were posted on the front door of the building; a further pair was assigned the landing outside the rooms. The rest of them enjoyed a large meal consisting of several dishes – when a member of the royal family stays at your establishment, Sarene mused, it would make sense to empty your larder to ensure they enjoyed themselves – and she felt stuffed for the first time in months.

Leaning back in her seat, she listened as the guards shared stories and told jokes. The Regent seemed to find each and every one fascinating, for once hanging back and allowing others to dictate the conversation. Jared offered his own experiences, as few as they were, but he was well received by his audience. Once again Sarene felt proud of how smoothly her brother could integrate himself with a crowd; his self-depreciating humour and natural timing lent his tales a charming quality. Even Glaithe told a brief anecdote of his early career, wisely selecting one unrelated to the Gathire.

Only Kanderil had not spoken, though she suspected he paid attention to every word.

The next morning, Sarene was still rubbing the sleep from her eyes as she stepped outside. The sunlight made her wince, but she smiled at the gentle wind which had picked up since the previous evening. She came upon one of the Royal Guards explaining something to the Regent and Kanderil. The guard was addressing the latter in a heavy western brogue.

"I went o'er room several times. I can't understand 'ow 'e

got free. There was not'ing to cut 'is bonds with. I tied 'em meself, too. Even the window were still latched on t'inside. Garios an' Pharai on front door din't see anything, either."

"There *is* another exit around the back of the guesthouse," Kanderil observed.

"Aye, but t'owner keeps it locked at night an' key wit'im when 'e goes bed. It were still locked this morning. Unless yer man picked it open, went through an' picked it shut again, then I'm sure 'e couldn't gone that way."

"You are saying he just disappeared?"

"I'm sayin' that I can't explain 'ow 'e escaped." The guard replied with a sour look. "But escaped 'e 'as."

Someone tapped on Sarene's shoulder. She glanced up to see Jared holding two apples for her. Taking them, she gestured towards the conversing group; he nodded in understanding.

"Is this Hawk important?" asked the Regent. He was impeccably presented even at this early hour, with his clothes unwrinkled and his hair combed and oiled.

Kanderil turned away, moving to his waiting horse. "He wants to kill me and kidnap Sarene. I suspect he will have a hard time of it with your armed escort around her. He should be no further worry."

The Regent clasped his hands behind his back, looking over at one of the officers. "Cembri, see to it those men on duty at the time of his disappearance are *thoroughly* questioned."

Responding with a quick salute, Cembri stepped away and called four of the guards over to him. They spoke in low voices that Sarene could not make out, but she could read their body language and expressions easily enough. While clearly shamed by Hawk's disappearance, none of them held any further answers to Cembri's inquiries. All four seemed truthful in their replies.

Biting into an apple, Sarene silently hoped that they never heard from Hawk again.

◄○►

Sarene dozed as they rode, leaning against her brother's back. Sleep was impossible, even with her eyes closed – it was difficult enough to achieve in a bed, let alone while straddling a moving horse – but the time seemed to pass a little quicker. The heat of the day was relaxing, complimented well by the gentle wind on her skin. She had caught the sun during her journey and she no longer felt her skin burning so easily beneath the tan.

It was at some point during the afternoon when Kanderil dropped back to ride beside them. He had tied his headband back in place and it was now damp with sweat. Sarene offered a smile he did not return, so she shut her eyes again.

"Have you noticed the position of the guard around us?" he said in a low voice.

"Aye," Jared responded in kind. "Never less than two in front and behind. Why do you ask?"

"Does it seem strange to you?"

"Not really. He's offered Sarene protection, after all."

Sarene opened one eye upon hearing her name.

"Indeed. But you and I?" Kanderil thumbed his nose, looking at the riders in front for a moment. "I slowed to check the kind of tracks we were leaving. Two of the Regent's escort stopped with me."

"So?"

"I dislike the idea that I am being herded to our destination."

Sarene felt Jared shrug his shoulders. "So tell the Regent to ask them to back off. Honestly, Kanderil, you're sounding a little paranoid." The words came with the briefest of laughs.

Kanderil frowned. "You are new at this game, lad. You should trust me." He paused. "The creature has not returned since yesterday, either."

"Spasmodic? No, he hasn't. Is that odd?"

Without reply, the woodsman turned his head to survey the southern landscape, where flocks of sheep grazed upon an extended incline. Shortly afterwards he heeled his mount towards the head of the column again, the horse's tail flicking behind it. Sarene leaned back to look past Jared's shoulder, watching him go.

"What was that about?" Jared muttered to himself.

Sarene sniffed, stretching. For the first time since they'd met, Kanderil seemed clearly agitated. That in itself was cause for concern. Right now she had enough to worry about. It was still daunting to consider that she was riding to meet with the Prince of Tamir. Not only that, but to be *presented* to him for judgement, to help make the case for offering her family sanctuary from the Gathire. The Regent Nichai had been pleasant enough, but the real authority with the kingdom lay with his elder brother. It would be Remelas who would decide her fate, and it was crucial that she made a strong first impression.

With Kanderil's misgivings in the back of her mind, the task became that little bit harder.

Not an hour later, a call came from the front of the column. Her horse clopped to a halt. Gripping onto Jared she leant to the side, looking up ahead.

There on the roadside was a large caravan. It was one of the most fantastic things she had ever seen. The vehicle was a deep, lacquered scarlet covered in painted flowers and etched stars of a detail she could appreciate even from four lengths back. Two snow-white horses dressed in feathered headwear were harnessed to the far side. Fixed to the top of the caravan was a wooden sign which had been carved to read '*THE GREAT MANDRAIK!*' It was embossed with gold leaf, some of which had flaked away. It seemed ancient and new all at once. Sarene grinned and patted her brother's arm in excitement.

"Ho, travellers!" came a compelling voice. Emerging from the other side of the caravan was a man wearing a blue waistcoat over a yellow shirt. A matching top hat of bizarre length sat upon his head and added three feet to his height.

He was handsome and radiated self-confidence. As he approached, he twirled a hook-handled cane with startling speed.

"Ho!" Savarn had wheeled his mount around and now faced the opposite way to the rest of the column. He walked his horse to place himself between the caravan and the Regent. "Might we help you at all?"

"You might indeed," the outlandish man replied. "You might take a short break from your journey to witness one of the finest exhibitions in all the lands. You might take pause to see the wonder and the spectacle of my travelling carnival show. And you *might* wish to consider this your lucky day, for it is not often that a gentlemen finds himself in the presence of the marvellous, the magical, the magnificent..." - the man took a deep bow of such poise that Sarene hiccupped a laugh - "Mandraik!"

"Oh, bravo!" she heard the Regent say. She presumed the rapid, joyful applause was also his doing. "I say, why not! It has been quite a dull ride and I could use some entertainment. What say you, Glaithe?"

Glaithe shook his head. "My lord, I really think we ought to c--"

"Splendid!" the Regent brayed. "It's settled then. *Dismount!!*"

The guards complied with a distinct lack of enthusiasm. Sarene dropped out of the saddle, running ahead even as she heard Jared's command to wait. She ignored it and hurried towards the caravan, eager to get a prime viewing position.

She ran into a solid force which almost knocked her from her feet.

Bewildered, she blinked. Then she realised that she had collided with Kanderil's hand. The woodsman now held her in place.

"Stay close to me," he said. His face was like thunder and the words were severe. Twitching with eagerness she nodded, her eyes returning to the magnificent Mandraik. Kanderil relented, walking with her towards the group now assembling before the caravan. The Regent came to find her.

He seemed as excited as she was, his hands clasped to his chest in an effort to contain himself.

The guards gathered in place. Jared joined her, Kanderil and the Regent. Glaithe was the only one to remain on his horse, leaning forward on his pommel. Looking around she noted that few of the guards expressed interest in the show they had been promised. She disregarded this, deciding they were too full of soldiering to enjoy a carnival show.

Up close, the paintwork on the side of the caravan was incredible. The flowers had small faces in the bud, surrounded by petals of painstaking shading and colour. The vines appeared to pulse, thickened and thinned with varying amounts of textures, climbing along the frame and the wheels. The stars in the upper portion of the picture shone somehow, an ingredient in the paint reflecting the sunlight above. Sarene made out various pictures as the different objects came together, creating a larger mosaic which changed depending on which part of the caravan she focused on; a woman's face here, a dragon roaring there, a cherub up above and a fish down below. It was impossible and yet she bore witness, entranced by the view.

"Now, ladies and gentlemen – well, *lady*," Mandraik said with a wink to her which made her giggle. "What I have in store for you today will be something to remember tomorrow, the next day, and each and every day after. You will see things you may not believe. You may see things that frighten you, but know that I will not judge you should you scream in terror." Mandraik strode before his crowd, seeking the gaze of each man. The cane continued to whirl as he reached up to tip his extraordinary hat. "Many would, but not I."

Nobody laughed except the Regent, who *squealed*. Sarene flinched before nudging him to be quiet, grinning.

"But, I can see that you folks are in a hurry," Mandraik continued, standing upright and stepping back, "and I am sure that *you* can see that I am the sort of man who could talk the hair off a horse's arse, so I will at least seek to restrain myself and simply say..."

He paused for effect. A sly wink was offered to the audience as he peered out at them from beneath the brim of his hat.

"...Let's get started."

Mandraik tapped the caravan with the bottom of his cane. The sides collapsed. Sarene jumped. The front and rear of the caravan folded out and the wall nearest to them fell forward with a jarring *thud*. Suddenly they were watching a stage so packed and animated that it was difficult to believe it had all fit inside the trailer.

The stage was full of odd props and gaudy colour created by paints and fabrics. The background of the stage was a deep blue made to resemble the sea, bordered with hanging scarves and transparent drapes of pink, red and gold. Four figures in skin-tight clothing, completely black from head to toe and decorated with silver stars, were already dancing in flawless symmetry. They moved in time to the sounds of tambourine and violin which had commenced the moment the caravan had unfurled. At either side of the stage were two people of such short stature that Sarene at first thought them to be children. In unison they raised a thin rod with a block of burning pitch at one end and blew hard on the flames. A huge roar of fire burst into life above them and she heard some of the crowd gasp or curse in laughter. They crossed each other as they scurried along the stage before performing the same trick again.

Appearing from behind the upright back wall, Mandraik stepped between the dancers without any effort despite the limbs which curled and twisted inches from his person. He gave a deep bow, holding his hat in one hand to reveal dark hair tied in a bun atop his head. Sarene had never seen a man with such a hairstyle before.

"Lady and gentlemen," he called again, "know that it is indeed flattering to present our show to royalty. I have always said to myself, 'Mandraik, one day you will bring your wondrous show to the royal court'. Haven't I always said that?"

The two small people nodded at him enthusiastically,

kicking an abrupt jig. The black figures continued to dance, fluid and enthralling.

"And finally, here we are, proved right and proved justified. A great honour to receive you as a guest, your Highness." He offered a humble gesture of respect to the Regent, who laughed.

"The pleasure is mine!" he yelled in return. Jared covered his face with a hand.

Sarene scanned the plains, searching for Spasmodic, but it was nowhere to be seen. She sighed. The creature would probably have adored a spectacle like this.

"Most kind! Yet onwards we must go. As much of an entrance as I know this little prop of mine grants me," Mandraik continued, tapping his cane on the stage, "I appreciate that not following up with a trick or two would be a travesty, deceitful in its promise. For that reason..."

Mandraik removed his hat again, twirling it in his hands with the same practised skill as he did his cane. He flipped the huge hat in the air, caught it by the brim, and lifted it above his head as if trying to catch something falling from above.

From the hat flew two doves. They scrambled and fought for air, gathering altitude and flying away from the caravan. Some of the guards gave short, polite applause as Mandraik returned the hat to his head. Sarene clapped her hands with vigour, as did Nichai. Jared joined in, smiling down at her.

"Thank you, thank you," Mandraik drawled. "Now, perhaps you *fine* men of honour and glory would enjoy something a little more dangerous, eh?" He straightened, raising a brow as he returned the hat to his head. The violin and the flute continued to play, their song bouncy and melodic. All four dancers span around him, coming to the front of the stage as he stepped back.

"Please, if you would, give a round of applause to my wonderful assistants as they show you how to *really* handle a sword."

Kanderil's hand was on Sarene's shoulder in an instant. She glanced up at him for a moment before her eyes were drawn to the hilt of his knife, upon which his fingers hovered. She looked back to the caravan to see that each dancer now held a long, thin sword each.

The dancers stood in a row at the front of the stage. The two small people had positioned themselves at either end, this time juggling flaming batons. The fire twirled in a cross pattern in front of them, turning the dancer's silver stars to gold. The dancers adopted a stance with their feet planted shoulder-width apart. As one they raised the swords to point at the sky, their distance from each other perfect. The sunlight glinted from the blades, causing Sarene to squint for a moment as one reflected beam hit her face.

Together, the swords were spun and brought down. The blades disappeared into their wielder's throats.

Sarene tensed, her breath caught in her chest. She heard similar reactions from the crowd around her, sounds of surprise and alarm which didn't fit the image of a group of hardened soldiers. The handles of the blades rested on the invisible mouths of the performers as they lowered their arms to link elbows, forming a human chain. Their audience burst into applause at the sight, encouraged by the small people who cheered along with them. The Regent doubled over, slapping his knee and roaring approval through a hacking cough. Sarene joined in, exhaling at last, clapping her hands with great enthusiasm.

The dancers soon removed the swords, again in synchronization, the blades being withdrawn with deliberate care. Once clear, they were twirled in a single circle before being placed point down on the stage floor, their heads bowed like knights before their King. Sarene wondered to herself what fabric their body suits were made from, for there was no visible mark around the dancer's mouths where the sword must have penetrated. Their heads remained concealed in black and silver.

"Astounding! Amazing!" Mandraik took centre stage, his cane tucked under one arm as he clapped along with everybody else. "Did I not say I would promise you something you would never forget?

"Now, perhaps just one more trick before we depart. I can appreciate that a man such as the Regent Nichai must have places to be and people to see." He gave another elegant bow. "For this final act, however, I must have a participant from the audience."

Sarene stepped forward but was immediately restrained. She looked again to Kanderil, who regarded the master of ceremonies in the same way one would watch a hissing snake. She gave one attempt to wriggle free but the hand at her shoulder tightened, the grip like warm steel.

"I'll go," said Jared. He had noticed Kanderil's actions also. Her brother ruffled her hair before moving towards the caravan, giving a playful bow to the assembled guards. They jeered him on in good humour, laughing and joking with each other. She saw Mandraik grin. Jared pulled himself onto the stage, rolling to his side as he swung his legs under him.

"You could have used the stairs, my boy," the showman observed, tipping his hat. The guards cackled. Jared spread his hands in acceptance of the rebuke. Sarene sniggered.

"Most gracious of you to join me. What was your name?"

"Jared."

"Excellent. A fine name. Well, Jared, all you need to do is take this apple." The fruit in question was held before him, red and polished, in one white-gloved hand.

"Thanks very much," said Jared. He tossed the apple in the air, spun on his heel and caught it again. He winked at Sarene. A few of the guards gave a teasing cheer while she clapped.

"Splendid! You are a natural, my friend. Let's see if you're as skilled with the next step, which is to hold the apple in your mouth."

"What, all of it?" Jared asked.

"Yes. Just move to the end of the stage over there," – Mandraik pointed to the right hand side of the platform – "and grip the apple between your teeth."

"No worry, boy," shouted one of the guards, a large man with fleshy bags under his eyes, "just bite it like you bite yer pillow in the Kalethi barracks." A great cry of laughter rang out. Sarene wasn't quite sure what was so funny about the comment. She looked at the Regent, who was blushing even as he smiled.

Jared saluted, doing as he was bid. He walked over to the edge of the stage, his footsteps creaking on the wooden structure. Then he turned to face Mandraik, who had brought his hand to his chin, watching.

"No need to turn to face me, Jared. Allow your friends here to revel in your handsome features. Holding an apple in one's mouth does wonders for the cheekbones." Another laugh. Jared faced the onlookers, smirking.

"Hands behind your back, stand straight, chin thrust out."

Jared bit the apple. They heard his teeth puncture the flesh, the sound fresh and ripe. Sarene's mouth began to water. It was then she noticed that only her brother and Mandraik were on the stage. The dancers and the dwarves were gone and the music had stopped.

The tension began to build as Mandraik produced a small throwing knife. He held it between two fingers, bringing his arm up to cover the lower half of his face. With his smile hidden his eyes were wicked.

"A simple feat of agility and marksmanship," he said. "Surely it would be impressive were I to cleave the apple from my assistant's mouth? Think of what could go wrong, my friends. Think of the jeopardy inherent in this trick." He turned his back to the crowd. Then his arm came straight beside him. The throwing knife was gone.

In its place was a large meat-cleaver. The guards gave a collective murmur of disquiet. Sarene became nervous, her throat growing tight.

"Are you ready, Jared?"

Jared made a noise. The crowd laughed, but Sarene caught the unease beneath it.

"Of course. Well then, say your prayers..."

Mandraik threw his arm forward, hurling the cleaver. Sarene could hear the *whompwhompwhomp* as it spun towards her brother. The weapon passed him and something made contact. She flinched, raising her hands to her face, trying to hide from the scene she knew was waiting. Something had gone wrong; the blade was too big, the throw was too hard.

A great cry went up. She peeked through her fingers to see Jared standing with half an apple between his teeth. The other half had fallen to the ground at his feet. She gave a great sigh of relief, joining the others in their praise. Jared seemed unconcerned by the risk he'd faced. He took the remainder of the apple from his mouth and showed it to the audience. They gave another cheer.

"I think you tickled my nose," he said.

"Wonderful! Well done, Jared." Mandraik applauded along with the rest of them. Jared descended the stairs, walking over to her. She grabbed him in a quick hug.

"Well done," the show master repeated. "Now, I should let you all go. You surely have places to be. I hope you have enjoyed the show, my friends." He gave a bow, sweeping his hat again. This time he was well received.

Mandraik moved towards the stairs at the side of the stage, walking down them with knees rising like a trotting horse. As soon as his foot touched the ground the stage began to rise at the sides and the front as the platforms were pulled back into place, wheels and ropes creaking in rhythm.

Walking in front of the crowd as the applause petered out, he raised his hands to call for quiet. "I hope... thank you... I hope you enjoyed this little break in your journey and that I have not delayed you too badly. I do not want your money in return, so for the one or two of you who were thinking of sharing some of your hard earned pay, rest easy and sleep well tonight."

A ripple of laughter from the Regent's retinue.

"In all seriousness, my friends, all I want in return is the chance to provide a very brief, very important message." Mandraik clasped his hands together, bowing his head. When no protest was forthcoming, he looked up.

Directly at Sarene.

She gave a smile, wondering what this strange, exciting man had to say. He approached her with graceful steps, his hands spread. Dropping to one knee he gave a sweeping bow to present himself.

"Listen closely, dear, for my words are of profound significance." He smirked. "Will you listen closely?"

Sarene nodded.

"Good. Here is my advice. Tomorrow, you should make a truly concerted effort to enjoy life. Watch the sunrise. Prepare your favourite meal. Take a walk somewhere beautiful." He chuckled. "Whatever it is that means the most to you, you should do. I say this as a simple messenger, nothing more, nothing less."

Peering around at the others, feeling pressured to react, she gave the show master a warm smile. She nodded again.

"And one last thing," said Mandraik, leaning on his bent knee with both arms. He took a deep breath, uttering two words as he exhaled. "*Tyrrial comes.*"

Kanderil pulled Sarene behind him and stepped forward, seizing Mandraik around the neck and lifting him clear off of the floor. The man gripped the Hunter's wrist, holding on for his life even as it was being choked out of him.

"Who told you that?" Kanderil growled through gritted teeth.

"A-h, nnghget-*aack!*"

"*Who?*"

The ridiculous top hat fell off. Mandraik swung his legs, kicking out to try and find some purchase. The showman was by no means slight, but Kanderil had hoisted him like he was made of cotton. His face was turning purple and Sarene brought a hand to her throat, anxious.

Laying a hand on Kanderil's elbow, Jared spoke quietly but with impatience. "If you hold him that tightly you'll strangle him before he can speak."

Kanderil shot Jared a hard glance. "I told you to trust me," he replied.

A moment afterwards the woodsman let go, turning his back. Mandraik fell to the floor, coughing and spluttering, writhing like a fish stranded on the shore.

"Wha--" he wheezed. "I didn't... *coughoughough*" – he spat something onto the floor – "that m-message wasn't *me--*"

Jared stepped forward, reaching down to yank Mandraik up by his waistcoat. The Regent's guard were forming a circle around them, all business now, eyes surveying the tranquil landscape for any sign of an ambush. Nichai himself was watching this development, dumbfounded.

"You mentioned Tyrrial," Jared said. "Why?"

"A man," Mandraik said, gasping and holding his neck, rubbing at the red skin there as the blood rushed back. "A-a man came to me. He paid me... *cough*... paid me good m-money to be here at this hour." He was staring at Kanderil with fearful eyes on an angry face. Sarene felt the complete image made him look confused.

"Describe him," continued Jared.

"He... Tall. Handsome guy, blonde hair. Well s-spoken." Mandraik stood straight. "He, uh... He laughed a lot. He told me to wait here for the Regent... *cougough...*" – the man shuddered into another brief coughing fit – "...To pass that message on *(cough)* to the girl with him."

Some of Nichai's retinue glanced at Sarene. She shuffled her feet, doing her best to ignore them.

"Have you any idea who she is?" Kanderil asked, his words rigid.

"I've n-never seen her before," Mandraik responded quickly. "Should I know her?"

"No," said Kanderil. He waved his hand dismissively. "Take your caravan and get out of here. Enjoy your gold."

Mandraik needed no further encouragement. He ran around to the rear of the caravan. A moment later he was leading the white horses to the harness at the front. Two wiry young men had joined him. Sarene watched them work before movement drew her attention back to the mosaic artwork on the vehicle's panels. Two separate peepholes had been pulled back, one high and one lower to the ground. She saw two sets of eyes peering out at them from within.

"So what does that mean?" asked the Regent. "We have to be wary of carnival folk as well?"

"No," Jared said as Glaithe joined them, having dismounted. "The man was just paid to pass on a message."

"I can think of only a handful of people who would be able to make the connection of the Regent riding with a young girl," said Glaithe.

Kanderil grunted. "Seems we missed something."

"You don't think..." said the Regent, bringing a hand to his face. His gasp encouraged a dramatic response.

Instead he received a blunt one. "Either Tyrrial is in the area and sent the message himself, or he got someone to do it for him," said Kanderil. "Either way, we have been given a warning."

"The man he described sounded a lot like Hawk," said Jared.

"Aye, it did. Where Hawk would get the money to pay for a trick like this I do not know."

"I suggest we get moving," Glaithe said, focusing on Nichai as he spoke. The Regent's cheeks bloomed with scarlet. Sarene gave him a pat on the arm which he seemed to appreciate.

"No more stops." Kanderil was walking back along the column of horses. Some of the guards had already mounted, while others were at steady intervals along the convoy of horses, keeping watch over the surroundings.

Sarene looked up at Jared as they made their way back to their horse. He gave her a fond smile, reaching across to squeeze the back of her neck. She bit her lower lip to show him that she felt nervous.

"Don't worry, brighteyes. We'll get you safe." The words were said with conviction, and she nodded.

Within a few minutes they were heading east once more, just as the Marvellous Mandraik's beautiful caravan began to tumble to the west.

Chapter Eighteen

*T*hey arrived at the Leithar Grove barracks as the sun was setting the following day. The flag of Tamir hung flaccid from masts atop the pair of rounded towers within the stronghold. The sky to the west was a deep orange. A looping curve of cloud slashed across its path, a great shadow in the sky.

Leithar Grove was a winding trail of open countryside cutting a swathe through the encroaching forests. Glaithe had mentioned to Sarene that the Grove suffered a terrible forest fire several years previous, and the woodland was only now returning to its former glory. The barracks sat at the highest point in the area, a knoll overlooking the terrain below. Jared pointed out the sloping grassland between the barracks and the woods. For roughly ten yards in front of the forest Sarene could see the stumps of trees which had been felled and dragged clear.

"Killing ground," he remarked. "Any enemies which attacked the fort would have to charge uphill, you see. With no cover they'd get shredded by arrows."

Sarene sat back, wishing her brother hadn't shared that nugget of information. The images which came to mind were most unpleasant. She shivered.

The barracks themselves were larger than she expected. The upper section of the knoll had been flattened out to provide a level building ground. An imposing barricade rose more than twenty feet into the air. Unlike the walls around Tamiran these were not smoothed over, the chaotic pattern of stone lending the structure an iniquitous appearance.

A horn blew inside, the heavy note sustained for an awfully long time. The main gate of the fort, built into the eastern wall, began to open as the convoy approached. There was a mechanical clicking as the portcullis rose, the cogs strained by the wrought iron burden. The noise seemed alien to her. Sarene had never witnessed a gate this big actually moving.

As they rode through – with Nichai at the head of the column, Savarn alongside him – she saw several groups of men. Some were fully outfitted in the armour of the guard, others wearing only the linen underclothes of blue and grey. The majority were tall and strong with heavy brows. To her surprise a lot of them were young; within Jared's age range of twenty summers. Sarene offered a smile as she passed. A few of the soldiers nodded in return as they continued with their various tasks.

"Halt!" yelled Savarn. His voice had become familiar to her, barking out orders in the name of the Regent. Her horse came to a standstill, rearing its head as Jared tugged on the reins. The riders dismounted so she did likewise. As soon as Jared was beside her she made her way towards Kanderil. Ahead, Nichai was embracing a strikingly handsome man. He was dressed in a white shirt and black riding pants with matching boots. The shirt was open at the chest. His hair was a long, light brown with a slight curl. There was only one hint as to the man's identity; he wore a large golden necklace embedded with a ruby of such a huge size that Sarene didn't believe it was real. It matched the description of the Scion's Amulet, handed down through generations of the Tamir Royal Family. She was in the presence of Prince Remelas.

Glaithe stepped away from them to stand beside Nichai,

while she hung back with Kanderil and Jared. She watched as he was introduced to the Prince, who greeted him with genuine warmth. Shaking his hand, Glaithe said something which made Remelas laugh.

The Prince then glanced their way. Sarene met his gaze for a second before losing her nerve, turning her attention to the sky. It reflected her tension.

The two Royals approached them as servants arrived to lead their horses away.

"This is Kanderil, formerly of the Kalethi," said Nichai with a sweep of the hand. "The young girl is Sarene, and beside her is her brother Jared, currently of the Kalethi."

"Welcome to Leithar Grove," said Remelas. "My brother tells me you have had quite the journey."

"Aye," Kanderil responded. "You could say that."

"Well you can relax for now. You are safe within these walls. I regret that I have some matters to attend to, but I should be ready to speak with you at length within the hour."

Kanderil inclined his head without comment.

"Excellent." Remelas looked down at Sarene, giving her a quick grin. "If you will follow my page he will show you to our kitchen." He clicked his fingers and a young boy dressed in a royal tabard came hurrying over. "Our meal today was roast pig. I believe there is some left over. Nichai, would you walk with me?"

Sarene, her companions and the Regent's guard made their way after the page. The boy couldn't have been much older than she was, with mousey brown hair cut with a bowl. He scurried towards one of broad courtyard entrances, then had to wait for those behind to catch up. The idea of matching pace with them didn't seem to cross his mind.

"That was brief," said Kanderil.

"I expect he's a busy man," replied Jared. "He wouldn't have known we were coming, after all."

"If you had let us send word perhaps he would have been ready to receive us," Glaithe put in, walking behind the three of them.

Kanderil gave a sigh. "It was not a complaint. Besides, I could use a meal," he admitted. "We will see him soon enough."

"Military food is awful," said Jared, and Sarene grinned. At least her brother was honest enough to complain about *his* views. She tugged on his sleeve and mimicked poking a finger down her throat. Jared laughed, but slapped her hand away.

"Stop it, Sar."

They were led through one of the fort's inner doors into a long corridor lined with doors which had been carved out of the cinereous stone. The corridor's floor was paved with square tiles. Sarene imagined it must be cold in winter, but for now it retained the heat of the day. Most of the doorways were closed, but not all. Sarene saw a few rooms with stacked beds and latched trunks. The sheets were made and the floors were spotless. Even her mother would be impressed by the cleanliness of the place. She tugged Jared's shirt and pointed.

"Soldiers have to ensure their bunks are neat and tidy at all times," Jared explained. "It encourages high standards and sets a routine."

"Also trains those too ugly to find a wife to keep their homes in order," said Glaithe with a smile. Jared laughed. Sarene found the quip amusing but was intrigued by Jared's reaction, since few of Glaithe's previous comments and been well received. She didn't dwell on this for too long; the smell of roast pork was beginning to reach them, causing her mouth to water.

They entered the kitchen at the end of the corridor which now split into a T junction. Three long tables ran the length of the room, tables which Sarene had never seen the like of. Each ran for around twenty yards, parallel with benches on either side. She tried to imagine what it must look like when the tables were full. Her only point of comparison was the Shalith meals back at the valley, where everyone in her village would come together to feast and dance and sing.

This room would only accommodate the feast. Bereft of

decoration or luxury, it was devoid of charm. She sat down with the rest of the guards, wedged between Kanderil and her brother. Glaithe seated himself opposite them.

The page went into the kitchen area, where three servants were washing dishes and scrubbing pans. Beside them, on one of three great steel spits, Sarene saw the golden brown remains of a pig carcass. There was plenty of good meat left on it and her stomach rumbled in earnest. She heard the page explain that the men in the room were guests. The servants put down their cleaning tools and started collecting plates and cutlery. Slowly, food began to filter along the table as cuts of pork were passed along the rows, folded flatbreads beside them on the plates. Sarene licked her lips as four servings of food passed her before she received her own. She tore into the meat, which was gloriously warm. Juice dribbled down her chin and she tried to catch it with a handful of bread. Jared laughed at her.

"Calm down, Sar. It's not going to get up and run off, you know."

She grinned at him with a mouthful of food.

Her companions ate without talking, listening to the idle chatter of the guards. Sarene enjoyed their banter with each other. It was sometimes profane, often hilarious. She finished her meal before everyone else and wiped her finger around her plate in case she found any invisible pockets of flavour. Jared tossed a piece of his own serving onto her plate. She snatched it up, nodding her appreciation as she popped it into her mouth.

Nobody at the table left any food on their dishes. The servants cleared everything away quietly. Finally the guards stood, filing back out into the corridor. Only a few of the men said goodbye, but Savarn paused beside them.

"We have to go and sort out beds for tonight," he said. "When his Highness is ready for you, he'll send someone. Just wait here until you're called for."

Glaithe nodded. "Thank you."

Acknowledging them with an informal salute, Savarn followed his unit outside.

They waited until the sun fell behind the forests and the sky turned a deep, gloomy blue, visible through narrow windows along the back wall. The kitchen inherited a sickly yellow colour from the stuttering lanterns. Nothing much was said. Sarene guessed it was a combination of fatigue and apprehension. The meeting with Nichai had been important but their audience with the Prince would be vital. They understood, just as she did, that it was Remelas who held the power to grant her safety within the House of Tamir.

Kanderil sat with his arms resting on the tabletop, focused on his hands. He emanated that same, steady patience that she had come to associate with him. Not even a meeting with the Prince of Tamir seemed to faze him.

By contrast, Jared was as nervous as her. He tapped his fingers on the table, looking around the room and making little observations about the barracks to which Sarene listened and responded. Before long he got up to fetch some water, moving to the barrel without a cup in his hand. It took him a moment to understand the flaw in his plan. Sarene patted him on the arm when he returned. She was certain that Jared would slip into his usual, confident self when the meeting was underway. It was just the waiting which seemed to unsettle him.

Glaithe appeared calm. He was watching the three of them in turn, but looked away whenever she met his gaze, just as he had in the cabin. His conscious effort to avoid her eyes was... well, *rude*. She didn't understand his reasons and felt uncomfortable at the idea of asking. To distract herself, she started picking at the table with a fingernail.

Eventually one of the guards came for them, snapping to attention in the door and giving a crisp salute.

"Prince Remelas will see you now."

Together, the four of them stood.

They were led out of the kitchen and back down the corridor. Most of the doors were open now, the soldiers sitting on their bunks in casual clothes and chatting to each other. Kanderil heard the banter and the colourful language as they walked past, and looked down to Sarene for a moment before he caught himself. Cursing was the least of her worries.

He'd been catching himself a lot over the last few days.

Was it right that he felt such a strong sense of duty? A month ago this girl had meant nothing to him. He'd been asked to do a favour for a man whose home had been invaded. As requested, he had delivered her to her brother. With his promise kept he was free to move on. Kanderil could hold his head high.

He'd returned to Tamiran, the capital he so despised. Once they had spoken to the Regent and claimed his support he could have left, safe in the knowledge she would be protected. Jared would have ensured she had her audience with the Prince. Instead he found himself anxious to get back to her; to have Sarene under his watchful eye once more.

Why?

They exited the corridor and crossed the courtyard. Training had ended for the day. The area was deserted except for those on sentry duty and the few servants attending to mundane housekeeping tasks. The air had a heavy, soothing taste to it which accompanied the fresh night. The sky itself was a delicious indigo, a colour to match the oceans.

As a Kalethi, Kanderil was occasionally required to escort civilians across Tamir. Some in danger, some not. He'd shared the company of a few of these people for longer than he had Sarene, but once they'd been safely guided to their destination he would leave with no regrets. Never had he completed such a mission with an inclination to keep in touch.

With the girl it was different. He felt compelled to remain in her company, to walk beside her as she endured this improbable combination of events and circumstance. The fact that she was facing it at all was inspiring to him. To do so at her young age was *incredible*.

During his career he had heard grown men weep before

joining combat, scared for their lives. He had seen recruits complain and yell and stamp their feet at being given extra guard duty, like giant children in fancy dress. Once, Kanderil had witnessed a portly trader, easily into middle age, rolling in the mud of a street gutter, throwing an absurd tantrum after discovering his horse had been stolen. Yet Sarene was now shouldering the responsibility of being utterly unique within the world. She was still smiling, still playing, and still moving on. The girl displayed a maturity of will which he greatly respected.

You want to be here, he thought. *You found something new to believe in.*

Reaching the opposite end of the courtyard, the group made their way between two sentries who were flanking a broad staircase. They both looked at Sarene. They both looked at him. Jared and Glaithe were ignored. Seemed the latter two fit into the same category as everyone else in the fort – male, regular sized and military stock. Giants and females were the attraction here.

The soldier leading them stopped before a door with an arched top, knocking three times. A voice from within responded in a positive tone. After opening the door, he stood aside.

Kanderil followed the others into a spacious chamber. It had little furnishing, but what there was seemed most comfortable, illuminated by six paraffin lanterns hooked against the wall at regular intervals. A high-backed chair with embroidered cobalt blue padding faced a beautiful pine desk with a marbled, glossy finish. On the desk were six silver goblets on a tray beside two pitchers. Thick velvet drapes hung tied beside the open window, which looked over the grasslands leading into the surrounding forests. A bearskin rug, the head intact, lay snarling across the floor. Kanderil guessed it must have been colossal in life.

Standing in the centre of the room were Remelas and Nichai. The Prince and the Regent were both smiling, though Kanderil could tell that the younger of the two was copying the mannerisms of the elder. Nichai's gaze flicked across to the Prince every few seconds, changing his expression accordingly. He wondered if either of them knew how obvious this trait was.

"A warm welcome to you all," said Remelas, spreading his hands in greeting. "My apologies for the delay, but I was somewhat unprepared for your visit. It is rare my brother here ventures so far from home and rarer still that he brings guests." He clasped Nichai on the shoulder.

The Prince had pulled on a thin overcoat since they had last seen him. With his strong, attractive features and confident posture, he looked just as the heir to the throne should. Kanderil folded his arms over his chest, studying Remelas. He had heard great things since their brief encounter years previous. It was interesting to assess his development in person.

"No apology necessary," Jared said. The words sounded prepared. "We understand you must be a busy man."

"Indeed," Remelas replied. "Even so, my brother tells me that one of you is a most special guest."

Jared and Sarene exchanged looks. Nichai sniggered.

"Before we begin, may I get anyone a drink?" The Prince moved over to the desk. Lifting the pitcher he poured a cherry-coloured liquid into two of the goblets. "It's Cho'Nanj syrah. Some of the best wine I've ever had. I think you'll find it most agreeable." Remelas passed one of the goblets to his brother.

"Very kind of you," said Glaithe. He had stepped away from the rest of them and was leaning against the western wall.

"Please," said Jared, "but I fear my sister is a little young."

Sarene scowled at him, tutting.

"Completely understandable, and the sign of a responsible man to say so. Thankfully, I had some apple juice prepared." Remelas smiled, pouring once more. "Sergeant Kanderil?"

"Aye, thanks." That the Prince had named him was unexpected.

Once drinks had been handed out and all had complimented the taste – Kanderil had to admit the flavour was grand; robust, full and smooth on the tongue – Remelas took centre stage again, stepping back beside his brother.

"So I understa--"

Something jumped in through the window. Everybody turned to see Spasmodic land on the ground, bouncing upon its heels. It took a moment to survey the room before reaching so far behind its back that its shoulder clicked.

"What in the name of..." uttered Remelas, stepping back a few paces.

"I told you they had a demon!" Nichai chirped, clapping his hands.

"Where have you been?" Kanderil's calm voice contrasted with the royals.

"Busy." Spasmodic grinned up at him, rubbing its scalp with its palm. Stuff fell out.

"A little more specific, please."

"What are you, my mother?" It snorted abruptly, dislodging something from its nasal cavity. It rolled its tongue around its mouth before it swallowed. "I been busy. Kept me distance like you asked."

"You thought this would be a good time to return?"

"What, when you guys met the champ, here? This is why I'm hanging around with you, dummy. Getting to meet the movers and groovers of this world." It offered Remelas a sharp wink. "Hey there, guv'nor."

"An honour to meet you," Remelas said without missing a beat, snapping his fingers. "May I have the pleasure of you name?"

"Spasmodic. Does it give you pleasure?" the creature sniggered.

"It gives me something to call you besides 'demon', Spasmodic. I presume the term is not to your liking. There are a plethora of connotations associated with the word, few of them flattering."

"...I have no idea what you just said."

Kanderil, clearing his throat, sought to bring the meeting

back on track. Entering into a conversation with Spasmodic was risky at the best of times. "You were saying, your Highness?"

"Ah, yes. Forgive me." Remelas took a sip of his wine, savouring the taste before speaking. As he did he began to pace a circle around his brother, who looked on adoringly. "Nichai has informed me of both your situation and your appeal for help. You have asked that Sarene here be placed into our custody, along with her family."

"That's correct," said Jared, taking a light hold of Sarene's shoulder. She reached up to place a hand over his.

"I can appreciate the request, of course. It must have been unpleasant to have the Gathire chasing you halfway across the country." Remelas focused on the girl, holding his goblet in both hands. "Especially for you, Sarene."

She nodded at him, sweeping a length of hair behind her ear, shrugging in resignation. He held her gaze for a moment longer before continuing.

"While Nichai has shared his views on the matter, I do have a few questions of my own before I make a decision." He walked over to the window, taking a brief look outside before turning his attention to Kanderil. "You and... Spasmodic, here. May I ask your relationship with the girl?"

"She was put into my care by her father, after her family were attacked by the Gathire," Kanderil replied in a way which conveyed his poor opinion of the faction. "I was asked to deliver her to her brother, who now stands beside her."

"How did you know Sarene prior to this?" Remelas asked.

"I did not."

"I see. How, then, did you come to be in her company?"

"She ran away from home in pursuit of him." Kanderil inclined his head towards Jared. "I came across her alone and without much in the way of provisions. I decided it would be best to take her back to her parents."

"I would be apt to agree there," Remelas remarked with a smile. "And you, Spasmodic?"

"I just follow her around," it said, yawning.

"That sounds rather ominous."

Kanderil grunted. "It was created by Tyrrial and sent to kill the girl. Once it arrived it decided not to do so, and has travelled at her side since."

Remelas paused, looking to Nichai for a moment. Nichai grinned in a way that irritated Kanderil. The grin of a man who knows something and is eager to share it.

"Well, we can discuss that at length another time. I am sure it has good reason for declining to complete its mission, just as I am sure you have for remaining with her for so long." Remelas turned to Glaithe. The former Agent had a smoke stick dangling from his lips and had struck a match. He looked up as the Prince addressed him, the flame still a few inches from his face.

"You I recognise, Gathire. What is your part in all of this?"

"I was a part of the dispatch sent to Sarene's home and involved with the attack Kanderil mentioned, your Highness." Glaithe drew up one leg, resting his foot flat against the wall he leaned on. "May I?"

Remelas nodded. Glaithe lit the stick, puffed the newly formed ember into life and shook the match out.

"I was forced out of the Gathire after I protested against the treatment of her family during questioning. Justicar Chalimer discharged me upon my return to Tamiran. I then pursued her to offer my assistance, knowing that she would still be hunted."

"How noble of you," Remelas replied. "However, you are surely aware that the Gathire are under my command?"

"I am, your Highness."

"And yet, you freely admit to hampering their work?"

"We have been told that you did not give the order for the search," said Kanderil. "The contract was bought independently."

"Even so, they are still my men," said Remelas. He moved back to the table and replaced his goblet on the tray. "You three I can understand – you were entitled to run following these unwarranted crimes towards Sarene's family.

Which, while we are on the subject, I offer my most sincere apologies for." Remelas motioned first to Sarene and then to Jared. "Those responsible will be properly dealt with. That is not how things are done within the Gathire."

"As for you, Glaithe, I will speak with the Assembly regarding your conduct. You will be given the chance to plead your case. The fact that you brought Sarene and her companions to us before any further incidents could occur will weigh heavily in your favour."

Glaithe nodded, taking a long drag on his smoke stick.

"Incidents?" Jared sounded surprised but was too afflicted by nerves to add conviction to his voice.

"Yes. Incidents of violence. I presume that whoever hired the Gathire wanted to bring Sarene in for questioning, not execution." Remelas looked to Nichai for a moment. "You are convinced that she is the one? The babbling of those prophets has gotten you excited before, brother."

"I know, I know," said Nichai, holding up a hand in confession. He had also re-dressed since separating from the group, now resplendent in a blue silk shirt, dark pants and soft moccasins. "But this is the first time so many have spoken *together*! Besides, why else would a de--" He coughed as the creature looked at him, recovering fast. "Why else would Spasmodic travel with her? It is a creation of the Four."

"Tyrrial," said Kanderil.

"What?"

"A creation of Tyrrial. Not the Four. They work independently of each other."

"What makes you say this?" asked Remelas. The question was more of an encouragement.

"I would say your brother mentioned our meeting with Corliani." The Prince nodded. Kanderil continued. "Well, he lacked hostility. He merely wanted to meet Sarene for his own personal interest. If the Four were collaborating he would have taken her then."

"I thought similar," Remelas replied. "The chronicles of the Four always state they walked the lands as individuals."

"Tyrrial's a borin' old git anyway," put in Spasmodic. "Don't blame the others for hidin' from him."

Nichai blurted out a laugh. "Oh my. Quite the rascal, isn't it!"

Spasmodic looked at the Regent like he had just tried to put flowers in its hair.

Hiding his smile with a cough, Kanderil spoke up. "To answer your previous question, I cannot say whether the Seers are telling the truth or not. I consider them to be frauds, but that is irrelevant. Sarene *is* immune to the power of the Four. I witnessed this myself."

Remelas looked at him as if ascertaining whether he could be believed. Kanderil stared back. It was uncommon for any man to hold his gaze for long, but the Prince did not waver.

"Very well," he declared. "I will take you at your word. By sunrise you shall have a document granting you my protection and instructing the Gathire to break off the search."

"I have already done that for you," said Nichai, beaming.

Silence descended on the room. Kanderil focused on the Regent, his jaw clenching tight, waiting for the words which were about to come. Words he should have expected.

Remelas faced the Regent, arching a brow. "I beg your pardon, dear brother?"

"I called off the search for Sarene."

"You have no authority to do so, Nichai."

"I do, in a sense," Nichai said with infuriating self-satisfaction. "I simply withdrew *my* contract."

Jared took a step forward. Sarene grabbed his arm at once, trying to hold him in place. "You... You *bastard!*" The young man trembled in both voice and body.

"Hold your tongue, Kalethi," said the Prince, raising a hand.

"I think he is entitled to speak his mind," said Kanderil. He looked across at Glaithe. "Did you know about this?"

Glaithe said nothing, looking down at the stub of his smoke stick. He exhaled a cloud of blue fumes... and smiled.

Kanderil moved for him, furious. Glaithe stepped from the wall, placing a hand on his knife.

"*Guards!*"

The door burst open and two men entered, assessing the imminent conflict right away. Within seconds they had crossed there spears between the two parties, the weapons *clink*ing together. The Hunter made a grab for his target, who hopped back out of range.

"Kanderil, you *will* stand down," Remelas ordered, his voice booming inside the chamber. "We shall discuss this further, and I can assure you I desire answers from my brother a damned sight more than you."

Kanderil glared at Glaithe, who still held his knife half-drawn. The man was watching him, cold and calm.

"Stand down or I shall have you put into a cell." Remelas' voice was quiet this time but retained its assertiveness. Kanderil exhaled to release his anger, at last stalking back to Sarene and Jared. She was watching him with those huge eyes, reaching out for his arm, giving a few quick pats. Her expression spoke for her. *Please.*

"Guards, you are excused. Call for assistance and remain close by."

The two men took one last look at the situation in the room before departing. They took a moment to stare at Spasmodic, who was squatting on the floor in an aggressive posture, jade eyes fixed on Glaithe. As the door closed behind them Remelas turned to his brother.

"Explain yourself, Nichai," he demanded.

"I took out the contract to find her," the Regent started. He seemed like a deer caught in fright, his gaze darting from one person to the next. "I thought if I could bring her to you it would help you with your plans here."

Kanderil, pacing near the doorway like a prize fighter preparing for the ring, focused on him. "Plans?"

Nichai looked up at Remelas, stammering. "I-I-I mean... T-that is to s-say..."

"Someone wind him up, the great big boo-hoo" said Spasmodic scornfully. One of its claws scratched against the concrete floor.

Remelas sighed. He moved to place a hand on Nichai's shoulder, drawing his younger sibling into an embrace. Gently he whispered against the boy's temple. "Why didn't you tell me, brother..."

"I wanted to s-surprise you," Nichai replied, sniffing. He pulled his head back, a spiral of emotions crashing to the surface. "I wanted t-to do s-something to *help*, I..." He swallowed, producing a *guh* sound as he choked back a wail. "You keep telling me of all the w-work and a-all the, the, the..." At last, he fell into quiet sobbing.

Kanderil felt no pity for him.

"Sit down," Remelas said, cooing as if speaking to a child. "Come on. Sit down. Take a drink and calm yourself." He led the Regent to the large chair before handing over one of the goblets. Nichai downed the contents, liquid gurgling with each mouthful.

"I was not aware of this," Remelas said to the others. "I was not aware of the search, the reasons for it or my brother's involvement." He smoothed Nichai's hair with a palm. "In that you must believe me."

"Two of the men in this room are liars," said Kanderil, levelling his gaze at Glaithe. "Why should we accept you are not amongst them?"

"Because I tend to ignore the words of the Seers for what they are – unfettered drivel." Remelas straightened, hooking his thumbs into his belt. "Prophecy and visions mean nothing to me. And I would prefer not to be called a liar in my own kingdom."

Kanderil resisted the urge to retort as Glaithe folded his arms over his chest. The man's demeanour had changed. He was stony faced, lacking in the acerbic humour which had until now characterised him. With the secret revealed he was back to his true self; Gathire through and through. Kanderil's failure to see it was just as infuriating as anything else.

"They set us up," he said. "Both of them. I fell for it and I will be *damned* if I let myself be tricked again."

"Then how do you suggest we resolve this, Sergeant?"

Sarene stepped forwards then. The tension which had filled the room so suddenly ebbed away. She snapped her fingers, leaving a gap between each click, until Nichai looked up from his goblet. She spread her hands before her, her shoulders rising with deliberate patience. The question was evident, even for this cretin. *Why?*

"I c-couldn't tell you," Nichai blubbed. His face was swollen from crying. "I had to get y-you here, to her- to my brother." He sniffed. "I had to prove t-to-to him that I was *use*ful..."

To his sole credit, he repressed the wail which threatened to squeal into life.

Spasmodic giggled. "He's a fuckin' sap. How long we gonna sit here an' listen to this?"

"You have to understand something." Remelas addressed the creature directly at first, then the others. "My brother here has to live in the shadow of my father and me. As the second born, he has little authority over any official matters." He clutched Nichai's shoulder and gave a firm squeeze. Nichai gazed up at him, smiling through the tears.

"I share with him details about my ambitions for the nation, and he can do little to help. He is no swordsman; no great tactician. He has no martial skill and lacks the mind for organisation. I suppose that is why he falls in with superstition and prophecy... Perhaps this is my fault after all." The Prince sighed, stepping away from the Regent. Nichai took another loud slurp from another goblet.

"He mentioned plans," Kanderil stated.

"Yes. This brings us to our next issue. You now know who hired the Gathire but you do not know why. Why Nichai would want to bring Sarene to me."

Suddenly aware that she stood in the centre of the group, Sarene quickly back pedalled to stand beside her brother. Remelas watched her with a thin smile.

"Again, I must insist that I was not aware of this search, nor of any evidence to suggest you existed, my dear. But..." The Prince wagged a finger in the air. "Well. If what they say is true, you may well become an important part of my army."

"...Your army?" said Jared. For a moment Kanderil believed that would be the young Kalethi's only offering to the discussion, but further words followed. Jared found his voice. "Why would you need her in your army? If it's because of what Nichai says, then you have it wrong – she can't *do* anything. She doesn't have any powers. She can't fight on your behalf."

"Sarene would not need to." Remelas folded his hands together, fingers of the left massaging the knuckles of the right. "Think on this. If she is truly impervious to the Four, as you say, then it would be difficult for them to uproot an army she walks amongst, no?" He paused. "Perhaps I should put things into perspective."

The Prince started to pace once more, keeping his distance from Spasmodic.

"I intend to take my army east and invade the nation of Carthlei in the spring. My best estimates proclaim that they will surrender to us within two months."

"How?" said Kanderil. He found he was not shocked by this announcement. Instead he was beginning to understand some of the comments made along their journey. Major Rohad. The Kalethi scout. Fallerin.

"By crossing the border with the largest army the world has ever seen. My standing military now numbers thirty eight thousand."

Silence, then. Those before the Prince exchanged glances. Kanderil shook his head. Since the time of the Four no ruler had ever raised an army of such magnitude, fearing that they would be visited and punished. Even the few open conflicts between nations over the centuries had been fought by forces numbering hundreds, not *thousands*.

Thirty eight thousand men would smother any defending force like the tide across a beach.

Spasmodic hopped on his heels, giggling. "Hah! I knew I'd pulled a good'un here. Can you imagine how much *fun* that's gonna be?"

"You are the Prince of Tamir," said Kanderil slowly. "You are within your rights to go to war, regardless of how terrible an idea it is. But I will object to the girl's involvement. For now she is still my charge." He saw Sarene peer at him.

Remelas smiled. "My campaign will go ahead without her, Sergeant. I had little faith that the Four existed. Now you claim that they do, I am still hesitant to believe they will stop me. It will take more than your testimony and the presence of a strange creature to dissuade me from years of preparation." He gestured to Spasmodic. It winked in response, grinning like an imp.

"However, there is no harm in having some insurance, is there?"

Sarene shrank back behind her brother.

"My dear," the Prince said in a soothing voice. "I am not going to force you to do anything you do not want to do. I am not a tyrant. All I ask is that you listen to me." His gaze flicked up to Kanderil.

The request seemed to take the girl by surprise. With hesitation, she shook her head.

"You have travelled all this way," Remelas continued. "Please. Do not allow my brother's efforts to be in vain. Should you still find yourself opposed to my request after I have had a chance to explain myself, then I will still provide you the protection you seek. Just grant me your patience for a short time."

Jared muttered. "You don't have to do anything you do not want to do, Sar."

Sarene nodded her understanding. With an index finger she first tapped her ear, then her temple.

"She says she will listen if she can think."

Finally she pressed the palms of her hands flat together and rested her cheek on them.

"Because she is tired."

"By all means," agreed Remelas. He made to move to the goblets once more but Jared spoke again. Sarene had continued to move, and Kanderil watched her point to

Glaithe and Nichai before turning to gesture to the door, walking two fingers in the air.

"She asks that Glaithe and your brother must leave, also."

Remelas shrugged. "Of course." He leaned over the silver cups, checking the contents of each before selecting one. Prior to drinking he nodded at Glaithe, who remained silent. "Please escort the Regent to his room. I believe he could use some rest."

Glaithe did so, moving across to Nichai and helping him to his feet. He led the sullen Regent towards the door, opening it for him and ushering him out. Not once did he look at any of his former companions.

"Now then," said Remelas. "Shall we get to business?"

"What's so important about Leithar Grove?"

Hawk leaned back and sucked his fingertips, chewing. The chicken wasn't bad, all things considered. The rest of the carcass hung over the fireplace. He'd remove it soon, but for now it was crisping up nicely. The small cavern reflected the light and heat so that the walls seemed to be in a constant state of flux. Outside the night had settled, contrasting with the yellows and oranges around him. He felt like he was sitting inside an old brass etching, watching the ink of the sky blot into his scene.

The old man sat opposite, smoking a scrawny reed pipe. He puffed for a moment, a bitter haze around him. Just as Hawk started to think he would not respond, he removed the grip of the pipe from between his teeth and tapped at the air with it.

"It is where everything comes together," he said. "All the gentle nudging and coaxing of the last few years. It will all be ended with a minimum of loose ends." The old man chuckled. "Destiny is a funny thing, once you get to grips with it."

Hawk took another bite of the steaming chicken in his

hand. He took the time to chew and swallow before asking a second question, enjoying the warmth of the fire. Warmth which was sorely lacking in the man sharing his company. "How so?"

"Your Prince is gathering an army. He intends to subjugate one of your neighbouring countries."

The news came as a shock. If that were true, then Remelas was in a great deal of trouble. "Can you read minds?" Hawk asked delicately.

"I do not need to. I have spent a good portion of the last few years in Tamir. I had to refrain from using my particular talents, for the most part, but it is a simple thing to convince men to talk about confidential matters. The rate at which your nation is recruiting soldiers is alarming. When an army exceeds the necessary size required for defence, one can presume their ruler is being cautious. When it expands six-fold, it can only mean one thing. War. War, despite our teachings."

Hawk shrugged. "Not everyone believes in you these days, Tyrrial."

Immediately afterwards the bandit regretted speaking. The old man looked at him with an expression which made Hawk's stomach turn. It was neither fury nor surprise. It was no emotion he could read. But the icy stare was distressing, as though his very soul were being observed.

"You make a valid point," Tyrrial replied after a while. "It is precisely for that reason why Leithar Grove is significant. I could have simply dealt with the girl. I intended to, originally. But her current path allows me to remove her threat whilst also sending a message to the lands. Mankind will be reminded that the Four exist; that we are to be feared and that we are watching."

Putting down his meal, Hawk brushed his hands together. "Will I get to deal with Kanderil?"

"What do you feel about him now?"

"I want to..."

Hawk trailed off as he considered the poacher. Ever since his first meeting with the old man he now knew to be Tyrrial of the Four, he had lived with an uncontrollable hatred for Kanderil. But now, when asked to reflect, there was no emotional response. He raised his hands. They shivered slightly, but no longer trembled with rage.

"I feel nothing," he said, mostly to himself.

"Indeed you do not. That is because I have other uses for you now, and wrath is not compatible. I need you to be calm and focused."

The frank statement unsettled him further. "What do you have in mind?"

Tyrrial placed his hands on his knees. "I mentioned destiny. A month ago you were hunting lost travellers in the forests. In weeks gone by you have been seeking revenge on Kanderil. Now, I want you to help me ensure that Tamir is claimed by the right man after I have completed my work."

Hawk quirked a brow.

"It is your destiny to pass a message on to this Glaithe you mentioned." The old man reached into his robe and produced a folded, sealed envelope. "You are sure he holds Regent Nichai's confidence?"

"They arrived together and Nichai was speaking to him like an old friend," Hawk replied. "Can't say I'd have ever thought a simple royal stooge would be as forthright."

"Good. Then give him this letter. The guest rooms reside within the fort's eastern tower. You should find him there, assuming Remelas does not expect his brother to sleep in the common bunks."

A log cracked in the fire, producing tiny sparks which streaked like comets away from the blaze. Hawk nodded. "Done. I'm guessing you can resolve my current status as a fugitive?"

"Of course." Tyrrial smiled. "They will not recognise you."

The old man stood, pulling back his sleeves to expose weathered forearms. With his fingers spread wide, he held his palms out flat. "I will be honest, Hawk. This will hurt." His lips started to move and his brow furrowed in concentration.

An unusual sensation crept over Hawk's skin. It was as though the air around him was becoming thicker, applying pressure to his entire body. The feeling was unpleasant and his eyes widened in alarm.

"What are you doing?"

No response came. Tyrrial brought his hands closer together, pushing against an invisible force which lay between them. Hawk cried out as the pressure around him increased. It felt like his torso was being crushed and his shoulder blades were threading underneath his collarbone. The bones of his legs shifted and collapsed and he fell to the ground. Pain exploded through his temples as his teeth melted together, sliding up into his nasal cavity inch by terrible inch. His vision blurred and his skin burst into hateful, torturous agony.

"Now you see why I need you. I am not too fond of the shifting process." Tyrrial gave a short laugh, the sound wicked with amusement. Hawk receded into merciful unconsciousness just as he fell into himself and his arms bent backwards at the elbow.

Chapter Nineteen

*R*emelas leaned on the desk, his legs crossed at the ankles. One hand toyed with the beautiful amulet around his neck.

"How did you raise an army that big without anyone uncovering the truth?" asked Jared. He had helped himself to another serving of the wine and was making an admirable effort of drenching his nerves with it.

"It wasn't easy, and it took a long time," said the Prince. "Rotating shifts of training and reserves. I have squads out on manoeuvres in the west while drill training others in the east. Back in Tamiran and other larger towns there are more still on reserve. They study in the universities and build their bodies in the fields." He smiled. "One of the advantages of such slow development is that the men learn various skills and become better soldiers."

"People have noticed the increase in military presence," said Kanderil. "They just do not suspect the scale of it."

"Exactly." Remelas folded his arms, clearing his throat. "Nobody does. Tamir is a small nation. Our economy is based on agriculture, with foreign exports dominated by wheat and grain. We have no coastline and cannot readily utilise the seas for transport. Our lands contain few precious materials. There are barely enough resources on our side of the Laysine Mountains to sustain our production of tools, weapons and equipment. As we are we will never better ourselves. No one believes Tamir will ever stake a claim to glory within the world.

"Carthlei will solve that. If we absorb them into our rule we will be able to harness the power and the bounty of the oceans. We can mine the eastern Laysine ranges for our needs. But more importantly we can fuse our cultures. Our *heritage*. With the combined teachings of our schools and universities, with our scientists working as one, think of the advantages it would grant us! Tamir could begin to forge a new age as a great nation built on power and respect."

"But first there will be bloodshed," Kanderil observed. His voice was grave. "You would have war, a true war, be your legacy?"

"A short, necessary war. I will build my legacy on the fruits of that sacrifice, on the spoils of victory." Remelas held his hands out, reaching for his subjects. "I am not a conceited man, Kanderil. I have ambition but I do not believe myself arrogant. I do this for the good of my kingdom and my people. My only wish is to provide a brighter future."

"But you're tricking us. All of us," said Jared. Sarene looked up at him, her lips pursed. His words were loose and he waved a hand to his side as though referencing an imaginary crowd.

"Not at all," said Remelas. "I have nothing to hide from the people. I am within my rights as the Prince of Tamir to raise an army and undertake military campaigns, as Kanderil has said."

"Yet you *do* hide it," Jared insisted. "You're going to pull together this huge army and march east and our nation will know nothing about it until it's already happening."

"I know how my subjects can be," the Prince said, ignoring the accusatory tone. "Were I to announce we are to invade Carthlei, they would talk. Talk breeds rumour.

Rumour can lead to panic. The legends of the Four are embedded in our society. The Tamir people would fear that the Four will swoop down on us like a plague."

"What if they do?" said Kanderil.

Remelas put his hands against the edge of the table and straightened his arms. "How long has it been since the Four abandoned us? Five hundred years? Six? If they were going to act on this Commandment of theirs they would have done so when the Grashna sacked the town of Hisa twenty years ago. They would have stepped in when the Juu'ad massacred that island race back at the turn of the century." Remelas shook his head. "There have been atrocities throughout our history which the Four left unpunished. If they still exist, if they ever did, they have lost interest."

"How can you say that now?" said Jared. "After what you've been told?"

"The wheels are in motion. These plans have been growing for years. Generations before me have lived under the shadow of a tale which has become myth. I am merely going to show the world that we need not fear these fabled men any longer."

"Exactly!" Spasmodic crowed. It stood upright and pointed towards the window, stamping its foot. "Show 'em who's boss, boss. You get out there and make a *stand*, damnit!"

"Hush," warned Kanderil.

"Are you blind?" started Jared, but before he could elaborate Remelas cut him off. The Prince's words were tolerant but firm.

"If you are to address me you will do so with a civil tongue, Jared. You may make your point without insult."

Jared took a deep breath. "My apologies, your Highness. I'm simply frustrated." He walked over to Spasmodic and gripped a handful of its dreadlocks. It sneered at him. "Look. This is a creation of Tyrrial, one of those men you say don't exist. And you're still going to test them? This is *proof*."

"Hello," said Spasmodic, waving its hand.

Remelas shrugged. "Spasmodic was sent for Sarene, you

say. I cannot equate that with the superstition that these historical men will rain down fire upon my head for seeking to expand my territory. Tamir is small, poor and has reached a plateau in growth. I must do something."

"Jared, calm yourself." Kanderil. said, watching the young Kalethi.

"No, I can't calm myself," Jared snapped back. "It's this man's fault that my sister is being hunted in the first place. By everyone!"

"How do you figure that?" asked Remelas. The statement had irritated him and he scratched behind his ear to mask it. Sarene raised a hand to her mouth and bit on her thumb.

"Your brother hired the Gathire for you." Jared said. "That's obvious enough, but consider Tyrrial as well. Do you think it's a coincidence that someone with Sarene's immunity arrives in the same country which is breeding an army for invasion?" Remelas did not respond. "Come on, your Highness. Corliani came to visit my sister within the boundaries of your nation. Tyrrial sent an assassin after her. We've got someone else paying carnival men to pass on messages of Tyrrial coming here personally and you think this isn't related to your plans of conquest?"

"What are you saying?" asked Kanderil.

"I'm saying that *this* man, our Prince, brought their attention to this country with his ambition and his militaristic schemes. They might have left my sister alone had she spent her life in the valley, but instead the Four's seen two separate issues together and decided they're connected." His tirade came to a halt and he twitched, hands closed into fists. He laughed, the sound reflecting his obvious disdain.

Kanderil ran a hand over his mouth, looking back to the Prince. Sarene did likewise. She felt scared; her problems were being jumbled up into something much bigger than her, and she was losing track of them all. Jared's words were unnerving.

"He has a point," said the woodsman.

"He has a theory," countered Remelas. The words

preceded a sigh. For the first time since Glaithe and Nichai had left, the Prince looked at her directly. "Sarene. Please, step forward." He held out his hands to her. Cautiously, she obeyed. She was having trouble coming to terms with the discussion between them. It all seemed too much, too big of a mess. Everything was spiralling out of control.

"Don't do it," said Jared, stepping forwards to intercept her. It was Spasmodic who reached out to stop him. The tips of those lethal digits snagged in his shirt sleeve.

"You had your say, gorgeous," it said. "Let the bloke have a turn."

The creature had a peculiar look in its eye. Sarene wasn't sure why it would say something so *sensible*. She sniffed, turning her attention to the Prince. He took her hands in his.

"Sarene, listen. What I have said here today may seem difficult to comprehend. I pride myself on my good judgement. I fully appreciate what you and your companions have told me. I accept that you have had a most troubling journey and endured something I will never understand." He produced a modest grin. "How could I? I have never been hounded through the woods. I have never been chased by creatures of the night. I would not presume to know how it must have made you feel."

She shrugged, uncomfortable with the words. She tried focusing on the honesty with which they were spoken.

"However, I maintain that for the kingdom to grow and our people to prosper, I must make room for us to breathe. Tamir needs this. I only seek for the nation of Carthlei to be absorbed into my own. We will not destroy them or burn their lands down. My soldiers will not harm women or children or the citizens of the land. I cannot do this through diplomacy so I must do it with a show of force." He shrugged. "Ideally they will simply surrender at the sight of us, making them inclined to agree to my proposition. If I could achieve my goals without any bloodshed then it would be the ultimate victory."

She nodded. It felt like the right thing to do.

"If my brother puts so much faith in you then I must at

least entertain the idea that he is correct. If we truly risk the wrath of the Four and you *truly are* here to change the world... I would be a fool not to ask you to join with me."

Sarene stared at him. The Prince believed what he said. She could read it. Remelas was asking for her help. He was not demanding it from her, nor making threats against herself or her family. Back at the village she wouldn't have had such a choice. The decision would have been made for her by her father or the elders.

Here, the Prince of Tamir was requesting her aid.

Biting her lip, she moved back towards Kanderil. Was this what they had meant? What the Four feared? If she joined with the army and marched east to Carthlei, what would that prove?

Something clicked into place. It would prove that she was destined to perform her duties as foretold by these Seers. She was just a marionette playing to the dance of fate. They'd gotten it right so far. The Four must hold a reason to take such an interest in her.

What if Jared were correct, also? What if she'd been tugged into the plans of the Four purely by chance? It wasn't a ridiculous 'theory', as Remelas called it. If Tamir had thirty eight thousand soldiers at the ready – a number of men with swords and shields she couldn't picture in her mind – then perhaps the Four had decided to deal with the Prince directly. They'd realised that Sarene was in the same country, put the two pieces together, and decided to eradicate both threats at once.

Unless it was the other way around. They'd decided to deal with *her* first and punish the House of Tamir as an afterthought.

She looked up at her guardian. Even now, those same patient eyes watched her, eyes which saw everything, or at least appeared to. Tears welled to the surface. Everything she'd been through, everything she'd suffered, had led to this. Every choice they'd made and the roads they'd turned had brought them to this moment, in this room, with *this* man. This Prince.

At last she turned to face Remelas, tilting her head onto her flat hands for the second time that evening, and closed her eyes.

Remelas nodded. "You wish to sleep. Of course."

"Are you going to lock her room so she cannot escape?" Jared asked in a petulant tone.

"I will have guards posted to her quarters, but not to prevent her from leaving. She is being hunted after all, Jared." The Prince regarded her brother. "I appreciate why you are so protective of your sister. She has been chased through the forests for weeks, and those you thought were your comrades had their own agendas. I can see how that would be upsetting. But you are not my prisoners here. I am as shocked by my brother's actions as you are. Whether you believe me or not is your choice, but all I can do is speak honestly."

Sarene clicked her fingers, waving Jared towards her. He did as he was asked, moving to her side quickly.

"Uh, do I have to use the window again?" asked Spasmodic, pointing towards the wall behind him.

Kanderil shook his head. "Put up your hood and hide your hands." He opened the door, stepping aside to allow the others through. Sarene walked out with Jared close behind. She heard Spasmodic's booted feet stomping along with them.

"Kanderil, would you wait behind a moment?" Remelas said. Sarene looked back over her shoulder but could not see much of the chamber. Without a further word the door closed with a dull *click*.

———◄○►———

"Well," said Remelas. "What do you think?"

Kanderil turned around. He had appraised the Prince during the discussion with Sarene and Jared, purposely choosing to keep his words few. In conclusion, Remelas was simply taking a gamble. Success hung on the fallacy of a fable recounted during the Shalith celebrations. Remelas was a bold, ambitious and powerful figure. A man such as this rarely changed their mind. It was as difficult as convincing an alcoholic not to drink. All it was possible to do, in his experience, was act as a guide.

"Before I reply, why does it matter what I think?" he said.

"It matters because I admire you, sir." Remelas bowed his head a little, sweeping a hand through his ash-brown curls. "I cannot say I know much of your history, but to have navigated our lands with a young girl in tow whilst remaining a step ahead of the Gathire suggests you are skilled. More than most men, perhaps. I respect that."

Kanderil said nothing.

"Now, we've been through the academic study here. If you wish, we could debate further on the campaign's ethical implications. Alternatively we could discuss your claim that the Four once again walk amongst us. But I want to ask a simple question. Do you think that an army as large as mine can succeed?"

"I am sure you have advisors for such matters," Kanderil replied, aware that the Prince was trying to draw him into a conversation topic they could bond over.

"I have advisors for everything," Remelas admitted. "Advisors for the training, advisors for the equipment, advisors for the logistics and the timeframe and the organisation..." He rolled his wrist as he named each area. "I have advisors who would tell me the sky was pink if I made plans for it to be so. I trust my generals but I am asking you as a man who does not seem afraid to expressing his opinion. Can I succeed?"

Kanderil raised a hand to his jaw. What did it matter if he spoke his piece? The invasion would go ahead anyway; he was sure of it.

"You will swamp the opposing army. That is not to be questioned. Your slow build will ensure your men are more than capable of achieving what is expected of them. At least at first."

Remelas raised a brow. "Go on."

"Carthlei is a big place. Thirty eight thousand men will

dominate the battlefield, but what of the population? The Carthleid must number almost two million. Your final victory depends on taking the capital and overwhelming the *Fhei*. Only with his support will the people even consider falling into line."

Snapping his fingers, Remelas pushed away from the table. "Exactly! That is my main concern as well." He started to walk in the same, loose circle that he had earlier. "We will need to head for the capital directly. It will take them time to muster their defences properly. If we push on without becoming distracted by secondary objectives, Garonal believes we can be at Caragi within a fortnight of crossing the border."

"Where is Garonal?"

"West, at Jorulei. He tends to think of the bigger picture and as such tried to be everywhere as often as possible."

Kanderil brought his hands together in front of him, wrists crossed over his waist.

"How long did you remain with the Kalethi?" asked Remelas.

"Eighteen years."

"And you only made Sergeant?"

"I was offered promotion several times. I turned it down."

"May I ask why?"

"I was comfortable with my role."

Remelas nodded slowly. Kanderil could see the man's mind working behind his azure eyes. "Of course," he said, bringing a finger to his lips. "Of course. I'd wager you were a *damned* good Sergeant as well, Kanderil."

"I did the best job I could. I see little point in doing otherwise."

"Why did you leave?"

"Personal reasons."

"Such as?" Remelas persisted.

Kanderil took a slow breath. "I decided to enjoy my own company for a while."

"So after stepping aside from the Kalethi, you ended up

in this little situation of yours?" Remelas chuckled with genuine amusement. "Remarkable how life works sometimes, isn't it?"

Kanderil nodded once. The laughter petered out.

"I want you back in, Kanderil. I want you to captain a squad for me."

"Not interested."

"You would turn down a request from your Prince?"

"I would. It does not benefit me and you do not need more men for your army. You will win your battles."

"As you wish." Remelas shrugged. "I will not force you. May I at least provide you with another drink?"

Kanderil inclined his head. The Prince moved to the goblets and refilled one only. The pitcher was emptied, the last few drops of liquid sending ripples along the dark contents. Kanderil took the offered goblet and drained the contents in one swallow, drawing the cup from his lips to watch the man opposite, his focus unblinking.

"You dislike me?" Remelas asked. "Please, speak plainly."

"I like you just fine, lad," Kanderil replied, impressed by the direct question. "I simply do not trust you. That is not to say you are a liar. I just do not believe you have revealed your whole hand yet."

"I have shared the details of my spring offensive in the east. Nobody outside of my immediate circle has heard them, except for you and your companions. I have little else to disclose, Kanderil."

Kanderil shrugged his wide shoulders, handing the goblet back. "I have avoided people since I retired from the Kalethi. Glaithe and Nichai were amongst the first I have placed my confidence in for over three years. Both betrayed my trust, so you must allow me to treat your words with a certain degree of scepticism."

"Of course." Remelas replied.

"What do you think Sarene can do for you?"

"Did you ever study the legends of the Four?"

"I heard most of the fables as a child."

"Well then," the Prince stated. "When my brother told

me of the girl's immunity and how he believed it would help me – since he accepts the whole myth as hard truth – one of those tales came to mind. It was the tale of Haihachea the Stonemite."

Kanderil recalled the story. Haihachea had been the leader of a tribe of people tucked into the mountain ranges of Monethieia, far to the south western lands. It was said that Haihachea was so paranoid of the Four, having heard of their work in neighbouring regions, that he barricaded himself up in his cavern stronghold and enlisted every man of age to bear arms. When Mubuto eventually arrived, Haihachea sent his militia surging out of the mountains. They numbered almost a thousand strong, and were determined to kill Mubuto before he reached the fortress.

Mubuto had torn the very ground before him, opening a huge chasm beneath the approaching men. The majority fell screaming to their deaths. Those few who avoided the drop fled for their lives.

"I am aware of that one," said Kanderil.

"Then imagine if one of those men running down that mountain was *also* immune to the whims of the Four. By reason, the ground would never have opened up. Haihachea's force would not have been destroyed. Sarene would be like the tear in the net. Any spell cast on my army would be nullified and my men would survive."

"You're basing your belief on opinion, your Highness. Besides, your soldiers could still be killed one at a time regardless."

"Not that many. Surely they would not be defeated in such large numbers. If this recoil my brother mentioned really does leave the Four helpless when they attempt to affect the girl..."

"You would need Sarene in close proximity for that to work," Kanderil said coldly.

Remelas returned to the table to set down the empty goblet. One of the lanterns was running low on oil and the flame sputtered. "My offer to you will remain open, just as my request to Sarene does. Think it over. I will offer you a wage well worth your consideration. A home. Land of your own."

"You mean you will bribe me."

"Haha, Kanderil! Please. I respect your skills and I believe you would do a good job. I will review your Kalethi record to ensure it isn't just blind luck that you avoided the Gathire, but you have the manner of a man who is not to be taken lightly."

Kanderil chuckled. This would-be conqueror was persistent in his approach, if nothing else. "Kind words. Now I believe I should rest. It has been some time since I slept on a bunk."

"By all means." Remelas offered a gracious bow. "Tomorrow we will meet again to listen to Sarene's answer."

Kanderil moved to the exit. He twisted the handle but delayed pulling it open. Eyes downcast, he glanced back over his shoulder. "You understand that the girl will decline."

"I expect as much. But I have to ask, if only to give my brother's efforts a sense of worth."

Nodding, Kanderil left the Prince of Tamir alone in his tower chambers.

"So what do you suggest we do now?"

Nichai was sitting on his bed, watching Glaithe closely. They had retreated to one of the guest quarters. The room was sparse, but adequate for a short stay, with one double bed and a small oak desk.

The former Agent was standing at the window watching the fort at night. A guard strolled the ramparts, whistling to himself. A bat appeared briefly, flapping hard to maintain its ungainly flight, before vanishing into the darkness. The grounds outside the fort were peaceful, the stars twinkling through gaps in the cloud alongside the sliver of moon which fought to be recognised.

Glaithe was furious with himself for not warning Nichai to keep quiet about the contract with the Gathire.

The Regent had done a grand job of holding his tongue during the last two weeks of travel, revealing his role as the contract holder in a note passed over during the ride from Tamiran. He hadn't given any indication to Sarene's group that there was a secret to hide. Such restraint had been impeccable, much to Glaithe's honest surprise, and as such there had seemed little need to remind him to keep his mouth shut when they met the Prince.

The girl had been delivered to the royals and the terms of the contract had been fulfilled. Glaithe was all but signed back into the Gathire. All it had taken to cheat him of a flawless success was the overwhelming power of an insecure young man seeking the approval of an elder brother.

At the worst, questions could be asked of his involvement in the incident at Sarene's home. If pressed, Chalimer could reveal the true culprit. Remelas would feed a disgraced Agent to the dogs to appease the girl, if needed.

"Glaithe?"

"I'm thinking, my lord," Glaithe snapped.

Nichai flinched. His eyes were still red from sobbing and his make-up had run with the tears. The Regent looked like a waxwork bust of himself which had been left too close to the fire. Turning to look at him, Glaithe muttered. The sight was pitiful.

"Forgive me, Nichai," he breathed. "I am just thinking. Now they know we have betrayed them we have jeopardised our position. They will not trust us again. Kanderil especially."

"I did not lie," Nichai protested. "They did not ask me if I was involved. They were only interested in my brother."

"Regardless, they are now here through deception. The Prince may be able to stop them from seeking to settle the score but what then?" Glaithe threw up his hands. "I cannot rejoin the Gathire. Not without Remelas' signature. I cannot bring the girl back to Chalimer. What, pray, should I do?"

"You could come and work for me?"

Glaithe laughed. "A generous offer, but I am not a guard or a lackey. I have greater ambitions."

Nichai rubbed his nose, sniffing. "Then what?"

"I do not know." Glaithe faced the window once again. "I simply do not k--"

A silhouette filled the opening, fluttering and ruffled. Glaithe stepped back, holding his cry of alarm in his throat. He pulled his knife free of its sheath only to find that a hawk now sat on the windowsill. Its plumage was full and clean, with black spots through tawny feathers. Its head darted this way and that, beady yellow eyes gazing somewhere new each second. If Glaithe didn't know any better, he would have said it seemed distressed.

In its beak was an envelope.

Glaithe glanced at Nichai.

"Did we upgrade the messenger pigeons?" asked the youth.

Ignoring him, Glaithe carefully reached forward to take the letter. Before he could grab it the hawk opened its beak, dropping the thing. It flapped its wings, falling back out of the window. Soon it was sailing away, far out over the battlements.

He bent down to pick up the letter. Turning it over once in his hands, he slipped the flap free and opened it up.

Glaithe,
An associate of mine informs me that you have the ear of the Regent of Tamir. I therefore ask you, as a service to your country, to escort him clear of the fortress tonight. Do so without any witnesses. Return to Tamiran and await further news. I intend for the Regent to ascend to the throne in the near future. For your assistance, you will be rewarded.
Do not fail me.
- Tyrrial

He read the spidery handwriting three times over, then lifted his head to stare back out of the window. There was no sign of the bird.

"Well?" asked Nichai. "What does it say?"

"We, um..." Glaithe coughed gently. "We need to return to Tamiran. Tonight."

"Tonight? Why?"

"I do not know. But the letter comes from Tyrrial. I suggest we listen."

"Tyrrial?" Nichai bounced forwards. "Oh my. How do you know it is from him?"

"He signed it."

"Anyone can sign a *letter*, Glaithe." Nichai ran a hand along his slick hair, smoothing it down flat. "How can we be sure?"

Glaithe tossed the letter towards the bed. It just made it, landing on the edge of the quilt. Nichai leaned over to grab it, the mattress creaking beneath him.

"We can be sure."

Once the letter was opened it did not take long for the Regent to accept the authenticity. His eyes lit up and his mouth gaped wide. "How does it do that!?"

Glaithe shrugged. There was an outline of a fox on the lower right hand corner of the page. The inky shape was running on the spot, alive and fluid.

"That isn't important, Nichai. The message is. We need to get you back to Tamiran."

The Regent raised a palm to his forehead, reading the letter over. "But what about my brother? We have to tell him. He could be in danger. Why else would I become heir to my father's throne?"

"I do not advise going against the wishes of the Four," warned Glaithe.

"But if I leave now, what happens?" Nichai stood from the bed, walking in his stocking feet across the room, and patted himself down. He rubbed the back of his neck and scratched his arm, baffled, as though his conscience was warring within him so badly it was affecting his motor skills. "If something happened to Remelas I would never forgive myself. I have to at least show him the letter before we leave!"

"Nichai..."

"Without any witnesses as well! What if word got out that we escaped before something terrible happened? They might think it was me. That wouldn't do, Glaithe. It would not do at all."

"Nichai, listen. We have to consider all the options."

"Options?" Nichai was chewing on his fingernails, biting the quick. "What options? I couldn't just run out. I have to tell Remelas right now, so he can esc--"

Glaithe surged forward, ramming a forearm flat against the Regent's chest. The young man yelped in surprise as he was shoved back against the wall. When contact was made the Regent gasped, the wind forced out of him, staring at the Agent in shock. Glaithe leaned in close.

"Listen to me. Tyrrial has told us to get out of this fortress. He has offered to make you the King of Tamir and has threatened me personally if that doesn't happen. Now if you tell your brother then we are all targets. Do you really want to annoy the Four?"

"N-no..." Nichai wheezed, frozen in place.

"Good, because I refuse to become the bastard's next target. We are going to escape this place, we're going to do it now and you will follow *every* command I give you until we are safely on the road to Tamiran. Do you understand?"

"But..." Nichai started to cry again, his Adams apple bobbing up and down in his scrawny throat. "But my brother..!"

Glaithe brought his dagger up against Nichai's cheek. The Regent of Tamir whimpered in terror.

"The incident at Sarene's home? That was me. I cut her mother and beat her father. I am a man used to success but instead of a commission back into the Gathire I'm in a tower with a snivelling child who sold me out to impress his brother. On top of that, I have been given the opportunity to gain the favour of Tyrrial and to give *you* the throne. I will slash you right here and now until you do what you are told, Nichai, if that is what it takes." The edge of the blade was pressed against flesh. "I would rather take your revenge in Tamiran than Tyrrial's wrath in the forests."

Nichai nodded, tears falling. His sobbing was silent as if he was too scared to make a noise. Glaithe felt a surge of power run through his body. The last few weeks of holding himself in check and acting like a common mercenary had been torture. All he wanted was to return to the Gathire, regaining the authority it lent him. He'd wanted to cut down Sarene's pet demon, sever Kanderil's throat and put an arrow through Jared's eye. He'd wanted to drag the girl back to Chalimer and deliver her bound and gagged. He wanted *recognition*.

Now was his chance to impress Tyrrial.

"Are you going to do as you are told?"

Nichai squeaked out an affirmation even as he cringed. It was obvious from his expression that the Regent wanted to refuse and go to his brother. His tear-filled eyes exposed how strongly the sense of betrayal was eating at him. Cowardice was a terrible curse.

Glaithe pulled away the dagger. "Good. Then follow me."

Sarene couldn't sleep. This time it wasn't the dreams.

Jared had fallen quiet around an hour ago. She could hear his heavy breathing from the bunk above hers. She suspected the wine may have helped him get to sleep.

Kanderil lay on the bunk opposite. She felt sorry for him. The woodsman was clearly too big for the bed, with his legs dangling off of the end. By the scarce light of the moon outside she could see his eyes were closed. She decided not to disturb him.

Spasmodic was nowhere to be found. It had come down the stairs with them but by the time they had reached their dormitory it had disappeared.

Sarene gave a long sigh.

The offer from the Prince was great. Too great. She couldn't accept it, of course. The idea of being some kind of banner was distasteful. She was having visions of being led on a horse through a huge crowd massed along the streets of

Tamiran, the Prince himself holding the reins. The onlookers were cheering and clapping as Remelas waved at them. If she was part of his plan, he would revel in the adoration it brought. He would assure them safety from the Four. She was just his tool.

But the fact that he had *asked* for her co-operation nagged at her. He could have forced her to come along. He was the Prince of Tamir, a man surely used to having whatever he desired. If he wanted Sarene to ride along with his army like some sort of anchor, some magical shield, then he could ensure it happened. But instead he'd pleaded his case and allowed her to decide. Her own father rarely treated her with such respect and maturity.

The thought of her father made her smile. Remelas had promised they would be granted sanctuary whatever her choice. By rights she could be back with them by the end of the month, all safe and cared for within the House of Tamir. The notion was surreal. At least the Seers were useful for something, she thought to herself. They'd blabbed their way into giving her the favour of the royals.

The moment faded. She hoped her family wouldn't be mad at her. They had lived in the valley for all their lives. Even if they were moving to a palace, they would be leaving behind all they knew. All for her. They could visit their home, of course, but it wouldn't be the same. It was likely they would have to walk the streets with a guard in tow. *Maybe* they would be escorted everywhere they went. How much freedom would remain?

Perhaps they didn't have to move at all, now. The Gathire had been called off. Hawk had disappeared. The House of Tamir wouldn't help much against the Four anyway. Whether she was there or home in her own cottage, they could find her. They could come for her, or send more things like Spasmodic. Things which would follow through with their task.

She shivered, rubbing at her scalp. Then she yawned. Her body was tired but her mind wouldn't shut off.

"Still awake?" Kanderil's voice made her jump. Even his

whispers were immense. She grinned in the darkness, clicking her tongue to let him know she was listening.

"Aye, me too. Never did like these bunks." He gave a muffled grunt as he stretched, the frame supporting him producing a dangerously loud *creak*.

"Much better," he said, relaxing again. There was a long pause. Sarene lay with her eyes open, picking out the shapes in the darkness. Kanderil turned his head to face her.

"Whatever you decide to do, I will accompany you," he said. "If you go with your family back to Tamiran I will see you safe. If you go with this army I will remain here until you march in the spring. If you wish, of course."

He cleared his throat then, the sound anchoring his last word. Sarene realised what he had said with a broad smile. Reaching across the narrow gap between the bunks, she caught his shirt, tugging at it to show her appreciation for the words. She thought she saw him smile.

At the end of the room the wooden window blinds burst open. Spasmodic appeared, perched on the sill. The creature giggled, silhouetted by the moonlight of the sky and the torches of the fort. It shook with a nervous energy as Sarene looked at it, teetering in place.

"We're in trouble," it said, an anxious shiver in its voice. The chill of the night air swept in around it.

Behind it, something *exploded*.

Chapter Twenty

Shouts came from the men in the courtyard outside. Sarene fell to the floor, scrabbling for her things. Kanderil slid himself out of the end of his bed to avoid stepping on her and moved to the window. "What's happening?" he demanded as Spasmodic hopped into the small room.

Another crash came from outside. Something heavy thumped against the ground, shaking the floor, and the *tiktaktik* of shrapnel hitting stone ricocheted around the courtyard. Sarene pulled on her shoes and started tying her belt. It struck her as ridiculous that she was dressing herself so properly when something was happening which could cause the walls of a fort to tremble. She clipped her dagger into place as Jared dropped to the floor next to her.

Spasmodic was cackling. "He's so *pissed*, haha!"

Kanderil grabbed it by the lapels of its overcoat. "Who is?"

"Tyrrial!"

Sarene froze, staring at the door. She gulped.

"He's *here*?" Jared's retorted in alarm.

"In the flesh!" The creature pulled itself free of Kanderil's grip and smoothed down its shirt with its cuffs. "Hope you guys got a plan."

There was a great plume of light and heat from the window. Sarene couldn't see what caused it but she heard a guttural scream of agony seconds afterwards.

Kanderil grabbed his bow and quiver. "Move," he said.

They ran into the corridor. Men were sprinting from their bunks and racing towards the courtyard. Up ahead they could hear a man roaring orders, his booming voice a bastion amongst the yells of confusion beyond.

"*Secure your weapons, lads! Form into group, five at a time! Don't lose them and don't let them wander off! Kartei, get your arse out of that room and come here, now! You there, take Josan and Leathor and fetch us some damned arrows!*"

"We hiding out somewhere or joining in?" Jared had his sword in his hand.

"We need to get to Remelas," said Kanderil.

"What for? Let him burn. This is his fault anyway."

"He's still the Prince of Tamir. You think Tyrrial will stop looking for your sister when he's done?" Kanderil's voice was assertive, even when something else outside was sent tumbling. It sounded like a house being knocked down. Acrid smoke was filling the corridor. "Trust me on this. We need to get to him."

They started moving down the passageway. Kanderil all but hurled men out of the way, shoving them into rooms or against the wall. Sarene, Jared and Spasmodic followed along, trailing in his wake. One man ran the other way past them, scrambling through the throng of bodies. He had a sickening gash across his forehead which dripped blood along the ground behind him.

"They've returned!" he was screaming, his voice cut and sticky in his throat. "They've returned! We're being judged, lads! We--"

Spasmodic backhanded him across the jaw and he fell silent, slumping against the doorway of one of the bunk-rooms. The creature kicked him inside. Sarene was too shocked to react, being half-guided-half-shoved forwards.

They reached the courtyard.

Sarene had once heard a lecture of how things used to be before the Four walked the lands. There was a lot of talk about violence. There had been images in her mind of blood, fire and pain. The dreams she suffered even now, the dreams which disturbed her slumber so often, never remained in her memory when she awoke. But the scene confronting her brought them into sharp clarity. A contrasting stream of orange, black and red, dancing and spiralling around in her mind.

Now she understood.

The front gate of the fort had been blown from its hinges and was now embedded in the wall on the opposite side of the courtyard. Upon impact it had impaled a servant through the chest with one of the support girders. The floor around the gate was alive with flame, as though the sun itself had fallen from the sky to strike the barracks. The light it cast lit up the scene of chaos around them. Men were running towards the gate just as others were fleeing back inside. She saw one man clawing at the walls with bloodied fingertips, trying to climb out of the fort from the inside.

A soldier was hurled over the walls from the *outside*. The man was screaming in terror up until the point he impacted against the ground. There was a sickening crunch, the sound giving her the terrible, childish recollection of a snail being trodden upon, and he screamed no longer.

"This way!" Kanderil yelled, heading towards the stairs that led up to the Prince's meeting room. Sarene followed with Jared laying a protective arm across her shoulders.

"I ain't never seen a tantrum like *this!*" Spasmodic roared after them. It revelled in its cry, a vicious creature now in its element. Sarene caught a glimpse of it over her shoulder and shivered. It was never meant to follow her around and walk through the forests, taking orders. It was meant for this.

Blood, fire, and pain.

They ran on. One man came to them and tried to grab Sarene. She recognised him as Savarn, the Regent's aide.

Jared stepped in to fight him off but the man would not be denied. Sarene's eyes were locked with her assailant as he gripped her shoulders tight enough to make her grimace. Savarn tried to lift her from her feet.

"He's here for you," Savarn cried with a depth of purpose which brought her back to her senses. She started to fight, kicking and flailing at him. "He's here for you, Sarene. We hand you over and we live!"

"Let go of her!" yelled Jared, aiming a punch at Savarn's jaw. The crazed soldier took it and staggered back, dropping Sarene. She scrambled to her feet, reaching for her dagger to defend herself against the man who would give her up in his place, a sacrifice to appease the Gods. Savarn rushed forward once more, throwing a wild left hook which Jared managed to avoid followed by a straight right which connected. Jared fell and hit the ground, dazed.

Triumphant, Savarn reached for Sarene again. This time she was able to avoid him, ducking low and stepping back, her blade at the ready.

There was another huge crash and more of the wall went scattering into the air, peppering the floor around them. A burst of flame, this time much closer, detonated through a group of men who had arrived at the gate. Two of them caught fire. Three of them scattered, yelling their fear.

Spasmodic leapt even as she noticed Kanderil turning to head back towards them. The creature's right hand whipped around just as it had in Tamiran. Savarn fell to the ground moments after, blood pouring from his neck. She couldn't take her eyes off the body despite there being so many others already lying in the courtyard.

"You okay?" Kanderil asked as he arrived. She snapped her gaze to him to see he was talking to Jared. Panic touched her chest for the briefest moment before her brother got to his feet. His lip was bloody but he seemed otherwise intact. Jared nodded, waving at them to get moving again. She sheathed her dagger, then wiped her hand on her tunic.

As they ran, Sarene witnessed Spasmodic lick at its claw as if no-one was looking. Blood trickled along its chin. They weren't far from the stairs now. They weren't far.

Kanderil paused at the entrance to the Prince's tower. He was coaxing them forward, clearly wanting to be the last up, to cover the rear.

She liked Kanderil. He was a brave man and he had been so nice to her.

Something fell to the ground about twenty feet away. A swift assessment revealed it was a section of masonry from one of the corner turrets of the balcony. Beneath the masonry was the upper body of a man holding a crossbow, apparently perplexed that his lower half now lay crushed under tons of stone. His eyes were open as he died.

"Did you feel that hit the ground?" said Spasmodic. "Damn."

They pushed on up the stairs. Jared dragged her along and she did what she could to keep up. The creature was skittish behind her, bouncing from wall to wall. Kanderil brought up the rear, or so she hoped.

Ahead, at the door to the Prince's chambers, two sentries stood ready with weapons drawn. They looked shaken but Sarene knew they must be brave men to remain here despite the explosions and screaming.

"You think he's here?" Jared asked.

"This gives the best view of the court and the hill outside," Kanderil replied, catching his breath. "If he is not here he has fled."

"Or he's hiding under the bed," Spasmodic sniggered.

Reaching the top of the stairs, Jared reached for the door handle. One of the guards made to stop him when Kanderil spoke.

"Trust us, lad. We are not the ones you need worry about."

"We need to protect the Prince," the guard responded mechanically, tense and scared.

"We'll help you do that," offered Jared. "We need to get to him. He's vulnerable on his own."

"You aren't his guards," said the other one, his armour clanking as he moved.

"No, but there's a man outside who made your gate explode and is currently firing Tamir soldiers around like cannonballs. This isn't the time to worry about protocol!" Jared delivered the words like an officer reprimanding one of his own. "You two get down there and watch this stairway. We will protect Remelas and get him to safety."

"Do as he says," Kanderil urged, his own voice as heavy as the mortar falling outside. "The Prince needs you now. When the bastard comes, you make sure he needs to fight to get through here."

"Will we know it's him?" one of the guards shouted as they moved past the group, descending towards the entrance to the courtyard. Spasmodic smirked, clasping him on the shoulder. Its claws scraped against the man's spaulders.

"Yes, matey," it said. "You'll know."

———◄○►———

The door to the Prince's chamber flung open. Jared burst in, his sister hanging from him. She'd been disorientated by the attack and he wasn't surprised. Sarene had shouldered her burden for so long, and all this violence must have finally pushed her over the edge. The timing wasn't great, but there was little he could do.

The Prince was observing the events below from his window, wearing the same clothes he had during their prior meeting. A sword was in his hand. He turned towards them, his manner tense and worried.

"Thought about my offer?" he said thinly.

Jared shook his head. "You see what you've brought us to? This is your doing, Remelas. Now we're all to pay."

"The boy's right," Kanderil said as he came in behind them. He slammed the door, sliding the bolt into place. "You reckoned yourself above the rest and now Tyrrial is here to set us straight. I expect he will seek an audience with us."

Jared led Sarene over to the chair beside the desk, lowering her into it. She was steady enough to sit upright but looked exhausted, her cheeks pale. Despite that, she managed a weak smile. He ruffled her hair before moving across to the window. "Stay with us, brighteyes."

Down below was terrifying. Jared was reminded of the damp ditch forts he and Sarene used to make as children. They would spend hours building a castle, walls and a moat, sculpting it all into place with soft, wet earth. When they were done and after they had admired it Jared would start kicking it down, trampling over it, pretending he was a giant.

The fort they now occupied looked exactly like it had been kicked in. Most of the front wall was missing. Huge wreaths of flame were scattered around, like someone had built a fire on the wreckage and then thrown hot coals across it. Even the stone itself, the remains of the parapets and foundations, was ablaze in places. Bodies lay sprawled across the courtyard, human debris of death and loss. Some men still ran back and forth in a futile effort to douse some of the flames. Others tried dragging their comrades, their *friends*, to safety. Only a few still held weapons, howling in dread and anger at the figure situated in the centre of it all.

Tyrrial.

The man had close cropped hair which seemed golden in the flames, and wore a dark robe with broad sleeves. With hands on hips, he surveyed his handiwork. Even at this distance Jared could tell he was smiling.

"Shit," Jared muttered. Tyrrial looked up at him in the window.

Something went *boom* around his head. It was the last sound he heard.

Sarene opened her mouth to scream with a voice she didn't have. Jared dropped to the floor, sprawling across the bearskin rug, blood trickling from his nose. She fell forward from the chair and crawled on her hands and knees to clutch at him. Pulling her brother into her lap, she slapped at his face and shook him as hard as she could. Jared made no sound. The noises she made were worse than crying; her sobs and tears and yells came with only the heavy sucking and coughing of breath caught in her throat. She tugged again at her brother's body, trying to wake him up, wiping the blood from his skin.

Kanderil turned to the Prince, coiling his emotions tightly within him. "Is there any other way out of here? Any way we can escape?"

"No," said the Prince, watching Sarene cradle her brother in her arms, touching her forehead to his. "No, there's no way from this room except through the window."

Cursing, Kanderil slid the bow from his shoulder and notched an arrow to the string. He was glad to have the weapon in his hands. It gave him a swell of confidence, the sense that he could change the odds.

Then again, how much use would arrows be against Tyrrial? The man could probably just deflect them away with a wave of the hand.

"What can you tell us about him?" Kanderil said, looking to Spasmodic. The creature shrugged, pacing the room just as Remelas had done earlier that night. *Except the creature is enjoying this,* he thought.

"Dunno."

"Anything, lad! Anything at all."

Spasmodic whirled around, its coat spiralling around its waist. "I don't know anything! The silly old shit talked a lot and bragged a lot. He didn't show me how to fuckin kill him."

"So he's arrogant," Kanderil pointed out. "If we can get him angry enough we could buy some time."

"Have you seen it out there?" Remelas said, shaking his head. The Prince was in control, but his eyes were loaded with fear. "You want to make him *mad*?"

"Yes," replied Kanderil. "Trust me. We just need to delay him from killing us long enough."

"Long enough for what?"

The door to the chamber burst open. Remelas flung himself to the side to avoid being bludgeoned with it. It slammed against the back wall and clattered to the floor.

Kanderil turned to look down into the stairway, drawing the bow in his hands.

There he saw Tyrrial moving towards them. The two guards they had passed still stood ready, and Kanderil whispered a prayer to their courage. He hoped it met with whoever heard such spiritual words, for a moment later there was a sudden change in air pressure and the two guards were crushed against the walls of the corridor. Brickwork fell like crumbs around them and the candles went out, extinguished by the same abrupt indoor breeze.

Kanderil fired. Tyrrial waved a hand and the arrow changed direction sharply, hitting the ceiling and vibrating with its impact.

"Silly boy," he heard a voice say, a voice which seemed to fill the room he occupied. Just as Kanderil pulled another arrow from his quiver he was blown from his feet.

Sarene watched as Kanderil hit the wall. *Hard.* He knocked an indent into the stone, roughly the same size as his broad back, and then collapsed to the floor. Dust and brick fragments puffed from the point of impact, scattering around his body. Sarene shook her head, tears slipping from her cheeks. Jared's blood had left stains along her sleeves and trousers, and her hands were wet from trying to clean his face.

Tyrrial strode into the room. His face was stern and depicted someone who had seen little joy in life. Kneeling on the floor as she was, he seemed colossal; radiating a presence too immense, too unreal, to possibly exist as a man. After appraising those in the room, his small amber eyes focused on her.

"You," he murmured. Though he smiled at her, that unwavering gaze regarded her as a mortal enemy. Yet this was the first time they had ever met. She was petrified.

Glancing at Remelas, Tyrrial waved a hand. The Prince stopped moving, becoming statuesque.

Spasmodic lunged at its creator. It roared with venom as it threw itself into the air. Both claws swung in a savage ark, its talons splayed wide for maximum spread of contact.

Tyrrial moved his lips before it connected. The creature became stuck in mid air, its face contorted into a frenzied grin. Spasmodic's body swung upwards from the shoulders, as if an invisible noose had hooked around the throat. Frantically it clawed for purchase, trying to find something to hold on to; the floor was a couple of inches out of reach. It snarled despite not having the breath to spare.

"You ungrateful spawn," said Tyrrial. He stepped towards the creature. Another whispered word and Spasmodic's limbs froze as well. Tyrrial leaned forward to stare it right in the eye. The creature snorted, its features twisted in rage. "After all the effort I put in to create you."

The man studied the dreadlocked thing he had grown, built, made, *whatever*. Sarene looked down to her brother, her grief overwhelming her again. She tried to will him back to life, to push him back to the surface, but Jared remained motionless.

Then Tyrrial spoke again. "I send you on a simple mission and you decide to turn against me." A harsh contact of skin on skin made her look up as Tyrrial slapped it. The creature gnashed its teeth, gasping for air. "To think I ever believed that you would fulfil your purpose. To think that I believed you would do your job..."

"Yah--" Spasmodic wheezed, sucking in as much oxygen as it could between words, "Suck... assh P-Parent-" The hold on its throat tightened. Spasmodic struggled for support as much as it could within its constraints.

"I will be taking you back to your birthplace, Deliverer. Clearly I need to open that skull up and redesign you. Make you a little more docile, hmm?" He tapped Spasmodic on the forehead. The skin there split and began to peel open. Half an inch, one inch, half more...

"Personally..." came a quiet groan. "...I was expecting more."

Sarene saw Kanderil pushing himself to his feet,

wreckage from his landing sliding from his frame. "Sending that thing... out as it is." He stood straight, craning his neck to relieve a muscle there.

Tyrrial turned to face the Hunter, adopting a dangerous smile, leaving the bound and bleeding Spasmodic adrift in the air.

"Well, well. The Windfury. I was told you were quite the specimen, my boy. They weren't wrong. Look at you! I haven't seen one of your size for many decades." The ancient one approached, articulating his thoughts as though studying a prize-winning bull.

"On the other hand, I have met one of *your* kind already this month. Corliani." Kanderil chuckled, brushing cement dust from his clothes. "Personally, he impressed me more."

Tyrrial smirked, his lips tight. "Really." He leaned forwards. "Between you and me, Corliani was always the weakest of the Four."

"Perhaps," Kanderil conceded. "He certainly did not throw such impressive tantrums."

As Tyrrial's eyes grew wide, as this figure of legend became angered, Kanderil threw a vicious right hand cross to the man's jaw. The impact was solid, and his head whipped to the side. Sarene felt a faint flicker of hope, which was immediately extinguished by a wry sneer. He turned his head to face Kanderil once again.

"Care to try again?"

Kanderil complied, tearing an uppercut into Tyrrial's sternum. There was a crack, but it was Kanderil's face which tightened in pain. He withdrew his hand and Sarene saw an ugly bulge between two of the knuckles. It was as though the woodsman had stuck concrete.

Tyrrial responded with his own blow. The punch appeared timid compared to the larger man's effort but it connected against Kanderil's torso with such force that Sarene immediately realised her guardian would crumble. Something, more than a single something, snapped under the fist. Kanderil coughed, flecks of blood appearing at the lips, and dropped to one knee.

"I thought you would have learned your lesson," Tyrrial said, irritated. "I thought you might have kept your mouth shut." He tilted Kanderil's head back with a finger under the chin, and then threw another right hand. The collision of hand against jaw made her gasp. Kanderil slumped to the side, his eyes glazed over.

"What about you?" the fabled being said to the Prince, who was standing stock still. The question animated him. Without thinking, Remelas lifted his sword to attack. Before he could follow through Tyrrial narrowed his eyes and held out his hand. The sword turned an intense red and Sarene could feel the heat expelled into the air. Remelas dropped the sword with a cry of pain.

"You fool," Tyrrial spat. "You arrogant, closed-minded *fool*. You really believed we would just let you by, hm? That you could build your army and set off for conquest and glory?" Tyrrial left Kanderil lying and advanced on the Prince, reaching out to grab him by his shirt and lifting him clean off the ground.

Remelas glared at him in defiance. "Why now?" he pleaded. Sarene could see he was fighting with his fear, determined to speak his mind despite the potential consequences. "All the evils in the world and you come back now. You abandoned us, Tyrrial. You left us for so long and God--"

The arraignment was cut off as Tyrrial's body caught aflame, suddenly lashed with fire all over except for around the hand clutching the Prince. Remelas wilted, enraptured with awe and terror.

"God?" Tyrrial sneered. "You're calling to Gods now? Well, there's something even *we* could not prove existed, your Highness." He dropped the Prince to the floor, discarding him like a broken toy, and walked back towards the centre of the now ruined chamber, covered as it was in building materials, blood and dirt. "As far as you should be concerned, for your little remaining time, *I* am your God.

"I implored my brothers," he continued, his hands sweeping around him. The flames over him died away.

Tyrrial bowed his head, now giving sermon. "I told them that if we left mankind to its own devices then it would one day ignore our lessons. You would return to the same old habits." He shook his head, muttering. "Do you see? You're the precise representation of what I predicted centuries ago, Remelas." He regarded the Prince, who was staring up at him from the ground, propped on his hands. Tyrrial laughed quietly, the sound rich with contempt. "I told them we should keep you on a tighter leash. All of you. Without our presence, without our guidance, you would fall back into destruction and murder."

"M-murd-der?" Remelas stuttered through gritted teeth, speaking angry words he was terrified of saying. "For s-someone so benevolent y-you killed so m-many tonight--"

"*Silence!*" Tyrrial thundered. He took a menacing step towards the Prince of Tamir, who couldn't help but withdraw. "You listen to me, boy. You do not speak."

Finally he turned his attention to Sarene. She looked back through watery eyes. This was it.

"This one cannot speak. She is perfect. Listening without reply, absorbing whatever it is she is told. Isn't that right?" He grinned. The image was so full of dark promise that she shrank back from it, clinging to Jared's body for protection.

"You were the only risk, girl. I foolishly considered that you would pose a significant threat to us. Well, look at you now. Crying over a corpse and too scared to move. What was he, your brother? Cousin?" He smirked. "Lover?"

Sarene shook her head, swamped with self pity and disgust. She was too terrified to be angry or to fight back. The fight was lost now. She rocked back and forth, feeling every inch the child she had always been told she was.

"Useless. All of you, useless!" Tyrrial paced again, his robe sweeping around his body, Spasmodic continuing to choke against unseen bonds behind him.

"My brothers and I have shown you infinite patience. We have let you take so *many* indiscretions against us. No more. Not after this. You will fall in line once again, once word spreads of what has happened here. The world will not change and our rule *shall* remain absolute. Humanity *will* obey and any disobedience *will* be crushed. Tamir will be a shining example to the world."

Pausing, he looked at Sarene again, wagging a finger. "You, I think, should come with me. Perhaps I can learn something of you for future reference. I believe your physiology will prove most intriguing."

Tyrrial approached her. She sniffed, useless upon the floor, and did nothing to stop him.

Kanderil tried to open his eyes. Only the right one obeyed. The left was closed and felt sticky. His jaw was swollen, and his tongue felt at his teeth. Three of them were loose and bleeding.

He pressed against the ground in an effort to lift himself. A deep pain filled his chest and sides and he took a moment to collect his thoughts, which spun around his brain like a sycamore seed falling through the air.

He was injured, more so than he had been in all his life. Pain did not faze him, but he had never suffered to this extent. He found it difficult to breathe and his chest made an alarming *schlock* sound with each agonising lungful. Yes, agony was the word. The pain was growing as his consciousness returned to him. He pushed at the floor again and found it so difficult, so far beyond him. Kanderil sagged.

"The girl who would change the world," he heard a distant voice say. "How disappointing."

Sarene.

He was in a room with his companions, and Tyrrial was with them. The man had brought them all down with such ease.

Get up.

Fighting back would be pointless. He had completely underestimated his enemy. There was no matching the Four. They were all powerful. Tyrrial was immune to anything they could throw at him.

Immune. She's immune.

Jared was already dead. Spasmodic was out of the picture, choking to death in mid-air. The Prince was there but, despite his efforts, seemed too shocked to move. Tyrrial had won. Sarene was his.

She can do it. You need to show her.

Getting up now would just make it worse. Lie here and you'll live for another time. Another fight. Not this one. This one is too big. Getting up now will merely anger him.

You need to buy her time. Get up. She can do it. Get up now.

Fighting for each inch with enormous effort and a hoarse cry of pain, Kanderil pushed himself upright. He slumped back against the wall, what precious little strength he had ebbing away, but he had sat up. It was hard to breathe. He grinned, revealing his bloody teeth to Tyrrial, who had turned around to observe him.

"Still alive, hm?" the man said in a calculated tone. It made the Hunter shiver, and he forced himself to concentrate.

"I was won'ering," Kanderil mumbled, and his voice sounded far away. He took a moment to catch enough breath to speak the whole sentence he had in mind. He spat a mouthful of saliva and blood. Mostly blood.

"I was won'ering why ye... you punch like-ah whoreson," he forced himself to say. "Yo're nothing, Tyrrial. Nothing at all." His words became a soft, gentle chuckle. The effort of laughing was like boiling tar in his lungs, but he persisted. He had to make sure it riled the man up.

It did just that. Tyrrial moved towards him. Kanderil laughed harder. It was either that or cry out in fear, and he refused to do the latter. Any sign of weakness would break his spell. The only chance he had left.

"*I am the greatest of the Four!*" roared Tyrrial, grasping Kanderil by the throat and lifting him, sliding him up the wall. Held in place, Kanderil's feet still reached the floor but lacked the strength to support him. He was being strangled by a man less than half his size, and he couldn't do anything about it. If he fought to break free he would lose. He had to just take the intense pressure on his neck, take his swimming vision and his ailing thoughts and keep smiling, and he had to hope that it worked. He had to hope it worked. He had to hope because he could feel himself slipping away, he could feel his senses slipping further and further away and he couldn't hear anything and his chest was agony, filled with hot coals, and he needed to breathe, just breathe but he couldn't, he could just smile, there was something crushing his throat and the air, sweet air, wouldn't come he just neededtobreathebreathebreathe--...

———◀○▶———

Sarene watched Tyrrial choke Kanderil. The image was perverse. That such a small man was capable of it was wrong somehow. She kept urging Kanderil to fight back, but all he did was grin. He smiled at Tyrrial even as he was dying.

Her gaze flicked across to the Prince, wanting to grab him and shake him into his senses to help, but Remelas' eyes were wide with dread. Spasmodic wasn't moving, suspended in the centre of the room by Tyrrial's mere thought.

She was the only one left.

Despite the destruction all around them, Kanderil hadn't lost himself to fury like Spasmodic, nor given in to fear like Remelas had; like *she* had. He was battered and bruised and coughing blood even now, but he refused to give in.

Kanderil had protected her without reward and now she was watching him die.

With great reluctance, she gently slid Jared's head from her lap. She brushed his hair from his face. As it was, he looked like he was sleeping. Sarene patted the top of his head, aware that time was running out but determined to say goodbye. One last farewell before taking what could be her final action.

She had to believe it wasn't.

Anger touched her then. This man, this evil, horrible man, this bringer of wrath and death, had murdered her brother. Tyrrial had snuffed out the flame she was drawn to more than any other, the one person she loved over everyone else. Swallowing her tears and her sadness she looked up, glaring at the legendary figure. She focused on him just as Kanderil had. With controlled emotion. With harnessed rage.

Sarene scrambled to her feet, breaking into a run. Four steps later she leapt forward, seeking to tackle Tyrrial and push him away from her guardian, the man who had walked with her through the lands of Tamir when no one else could.

Tyrrial turned to her at the last moment, holding out a hand to push her away, infuriated.

Nothing happened.

She connected, arms wrapping around her terrible foe, and shoved as hard as she could. Something caught around her ankle and she tripped, falling to the floor, the farmer's daughter and the man of myth and fable at once coming together and breaking apart.

Kanderil collapsed back to the ground, catching a huge lungful of breath which was at once wonderful and torturous, his legs sliding along the floor to trip Sarene. She fell in a heap and lay there, ready to spring again, fiercely staring upwards. There was blood on her hands.

Tyrrial had staggered backwards; his hand, smothered in his robe sleeves, was clamped to his side. There was a look of shock on his aged face, an expression of impossible depth, as if he couldn't believe whatever it was that he had just experienced.

The sleeves moved. Kanderil saw the dagger which was revealed. Jared's Kalethi dagger, hilt-deep in Tyrrial's flank.

He looked down at Sarene, to the red smears on her hands, then to the blood trickling to the floor. It was beginning to pool at his feet.

"You..." he whispered. Tyrrial backpedalled one more step. He stood there, stunned, unable to comprehend what it all meant.

"No." He spoke with more power but the word did little to steel his resolve.

Tyrrial's lips moved once more. A hand slipped into the pocket of his robe. This time, he disappeared.

Spasmodic fell to the ground in a heap, gagging and choking. Remelas started to rise from the ground, laughing, hysterical relief pouring out of him. Sarene gazed in wonder at where Tyrrial had been not a moment ago.

Kanderil leaned his head back. All he could do was smile. They had survived.

"You did... well..." he murmured. "...*so well...*"

Sarene looked at him but he couldn't say any more. He had nothing left. She reached out to grab his hand, bursting into tears, as his vision swam away into darkness.

Chapter Twenty-One

*K*anderil opened his eyes.

The sunlight was like a needle to the brain, making him wince. He lifted a hand up to block it out and his chest flared in agony. Letting his arm drop, he instead turned his head away from the window.

Remelas sat beside his bed. The Prince of Tamir looked exhausted.

"Welcome back. I was starting to worry."

"How long have I been out?" Kanderil asked, his throat hoarse.

"Three days," said Remelas. "I would guess Tyrrial knocked a few years off of your life with those punches."

A servant came over with a cup of water. Kanderil forced himself up onto his elbows, ignoring the amazing pain in his side, and took the drink. He felt as though his tongue was sandpaper, and he enjoyed the cool water more than anything he had ever drunk before.

"So what is the damage?" he asked as he finished.

"Broken ribs, three shattered knuckles, a fractured cheekbone and probably a concussion, but you'll live. Oh, and I found two of your teeth in my chamber."

Kanderil explored with his tongue. Sure enough, there was a gap where Tyrrial had struck him. The exposed gums tasted of copper.

"The fort is useless and will take months of work to repair. We lost over half of the men stationed here." The Prince bowed his head. "Two hundred and sixteen lives, with dozens more injured. I cannot begin to consider how to make amends for this."

"The Regent?"

"Missing." Remelas took a deep breath.

"I am sorry." It was the right thing to say, even though he did not truly believe the words at that moment.

"You have nothing to be sorry for, Kanderil." Remelas raised his head, giving a smile devoid of amusement. "You came to protect me when you would have been within your rights to simply flee. Without your help I would surely be dead now. I owe you a lifetime debt for that. If ever you need anything, you come to me."

Kanderil glanced around. They were sitting in what was formerly the mess hall. Now it was an infirmary. Bunk beds had been dragged in and set up in rows, with injured men of varying severity occupying them. A few servants moved between the beds, performing the duties of a nurse as best they could. Only two of them seemed to have any real idea of what they were meant to be doing, and Kanderil presumed these were the ones with formal medical training. They, too, appeared immensely tired.

"Where is Sarene?"

"With her brother," Remelas replied.

"Take me to her." Kanderil swung his legs over the side of the bed and forced himself to stand, ignoring the wave of nausea which swept over him. He couldn't tell if it was a result of hunger or the pain which lanced through his chest. Remelas stood up quickly to grab his arm.

"You should not be walking anywhere," the Prince said. "You've just woken up from a serious beating."

"Someone else can have my bed," Kanderil replied, stubbornly. "I am sure there is need for it."

They made their way out of the infirmary, Remelas struggling to support the larger man, ignoring the protests of one of the acting surgeons.

They reached the courtyard soon afterwards. Kanderil, already short of breath, was surprised to find Spasmodic surveying the clean-up operation. Men were working to clear the fortress of debris, setting up horses and harnesses to cart away the remaining pieces of rubble. A large pile of salvaged rock was being collected in one corner of the yard. Huge sections of the barracks were scorched, the evidence of the flames which had raged with the attack. The overhead sky was grey and murky. It fit the mood of the place.

Only Spasmodic seemed in good spirits. The creature had its hood up and its hands were tucked into its pockets. As it turned to greet them Kanderil noticed the heavy bruising around its throat.

"There you are, ya lazy bugger," it said with a grin. "How you feelin?"

"Like I fell down a mountain," Kanderil replied, already light headed from the brief exertion he had made.

"Yeah, well, looks like you did, too."

Kanderil grunted, bringing one arm close to his chest. The other was wrapped around Remelas' shoulders. "Where is Sarene?"

It shrugged. "Still with her brother. I guess she's waiting for him to wake up or something."

Kanderil stopped beside it, letting go of the Prince and standing on his own two feet, locking his knees. His chest roared, his back ached and his head was throbbing but he ignored all of it.

"Pretty, ain't it?" Spasmodic giggled.

"No," said Kanderil.

"Aww, c'mon. You didn't see it when it was all smoking and stuff. I loved it." It sniffed. "Reminded me of my dreams."

"It is horrific," Remelas said. Somehow he had escaped physical harm but Kanderil believed he'd suffered perhaps the greatest injury: self-worth. The destruction of the Leithar Grove barracks had been devastating and Remelas watched the operations to clean up the destruction with a grim face. "My conceit brought us to this. It was my arrogance which drove these men to their deaths."

"You did what you felt was right," said Kanderil. "You stated your reasons. I felt they were misguided, but they were honest."

"The reality of it is the only result. I cannot tell these men that my choices were well-meaning. All I can do is work to ensure this does not happen again."

Kanderil looked at him, taking the measure of the man, but did not speak further. They waited. He wished that he could take part in the effort to rebuild the fortress. These Tamir soldiers had acted with courage in the face of an unstoppable foe. His mind recalled the two sentries who had died in a futile effort to protect the corridor to the Prince's chambers. They must have known they would not survive, and yet they stood their ground. Such bravery was inspiring.

He considered his own position now. His retirement had led to where he stood. Had he remained with the Kalethi he would never have found the girl in the woods. He would never have been involved in her peculiar situation or her journey from her valley home to Leithar Grove. Having abandoned his responsibilities to seek a quiet life, he instead found himself in the middle of an event which could change the course of history. Everything the Four had feared. Everything the Seers had cried. It was all coming to pass and he was a part of it now.

Those two sentries. They had accepted their fate. Would he, now, after everything he had experienced?

The answer danced on the edge of his tongue.

"I'm hungry," said Spasmodic. "You guys hungry?"

"No," said Kanderil. The creature huffed and folded its arms back across its chest.

"Fine." It paused. "You think he'll be back?" The words came with a hesitance at odds with its usual demeanour.

"Tyrrial?" Kanderil shrugged, immediately regretting the

motion as fresh pain ignited. "If he survived, perhaps. We do not know how severely Sarene injured him."

"Weird that he ran," Spasmodic said with another sniff. It wiped its small nose on the back of a sleeve. "Only a stab wound, like."

"Not really. Think about it. Tyrrial had everything his way all these centuries. I doubt he has ever suffered a wound like that despite all the conflict he must have encountered. None of us could touch him. He likely panicked and fled in shock."

They watched the remains of the carnage. The ruins were the same colour as the sky above. Rain was threatening and it felt colder than it had been in months. Nobody spoke for several minutes.

"You know where to find her?" Kanderil asked eventually.

"Yeah. Out behind the back wall."

The words gave the final confirmation he needed. Kanderil sighed, nodding. The three of them headed for the gaping hole that was once the main gate.

Sarene sat before her brother's grave. The freshly turned soil was damp. The marking was a simple wooden stake, along which she had carved the word *Jared*. A lock of her hair had been fastened to the stake by a length of string, as was the Tamir custom when burying a loved one; a sign to others that the bereavement was fresh. Her cheeks wet with tears, she clutched her pan pipes between filthy hands. She was tired, exhausted to her bones, but she couldn't bring herself to walk away. Not yet.

Dimly aware of people approaching her, she did not look up. Instead she stared at the name engraved on the wood, the letters stained with charcoal, unable to come to terms with the reality of the situation. Everything had been like a dream. The encounter with Tyrrial kept running over and over in her mind but it was detached and hazy. She was completely numb.

The ordeal they had endured was a mockery of her brother's life. He shouldn't be dead. None of this should have happened. She was no threat to anybody despite whatever plans people had for her. The Four be damned. Sarene was not going to change the world. They'd just used her as an excuse; a catalyst for other people to rise up in her name. Humanity would rebel against the Commandment of the Four and use her as their standard. If everybody had left her alone then she would be with her family. Kanderil would have brought her back to her village and then walked away. All these people would still be alive.

Now she was left with nothing. Jared was gone. Her family would be in danger if she returned to them. She was without purpose and without hope.

Someone knelt down next to her. Reluctantly she glanced at them. It was Remelas.

"Sarene," he said. "Please, forgive me for intruding."

The look in her eyes must have troubled him, for he flinched before continuing.

"I, uh... thought in my pride that I could march across the land with no opposition from these men, these awesome men. Despite the evidence you brought I had started to believe that the Four would not dare to touch us." He exhaled, gathering his words.

"Without my plans, my brother would not have sought you out. Your family has suffered injury and loss due to our actions, and I take full responsibility for those crimes."

At first there was no reply. Then Sarene nodded. It was such a simple gesture.

"I will still provide the sanctuary you first asked for, should you wish it. I can have your family living in the House of Tamir within the fortnight. I will do everything in my power to atone for this, even though I accept that nothing I can offer will ever be enough."

She wiped her cheeks with the heel of her palm, one after the other. Then, with a deep breath, she reached out to place a hand on his shoulder. Sarene did not hate him. She didn't even hate the Regent. They had acted without malice. The results were merely tragic.

The Prince of Tamir arose, wearing an expression of solemnity.

"Just say thank you," said Kanderil's voice. Sarene twisted where she sat to find him standing beside Spasmodic.

Kanderil had survived.

A rush of emotion hit her then. Her face screwed up and she scrambled to her feet, launching into him. She gave a fierce hug, holding to him as though she would surely be lost if she let go. Kanderil grunted in pain at the connection but did not pull away. His huge arms wrapped around her shoulders and he held her lightly, massaging the nape of her neck. She cried into his chest, the floodgates opened, plunging headlong into devastating grief.

Nobody spoke for a long time.

Eventually she leaned back, her eyes red and her throat sore. She sniffed, catching her breath. Kanderil watched her with the patience she had come to expect from him.

"I cannot fix this," he said. "I wish I could. But know one thing, girl. I will walk with you wherever you go. I will do my best to protect you and to grant you protection against any who would do you harm. You have my promise that I shall keep you safe for as long as you need."

She nodded, stepping back and mopping up her tears with her sleeve. Then Sarene smiled, the first she had given in three days. She turned her attention to Spasmodic, who was chewing at one of its locks.

It coughed. "I'll... y'know. I'll be around. Somewhere. Probably." It shuffled its feet awkwardly. She merely nodded once more, reaching out to poke its arm. It gave a sudden grin, winking at her with emerald eyes.

Sarene glanced over her shoulder at the grave. The word *Jared* stood out against the marker.

To give up now would make his sacrifice worthless. Surrendering to those who hunted her wasn't an option. It was essential to stay strong and keep going. Her brother had done everything he could to see her safe, always ensuring that others treated her as an equal.

She had believed in him, just as he had believed in her.

The memory of Jared, still so fresh, stirred a glimmer of hope within her. Sarene ran her gaze over the three of them in turn, settling on Kanderil. He met her eyes. This time she did not look away.

One day. Perhaps one day she would find the peace she had once longed to escape.

About the Author

Ben Hennessy is an exciting new author from Essex, England. Brought up on a literary diet including the likes of Stephen King, David Gemmell, Terry Pratchett and David Eddings, he looks to take all these elements and create a unique style of fiction which blends heroic fantasy and a subtle sense of wry humour. Having spent the last decade working various jobs in locations such as Ireland, New Zealand and Vietnam, he is now hoping to forge a new career as a full-time writer.

When he is not poking his keyboard, Ben enjoys travelling the world, finding new music and crashing parties.

Author Website: http://www.hennessywrites.com
Author Twitter: @HennessyWrites

Lightning Source UK Ltd.
Milton Keynes UK
UKHW012028080922
408463UK00001B/32